MOONBURN

MOONLIGHT IN GLENWOOD
BOOK ONE

AYNSLEY J. FRASER

LITA HUNT

ISBNs
EBook: 979-8-9870098-1-9
Paperback: 979-8-9870098-0-2
Hardcover: 979-8-9870098-2-6

Cover by Tina Fulton

Edited by Ashley Chapman

Beta Readers and Contributors

Disc, Duck, Flicka, Hay, Mono, Rhianne, Kung Fu Alan, Lou, Ro, and A. Sherriff

Special Thanks To

Darren at Imperial Outpost Games for chasing people away so we could write, Aynsley's parents for giving up their dining room on a Sunday, and Lita's parents for the use of their library in a pinch.

All our various caffeine providers this wouldn't have made it to paper without you.

For everyone who encouraged us, this is for you.

INTRODUCTION

TLDR: Imagine that in the 1950s, supernaturals stepped out of the shadows and joined society. Now, werewolves, witches, vampires, elves, and dwarves are all on your doorstep. Fast-forward to modern-day Los Angeles, where the supernatural is commonplace. You have neighbors who turn into wolves and magic that keeps your coffee hot or cold all day long.

But what do you do when the werewolves down the street start a brawl? Call the police? Of course, you do! They will send the Multi-Operational Organized Network of Supernaturals (MOONS) to handle the dispute. Who better to deal with super strength than another werewolf? The supernaturals who work for the MOONS are affectionately referred to as moonlighters. Now you know everything you need know to skip the rest of this explanation. Unless you enjoy reading textbooks then keep going. Otherwise, see you in Chapter One!

— — ·— ◡ —· — —

The first half of the 20th Century was fraught with disease and wars on the global stage. As people attempted to recover in the wake of the Second World War, a famine hit Europe in 1946. Crops began to die off in waves. The blight rippled through the continent and spread across the rest of the world. Starvation tore across borders far worse than any infection could. No one was immune to hunger. Within two years, the blight covered both hemispheres, leaving nowhere untouched.

Humanity began to die off in droves... but help appeared from an unexpected place.

In 1950, Supernaturals stepped out of the shadows to save the human race from extinction. Monsters from storybooks and fairy tales came to life before the eyes of the world. One day people knew that werewolves didn't exist, but the next, they learned that their reclusive neighbors turned into wolves. Vampires, werewolves, witches, elves, and dwarves, colloquially referred to as the Big Five, stepped in to halt the collapse of modern society. There were whispers that others beyond these five races existed, but no more stepped forward.

The Big Five had always been there, hiding alongside humans for millennia. Their existence was a well-kept secret from all except a few to ensure their survival. But even before a global famine brought panic, the writing had already been on the supernatural community's wall. Technological advances continued accelerating faster than ever before. First, cameras were invented. Their ever-evolving contraptions got quicker at capturing the truth. Then wires stretched over the land connecting coasts with telegraphs and telephones spreading their stories faster. The world grew smaller and smaller with each passing year, as did the Supernatural's ability to pass undetected. Even the most human-like creatures such as elves, found less isolated communities to hide their long lives in. However, as governments floundered in the face of overwhelming chaos, the Big Five stepped in to pick up the pieces.

Monsters became heroes in the eyes of humanity. The scared

housewife discovered she didn't care that her mailman actually upset the family pet because the dog smelled a werewolf. Not when that mailman could send looters running with little more than a growl. The sick learned a doctor who drank blood was better than one who didn't. Especially when that quick sip could pinpoint your disease and get treatment underway. The most religious of men could not dispute that having a witch in town was a blessing. Especially when the woman's magic could restore the failing crops while still coming to mass on Sunday.

Rather than wait to be dragged from the shadows kicking and screaming, a contingent of Supernaturals from the United States' West Coast took the initiative. The leader of the Los Angeles Coven of Vampires drafted a plan for integrating into human society and brought it before the other members of the West Coast Council of Supernaturals. The plan needed the cooperation of every race if it was to work. Once the Big Five were in agreement, they approached the rest of the world with an offer.

At first, the United States government reeled in shock as monsters from their nightmares appeared at the doorstep. President Truman's jaw hung open in disbelief as his secretary swore a gruff toned dwarf was threatening to remove the door's hinges if their group wasn't let in. Within the hour, multiple people of his cabinet assembled before an uncharacteristically informative Director of Central Intelligence. He briefed them on Project Moonlight, which was the country's attempt to find the truth behind supernatural creatures. That day President Truman met his first Supernatural. That week a deal was brokered between the United States and the Supernatural Powers. If these monsters could stabilize the country as they promised, the USA would welcome them with open arms.

The integration of Supernaturals was smoother than anyone believed possible. Powers beyond the best humanity held, mixed with the ability to do so in the open, had life-saving effects. The government extended full rights and protections to their Supernatural citizens without hesitation. Even those who lived off the radar were given sanctuary under federal law. In exchange, Supernaturals would adhere to the same laws and regulations as the rest of the population. A policy of forgiveness for any previous crimes was adopted for minor or unprovable infractions. Advances were made to ensure a clean transition such as artificial blood, which a vampire could live on without feeding on their neighbors. As obstacles fell to the combined ingenuity of every race working together, the United States started down the road to recovery.

The 21st Century has found Supernaturals as a whole outed worldwide. But how each country chose to handle them is vastly different, even in places most people would consider progressive. Middle Eastern countries banned werewolves, causing them to flood into Asia and Africa. Old grudges in European countries saw their witch populations moving out quickly to avoid ancient laws resurfacing. The global rules of engagement were immediately revised to include anyone with powers as superweapons. Supernaturals were banned in war after a squad of dwarves single handedly pulled neighboring countries into Latvia's territory. In contrast, some states even elected supernaturals to their government, such as when a vampire swept the Brazilian election.

While the United States stands as an exemplar around the world, there are still struggles. Both humans and supernaturals have millennia of superstitions they are slow to shake free from. The Big Five races are not always welcome in every field and the most notable is law enforcement.

While people might not mind that their neighbors turn into giant wolf monsters, what do they do when those neighbors get into a domestic dispute? The average human police officer is ill-equipped to handle a werewolf shifted into their hybrid form and using super strength to throw people through walls.

The solution?

They call in the Multi-Operational Organized Network of Supernaturals to do the heavy lifting. MOONS are contractors that work in tandem with local police departments. They lend supernatural powers to support everything from tracking a missing person to breaking up a riot. Rather than expect the police department to memorize every way that magic can be used to break into a bank, they can call in a witch specialized in that knowledge. Who better to hunt an assailant that disappears in shadows than another of their kind? The supernaturals who work for the MOONS are affectionately referred to as moonlighters, after the old project once set up to find out if they even existed.

CHAPTER I

DISTURBANCE

Laika
September 1st, 2018
Night Claw Residence, Glenwood, CA

CRACK!

The leg of the coffee table snapped as Laika went through the bargain-brand wood. There went another piece of furniture, sacrificed to the gods of training. Her dark hair splayed around her like a halo while she lay on the ground, groaning about lousy aim. Splinters from the broken wood dug into her palm when she pushed herself up again. A smug Evie stood on the large padded mat that had pushed the couch, television, and everything else in the room out of the way. "Point to me," she half sang, pumping a fist into the air.

"That was a good throw, but could you aim at something softer next time? Like the training mat?" Laika growled playfully, staring up at her friend.

"You should try aiming your landings better," the woman shot back with a confident toss of her red locks.

"How? I was in the air?"

The other woman shrugged, "Training?"

"Haha," replied Laika dryly. She studied the slivers of wood embedded in her hand with a grimace. Nails picked at the tiny pieces, trying to pull them free.

Her action was met with an eye roll from Evie. "You are a big bad werewolf, and that was a fragile IKEA table. If you huffed and puffed at it, then you could break it."

Their exchange was cut short as the light above them flickered for a moment before going dark. All sounds of electricity in the house faded, leaving the pair standing in silent darkness. "Did you pay the bill?" inquired Laika as she begrudgingly pushed herself to stand upright, splinters of wood now forgotten in the face of real calamity.

"Of course, I did! I paid the damn bill on the 20th!" Evie defended.

They were due to start the season finale of Love Pack in just 20 minutes. Which meant the internet would be rife with spoilers in a mere hour and 20 minutes. Laika's forlorn look was lost in the dark. She handed Evie her phone from where it sat discarded on the couch.

Her friend squinted at the phone's bright light in the dark while she pulled up her account.

Laika's amber eyes read over Evie's shoulder. "20th of July or August?"

A pause hung in the air while the redhead counted back quickly, pale fingers counting out months. Evie smiled coyly as she reached a realization. "Uh... June, I think. I definitely paid the water bill last month, though."

No attempt to deflect could stop the annoyance bubbling up in Laika. She was a flurry of motion before the sentence even finished. Her body shifted to the left, allowing her to plant a foot on the couch. "It's the 1st of September!"

"I know!"

Cushions helped launch Laika up and over the defensive hands of Evie. She clasped her friend's arm, pulling the limb sharply up with a mock growl, "August is your month! That's why I've been buying dinner!" Their meal of ramen was nestled between a luke-warm six-pack of beer and chips on the couch. On the dregs of her paycheck this was the best Laika could offer.

"Off!" shrieked Evie.

"No!"

The playful moves from their training took on a more serious edge. Laika's hold was broken with a jerk of Evie's arm then she stepped back. A follow up high kick was also deflected into a nearby lamp. Laika's balance slipped on contact with the light. She'd expected a more solid impact so she scrambled for a better footing. However, the dark bulb smashed when it hit the floor, sending shards in all directions. Another leg on the coffee table cracked as Laika slammed her foot down, regaining her stance.

Evie saw the counter too slow. Laika was able to outmatch her best friend's blackbelt with raw strength and speed. There was no time to prevent them toppling as Laika's shoulder drove into the friend's chest. Cans and chips crumpled under the weight of both werewolves. A soggy mess of ruined food erupted below them.

"Stop! It's getting in my hair!" shrieked Evie.

Laika looked down at the other werewolf, whose red hair stuck out in odd angles and her fair skin had a few cuts from broken glass. Then her gaze raised to survey the damage they'd done to the living room. Had either of them landed even half a foot to the left, then the television would have been another casualty of their war. Silver and amber eyes connected once more causing them to burst into laugh-ter. What had they even been fighting about? A late bill?

"Okay," Laika relented as she flopped backwards onto the carpet, "We can call that one a tie?"

"I won't go so easy on you next time."

"In that case, I'll make sure to use my full speed."

They jabbed at each other with companionable quips and matching grins for a little longer. No fight between them ever lasted. Finally, one of Evie's finely manicured hands ran fingers through the wet strands of hair with a scowl. "I'm going to take a shower. You call Owen. We'll see if he's got any work he can throw at us this weekend... please."

As Laika sat up, she rolled her eyes at the bossiness but called after her friend all the same. "Yeah, maybe he and Aaron are having a bad weekend. That'll mean a good payday for us."

"We can only hope." Evie's voice was coming from the hallway to her bedroom now.

Laika stood back up, picking up the crushed bag of beer-soaked chips as she did. She gave them a quick sniff before taking a bite. Dinner would taste unusual, but be edible. A loud scream of frustration echoed down the hall, causing her to wince.

"Laika! Call Owen now!" Evie stormed back to the living room.

"What's wrong?"

"The water is out as well!" Snatching her phone back up, Evie scrolled for a second then dialed. Her tone changed to her very best 'I have no idea what's wrong?' voice.

Laika watched Evie pace back and forth, her superior hearing picking up both sides of the conversation. Her friend had called the water company and was swearing up and down the check was mailed two weeks ago. If only they could turn on the water for tonight, their money would surely be there in the morning. Taking that as her cue to give up on cleaning, Laika searched through the overturned couch for her own phone. The third number in her speed dial was labeled 'Best Brother Owen,' referring to their favorite Glenwood police officer.

"Kirkland speaking, how can I help you today?" answered the playful tones of Owen on the other side. The amusement curling his lips could be heard even over the phone.

"Hey Owen, how is my Best Brother doing today?" replied Laika sweetly.

"I'm not your brother," reminded the man for the hundredth time even if his happy tone never dipped, "I'm your boss... kinda.

What pair of shoes did you see at the mall that now makes you want a job?"

The edge of the dark-haired woman's mouth curled up at the usual greeting. She teased him with an overly dramatic tone, "Can't it be both? Alas, I'm not calling about shoes today."

"What's up? You only call me when you need something. Or feel like drinking. By my count, you don't get paid for another four days, so drinking doesn't seem likely."

Laika scoffed, "Are you calling me a liar?"

"Why would I do that, *Lie*-ka?" Owen answered without missing a beat.

"Our power might have turned off tonight... and the water turned off this afternoon as well. We really need bill money." In her head she silently added, '... *to see the Love Pack finale.*'

"Shit," swore Owen, "That's bad. I was going to call in Blood Fang for this domestic, but I guess I could give it to the Night Claw pack instead."

Laika glanced up at Evie, who was still on the phone playing dumb to the point the water company representative was getting frustrated. Either they'd get water tonight or be hung up on. "That would be amazing if you could," cooed Laika, turning up her charm, "Please, Owen, this would mean so much to us and just prove you are our Best Brother." She knew that the job was already theirs though, as he wouldn't have brought it up otherwise.

"Yeah. Alright, I'll ask for Night Claw when I put in the request... and you should get a call in a minute or two." Owen went quiet as he started typing quickly.

Evie hung up. "We're back in business for the night. How about you?"

Laika muted her phone. "Domestic Dispute in progress, and it's all ours. I'm just waiting for confirmation."

"Amazing!"

"The only issue is you don't have time for a shower." Laika's smile faltered.

"Ew, no. I always have time for a shower," corrected Evie, twisting her lips while her nails picked at the beer-soaked strands clinging to her neck.

Owen interrupted them, "Okay, one requisition for MOONS in your name. Just don't do what you did last time." His tone held an air of warning.

"That wall was broken when I got there!" Laika exclaimed.

Evie
September 1st, 2018
Domestic Disturbance on 8th Street, Glenwood, CA

Evie pulled her shabby Saab into a parking spot down the road from the disturbance on 8th Street. Most people assumed nothing exciting happened in this suburban town nestled between Los Angeles's outskirts and the wooded foothills. But the moonlighter knew better. Worldwide the non-humans made up less than 5% of the population, but Glenwood had a higher than average supernatural community with werewolves and dwarves being the most common, followed by witches, elves, and vampires.

In California there were really only three options for any were-wolf when looking for company. You could join a domestic pack, which usually consisted of 5 to 10 families that took over a street. They hunted for sales, not wild prey, and barbecued on the holiday weekends. Next, there were the Mega Packs like Crescent Bell which consisted of hundreds of domestic packs with centralized leadership. They tended to have their own schools and werewolf-only clubs. Or, like Evie, you were in a Moonlighting Pack.

The houses on 8th Street were predominantly owned by were-wolves from one of the many domestic packs in Glenwood. Tonight their street was empty of the usual people taking a walk or catching up with neighbors. Instead, the neighborhood stood clustered behind a police barricade across from the third house on the left.

Two cruisers from Glenwood's Police Department were parked in front as well, with red and blue lights flashing in the night. A signal for them to follow.

"I think this is our stop," teased Laika from the passenger seat, barely containing her excitement. Evie could read the anxious energy coming off her friend. A door slammed as Laika bolted to get their gear. Evie was almost surprised that the tawny-skinned woman had held still until their car was in park.

With a pause, Evie checked in the driver's side mirror that her beer-soaked hair was still tamed by a scrunchie. Her sparkly shorts and orange-colored shirt had snaps up the sides to help with a shift. She longed for proper shifting clothing that wouldn't require redressing in the street every time; the larger hybrid forms were too big for her regular clothing, so she'd gotten creative by buying stripper outfits. The tamest ones she could find, naturally. If her shorts had to come off, at least they wouldn't be torn to shreds.

She gave herself a shrug of acceptance before eyes turned to scan the scene laid out before her. There was a small quirk of her lips, feeling a swell of excitement herself before she joined Laika in retrieving their limited gear.

The trunk held both of their tactical vests at all times, even when stuffed between ramen and milk. Last year they'd both finally sprung to buy their own rather than keep borrowing the MOONS loaner vests, and Evie would never regret that decision. The other vests had been unisex messes that smashed her breasts to her chest when tightened or hung off her shoulders when loose enough to breathe correctly. And after a few mishaps of forgetting the protective gear only to be sent home from a job, Evie had ensured the vests only left the car for cleaning and work. She held up the flexible kevlar blend vest for a quick inspection. Satisfied, she pulled it over her shoulders. The vests had many buckles, pockets, and snaps all over, but the woman ignored most of them. She'd never bothered with the 20-

page manual. How complicated could a vest really be once you figured out how to put it on?

Laika was already strapping her gear in place tightly so it wouldn't impede her speed when she moved. She rolled her shoulders, testing her range of motion. "Hurry up! We don't want to be any longer, or Owen will regret calling us in."

"I'm almost finished." Buckles clicked into place swiftly. Evie had to be careful not to snag the delicate fabric of her shorts. Her friend's denim shorts were more durable, but Laika tended to spend more when inevitably replacing them.

The werewolves quickly made their way to the police car parked in front of the double story house with red bricks. Aaron Leaven-worth and Owen Kirkland were standing by their cruiser. Both were in their uniforms, with a reflective 'MOONS' on their shoulders. They were perpetually at every Moonlighting job they'd ever had; as the Glenwood Police Department's MOONS Liaisons, the men were responsible for overseeing the moonlighters of MOONS' work.

Unable to keep her face from brightening with excitement, Evie greeted the pair with a wide grin. She was ready to get the lights turned back on, but also importantly, she wanted to get to work.

Aaron was only a few inches taller than the women. He had the look of someone who rolled out of bed with perfectly messy brown locks and a confident air around him. Evie was always impressed that Aaron had no fear of the creatures more powerful than him, despite working with supernaturals daily. He looked up from the laptop perched on the hood of his car, "Miss Belle, nice to see you again."

"Evie. 'Miss Belle' sounds like someone receiving the Glenwood Chastity Award, and we both know that's not me." She waved her hand dismissively. She'd been pushing for him to be less formal with her for the last five years. Only in the past few months did the man finally agree. The offered smile made up for any misstep on the officer's part a moment earlier. Her supernatural empathy picked up the familiar warmth coming from him.

"Sorry, yes, Evie. Old habits."

Next to him, a woman with long blonde hair leaned against the cruiser wearing an EMT jacket. Evie usually wouldn't even take a second glance at whichever medical professional drew the short straw to be on call tonight. But the striking woman joining them was hard to ignore. Tattoos covered the exposed olive skin of her neck and wrists that peeked out from her jacket.

Aaron noticed where Evie's gaze had drifted to and added, "Oh, have you never met Melinda before? Evie Belle, this is Melinda Vaas; she's our backup for the night."

"Hello, nice to meet you." Evie extended a hand politely.

"You shouldn't shake hands with creatures you don't know," Melinda responded while staring down at the extended greeting. Her steely blue eyes pondered the appendage apathetically for a moment, then returned the handshake.

Evie got a better look at her tattoos now and contact brought strange feelings. The thick black lines looked arcane in nature. Maybe magic? Melinda had a prickle of power and sadness coming from her; this had to be a witch.

"Melinda handles our more dangerous cases-" Aaron attempted to explain.

Evie interrupted. "Hang on, how dangerous is this?"

No answer came because Aaron was looking past Evie where Laika and Owen were exchanging shoulder punches. Each trying to get the other to give up. He frowned, "Officer Kirkland. We've got to brief them on the scene. Stop messing around."

"Lighten up; this barely qualifies as needing moonlighters."

"There are still people in danger," countered Aaron.

Owen scoffed, "The guy has what? Thrown around some furniture? As mad as he is, I don't see him raising a hand to his wife. Werewolves know their strength, and they don't hit humans."

An eyebrow raised as Aaron glanced between Owen and Laika. "Because we've never been called to a scene where a werewolf hit a human?" Owen looked ashamed. The blonde man stopped joking around with Laika so his partner could explain the scene.

Aaron began to brief them. "30 minutes ago, we received multiple calls from the neighbors stating that Mr. Brian Abbott put his dining room table through his patio doors. There have been several screaming matches between him and his wife, Derdria Abbot, in the last month. He's registered as a werewolf, and his wife is human. We have been told their son, Jerome, is almost eighteen and is showing signs of being a wolfkin."

Wolfkin appeared if at least one parent was a werewolf, but unlike that parent they didn't turn once reaching adulthood. Every big werewolf family had some wolfkin siblings and cousins running around.

Aaron's mahogany eyes flickered to his partner. Owen just calmly played with his radio, ignoring the word as though they were talking about the weather.

After the briefest pause, Aaron continued his explanation for the moonlighters. "The fights have been escalating to the point of destruction of property and neighbors have said that they hear a lot of yelling about Jerome. We just need to get him out of the house then check on the wife and son. So far he's been responding to attempts to communicate, but hasn't left the entryway. He's denying that his son is a wolfkin or that there are any issues."

"Because being a wolfkin is somehow shameful or even his kid's choice," grumbled Owen, finally allowing himself the indulgence. "Besides, he's not even 18 yet and could have a more subtle power like a faster shifter. You wouldn't see that until the boy actually turns around 20-22."

"He could easily be like me with empathy," added Evie, redoing her hair. Her empathic powers had taken her well into her 20's to figure out. Her eyes flickered back to Owen reading annoyance off of him, but not commenting on it. Laika patted the man on the shoulder but knew better than to try cheering him up. There wasn't really a problem with the wolfkin police officer. He'd been born from a werewolf family, but Owen never felt the wild's call to turn into a wolf. No wolfkin did.

"Yes, it is very possible," agreed Aaron, "Right now we need to deescalate no matter the reason."

Evie sighed, "This is a stupid reason to destroy your home. Do you know how much a new dining room table costs?" She turned to her packmate, "I could go to the front door? See if I can get Mr. Abbott talking long enough to step outside?"

"If the back door's already destroyed, I could sneak in there?" offered up Laika with a grin.

Evie knew if she didn't rein in her friend's impulses quickly, then more than a table was going through glass tonight. "Yes, you could do that and get Mrs. Abbott out of the house while I get Mr. Abbott to surrender peacefully."

"Yeah... that works too." Her eyes lost a bit of their fire. Laika wouldn't have as much fun as she would ambushing the offending werewolf onto the lawn...

"Alright," Aaron acknowledged with a nod, "Then we have a plan. Evie, you come with me."

"Don't break anything," warned Owen as he gave Laika a sharp look.

Aaron shook his head. "I don't care about any broken walls, only bones. If he turns violent, both of you are cleared to use any form to keep humans at the scene safe."

Owen groaned audibly at his partner's statement.

Melinda spoke up, "If you screw up and break bones, then I come into play." She put on a pair of leather gloves decorated with pieces of jade.

"Are you a Green Witch?" Laika immediately asked with a spike of excitement.

"Not right now, Laika," interrupted Evie. Despite werewolves having no affinity of their own, the redhead knew her packmate was fascinated by magic. She'd be going nonstop for the next hour if given a chance.

Aaron ran a hand under his chin, getting his game face back in place. "Alright, everyone please get into position and be careful."

"Yes, sir!" Evie saluted before she could help herself. She fell into step towards the red-painted door.

Once they were out of earshot, Aaron whispered, "You reek of beer. Are you sure you are up for this?"

"Shut up, I would never show up drunk to a job. Half dressed like a 'dancer,' yes, but not drunk."

The pair chuckled at her words while passing the yard fence. Ahead the door had a large crack running down the wood, but the hinges were still intact. A domestic pack neighborhood like this would have werewolf-proofed upgrades everywhere. From the corner of her eye, she saw Laika slipping down the street like a dark shadow.

The house seemed well-kept until Evie got closer. A small jungle of weeds grew in the yard and the trim was a few years overdue for a fresh coat of paint. Still, she believed this had been a lovely home at one point because the warm feelings of family hadn't faded yet. She could imagine that Mr. Abbott would be home on time every night. They had family dinners and everyone would talk about their day. Happiness like that left a mark. But now it was overshadowed by a dark cloud of roiling emotions.

Evie paused just short of the brick steps up to the front door and let her escort go first. "Mr. Abbott," Aaron called calmly through the door. He didn't wait for a response before continuing, "I've brought someone to talk with you. Her name is Evie, and she's a friend from MOONS."

"YOU CALLED IN LITERAL MILITARY DOGS ON ME!?" There was a bang against the wall, strong enough to crack the plaster.

Evie could feel boiling anger behind the doorway. Other emotions mixed into it were frustration, fear, and anxiety. Nothing unexpected in a situation like this. "I should just take this door off the hinges at you both before she breaks it anyway!" But Mr. Abbott didn't follow up on his threat just yet.

"No, sir. Moonlighters work for Glenwood; it's not military. Evie hasn't served a single day in her life," Aaron assured, glancing at the woman for confirmation he hadn't been lying.

Evie kept her voice as soothing as possible. "Good evening Mr. Abbott. It's Evie. I'm not here to break down your door. If Glenwood PD wanted that, they would have called in someone much heavier and scarier than me. I'm not a six-foot-tall bodybuilder, I swear."

"You sound young?" responded a surprised voice, clearly expecting someone else.

"What I lack in age I make up for in my charming personality, I promise."

Silence met her words.

"I'm here to talk to you about what's happening inside. I would really prefer it if we could have this conversation face to face. Would you mind opening the door?" Evie let her empathy guide her words.

"I'm not sure that's a good idea. I open this door, then your ten packmates rush me, right? I've heard that's how you moonlighting wolves do it." His tone was hesitant for good reason. But Night Claw was a pack of two, so an overwhelm tactic wasn't in the cards.

"How many people can you hear out here? Two breathing from this distance," she gave him a moment to check for himself.

"Yeah, two..."

"Hopefully, we can resolve this situation without anyone getting hurt. I don't want to fight you. I'm a trained moonlighter. You're a suburban dad. The optics are terrible for both of us if that happens. Don't get me started on the paperwork either." Evie joked, feeling amusement break through the waves of anger.

"Good job," Aaron mouthed silently. He seemed confident in his choice to send Evie to the front door.

"Evie?" asked Mr. Abbott, "Am I going to jail tonight? Since you had to show up here?" She looked at Aaron for an answer, but he only gave an unsure frown. "It's only my furniture that got broken." Mr. Abbott's words rang with concern.

"No matter how mad you are, breaking the dining table isn't

right for the family. Where will you have dinner tomorrow? I suppose you all could picnic in front of the TV." Evie tried to lighten the mood since the other werewolf was done screaming. She knew they weren't past the line that Aaron had to get the cuffs out. As long as no one swung a fist then the night could be salvaged.

A small laugh came from the other side of the door.

Aaron assured, "It's standard procedure in situations like these for you to come down the station for a few hours, Mr. Abbott. I just need you to answer some questions. Maybe we can get you connected to a few resources to help you with that anger."

Finally, the door cracked open an inch allowing Evie to see tired eyes in the backlight. Mr. Abbott didn't seem close to a frenzy, just a soccer dad in over his head. Everything about this situation seemed wrong. If he'd been escalating fights for the last month, he should be foaming at the mouth, but his anger was a smokescreen for a deeper fear.

Werewolves ready to lose themselves to a frenzy were on the edge. They couldn't control themselves and got overtaken by the wolf inside. Unable to tell between family and foe, they attacked everyone in sight until they ran themselves into the ground. They were the most dangerous missions you could get because you couldn't reason with a werewolf in a frenzy.

Evie followed her hunch. "Mr. Abbott, did you really put that table through the back door?"

Mr. Abbott's eyes went wide in surprise when the moonlighter's question struck true. The older werewolf hadn't been responsible for the damage. No doubt the very human Mrs. Abbott hadn't been either. Which only left one more person in the house... Both of them realized the other knew the truth at the same time; that's when Mr. Abbott's eyes shifted. His irises expanded all the way to the edges, swallowing the white. Fear mixed with panic, resulting in a bad decision.

Evie and Aaron recognized that as the first sign of a werewolf shifting.

The moonlighter pushed herself into the door frame, shielding the officer from any wolf about to try and dash past her legs. But to the moonlighter's surprise, the tired Mr. Abbott didn't begin to shrink; instead, his shoulders rose slowly as his chest expanded.

Mr. Abbott had learned how to use his hybrid form. While not uncommon, most domestic werewolves never bothered with the difficult skill. Rather than condense their bodies down into a giant wolf, the hybrid form was a massive combination of human and wolf traits. Every aspect of it was designed for combat.

Transforming into wolf form took most werewolves two to three minutes. If they were brand new to shifting, then the turn took even longer. Hybrid forms were not an innate skill; it took months, if not years, of practice to learn. The hybrid transformation took at least 10 minutes minimum. There was a significant difference between MOONS werewolves and most of the population, however. In order to be licensed, moonlighters were required to master hybrid forms, which meant a lot of practice turning fast. Even a moderate shifter like Evie only took 2 minutes. She could have beaten Mr. Abbott to the end, but stopping his transformation meant no fight.

A snout pushed out of Mr. Abott's face, while fur spread out to protect delicate human skin. Human hands remained at the end of muscled arms, but feet gave way to wolf paws. Both bristled with rending claws.

Evie sprang into action, quickly swinging a foot up at the spot just above her opponent's knee. The impact forced Mr. Abbott's leg back, breaking his balance as he started to shift. When he fell forward, Evie grabbed the back of his head, letting his momentum pull him down to the ground in a single motion. Swiftly she pulled both of his arms up once she was sure the move hadn't broken his nose or teeth. Evie wasn't a tiny woman, but most male werewolves still towered over her as they came built tall, and this worked almost every time.

Aaron handed her a set of reinforced handcuffs. With a snap, Evie bound the werewolf below her, knowing that he'd have to break his arms to keep turning. Only the most hardened of wolves would even try.

"Shit!" Evie swore. "We've got a problem. He's not the one we need to be worried about."

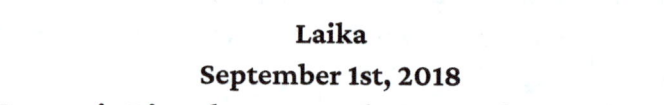

Laika
September 1st, 2018
Domestic Disturbance on 8th Street, Glenwood, CA

While her packmate distracted the family at the door, Laika's approach went unnoticed. Slipping through the neighboring backyards, she crept up to the chain-link fence surrounding the red brick house. Keen eyes spotted the broken back door. Fragments of the dining table that had brought her here were scattered around. But the dark-haired woman spied pieces of more than just a table in the dirt yard. All the chairs, the refrigerator, and so many family photos lay in shattered frames all around.

Her attention turned back to the fragile wall in her way, determining that climbing over it was a nonstarter. The metal links would screech under her touch. Instead of climbing over the trap, Laika backed up a dozen steps then launched into a running jump. Bare feet soared over the top of the chain-links. The werewolf tucked into a rolling landing with a small muffled thud. She perked up her ears, searching for any signs her entrance was heard. Hearing no reaction, she carried on with her approach.

Houses to the left and right were emptied into the streets out front, leaving no one to distract Laika's tracking. Inside the red brick house, she could hear Mr. Abbott talking at the front door, but his tone never changed as he spoke to the 'young girl'.

Worried feet pacing in the same hallway almost escaped her

sensitive ears. Any other werewolf might have missed the small sounds, but the moonlighter had superior hearing. She could correctly pick out all three household members' positions. Her ears pinpointed the locations of Evie and Aaron standing up front as well. Conversations being held on the other side of the house were possible to hear if she focused on the voices.

She could hear Evie making jokes about dinner in front of the TV. But that appliance lay broken in the backyard already. Her eyes peered around the edge of the sliding door taking in the trashed kitchen. Anything not bolted to the floor had been toppled or thrown around. She guessed the living room was in a similar mess, judging from the couch stuffing strewn on the floor. Someone had lost their temper and left a wake of destruction throughout the whole house. How they hadn't lost themselves to a frenzy was beyond her.

Careful to avoid any broken pieces of glass, Laika moved forward like a shadow. Her goal was to get Mrs. Abbott out of harm's way in case this situation turned violent. Before stepping a foot inside, Laika heard her packmate ask Mr. Abbott if he'd actually destroyed his house. Her foot hovered over the edge of the broken glass. Why would Evie ask him something that Aaron had already explained to them?

An obvious answer hit Laika like a ton of bricks.

She bolted back into the yard to get a good view of the windows on the second floor. There was a third person in that house who hadn't come downstairs. Even if he was a wolfkin, Mr. Abbott's son would have enough strength to throw around the table. He wouldn't be able to frenzy either if he hadn't shifted yet.

The supernatural who was actually a danger to the neighborhood wasn't the werewolf at the front door. It was the teenager upstairs who had the power to do a lot of damage to both his home and his human mother. The evidence lay at Laika's feet: dozens of pieces of broken furniture and glass. If the police did something like haul in his father for questioning, they'd leave an angry boy at home with his unprotected mother.

A house like this had narrow hallways with squeaky wooden boards that announced everyone's movements. There was only one way that Laika could make her way to the boy without him noticing. Her hand reached out to test how strong the red bricks were, pleased to find they were stable. The werewolf found the lowest part of the roof then backed up a few steps. With a bolt of intense speed, Laika pushed herself into a run up the wall. Fingers reached out for the lip of the roof, pulling her soundlessly onto the shingles.

Once more, Laika paused to ensure no one had heard her ascend to the upper floor. She could catch Mrs. Abbott screaming at Evie to let her husband go. Her packmate must have detained Mr. Abbott. Now she could hear Evie's cautious steps on the squeaky floorboards.

Laika's eyes could see two windows from her position. Through one, she could see the teenaged boy had heard the same commotion. He leapt up from his bed. She hid just out of sight under his window, peering over the edge.

The boy had dragged a heavy dresser in front of the door to block Evie's entrance. While her friend could have moved the furniture, she would have a more challenging time pinpointing the teenager's location. Evie would never risk toppling that much weight onto him by accident. She'd try to talk him down instead.

Laika could see how panicked the boy was becoming. Before anyone could make it through that door, he'd either hurt himself or jump out the window.

"Jerome? Are you in there?" Evie's patient voice called.

"JUST GO AWAY!" Panic bled from the teenage boy's voice.

The voice of her packmate continued calmly, "I'm not here to hurt you. I just want to talk."

Every inch of Jerome's posture looked like a cornered animal about to bolt. There was no way he'd get past everyone blocking his bedroom door. The boy only had one way to go; the window Laika was standing by.

While the moonlighter had jumped up here, Laika had physical abilities on the high end of werewolves. A wolfkin kid might break his neck if he attempted the jump down. Another minute and he'd be going through the glass if she didn't stop him. Laika made a decision and slammed her shoulder into the fragile glass of the window. Her body rolled through the opening. Her vest was all that touched the jagged frame, leaving the werewolf uncut.

Breaking glass made Jerome turn around, only to find the werewolf had already crossed his room. She detained him easily. He never stood a chance against a trained moonlighter.

"Clear," called Laika to the others as she held Jerome's hands behind his back.

"Was that glass?" Owen barked. His fist pounded on the door, but again it didn't move.

"The door's blocked," Evie reminded. To underscore her point, the doorknob jiggled as Laika's packmate pushed lightly against the door. The dresser didn't move an inch.

Owen cursed before begging, "Please don't break the door too!"

Laika looked down at the boy and back at the dresser. She stood, helping Jerome up as she did. He was no danger to anyone now, just a scared kid. One hand held his arms so he didn't decide to try for the window while her other hand pushed the dresser out of the way.

Jerome swore at the moonlighter's casual display of strength. Any thoughts of escape seemed to disappear as the boy's shoulders sagged. He was outmatched in strength by far.

"I've got him." Laika opened the bedroom door with a wide grin.

Evie stood poised for an attack outside the door. Owen and Aaron flanked her with their tasers drawn. No one had wanted to go through with force to retrieve the teenager, so a collective sigh of relief flooded the group. She saw Aaron slip his handcuffs back into their protective bag.

"Did you do that?" Owen hissed as he pushed through to inspect the destruction.

"The window?"

"Of course the window!" Owen hissed. His head was snapping left and right looking for any more damage he'd have to document.

Laika shrugged, "It was getting broken either way. Trust me."

"I was literally two minutes from not having to file any damage paperwork. Now I have to catalog everything broken in this house so I can assign blame for your insurance!" He put a hand carefully on the bottom of the frame and pulled it open. "The window's not even locked! You could have just opened it!"

"But what if it *had* been locked?" defended Laika. She had enough grace to look embarrassed by not even checking the window first. In the rush of adrenaline the werewolf hadn't thought about anything but lining up her tackle.

Owen scrunched up his face in frustration, "But it wasn't!"

"But if it had been, then he might have heard me. Then I would have lost the element of surprise."

"I swear to the moon and back, your insurance is going up for sure this time when I file this claim." Owen pulled his camera out to document the damage.

"Look. More importantly, Jerome is fine." Laika still had a hand on his arms. She had checked him over for any stray cuts or bruises from her ambush.

Aaron motioned for her to let the teenager go. He put a hand on the boy's shoulder to lead him away. As usual the officer was kind, not cuffing Jerome now that the situation had been defused. He did spare a glance back at his partner, a wry smile on his face, "You know she's right, Owen."

"Don't you start too! I'm filing this claim."

Laika groaned before giving up on trying to convince Owen. As much as he teased, there was no way Aaron would stop him. There wasn't a more law-abiding officer on the force.

Her attention turned to Evie who waited by the door. Laika said with a sheepish grin, "I think we might need a roommate to help with the bills."

CHAPTER 2
INTERVIEWS

Laika
September 3rd, 2018
Night Claw Residence, Glenwood, CA

Laika always remembered fondly how the Night Claw pack was formed. Back in college, she had suffered in dorms from day one. Her keen hearing was far beyond even most were-wolves, making the paper-thin walls practically non-existent. She never wondered what the party down the hall was like because she could hear every word and bass drop.

When Evie came into her life they had a very drunken 4th of July, spiraling into getting matching tattoos and moving in together. Their friendship had saved her from dorm life and brought her the best friend she ever could ask for.

Now Laika sat crossed-legged on the floor of her home with a roll of silver duct tape in hand. The pieces of the coffee table lay around her waiting for repair. She and Evie had wrecked their rental house a hundred times over by now. It was just a hazard that came along with rambunctious werewolves. At this point, she had gotten very good at triage with tape and spray paint. Her amber eyes couldn't see the damage even this close. At the very least, their landlord had never noticed before.

"Are you done yet?" asked Evie as she stuck her head out of the kitchen. Every red wisp of hair was swept up into a messy ponytail. A faint scent of chemicals clung to her as she'd spent half of the morning cleaning.

"Just about. Unless you really stick your nose under the table, you can't smell the paint."

Amusement flashed over Evie's face, "You've got spray paint up your arms... and your face. I am pretty sure even for you that's in bad taste."

"I'll go clean it off," promised Laika while she wrapped her duct tape around the last broken leg. A few puffs from the can of paint hid any mismatch of colors. Once more, their coffee table was in a single piece and she stood up. Then pulled up the tarp she'd used to protect the rest of the room over her arm. With a glance around, the woman was quite pleased with how normal the living room seemed. "Looks good, yeah?" she asked her packmate with a sweep of her paint-stained arms.

"Yes," agreed Evie sarcastically, "You've got our place looking like normal humans live here. Now go clean up before anyone arrives. We just need to convince one person that this is a home they want to live in!" The redhead's hands raised to pull her hair loose from the scrunchie, fingers fluffing it out into her signature feathered style.

"I'm going to clean up. Just don't start with all your 'no SOs staying over', 'no dishes in the sink', etcetera. Then we might stand a chance at finding a roommate," Laika warned. She headed for the guest bathroom that served as hers to wash off. The sounds of Evie rearranging the living room floated to her ears, but she ignored them. In the house, everything was much quieter with their thick dwarven-made walls.

As Laika walked the hallway, she paused to place a forlorn hand on the door that would soon belong to whomever they picked for a new roommate. Their rental house was actually a three-bedroom, but both women had run out of closet space years ago. Right now Evie had the master bedroom, Laika had the one closest to her bathroom, and the last one they used as a shared walk-in closet. Under Evie's guidance, both had grown quite a taste for the latest fashion. But it was Laika's impulsive nature that pushed them to buy before they checked if the bills had been paid. The combination resulted in a massive overage of outfits only worn once. Giving up 'the closet' to get a roommate had been like asking Evie to cut off her own arm, but ultimately having a 3rd paycheck meant stability.

Water did nothing to the dark pigment that stained Laika's hands, so she stood over the sink for a long time, scrubbing with rubbing alcohol. Splatters of the paint chips stained the basin leading Laika to waste further time cleaning them up yet again. Minutes evaporated, and before she knew it, the familiar chime of the doorbell rang through the house.

Cursing, Laika splashed water on her face and smoothed her hair down. Had that been a motorcycle engine she heard? She really hoped not. A noisy vehicle was the last thing they needed in a roommate. She was stumbling out to the living room in a mad dash as Evie opened the door.

"Hello there!" The chipper voice of her best friend rang out as she extended a hand to the stranger standing on their doorstep.

"Hey, I'm Tor. I'm here about the room." Her voice was laidback with a confident smirk and black painted nails took the offered hand.

Laika watched her packmate sweep long gazes up and down the woman. Her friend was nearly drooling over the black leather and piercings wrapped around snow white skin, dark hair, and a lean frame. Her eyes glanced past the newcomer to the shiny black bike sitting on their driveway. Laika barely resisted groaning as she recognized the look on Evie's face. Not again...

"I'm Evie and that's Laika," Evie gestured over her shoulder with a quick nod, "Please come in. Can we get you something to drink? Tea or coffee?"

Rolling her eyes, Laika recognized her friend's Bel Air charm being laid on thick. They had been friends for years now, and it had become effortless for Laika to spot when the other woman was interested in someone. She had sworn off cleaning up after the redhead's conquests many years ago. Evie didn't do relationships; those that tried got destroyed and Laika had to set them straight.

"Nah, I've heard about the stuff werewolves drink. Far too strong for me." Tor laughed as she strode into the living room, giving the room an appraising look. If she noticed the hastily repaired coffee table then she gave no indication she cared.

Both werewolves paused, baffled by the statement for a second. Supernaturals hardly broadcasted what they were, even in this modern age. Millenia of evolution ensured they blended into humanity smoothly. After a beat, Laika recovered from the shock. "How did you know?"

Tor laughed easily again, "Your ad says 'Werewolf Friendly,' and I took a guess, but it seems I hit the mark."

"Oh, yeah, that makes sense."

The raven-haired woman sat down on the couch before propping her elbows up on the back, looking very comfortable already.

"Is Tor your real name?" asked Evie, sitting at the other end of the couch. She pulled up a leg so she could face the woman.

There really was only enough room for two people comfortably which wasn't a problem before. So Laika sat on the floor as they didn't have more seating in the living room. That was something that would need to be remedied once they secured a roommate.

"Yeah," answered Tor simply, with a raised eyebrow, "Is that a problem?"

"No, no," blushed Evie, waving off the question with her hand.

Laika internally groaned, realizing that she would have to set down the rules of no sleeping with housemates. Otherwise her packmate was going to pursue this woman. This time they'd be out a paying roommate. She pulled open her phone to check the emailed application to check the names. Tor Baker was on the first one in her inbox.

"What questions do you have for me?" asked Tor, keeping that playful smirk on her face.

"Do you like Love Pack?" inquired Laika immediately, deeming that the most critical question.

"The Werewolf Version of the Bachelor? I've only seen a few episodes, but yeah, I've liked everything I saw. That Brandon guy is a moron because Sophie would be way more fun long term than that prude, Isabelle."

"Take that back," whined Laika as her favorite couple was trashed by their applicant, "Isabelle is a cinnamon roll; she only deserves good things in her life."

Meanwhile, Evie laughed loud enough that it became a snort. "You heard her. Clearly Tor has good taste! Score one point Evie." The werewolf did a little dance in her seat, enjoying the look of defeat on Laika's face.

There was another quirk of an eyebrow at the comment about points, but Tor didn't inquire about them. Instead, she asked a different question, "Do you guys take rent in advance?"

"Yes!" Both werewolves responded in unison, eyes now glued to this prospective roommate. An advance in rent was the perfect solution for the utility bills that had fallen behind. They could pay those off now, and handle future rent with their own paychecks.

Laika recovered first, clearing her throat softly, "What we mean is, of course, we'll take early rent if you have it."

Tor was unperturbed by the excited reaction from the werewolves. "And the room is available, like, now?"

"Yes," Evie answered, just a little too quickly, like a happy puppy. Her eyes all but sparkled as they gazed at Tor.

Laika shot an open glare her friend's way.

"...of course, assuming you're the best fit," Evie backpedaled.

As far as Laika could tell, no one else would hold a candle to the leather-clad siren sitting on their couch. Evie looked like she'd move

Tor in now if she could get away with it. A thought struck her, and the curious woman began to ask, "Are you hum-?"

"Laika!"

"What? It's a valid question." Laika rolled her eyes at the dramatics.

"I'm human," Tor cut them off with a shrug.

"Oh... okay then," Evie attempted to get them back on track, "So Tor, how do you feel about The Nine?"

No more real questions passed in the conversation as the women devolved into idle gossip about their favorite clothing, clubs, and TV shows. The interview itself wasn't terrible, but uninformative about the important aspects of Tor moving in.

Twenty minutes later Laika closed the door as Tor left. The sounds of a roaring engine peeled down their quiet street, signaling that the raven-haired human had left. Laika declared firmly, "That woman is dangerous."

"I know," Evie agreed with a much more excited expression, "I think she's perfect."

"She's really fragile, though," warned Laika, unsure that her packmate was thinking straight. If they had a human roommate, they'd have to be far more careful with their strength.

"You're being dramatic. She's not a paper doll."

Laika frowned. In her experience anyone who wasn't a werewolf broke too easily for her liking, but she changed the subject. "We have two more applicants today, so let's not make our choice until the end."

"Yes, yes," Evie waved a hand dismissively as she swept around the room, scrutinizing the repairs they had made. Nothing had been disturbed during the first interview, and Tor hadn't commented on the piecemeal repairs.

Laika would put good money that the next two applicants could be billionaire genius philanthropists, and Evie would still pick Tor at the end of the day. Her ears were focused on the street, waiting for another car to arrive. "You're not thinking with your head."

"I already said we'd decide after we talk to the other two. But I mean, what's wrong with Tor?"

"The next one is here," Laika announced, ending their conversation. There would be time to discuss the complications of a human roommate later.

A light knock at the door revealed a blonde woman, half a head taller than Laika. Pointed ears peeked from behind the flaxen hair, declaring the woman to be an elf. Bright blue eyes, the color of rain, sparkled with surprise and intelligence as a momentary flicker of annoyance crossed the elf's face. Then the woman beamed brightly. "Good afternoon, I'm Becky Hargrove. I am here to meet with Evie and..."

Laika realized the woman was waiting for her name. "I'm Laika, nice to meet you."

"Nice to meet you, too."

"Come on in," the werewolf stepped aside to wave the elf inside. Her eyes swept up and down, amusement trickling through Laika's mind. Becky reminded her of Evie from way back when the two werewolves had first met. Her outfit was the height of Bel Air fashion, and the colors mirrored those of Evie's own shirt. This was like looking at a blonde elven version of her friend.

"Hello Evie," Becky attempted to greet her fashion doppelganger.

Laika rolled her eyes at her packmate when Evie proceeded to ignore Becky, clearly still distracted by the pretty human. "Please have a seat."

"Thank you," Becky answered politely as she focused on Evie once more. Her eyes scanned the woman for a moment before complimenting, "That is an adorable jacket you have on."

"Oh," Evie joined the conversation finally, "Thank you. I like your shirt, it's a great color."

Laika knew her friend had just grabbed at the easiest compliment she could find. The woman was barely focused on the elf sitting in her living room, practically snubbing a potential roommate.

"Thank you so much. It looks better on you though."

A subtle kick darted out to hit Evie's leg before Laika settled herself back on the floor to start the questions. She could feel her packmate's glare burning holes in the back of her head but ignored her. "So Becky, do you like Love Pack?" the werewolf asked brightly.

"Oh yes, I'm a big fan! It is so much better than the elven version."

"Are you a Sophie or Isabelle shipper?" prompted Laika, still hoping someone would side with her today. If nothing else, maybe talking about their favorite show would get Evie to engage with the elf.

"Isabelle," answered Becky, but she seemed unsure of her answer. Her eyes glanced between the two werewolves watching her, "At least at the start of the season... I like Sophie better now."

"See, everyone loves Sophie," Evie pointed out smugly as another person agreed with her favorite couple.

"She's so fake," whined Laika.

The suspicious wolf leaned back against the couch, pulling out her phone. Then a quizzical expression warped Evie's face for a moment before she asked, "Your application says you work for Evergreen Pharmaceuticals?"

Becky lit up at the question, supplying a swift answer, "Yes. I've been an intern there for the last three months. I just got my Masters in Pharmacology, then went to work for my aunt."

"Why do you need a roommate?" Evie's tone bordered on interrogation with the last inquiry. The woman could be blunt when she wanted, but in situations like this, she was usually the picture of charm. Something must be sitting wrong with what her friend was reading.

Laika sat on the floor between them, feeling confused by the exchange. She knew that Evergreen was a huge elven owned corporation, but they didn't make anything particularly controversial. If anything, Evie should be happy their potential roommate was well employed. Her focus flicked between the other two women, trying to figure out what the problem was.

"I'm more looking for companionship with a good person than to live alone," the elven woman explained demurely. A pale hand brushed a loose strand of hair behind her pointed ears.

"That's sweet," Laika cut off Evie before she drilled in with another question. The look in her packmate's eyes said that she was gearing up for an inquisition. No matter what she was feeling, there was no reason to warrant this level of hostility.

Silver eyes suddenly cooled, and Evie stood up. "I think that's all the questions we have. Thank you so much for coming all the way out here to Glenwood, Becky."

"Of course, Evie," responded the elven woman with a soft smile. "This was hardly a problem. Thank you so much for your time. Please let me know if I'm selected for the room. I can provide more references if you need them."

Laika held her tongue until Becky was safely gone. "What the hell?" snapped the dark-haired werewolf the moment she heard the engine of the car outside start.

"Oh," Evie waved dismissively, "There was something wrong with that girl, she wasn't on the level about anything. Even you noticed her changing her Love Pack answer, fishing for the 'right' one."

"Seriously? You didn't like her Love Pack answer? She agreed with you!"

"She was lying about it," shrugged Evie.

"How is that a crime? Maybe she's just awkward at interviews... You didn't even let me get past the first question! I don't know anything about her except her name!" Laika hissed.

Evie frowned as she set her phone back down, "Evergreen pays more to their interns than we make combined. She'll be just fine for housing."

Throwing her hands in the air in sheer frustration, Laika flopped down onto the couch. "Did you kick her out because she makes more money than you? Because most people make more money than us."

"No, Becky just doesn't need us. We want a roommate that needs us as much as we need them. Or we'd always rely on her for the bills. I'm just saving us from a more awkward situation in a few months," Evie replied. Laika could tell her friend was being sincere.

"So she lied about Love Pack, but not her job or references right?"

"Yeah, nothing read wrong when she explained her degree or work," answered Evie.

Laika wanted to push back again, feeling pretty sure that the bombshell named Tor played more than a minor role in this decision. But there was nothing to be done; the elf was gone now.

"Let's just get all the way through the next interview, even if you don't like the woman?" pleaded the werewolf, reaching out to shake Evie's arm.

Evie deflated a bit, realizing she may have overstepped with that abrupt dismissal. "Unless I'm certain the next woman is some psycho serial killing stalker, I'll let you ask all the questions on the list."

They managed not to fight until their final candidate arrived. At the knock, Laika realized she hadn't heard a car approach or park. Had they come on foot? Evie opened the door to a short woman with uneven brown bangs. Freckles decorated her face and arms. She looked like she'd tanned in the actual sun, but she lacked the rest of the beach bunny appeal. No sun bleached blonde hair or vacant stares. After a moment, the pair recognized the newcomer as a fellow werewolf. Evie's voice was a note warmer as she made introductions, "Thanks so much for coming. I'm Evie, and that's Laika."

"I'm Shelly," replied the brunette, after a moment, she added, "Conner." The woman didn't seem to be well versed in the art of small talk.

Evie prompted for more information, "Nice to meet you. Where do you come from?"

"The East," Shelly answered, shifting her gaze around the room.

"Like Florida East or New York East?" Laika asked.

"Nowhere you've ever heard of, trust me on that." After assessing the place, Shelly seemed to warm up.

Laika placed herself back in her usual spot on the floor between them. She was happy at how well this interview was going compared to the last. Keen eyes were dying to know this werewolf's views on Sophie versus Isabelle. "So Shelly, do you like Love Pack?"

"What's Love Pack?" asked Shelly sincerely with a crinkle of her brow. "Is that one of those trashy reality TV shows?"

"More like the greatest show in existence," Evie exclaimed as both hands flew up to her face, exaggerating the expression.

"Oh..." Shelly said warily.

Evie pressed. "Do you not like Reality TV? It's so amazing and you get to see how not messed up you are compared to some killer train-wrecks. Who the hell goes on TV to date the same guy as 20 other women?"

"No, it's not that I don't like it... I just haven't seen a lot of TV shows." The brunette put up a hand in her defense.

"What do you watch then?" Laika took over the questions.

Shelly gave them an awkward grimace as she tried to explain better, "There wasn't cable back in the East."

"There wasn't cable?" echoed Laika trying to wrap her head around that. She came from small-town Colorado, and even then, her family had cable. Curiosity bubbled up, wondering how small of a town Shelly had come from, followed by a flash of camaraderie for another small-town wolf.

Her response was flat. "No, we didn't have cable, so I haven't seen things like Love Pack. My father thought shows like that were the work of the devil." The simple statement of fact conveyed Shelly's lack of belief in her father's view on the matter.

"Laika," Evie said, grabbing at her friend's arm with a shocked expression, "Do you realize what this means?"

The woman looked up in confusion, watching as her packmate's face shifted to genuine excitement. "What?"

"We have a real reason to rewatch every episode from the beginning!"

Laika's grin grew to match her friend's in seconds as her brain caught up. "You are so right! And if she's never seen Love Pack, then she's never seen By Daylight, or The Nine, or anything good."

Shelly's head whipped between them, watching this manic conversation unfold. She still seemed cautious about these two strangers that were too excited about trashy TV shows. Still her interest was increasing with every word, "What's By Daylight?"

"Just the best soap opera ever created," Laika informed the woman. "It's about what vampires do during the day when they are stuck inside. So much drama." The show had been running for nearly a decade, and somehow had not run out of storylines of vampiric drama.

"I've never met a vampire. I've never really met supernaturals outside of my family. You're like the 3rd and 4th werewolves I know that aren't related to me in some way." Shelly seemed sheepish at the admission, the faintest bit of color tinted her ears.

"That's fine," Laika assured quickly with a wave of her hand, "We only know Tony, and he barely counts. Here in Glenwood, vampires are super rare. But we do have werewolves everywhere! I think there are like 20 plus packs."

"Are you two part of a pack?" asked Shelly, her eyes guarded while waiting for the answer. There was a small uncomfortable shift in the air. Her brown eyes flicked minutely between Evie and Laika, as if the other wolf could glean the response from the air itself.

"Yep, we're the two members of the Night Claw Pack!" Laika exclaimed proudly, raising a hand to touch the tattoo peeking from under the strap of her tank top.

Steel laced Shelly's response, almost as if she put up her hackles to challenge the very idea of a pack. "I'm not joining your pack if I move in here, and I do not do pack drama either."

That left both women speechless for a moment. Neither expected her to sign up on day one, or even join their pack later. In the seven years that Night Claw had been together, they'd never recruited once. Laika found her words first, raising a hand reassuringly. "That's fine. We aren't looking for new packmates right now. Just a roommate to help with the bills."

"Okay, cool," replied Shelly, some of the fire in her words dying down.

"Cool."

As quickly as Shelly had gotten riled up, everything was relaxed again. "What's the WiFi like here? I need it for my job."

Laika shrugged. "Not great. We have the most basic plan, but as long as all of us aren't trying to stream something, it buffers pretty fast."

The brunette pulled up a smartphone that looked 10 years old. After a few moments tapping on the screen, she spoke again. "No, this is terrible WiFi. Would you guys mind if I upgraded the plan if I get the room? I need something at least ten times faster."

"Ten times?" Evie inquired. Any awkwardness at the pack situation already faded, replaced with curiosity about the WiFi.

"At least, I'll pay for it myself, and I don't care if you guys use it. As long as you don't torrent anything. I need my data stream unimpeded, and that shit brings a lot of attention."

"Like Limewire?" Laika knew how the internet worked but not exactly how 'torrenting' worked.

"Yeah, like Limewire." Shelly almost seemed amused by the answer.

"We just stream it on Netflix if we want to watch something."

That seemed to end the topic. Shelly asked, "Do you have any other questions? I have an appointment on the other side of Glenwood, and if I want to run there on time, I need to leave soon."

Laika glanced up at Evie, but nothing relevant came to mind at the moment. "No, I think we have all we need. We'll let you know in the next few days. Is that okay?"

"Yeah, no problem. I should tell you I'm interviewing at a few places, and I'll probably take the first that agrees. No hard feelings if it isn't you." The brunette picked herself up from the couch. The women showed their last applicant to the front door, watching as she walked down the street. Laika realized the run comment was a literal statement about Shelly's method of transport. She was no stranger to lacking a car in Glenwood.

Once the door closed, the woman swore as a realization crashed into her, "Shit. Evie, do you think we were supposed to ask these people if they'd committed a felony before? That could affect our Moonlighting, right?"

"Oh..." Evie trailed off as her cheeks flushed at their stupidity, "And maybe we should have asked if Tor had a job."

CHAPTER 3
ROOMMATES

Evie
September 4th, 2018
Taran Estate, Los Angeles, CA

Evie drew in a breath as she stared down at her phone. Annoyance was seething in her chest. Why did picking a roommate have to be so complicated?

Her debate with Laika had been raging since last night. The two wolves had spent hours running in circles through the same arguments over which one of their applicants was the best fit. Sometime around midnight, Evie had literally thrown her hands in the air and stormed off to bed.

Now she sat at work, waiting for her employer to finish getting ready. Her mind was still preoccupied thinking about the mess last night had been. Her best friend had insisted on checking in on employment and criminal records just to be sure of no surprises, so after everyone had left Evie had shot off a few text messages to all three of their applicants. The conversations had gone lukewarm at best.

EVIE

Hello, can you confirm your employment and that you have no criminal record.

Becky had responded within the hour, the text message chime followed swiftly by a ping of Evie's email. The promptness of her response got an eye roll from the redhead. Evie hadn't been completely honest with her packmate; she thought the elven woman was trying too hard to find friends. Becky had a desperate aura and while normally Evie would be kind to someone like that, they were trying to find someone to live with, not a hanger on.

BECKY

I've emailed you 3 months of pay stubs and a pre-signed consent form for a background check.

Let me know if you need anything else. I really hope this works out Evie!

Tor had gotten back to them just before the sun went down with a simple answer.

TOR

Yeah on the job and No on the crime

That had gotten a better reception from Evie. She'd pointed out the succinctness of the information as a selling point. Laika hadn't been so sold about the message, forcing yet another inquiry.

EVIE

Does your job pay enough to cover your 3rd of rent and bills a month?

TOR

Yeah

Evie felt that the woman had such a calming aura and alluring personality. But she and Laika had fought more after and her friend warned if she wanted to ask Tor out then do it. Don't move your crush in on the first date.

Shelly hadn't gotten back to them until after 11 pm with an answer. The delayed response had only soured Evie's mood further. At that point, the roommates had spent hours bickering back and forth.

SHELLY

I make around 10 thousand on a good month. What counts as a disqualifying crime to be a roommate?

EVIE

Anything on your police record

SHELLY

Then nope, I've never been caught committing a crime

That answer had sparked another explosion of disagreements. Laika was in favor of Shelly, the only werewolf of the three candidates. Evie was less sure, however. The other werewolf had been hard to read, but Evie had to admit nothing had been insincere.

Evie was exhausted this morning after a terrible night of sleep and feeling irritable towards her friend. She hadn't been so cruel as to not wake Laika for work before leaving, but she hadn't given her a ride to the warehouse either. Just as she finished reading back through the text messages again, her employer finally sauntered down the stairs.

Arik Taran was an actor who used to be renowned for his roles in hundreds of romance movies. The increased lifespan of full-blooded elves came with the benefit of extended youth, which Arik had traded on to make a name for himself in Hollywood. The man's catalog spanned across Hollywood's history, even boasting black and white films. From the most tear-jerking love stories to romantic comedies, he'd done everything the genre had to offer. Unfortunately, the current generation just didn't quite swoon over him like their mothers and grand-mothers had.

Evie acted as his daytime assistant, showing up every morning with fresh coffee and a perky attitude. She carried his bag to engage-ments and kept the flighty actor on schedule. The work was simple and had decent pay; however, before she came along Arik had gone through a new assistant every month. No matter the level of tantrums, he'd failed to run off Evie so far. She could see his mood turn before he could act on it and that made her highly effective at staying employed. Her mother had said worse things to her at an ordinary Tuesday breakfast than Arik could muster even raging drunk. When push came to shove, the woman was a werewolf and he was only an elf. Evie could muscle him around as needed, ushering him off the scene before his dramatics caused too much damage. In the last few years her employer had even seemed to become aware she was the same assistant coming to work every day.

"Ready to go?" asked Evie as she surveyed him for a hair out of place. Every long blonde strand was pulled up precisely, and not a wrinkle was found in his outfit.

"If we must. Let's get this over with," groaned Arik, not excited about the day's activities. The man gave a shake of his head, long golden hair fanning out behind him as he raised a hand to his fore-head dramatically.

"I'm sure you'll have lots of fun at this interview." Evie internally grumbled while plastering a cheery smile on her face.

Arik did not dignify that with an answer. The elf simply sighed again while waiting for her to get the door for him.

The werewolf reminded herself she really needed this job, because moonlighting didn't pay all the bills. Her phone vibrated in hand with a message from Laika. Despite her best friend working on her feet in a warehouse, she always found time to text. The fact that Moonbeans Coffee was owned by the Lowell family probably helped keep her out of trouble.

LAIKA

We got an unscheduled truck today, so dinner's on me.

Evie had been expecting a different message. She eyed the phone skeptically before responding.

EVIE

Okay?

LAIKA

I made a bet with Boss that I could empty it before lunch.

EVIE

He's going to regret that.

Evie's expression softened a bit at the normal text messages. She liked Bostjan, or Boss as they called him. He was a thickly built man with bulging cords of muscle wrapping his arms, a testament to his dwarven strength and work ethic. If Boss was making this bet then he must think it was a sure thing... Woe to him when whatever trap Laika had laid sprung.

LAIKA

Also! We need to pick a roommate today!

There it was... Trying to butter up Evie before she pushed the subject. Laika could be so predictable.

EVIE

Why?

Evie sat opposite of Arik while the elf's heavily tinted car rolled smoothly down the driveway to the main street towards his appointment. Tony was behind the wheel using his powers to avoid every cop in a five mile radius while breaking the speed limit. The drive went from smooth to hectic as soon as he got on the open road. No one in the back seat cared since this was a normal drive for them.

Even as Evie rattled off her boss's list of questions for the interview, her fingers danced across her phone to keep the conversation rolling.

LAIKA

Because if we don't they'll get picked up by other people

Then we will have to interview again

Don't make me do that again

EVIE

If you would just agree to Tor!

Becky was all the wrong types of friendly, and Shelly would be a project Evie didn't have time for right now. Why couldn't her friend understand that?! They needed stability, which Tor seemed like she would be.

LAIKA

Why are you so set on Tor?

EVIE

Because she is perfect for us!

She has a job!

The circle of debate continued for the entire drive. Both women were trying to bend the other to their line of thinking. Neither was making progress, only managing to frustrate the other.

Evie huffed as she stepped out of the car. She ducked into Last Drop Coffee Shop to retrieve a fresh latte for her boss. She knew Laika had hang-ups about how delicate other races could be when it came to werewolf strength, but this aversion to a human roommate was absurd. One of Evie's hands held out a card to pay for the drink. The other held her phone up so she could await the latest counter-argument from Laika.

LAIKA

But Shelly seems like she could use a
good home

EVIE

We don't need a charity case

If they were standing in the same room, Evie would have felt the waves of irritation coming off of Laika by now. She wouldn't like that last sentence, but it was true.

LAIKA

It's not charity!

She's just a new wolf in a new city

Plus she's a werewolf so she'll understand
all our weird!

"Damn it," mumbled Evie. She had to admit that point. Tor was thrilling but Shelly wouldn't be surprised by anything they did.

EVIE

You aren't wrong...

Why is this so complicated!?

Evie sighed as she picked up Arik's latte, quickly raising it up to double-check that the barista had added a magical glyph to the bottom of the cup. The tiny upcharge for the charm ensured the coffee would stay perfectly hot for hours. A worthy charge when your boss had a tendency to throw coffee that dared to be lukewarm at you. Trotting back to the car, she pondered Shelly again. It would be nice to have another wolf in the house, one that was less wild than Laika...

LAIKA

We could just pick Becky and compromise

EVIE

Nope. It's Shelly or Tor

We only have one open room

LAIKA

... We could make space for both?

Comfortably seated back in the car, Arik was going off on his distaste for Pumpkin Spice. The cafe had thrown in a scone for the man, as the owner was a big fan. It only set the elf off on a passionate explanation on how there was no such thing as 'Pumpkin Spice.' The coffees and scones were all simply marketing. Evie just nodded along, her attention still on her phone. She liked Laika's offer for a compromise. Splitting the rent four ways would be even better. Perhaps the pair could then afford to put some more TLC into Evie's aging car.

LAIKA

I know! We could make the basement into a room?

EVIE

No way! Do you remember what Fred said?

You do not open that door in the basement!

We can't make someone live down there!

LAIKA

I could sleep on the couch?

EVIE

What?

The car pulled to another stop and Evie hurried out. Arik took off at a fast pace for a man who didn't want to be here. He swept through the double doors with his usual diva-like flair, leaving Evie and his entourage behind.

She took a seat on a slick metal chair, not bothering with anyone else. Her nails drummed against the back of her phone. Her silver eyes fixated as she watched dots pop up and disappear while her roommate composed a response.

LAIKA

I could put my clothing in your room and just get a pullout

That way we get two roommates.

EVIE

Are you out of your mind?

Should we just all step over your passed out ass on a Saturday morning?

Evie waited on a response from Laika, checking her phone every few minutes. But after offering to move to the living room, her friend had gone radio silent. She was tempted to call if she didn't get an answer soon. Arik's interview was going to take at least an hour. Calling Laika would make it easier to tune out his scripted responses that were wafting out the double doors.

Tony leaned over Evie's shoulder to read her text messages. He was Arik's head assistant and technically Evie's supervisor, but the two had settled into a comfortable friendship years ago. Alabaster fingers swept through his short golden hair, the picture of nonchalant glamour in his flashy blazer. "So tell me, honey, why is your girlfriend sleeping on the couch now?"

"She isn't my girlfriend and I'm not letting her do this. It would be so stupid. Also leave my drama alone," Evie snipped but she didn't pull her phone away.

"But it's so delicious." Bickering with Tony was just part of Evie's daily tasks, and while he was dramatic, nothing ever came of the little fights.

"Stop it!"

"Stop what?"

"Feeding on my tragedy!"

Tony flashed a smirk composed with tiny fangs. He was a

vampire. But not the kind most people thought of at the word. He was a daywalker that survived by feeding off the emotions of others around him. While he could drink blood to sustain himself, the vampire had found an excellent niche in Hollywood surrounded by all the drama required to fill his needs. "But you two are always a five-course meal all by yourselves."

The phone in Evie's hand finally buzzed again with the long-awaited answer.

> LAIKA
>
> It's a perfect plan and you know it!

> EVIE
>
> Shut your damn mouth!
>
> You are not living in the common area

"Is another roommate really worth this?" Tony gasped. Still reading over her shoulder, he held his hand up to his mouth in mock horror. Even though the flashily dressed man wasn't getting a response from the wolf, the vampire was quite content. The emotional waves rolling off Evie were delightful and he basked in them lazily.

> LAIKA
>
> There is the shed?

> EVIE
>
> We could make them share a room?
>
> I think Tor and Shelly would get along great?
>
> Like leather and lace!

> LAIKA
>
> Evie! Stop thinking with your legs uncrossed!
>
> We could though...

> EVIE
>
> We could what?

LAIKA

We could share the master bedroom?

EVIE

As in we somehow fit all your clothes in my closet and we drag in your bed?

LAIKA

We share half our clothes anyways!

EVIE

We could just push both beds next to each other and turn the twins into a queen?

LAIKA

Yep!

Then we could have both!

EVIE

Then we could have both!

September 13th, 2018
Night Claw Residence, Glenwood, CA

E vie sat on the couch, head lolled back with her eyes closed, having kicked her heels off after an exhausting day at work. Her boss had run her ragged with errands; the elf clearly had some new hare-brained project he was working on, even if he wasn't sharing details. She just wanted to go to bed and sleep for days. Unfortunately, it was only Thursday.

The last week had blazed by with offers made to Shelly and Tor. Both had accepted, paid their first month's rent, and started to move in. Finally, when all the boxes were unpacked, Evie's predictions came true. She'd had to take Shelly shopping.

Her new roommate had moved in with a duffle bag of clothing and no mattress. For the woman making the most money in the house, Shelly didn't live like it. After the first trip out to the closest big box store, a whirlwind had started in the living room. It was as if Shelly had realized for the first time in her life she could just buy things. A new TV, a new couch, a second armchair, a new coffee table, and new TV trays appeared. Her room had very much gotten the same treatment. Even Evie got a little present; Shelly wanted her own TV in the living room because it was bigger and clearer. So a new TV stand was purchased for Evie's tiny TV, which moved into her newly shared room.

Meanwhile, Tor had surprised them by unpacking a pile of boxes into the kitchen. The barely used cupboards were bursting with shiny pots and pans. A colorful spice rack took up residence where their stack of instant noodles had sat. If that wasn't enough, Tor paid for a full year's rent in advance. The shoulder bag stuffed full of 5's and 10's was in the hall closet waiting to go to the bank, assuming it could be deposited.

"Hey, don't fall asleep," Laika had appeared, leaning over the back of the couch.

Evie forced her eyes open and muttered, "Why?"

"Two reasons... well three reasons. First, Tor is making us curry tonight and trust me, she can cook," Laika explained. The aroma of spice wafting to every corner of the house backed up that claim.

With a grunt of effort, Evie pushed herself out of the middle of the couch to make room for her best friend. She had no argument against a free dinner. "Okay, what else?"

"Second, we are going to watch Love Pack, and I heard tonight's episode of The Nine is going to be a-maz-ing," Laika continued.

There was a sound of agreement from the new armchair, where Shelly sat typing away on her laptop furiously. "I'm telling you, Ray is the alpha," she said in a slightly distracted voice.

"Ugh, no!" Laika protested, hopping over the couch to settle in next to Evie. The athletic wolf spread out lazily, throwing a leg over Evie's lap to claim more space. "The whole point of the show is that NONE of them are the Alpha! Why else would we watch it?"

"Nothing on TV is real," chided Evie as she left the offending leg in place. "Even those Love Pack couples don't last."

"Shhh," whined Shelly, covering her ears dramatically, "Don't tell me that. I want to believe in love stories."

So far both reasons to not crawl into bed early were solid. Dinner and some Trashy TV Thursday with new friends on the couch was enticing. But Evie knew better. "And what's the third reason?"

"We need to talk about Jonas," answered Laika.

"Who the hell is Jonas?" Evie shot a glare at her best friend. She'd never heard that name out of Laika's mouth before. Plus there was a nervous energy starting to spread out from both women in the room, which wasn't helping.

"He's Tor's ex-boyfriend and he showed up today," Shelly explained, her eyes never leaving her screen. When no one expanded on why Tor's ex showing up was bad, Evie threw Laika's legs off her lap and sat up straight.

"There's a chance that Tor stole the money from him," admitted Laika. She fidgeted with her phone before showing off a picture of a plaid man dressed in black with crimson trim and a scarf wrapped around his lower face.

Between the possibility of stolen money and a vampire being at their door, Laika now had Evie's full attention. "You mean her rent money?"

Laika nodded, "Yeah, he mentioned it when he was looking for her. He swore he didn't want it back. I let her know that he'd shown up, but Tor doesn't want to talk to him. What do we do?"

"We don't invite him inside and just say get lost if he shows up again. Unless he shows up with the police looking for his money," reasoned Evie.

"Coming through!" Tor's voice called as she swept into the room, juggling four steaming curry bowls. All eyes turned to her with various levels of guilty expressions.

"What?" Tor pressed, she stood casually with all the food not even phased that three werewolves were staring at her.

"I was just telling Evie... about Jonas and the bag," Laika admitted.

"He doesn't want the money back, he wants me back. He's not getting either so don't worry about it," assured Tor. Again her aura was casual confidence without anything Evie could attribute to lying. Soon each wolf had a bowl in hand, and Tor claimed her spot on the remaining armchair.

A tiny bit of guilt pulled at Evie, but she requested, "Just don't bring a vampire home? Please?"

Tor nodded with her fork in mouth.

"Jonas was a vampire?" Shelly looked surprised. Somehow she hadn't realized the pale man with sunlight proof clothing wasn't just a human at the door.

Internally Evie worried. Their new roommate knew even less about the supernatural world than she'd expected. This wasn't the first time in the last week a statement like this came up. She and Laika would need to crash course Shelly on basic California Supernatural Safety so she didn't end up kidnapped.

Then Evie remembered she had a topic to bring up too. "Oh... So, Becky is stalking me."

"What?" Laika stopped eating and gave her a skeptical look.

"Who?" Tor questioned. She was less concerned and more curious.

"Becky was the other applicant and today was the third time I saw her at the coffee shop. She was standing in line behind me, like two people back, and I swear she was staring at me. It's getting to crazy levels how many times I see her now," complained Evie.

Laika tried to soothe her, "Are you sure she didn't go to the same place before? And now you just recognize her?"

Evie was about to smugly reply that she remembered everyone who stood in line daily with her. She recalled the eighty-year-old lady with pink streaks in her hair that always got tea. A balding man with a kitschy tie that was never the same, who picked up 4 coffees with a carrier to take back to his co-workers. Even the perfumed horror, a woman who wore far too much rose-scented everything she could smell coming. Then a realization struck her.

"Okay... so there might be an Evergreen building nearby," admitted Evie.

"Didn't Becky say she'd just gotten a job there? And you're at the best coffee house in the area," countered Laika. Her friend had gone back to eating.

"Yeah... I'm probably overreacting right?" Evie hoped.

"Probably," agreed Laika with an apologetic look. "I'm sure it's awkward since you told her she didn't get the room."

"Oh, yeah," muttered Evie. She felt her face going red because she'd never actually sent Becky a message about the room.

"Evie," scolded Laika, "You told her she didn't get the room right?"

"Yep," Evie lied quickly. She'd need to send a text in the morning and then she'd hopefully get fewer creepy stares.

"Good, now onto Trashy TV," Laika moved the conversation on.

The TV was turned up as the title music of Love Pack began to play. Immediately bickering about the best pairs and who was alpha began, only interrupted by breaks to devour bites of the delicious homemade dinner.

If someone had asked Evie even two weeks ago if she had wanted her life to change so dramatically, she would've scoffed in their face. But as the cheerful voices surrounded her, wrapping the room in a bubble of camaraderie, Evie could not deny how happy it made her. It almost felt like family. And inwardly, she hoped it would stay this way for a long while to come.

INTERLUDE - KINDLING

The Ritualist
September 9th, 2018
..somewhere in Glenwood, CA

Whter chalk marked the path that the Ritualist was going to carve into the wooden floor. For someone else, painting it in place would be enough to create a ritual circle. But given her limitations, the Ritualist needed to do something more permanent.

A ceremonial knife was ready to start the process as soon as the outline was finished. This was just the first step in a long list of traditions that had to be followed if there was any chance of success. Old books, paper scrolls, and notebooks filled with translations were scattered around the room for reference as well. There was just so much still to do and what if it didn't work?

Would her Love forgive her for a failure like this? Would the family continue to ridicule her for her lack of skill? If her father had taught the Ritualist anything in life, it was that she always had to take the longest path to victory. Not because she wanted to, but because she had to. When you failed at the simplest things there were no shortcuts.

Magic like this didn't come naturally to her.

Hours passed as the Ritualist obsessively set up her spell, going from book to scroll and back, trying to keep the details straight. Finally, she was ready to try her hand at this particular brand of magic. Hopefully years of research weren't about to go to waste. The Ritualist raised her ceremonial knife high and took a deep breath. If this didn't work then she didn't know what she'd do next. Go home and get married? She rather ram this knife through an eye socket.

As the blade fell towards the center of the circle she felt a... spark? Like electricity running up her arm. When the tip touched down, all at once the magic flared to life... Her spell had actually worked this time?!

The Ritualist still had a long way to go, but she'd show her father how wrong he'd been!

CHAPTER 4
LIGHTNING

Evie
September 14th, 2018
Night Claw Residence, Glenwood, CA

Evie picked up her phone, reading the screen with a small groan. Usually, she loved to see 'MOONS' on her Caller ID, but the week had been long already. Thankfully today had been a half day at work; Arik had been a terror, so when Evie was released at noon she had intended to cherish every extra hour of downtime.

But not taking this call would mean a small hit to her reputation and paint her pack as unreliable, and getting work was hard enough. Glenwood MOONS had plenty of werewolves in their ranks; there was even another pack at their level. Ignoring the ringing meant handing that job over to them without a fight.

"Hello, this is Night Claw," the tired woman chirped as her finger hit the screen to begin the call. She managed to pour perky energy into her words, even if her face wasn't reflecting it.

"Good afternoon," intoned the no-nonsense dispatcher on the

other end, "I have work for an Empath. Is one available from your pack today?" This woman had literally been at the end of the phone every time MOONS had called in the last 5 years. She had never once given her name, so Evie and Laika referred to her as Julie and assumed she worked for the Glenwood Police Department.

Internally, Evie groaned but pleasantly responded, "We have one of those. Is this an active scene?"

"Yes, this is an urgent call," answered Julie while clicking away on her keyboard, loud enough for the wolf to hear. Then the woman added stoically, "Initial reports from the scene say that we have multiple confirmed dead. Do you still want this case? My records show that Night Claw hasn't dealt with murder cases previously." There was a pause in typing.

The redhead sat on the couch in the middle of the living room, with Laika practically crawling into her lap to hear every word. Shelly occupied the plush chair nearby, her laptop open on her knees, looking up curiously. Evie felt pinned in place by their stares. Did she want to move up in the Moonlighting ranks? Yes, but she hadn't expected an active scene with dead bodies when she got up this morning. "Is there any danger on the scene?" the werewolf asked tentatively.

Laika threw her hands in the air flashing her packmate an annoyed expression. The impulsive werewolf was dying for them to get some 'real' action while Moonlighting instead of the same single-target disturbances or hunting cold trails.

On the other end of the phone, Juile paused again as she consulted her computer before giving an answer, "No. The scene is being cleared for entry now. Do you want this case?...We don't have any other active empaths on call in Glenwood."

"Okay then," Evie agreed, caving to the heap of guilt thrown at her. "Night Claw will be there as soon as you send the location." A small buzz in her ear alerted Evie to an incoming message. The dispatcher had already sent their destination to her phone.

"Don't take too long," signed off Julie before abruptly hanging up the call. A few years on the job had taught Evie that Julie wasn't one for small talk; she just moved onto the next call on her list because pleasantries could cost someone their life. The Night Claw wolves held no ill will anymore when the line disconnected without a goodbye.

"Did we finally get a murder?" asked Laika as her eyes lit up at the thought. While she wasn't excited by the concept of death and murder, getting sent to a scene like that meant they could move up the rankings.

"Yes," Evie admitted, pushing her packmate back out of her personal bubble with her foot. A chill was running up her spine already. "But it's not like we are hunting down a killer right now. The danger has passed. We are just going to a scene because they want a lie detector on site. Probably already caught the killer!"

As the women descended into their usual good-natured bickering before a job, Shelly interrupted them. "Could I tag along?" she asked, looking over her laptop curiously. The brunette hadn't said anything about being interested in Moonlighting during her short time with them. She'd listened politely to their stories, but that was all.

"To a murder scene?" Evie asked instead of answering the question. Even if their new friend was looking for different experiences, that might be too much of the deep end. Pizza and trashy TV were one thing, and Evie wouldn't have even batted an eye at taking Shelly to one of their usual missions. But this particular job?

"Yes?" Shelly answered, unsure if she'd overstepped by the tone of her voice. Her eyes flicked between her two roommates, trying to gauge what they were feeling. Most of the wolf's requests had been met with exuberance and excitement, rather than a follow-up question.

Laika turned big amber eyes on her packmate then pleaded, "Oh Evie, let her come. Imagine if we could show up with three people!" One of the major hurdles holding back their tiny pack was the size.

"I'm not joining the pack," snapped Shelly as if reading Laika's mind with a glance.

"No," Evie snapped then clarified quickly. "No, you aren't joining the pack for real. Just don't disagree if anyone assumes you did. We aren't supposed to bring non-pack to these things... but just this once we can make an exception." There was a slight sigh as her shoulders slumped. She always had a hard time telling Laika 'no' on things like this.

The dark-haired werewolf cheered, throwing arms around Evie in victory. Laika cried out joyfully, "This will be a perfect first mission for Shelly. Absolutely no danger, and we'll get to play in the woods."

"Actually," Evie corrected while checking her phone, "We are going to the nice part of town. I guess it's a murder at an apartment building?"

---—◡—-- - --

September 14th, 2018
Fulmino Apartment Complex, Glenwood, CA

Glenwood was mostly suburban with plenty of neighborhoods just like theirs, packed with cookie-cutter houses. There were only two or three areas that Evie could think of for apartment-style living, and all of them were expensive and fancy.

As her little Saab pulled into the parking lot next to a GPD cruiser, Evie looked up. The complex rising in front of her had to be 12 or 13 stories tall, with a penthouse atop. Tall glass windows circled that upper floor giving a view in every direction. Evie felt a pang of envy thinking back to her small rented house. She had to remind herself that the house was feeling more like a home every day. Turning her head to talk to Shelly in the backseat, she explained, "The doors don't open from the inside. I'll let you out in a minute."

"Shit," Laika suddenly snapped from the front seat, drawing the car's attention. Her nose was pressed up to the window as she glared daggers at a pretty silver BMW on the other side of the police car.

Shelly leaned between the seats to get a better view. "What's wrong?" she asked, concern creasing her features.

"Why is Blood Fang here?" whined the dramatic werewolf grabbing Evie's arm, "I thought this was our mission."

Evie frowned, "I don't know. I didn't think they had any empathic abilities at all. They are muscle and trackers, and this scene is active but not dangerous." She'd be having a word with Owen about this one as soon as she could get him alone. Night Claw didn't need backup from inferior packs. Especially not when her pack was only called to the scene because they had the proper powers.

"Blood Fang? Is that another moonlighting pack? Do packs not usually work together?" Shelly shot off rapid questions, gaze quickly moving between them. She was trying to soak in as much information about Moonlighting as she could. Until now, Shelly had never met moonlighters, so her roommates served as the only window into that world.

"Moonlighting packs can work together, but they're just a group of morons," explained Laika opening her door. "They're the only other Glenwood moonlighters 'on our level'. Everyone else is way above in rankings, so we end up competing with them for every job. Just because they have 5 wolves, they think they are owed the work." The words dripped with venom as the wolf kept her glare firmly fixed on the offending BMW.

Evie opened the back door for Shelly with a huff of her own. "There might be more of them, but we are better moonlighters. Our rankings prove that." She straightened up, sweeping her hair out of her face as she rattled off a few of the specialties moonlighters had. "All of us are tested for our skill with certain aspects of the job. You know... Combat, Investigation, Tracking, Search and Rescue. Every job needs different skills, and MOONS use the rankings to determine who would be best suited to handle them. The higher your ranking the better you are at something, and the higher the average of your pack's skills the higher paying your missions are."

"Evie's power is all about her heightened sense of emotion. All the auras and body language we give off, she picks up better than the rest of us," Laika tapped her temple as she took up the explanation, feet turning to march towards the front door of the building.

"So I've got a pretty good ranking in Arbitration Skills. Laika can hear the length of a football field when trying..." Evie trailed off as the door to the building ahead opened. Two figures appeared, stepping out into the afternoon sunlight. Aaron Leavenworth and the tattooed witch from the other night were in deep conversation just outside the doors. Evie could practically see an aura of concern hovering around them.

For her part, Melinda seemed disinterested in whatever Aaron was saying. She had her phone out and was checking her messages as she offhandedly replied, "There is nothing dangerous happening there now. You can take people upstairs to do all your checks. But that's some deep magic. None of them are going to get you anything I didn't already tell you. Wait until he gets here, and you'll get answers. I need to get supplies, and I need to go now."

"Good afternoon Officer Leavenworth!" Evie chirped, a spring in her step as she walked forward to meet them. She was trying for an air of professionalism with this case being an active crime scene.

Aaron opened his mouth to reply to the witch, but the arrival of Night Claw pulled his attention. "Ms. Bel... Evie, Laika, I'm glad you got here so fast." He pulled open the front door, holding it for them as his brain caught up to the third werewolf in tow. The new face gave him a momentary pause, but he didn't comment. His head turned to try and finish his conversation with Melinda, but she had already taken advantage of the distraction. Her car zipped out of the parking lot before any of them had even crossed the threshold.

"There's magic?" asked Laika, her excitement growing.

With a sigh of defeat, Aaron turned his full attention to the pack of wolves. "Maybe. There isn't anything active right now, and

Melinda just explained... wait. It's best that I don't share any details right now." He held his hands up, cutting himself off quickly. A familiar smile fixed into place while he pressed the elevator button. They waited to see which of the building's two elevators would make its way down first. He looked at Shelly while extending a hand, "I don't believe we've met. Officer Aaron Leavenworth."

The brunette werewolf gave Aaron an appraising eye before taking the hand. The handshake was awkward like she'd never tried before. "I'm Shelly. The new roommate."

"Welcome, Shelly," the officer greeted, "I wish we'd met under better circumstances. Today is proving to be a doozy." The first visible sign that upstairs was weighing on Aaron shone through in those words. The ordinarily unruffled officer seemed uneasy during their trip in the elevator.

Evie claimed the spot next to him as they ascended, trying to pepper him for details. "Why did you call in Blood Fang as well?" she inquired, wondering if a hand on his shoulder would help. They tried not to cross the line with physical contact.

"It's not just Blood Fang," Aaron deemed to answer that particular question. "We called in Moonscent and Dark Wind as well." He ran a hand through his hair, trying to brighten up. "Every big gun I could talk into showing up is going to take a look. I'm glad you managed to make it as well. I was pretty sure your day job didn't end until a bit later."

"Must be fate," Evie quipped, knowing she hadn't wanted to be here. As the elevator doors popped open, she was hit by a wave of tension from everyone waiting.

"Game faces," Laika muttered, her stare fixed ahead.

The 10th-floor was serving as a waiting room for people heading up to the penthouse floor. Everyone looked in their direction when Night Claw arrived. Evie recognized two members of Blood Fang leaning against the wall. Randall glanced in her direction, scowling as the women appeared. His dreads were pulled back into a ponytail, and he wore a vest over his usual pants and a button-down shirt, trying to look smarter than he was. Thad was the opposite with short spiky blonde hair, rosy cheeks, and every bit of his outfit today screaming preppy moron.

Blood Fang were subpar moonlighters and barely passable werewolves. Evie found that the most annoying aspect of her rivals was that all of them were gorgeous. They were something out of a teenage dream, with a different flavor for every girl out there.

There was also a very young girl that Evie had never seen before playing on her phone. She had white feathery earrings peeking out of her curls that contrasted with the girl's dark hair and skin. Her clothes were bright and colorful, and she wouldn't have looked out of place in a high school. Typically, Evie wouldn't judge, but the girl couldn't have been more than eighteen. Far too young to be a certified moonlighter.

Before anyone could speak up or start an introduction, the second bank of elevators lit up, announcing another addition. Owen and yet another werewolf exited as the doors opened, having a calm conversation. The newcomer was recognizable as a man named Mike, who belonged to the top-ranked pack in Glenwood, Dark Wind. Despite the salt and pepper color of his hair and deep lines around his eyes, the werewolf was a better moonlighter than anyone else present. His movement spoke of the graceful predator he could be when provoked.

"Sorry Owen," Mike apologized in a cheery tone that didn't match his aura, "I really haven't seen anything like that before. I'll be seeing that room in my nightmares tonight for sure."

Any venom that Blood Fang and Night Claw had been gearing up to spit abruptly stopped at the appearance of Mike. Neither of the lower-ranked packs would purposefully make themselves look bad in front of Dark Wind. Laika's face alone blossomed into open hero worship for the veteran werewolf. Unlike Evie, her packmate didn't have to suffer feeling the fear and worry consuming this hallway. This just seemed like an exciting mission to her.

"It's fine, we are trying out anyone who can make time here. The last thing we want to do is ask LA for one of their witches," Owen assured the older man with his usual natural grin. His fist clenched in mock fury at the thought of asking another MOONS department for help.

"If there is any other way I can help, let me know," Mike replied, slapping the wolfkin on the back as they spoke. "We have to do all we can to stay ahead of Los Angeles MOONS."

"Exactly," agreed Owen.

"Ladies," Mike greeted, realizing there were more people here than before. He gave the women a polite nod, "Nice to have you join us."

"Hi," squeaked Laika, who immediately turned red at the sound of her voice. She then buried her head in Shelly's shoulder to hide her embarrassment.

Evie kept a more relaxed head; while she thought Dark Wind was a fantastic pack, she needed to at least pretend to be confident around them. "Hello," she responded with a gentle wave, "Is it bad up there?"

Mike gave them a half-smile then answered, "I've been told to keep it to myself. Not supposed to give you any ideas before you see the... uh... scene."

The two officers were whispering by the bay of elevators about their next steps. Aaron checked his phone and said, "We've got one more coming. I'll go wait for him downstairs. Can you take the next one up?"

Owen groaned, "Can't I go wait downstairs and you go back up?" His shoulders were tense, showing that this wasn't just his usual whining. The wolfkin didn't want to go back up to the penthouse even if someone had to. Evie could tell Owen was bothered enough that he hadn't even noticed her or Laika yet.

"Oh," Aaron blinked as gears clicked in his head, "Sorry, Owen, I didn't realize it was getting to you. You can go down and wait for him. I can take the next moonlighter upstairs."

"No, it's okay. I can do another round." Owen waved off the concern.

They reached an agreement of assignments as the first elevator arrived, spiriting away Aaron back down to the lobby. With a roll of his shoulders, Owen turned back to the wolves waiting, "Alright Mike, Melinda has gone for supplies. I can't let you go until another Senior Moonlighter arrives, even if the danger has passed."

"I can wait a bit longer," agreed the veteran moonlighter, "help you keep an eye on things until more magic arrives." His blatant glance in the direction of Blood Fang and Night Claw gave away his real intentions. The rivalry between the packs was well-known around Glenwood. While the junior packs tended to keep their squabbles from interfering with jobs, Mike seemed keen to ensure that was maintained today.

"Right," Owen readily agreed, glad for the help. He didn't look at the wolves in the hallway as he checked a list on a clipboard. The officers were hard-pressed today, juggling so many moonlighters. He pressed the silver button to get their ride to the top floor, "Keisha, let's get you up there."

"Yes, sir," said the young werewolf Evie hadn't previously recognized. The umber-skinned girl put away the phone she'd been looking at, the corners of her mouth quirked up. Her feathers fluttered as Keisha half-skipped past the older wolves to join the police officer. The pair disappeared behind sliding doors a moment later.

Evie had directed her entourage to stand along the wall opposite of Blood Fang. She kept her expression schooled to calm indifference, waiting patiently for the officers to return. Next to her, Laika leaned half in her shadow, still looking at Mike with open admiration as he stood casually in the middle of the two packs. The rookie moonlighter's admiration of Dark Wind was part of the reason she'd moved to California for college.

Silence descended on the hallway. Neither side was going to make the first swing here, and the best way to do that was to simply not talk. Unfortunately for Night Claw, that idea didn't last long.

Shelly was curious, and even with the earlier warning, she was studying the two Blood Fang wolves.

Feeling the gaze, Randall's eyes flickered to Shelly and then back to Thad. There was an almost imperceptible eye roll from the blonde, and then a moment later, Randall was leaning forward to extend a hand to Shelly. "I don't think we've been properly introduced. I'm Randall. Are you... with Night Claw?"

Laika's expression soured, her annoyance spiking as the boys approached their new friend.

"I showed up with Night Claw," Shelly responded, unable to stop her smile at the pretty boy. She folded her arms over her midsection before adding, "I'm Shelly. Nice to meet you."

Awkwardly withdrawing the extended hand, Randall asked, "Are you a moonlighter?"

Evie internally groaned as another girl fell for Blood Fang's charms. Her eyes flickered between everyone in front of her then back to Laika, giving an almost imperceptible shake of her head. Frustration boiled just under the skin as she watched Randall probe her new friend for information on Evie's pack. But Evie knew the moment Thad opened his mouth the spell would be broken.

Before the woman could save Shelly, both Laika and Thad snapped their heads upwards. Even Mike glanced up with a small frown creasing his lips for a moment. Thad mumbled at whatever had drawn the attention of the wolves with better hearing, "She didn't last long."

Laika hissed at him, forgetting the presence of Dark Wind for a moment. "Don't be so rude!"

Mike cleared his throat to end the brewing fighting between the two werewolves. The pair had enough grace to look embarrassed for a moment before turning away from each other. Meanwhile, the veteran moonlighter was moving towards the elevators.

The lights above it showed the machine was already underway on returning to this floor. Metal doors slid open a moment later and Keisha came stumbling out, supported by Owen's hand on her elbow. The young moonlighter looked pale and her eyes were wide in shock. Whatever awaited at the top of the elevator had clearly rocked the poor girl to her core.

Evie felt the wave of terror that followed them out. Keisha had heaved up her stomach upstairs; the acidic smell clung to her as she'd fled. She knew what Laika had heard and wished her packmate had warned her.

"You're alright," Owen said soothingly in a quiet voice, even though the floor of werewolves would all be able to hear. No one dared a mean word as Mike reached the pair, the older werewolf leaning in to comfort Keisha.

A ding of elevator doors behind them pulled the attention of the other packs, their eyes flickering back to see Aaron had returned with a newcomer. The man walking with the officer was clad in a long leather coat and every inch of skin was covered, including an almost gasmask-like helmet. Evie had so many questions of the mess unfolding in front of her, but she never got a chance to voice them.

"Come on, I'll take you home," Mike informed Keisha, putting a hand on her shoulder to lead her. He navigated past Aaron and the leather-clad man, who both moved quickly out of the way. She heard him mumble something like 'tag' to the new person before taking off.

Owen followed the Dark Wind werewolf into the elevator, but he paused, raising a hand to hold the metal door. "We're making sure Keisha gets out of here safely. She had an accident in the entryway," the wolfkin explained with a sympathetic glance at the young girl, "I'll call her pack before she makes it home. Just keep this moving, please."

"Of course," Aaron agreed, before addressing the man who had come up with him. "Do you mind waiting until last? I know this is a bit of a longshot, but these packs have spotted things at a scene I've missed plenty of times... and it's a weird one."

The man simply nodded despite the heavy mask he wore before walking past the werewolves to get himself a bit of space. He didn't find a wall to lean against like the rest; he just waited where he had a clear view of everyone and the elevators. Given how confidently he walked, avoiding the others, he seemed to be able to see out of the pitch-black glass on his helmet.

Aaron turned his full attention on Evie, "Have you gone up?" Confusion flickered on his face as Evie shook her head. He summoned another elevator to take them up to the penthouse. "You should have gone before Keisha. We need you up there."

Evie looked to her friends, but Shelly shook her head, quickly waving her arms in front of her body. "No, thank you," the brunette whispered, "I was interested until the moonlighters started losing their lunch." There was an apologetic look on her freckled face as she'd begged to come, and now was backing out.

"Laika?" Evie urged, her gaze shifting towards her packmate, "Are you coming?"

"I'm good, I'll keep Shelly company down here," her friend replied distractedly. The reasoning seemed sound, especially for Laika, but Evie could see her attention was elsewhere. Her packmate was pointedly trying to not watch the man in the leather coat, which just elicited an eye roll from Evie. Laika could be too curious some days.

"Just us then," Aaron confirmed, holding open the metal door. His calm demeanor still had a sense of urgency. He waited for Evie to join him before punching the button for the top floor.

Evie peppered Aaron with questions on the short trip up, but the man struggled to explain why she was needed. She sighed and put a professional smile in place as the metal doors slid open to the penthouse apartment.

The owner had decorated the front entrance with art everywhere. There were paintings, sculptures, and even a mural on the doorframe above the arch into the main home. Her eyes scanned the room carefully as she envied the collection. Whoever lived here had exquisite tastes, minus the gaudy centerpiece blocking the doorway. Evie barely glanced at the tacky sculptures of two black glass skeletons holding hands that stood in the middle of the arch. They pulled too much attention away from the rest of the room.

She could smell rotting food from further inside. There was something wrong with this room but she couldn't place it. The smell alone wasn't enough for the feelings she was getting. Not until names were placed on a few scents far out of place; Ozone, ash, and vomit hung in the air, saturating the entire room.

Dread dragged her attention back to the gaudy sculpture in the middle of the entryway. Evie realized the intimate picture was not fictional as her gaze lowered to the ground. Some time ago, had these two been living people leaving the apartment together? Piles of ash pooled around both skeletal feet. They didn't seem to be wearing anything. No clothing, jewelry, or even shoes. Had it all burnt away?

"Are these..." Evie trailed off, unable to finish the question.

"Yes," Aaron answered, following her every movement carefully.

Evie's stomach churned, threatening to create a repeat of Keisha, but she held herself together. Gently, she leaned into the grotesque figures taking a closer sniff. The sharp tang of ozone was coming from the glassy surface, reminding her of a stormy night. The moonlighter glanced at the police officer, asking, "Was there a storm around here this week?"

"No," Aaron answered quickly, "Why do you ask?" He paused their advance to see if she had found a clue he'd need later.

Her lips twisted into a deeper frown continuing, "There is this smell, like lightning in the air. Just after it struck the ground. Plus, they left out some food which is rotting now, so no one found this for a while."

The police officer confirmed, "The cleaning lady found everyone like this a couple hours ago when doing her rounds. Otherwise, I don't know how long the discovery would have taken. Mike said he could smell the same."

Evie pinned her bangs up out of her eyes to give herself a moment to steel her nerves. If she wanted to go further as a moonlighter someday, then today was a good day to start. A composed expression managed to find its way onto her face as she replied, "Okay. Where do you need me?"

The penthouse owners must have been having a party because the next room was filled with people. Or at least... the remains of people, illuminated in the setting sun from the wall of windows. A string of letters tacked up on the glass read "Happy Birthday Harry," confirming her suspicion.

Evie counted four people on the couches by the TV and another two lying on the floor nearby. One of the blackened skeletons stood poised to take a shot at the pool table on the other side of the room. Their cue was still raised over the pristine green felt; she assumed the table had only been used a handful of times. More people stood around in groups, gossiping just before their deaths. This was like some modern art installation about how everyone was fragile on the inside or something.

Evie's brain kept telling her something was wrong with the room, but she couldn't put words to exactly what yet. The woman crossed the party carefully to not touch anything, looking at the glass people. Ozone and ash clung to them the same as before. "You know what this reminds me of?"

Aaron stopped at the door to a room off the main area. He looked back at her, "What?"

"Have you ever seen sand after lightning strikes?" Evie tilted her head to examine a skeleton.

Shock ran across Aaron's features as he realized what Evie was implying. "Yes," he agreed, "It's like when the sand turns to glass, as though all of these people were struck by lightning."

"No broken windows, though," Evie commented with a gesture at the large glass-windowed wall. She trailed off in the middle of her thought, realizing finally what was wrong with the room. Or, more specifically, what *wasn't* wrong with the penthouse. Quick steps took Evie back to the pool table to verify her reasoning. "If lightning had struck the night they died and managed to reach the people inside, those windows should be destroyed or there should be scorch marks around any conductive surfaces they might have been touching... but nothing in here is damaged."

"What do you mean?" asked a confused Aaron. He'd walked the whole penthouse a few times. These poor people were all dead, so he couldn't agree with her sentiment.

Evie pointed at the clean pool table, "I mean nothing has been destroyed," she repeated. Green felt without a mark covered the wooden and leather frame, not an inch of it scorched. Gracefully quirking up an eyebrow, she continued, "Even if a freak lightning storm raged through here, turning people to glass and incinerating their clothing, why is nothing else damaged?"

"Huh," the police officer managed before starting to write in his book once more. Aaron murmured aloud to himself while scribbling, "How does that happen? What sort of magic?"

After one more glance around, the final count in the room was sixteen dead partygoers, which turned Evie's stomach. Who could have done this? Why would anyone do this? Nothing at the scene said this was anything more than a fun party for Harry. She wondered which of the many skeletons was the birthday boy.

"Evie, there's more."

"More?"

Aaron didn't reply as he led Evie across the apartment. "Harry," he called gently through the door he'd led them to, "I'm coming in with another friend. She's here to help you."

"He's still alive?" All attempts at professionalism faded at the horror-struck look on her face.

"We're not sure, I don't know how to explain."

"What does that mean?"

Aaron slowly opened the door to a bedroom, revealing the blackened legs of a skeleton. But as Evie's eyes traveled up the body, his shoulders and head still had skin. A vacant expression of fear marred the man's face. There were burns covering what was left of him and his head was moving.

"He needs medical attention!" shrieked Evie, rushing past the officer. She had no idea how to help but she couldn't ignore someone in pain.

"Melinda explained he isn't alive," Aaron commented as he quickly stopped her from touching Harry. "There is residual magic keeping him animated... she thinks he's dead."

"Why am I here then?" The redhead let him pull her back a step.

"I need you to confirm that... "

"Can't Melinda do that?"

Aaron grimaced as he explained, "She's gone to get supplies to try and save him if he is alive. But her powers don't work like that and you were the closest person with anything remotely like what we needed."

Evie gave the man a hard look, not her usual polite as he stated what he wanted her to do. "You want me to feel into his aura and see if he's still thinking... what if he is?"

"Then we'll do all we can." There was a glint of steel to the man's words as he let go of the werewolf, "But I need to know if I should be spending time on his life or finding his killer as soon as possible."

"Alright," mumbled Evie, feeling the resolve coming from the officer. Again she took a step towards Harry, lowering her voice as soothingly as she could. "Hello..."

The body on the floor twitched almost like he was trying to turn to the sound of her voice. His jaw clicked in a silent response before falling still once more.

"Happy Birthday Harry," Evie tried again. "Seems like you had a wild party." Her senses reached out to feel for reactions to her words. Nothing. His jaw clicked again and this time managed to turn his face in her direction. "Did you have fun?" the werewolf asked. But again, she got no emotions in return. She suppressed her tears and reached out to smooth his hair gently being careful to avoid his pointed ears.

"Anything?" Aaron asked, having retreated back through the doorway to give them more space.

Evie just shook her head, "He's gone."

CHAPTER 5
CLICK

Laika
September 14th, 2018
Fulmino Apartment Complex, Glenwood, CA

Laika stared openly at the leather-clad man. She'd never seen a moonlighter dressed like this before, in layers upon layers of padded leather armor. Werewolves needed gear that would shift forms with them and she couldn't imagine that leather would accommodate such a transformation. The man was simply too tall to be a dwarf and too broad to be an elf. The only witch they'd ever met on the job was Melinda, who had dressed in her EMT uniform. Perhaps this was another witch moonlighter? Maybe that leather was all fireproof for a red witch?

"Why aren't you going up with Evie?" Shelly interrupted Laika's thoughts. Her roommate leaned uncomfortably against the wall, fidgeting by crossing her arms repeatedly. She looked nervous, but Laika wasn't sure if it was from Blood Fang or the unknown man who'd joined them.

"Uhh... Well, that's a long story," Laika hedged absentmindedly, still fixated on the newcomer.

An answer came from across the hall. "It's because she's useless at anything that isn't a flat out run. I don't even know why she's here," Thad sneered. He had a smug expression that annoyed the female werewolf.

"Most of my scores are better than yours," defended Laika, feeling an angry flare in her chest for a moment. Her self control barely held the woman back from growling at the Blood Fang pack.

"Thad," hissed Randall, nudging his packmate in the ribs, "Keep it down!" The umber-skinned man seemed more on edge than the rest of the werewolves.

His blonde packmate ignored him, "Your tracking score is absolute trash. Did you even reach Rank 1?"

"You can't track?" Shelly asked with open curiosity. Hearing that Laika wasn't able to do a basic werewolf skill seemed to shock her. Werewolves were known as natural-born trackers; all wolves were born with keener noses than humans and other supernaturals.

Randall again punched his friend's arm, but was ignored. "Humans have a better sense of smell than her," Thad chuckled. His eyes looked back at his packmate as he smirked.

In response, Randall rolled his eyes dramatically while pulling his wallet from his jeans. He handed over a twenty-dollar bill to the blonde man. "Fine, you win." He still seemed on edge, but was getting swept up in the usual pack rivalry.

"I told you so," Thad gloated.

"I can scent track just fine," Laika snarled, feeling her control slipping as she watched them make bets about her pack. Clearly, they pegged that Shelly wasn't an official member. Or they were passing around money just to piss her off. She glared sharply, knowing that these two had faked bets in the past just to antagonize her and Evie.

Randall glanced at Laika before his face turned sour, "No, you can't. You literally have a 0 in your tracking score. Owen and Aaron can't send you on anything that needs tracking." His attention turned to address Shelly, "You picked the wrong pack to start interning for. Night Claw can't bust out of the bottom ranks."

"I'm not joining any packs," snapped Shelly taking a step forward, shoulders squared. There was a distinct lack of fear in her despite facing off against two trained male werewolves.

Laika chimed into the conversation, "I can track! So what if I don't rely on my nose to do it? I could run circles around you city wolves, and still take down the target miles ahead of your pack!"

The tension in the tiny space had escalated quickly. Thad and Laika were gearing up into a screaming match. Randall kept trying to keep the peace despite throwing his own insults. All of this seemed to antagonize Shelly as much as she didn't want to be in a pack; the insults to her friend were too much.

A sudden click of metal on metal broke the strained atmosphere, as if someone had opened the pressure valve on the hallway. Four sets of eyes turned to the leather-clad man, who had unlatched his helmet from his neck guard. If his hands hadn't touched the armored plate, Laika wouldn't have noticed it between the mask and coat. With how much gear he was wearing, how did he even breathe in all of that?

As the gasmask-like helmet pulled away, a handsome face with blue eyes appeared. Raising a gloved hand, the stranger smoothed his dark brown hair. He almost had a severe look between his sharp cheekbones and the dark circles under his eyes. When the man smiled politely, the effect was softened.

There was an air of nonchalance as the stranger spoke, as if the hall around him had not been exploding with werewolf aggression. He spoke calmly, allowing them to see a long set of fangs. "I rarely use my nose to track. I have always found my ears will take me in fewer circles than a scent trail."

The sight of his fangs chased thoughts of Blood Fang from Laika's head as her amber eyes went wide. The stranger was a vampire! She'd never met a vampire moonlighter before; in fact, the only vampire she knew was Tony. And he wasn't much different than a human and certainly didn't have fangs like this man.

The wolf in the back of Laika's mind growled low, sensing danger from the unknown threat. A flash of fear tried to push through to the forefront, but she ignored the instinct. Instead she was fascinated.

As an echo of her thoughts, she heard Shelly whisper, "I've never met a vampire before." The other wolf had retreated a step, brushing against Laika's elbow. Her brown eyes were apprehensive as they glanced at the vampire who was sharing the hall with them.

"Well, it is nice to meet you too," the vampire spoke once more, his air of politeness not faltering an inch.

Shelly's cheeks went red, realizing her misstep too late. The man had just said he tracked with hearing after all. What good was whispering when you were less than 10 feet away from someone like that? Laika grinned broadly at the good-natured response. She firmly stifled the wolf growling warnings in her head. How could someone with a sense of humor like that be a danger to them? He was a moonlighter too, after all. Stepping forward, she extended a hand, "Hi, I'm Laika. I don't think I've seen you moonlighting before... Just how well can you hear?"

"My name is Alfred," responded the vampire, keeping his smile in place. He swiftly shook Laika's hand, but the action gave her no new information about him. The gloves were leather, and his strength appeared in line with that of a human. "You could say I have been Moonlighting in Glenwood for a while."

Laika noted that his expression only read as polite interest while they spoke. Werewolves were good at catching non-verbal communication, but the vampire before her gave away nothing.

Someone who had been moonlighting a while? Laika pondered that piece of information carefully. She and Evie had been working in Glenwood for nearly 5 years. With their rankings they didn't run in the same circles as the professional moonlighting packs like Dark Wind. However, Laika prided herself on keeping up on the local moonlighting heroes. Whoever this was, he must not have been ranked very high... Or had been away for a very long time. Rather than let her mind scrape around for clues, Laika decided to just ask. "What's a 'while' for a vampire?"

The edge of Alfred's mouth quirked up for a split second before settling back into a polite expression once more. This seemed to be his default state so far. If her attention hadn't been trained on his face so carefully, she would have missed it.

Behind her, Laika heard Randall whisper with acidic annoyance. "Could you get any ruder?"

Laika's head snapped back glaring daggers at Blood Fang. A thousand comebacks were tumbling through her head, but the vampire defused them again. "A while is usually longer than your lifespan so far. Assuming I am correct in my estimate of your age," Alfred explained without actually giving her a specific number. Everything about Alfred was polite, from his words to his calm demeanor. And yet, he hadn't answered either of her questions. Both times he'd just side-stepped with his pretty words.

Laika could be antagonized by Blood Fang during any mission, so she decided to ignore the other wolves. The mystery of this 'new' moonlighter was far more deserving of her attention. Placing a hand on her hip, Laika tipped her head to one side and raised an eyebrow. Her grin never wavered, even if her tone had switched to be more teasing, "Are you going to actually answer my questions?"

Silence filled the hallway before Alfred spoke. "Decades and days have the same meaning when you do not age anymore. A while today means longer than you have been alive. However, I will not voice my actual guess on how old you are. Firstly, werewolves are notoriously deceptive in their ages, like vampires and elves. Secondly, you never say a woman's age out loud even if you are correct in your guess." Alfred's mouth had curved into a wider smile and had no hint of annoyance. "And my hearing is superior to most. Did I miss anything?"

Laika's eyes lit up as she laughed and she was pleased to get her answers. "No. I don't think you did." Alfred the Moonlighting

Vampire had very much captured her interest. Laika came from a family full of werewolves with keen hearing, and there was a flare of pride mixed with curiosity at his assertion that he might be better. A challenge to his claim hung on her lips, but again her attention was pulled. Her own ears picked up the sound of the elevators returning to the floor.

"It seems Officer Leavenworth and your packmate are return-ing," Alfred commented, without so much as a glance towards the elevators. He could at least hear the car scraping down the shaft the same as Laika. As predicted, the metal doors slid open to reveal a slightly green Evie. The sight of her friend in distress managed to pull Laika away from the vampire. She hurried to Evie's side, trying to take the woman's arm.

"Are you okay?" Laika asked, starting to fuss over the ill hue to the redhead.

"I'm fine," insisted Evie, pushing away the hands. A subtle glance towards the other werewolves gave Laika all the answers she needed for the short response. Her best friend was trying to keep it together in front of their rivals.

Thad chuckled, whispering to Randall, "She's not going to make it to her car before we get a repeat of Keisha." The look he gave Night Claw screamed he believed Evie was just being dramatic about her encounter upstairs.

"I'm shocked she made it back down here without blowing chunks," Randall agreed, still keeping his voice down. The two were speaking quietly enough that the words would be barely a whisper of noise to Aaron and the other werewolves.

But Laika could hear every insult being thrown back and forth, which only served to piss her off even more. A stomp of her foot caught the attention of Blood Fang as the werewolf rounded on them. "Like you're any better! How many murders have you been at?" She'd recovered from her earlier distraction and was winding up into a proper fight now.

"Let's just go," mumbled Evie, tugging at her friend's arm.

Glancing back at her packmate, Laika was surprised. Evie never backed down from quarreling with Blood Fang. Did the scene upstairs really have her off her game?

"They aren't about to do any better. Ten minutes and they'll be just as sick," Evie urged softly for only Laika's ears.

Thad laughed snidely, pulling Laika's attention back to him. The two werewolves were preparing to square off against one another, tension pulling tight as a piano wire. Laika tried to figure out her first move. She didn't know if Shelly would help her if the fists started to fly, but Evie was in no condition. Randall would undoubtedly come to his packmate's aid in a fight. Laika had a higher combat rating than both of the men. She could take them as long as she played smart.

Any explosion of aggression was stifled once again by the level and courteous voice from Alfred.

"Officer Leavenworth," he caught everyone's attention, "I can see the Night Claw moonlighters to the other elevator as you take Blood Fang upstairs, if that is alright? You do not need them any longer, correct?" While posed as a question, there was an edge of command to the smoothly delivered sentence. He'd created an opening for the GPD officer to defuse the situation.

"Right, this way please," Aaron spoke up quickly, summoning the elevator back to usher the two male werewolves from the hallway. For a moment, Thad didn't back down from the brewing fight. A low growl was barely suppressed under the surface of his usual smug calm. Night Claw and Blood Fang had never come to blows before, but the tense nature of this job had both packs riled up. Finally, Randall placed a hand on his friend's shoulder and muscled him into walking forward. Disaster avoided, they disappeared up to the penthouse with Aaron.

Laika glared as the two retreated and silver elevator doors slid shut, ripping them from her murderous gaze. Once the source of her anger was out of view, Laika shifted her attention back to her friends and the vampire. "Umm... sorry about that," she mumbled with the slightest hint of regret. Pack rivalries were well known in Glenwood MOONS, but showing how bad the fighting could get with a few well-placed insults was embarrassing. Not a grand introduction to the pack for a fellow moonlighter...

"No matter," Alfred replied kindly, his eyes flickering up as the other elevator arrived. He steered the werewolves towards it. His presence alone caused Shelly and Evie to move, while Laika's shame drove her forward.

Evie looked distracted as they crossed the threshold. Usually she'd have something to say no matter the job. But as her eyes stared blankly at the wall, her packmate ignored the group for the refuge of her own thoughts. Similarly, Shelly kept a step ahead of Laika, refusing to acknowledge the weirdness from before. Eagerness to get away from the place radiated off of her.

Laika walked casually now that she'd rebuffed her emotions for that little outburst. No lingering sickness or shyness kept her from offering up an appreciative smile for their escort. "It was nice to meet you," she said lamely, as the doors began to slide shut.

"As it was to meet you," Alfred replied, just as polite as ever. He made no attempts to join them as he hadn't taken a turn at the scene yet. The doors were more than half-closed when an impulse struck Laika. The wolf put her foot out, jamming them open.

"Wait," she said as she fumbled for her phone, before holding it out to Alfred. "Can I get your number?"

"My number?" repeated Alfred as a dark eyebrow raised. That was the most significant reaction he'd really had during their first meeting.

"If I have more questions?" Laika threw out the first reason that came to mind. So far, she'd learned more about vampires in two answers from him than Evie had in seven years with Tony. The phone stayed held out between them, waiting for an answer.

Finally, Alfred took the proffered cell phone and pulled his hand free of his glove. His fingers tapped on the call screen quickly before dialing. A faint buzz sounded from the depths of his leather coat.

Laika retrieved her phone, happy to have her prize in hand. She wasn't sure what possessed her to ask him so forwardly, but the woman was thrilled he'd agreed. He'd even confirmed the number was real for her. "Thanks," she cheered.

"Have a lovely day," Alfred offered amiably, before the last bit of the doors blocked him from view.

"He was nice?" Shelly tried to joke, but her voice was a bit flat from all the pack drama upstairs.

Laika laughed, her dark hair swinging around her before adding, "I'm pretty sure he can still hear you, Shelly." Which elicited a groan from her new friend as red embarrassment spread up her face and ears.

"Who was nice?" Evie asked, joining the conversation at last. "I know you aren't talking about Blood Fang and I'd be shocked if you managed two words to Dark Wind."

"Alfred, the Moonlighting Vampire," Laika replied as she typed the name into her phone, laughter still dripping from her words. It was only then she realized that her packmate had missed everything that happened in the hallway. She rarely got to say that she was the person paying the most attention, which only served to amuse her more.

CHAPTER 6
PAPERWORK

Evie
September 21st, 2018
Glenwood Police Department Station #1, Glenwood, CA

Evie glanced in the rearview mirror of her Saab and gave herself an appraising look. Her eyes continued to dart to her reflection at every red light, checking the details of her appearance. She needed to look composed at the station. Instead of like the walking dead... Maybe her new lipstick would help? If anything, she looked like someone who had been on the run for a while. She hadn't gotten a lot of good sleep for the last week; her dreams were haunted by a clicking sound. Departing from the scene immediately instead of doing her MOONS paperwork had led to today's visit to the GPD. Evie had no regrets; a little distance and some old-fashioned retail therapy had given her time to process the grisly scene.

A jarring ringtone chimed through the car from Laika's phone; it sounded like a metal click. Evie knew it well. It was reminiscent of Harry's clicking jaw. Every message sent a small shiver up her spine, a constant source of annoyance for the last week. "We should be there in ten minutes," Evie advised her friend while flicking her bangs to the side.

"Okay," Laika replied absentmindedly as her fingers flashed on the screen. She was sprawled across the beige seat with sneakers up on the matching dashboard. Even after finishing the message, her attention remained trained on her phone. The metallic ringtone sounded again barely a minute later.

"Do you think they've caught the killer?" Evie asked, ignoring the frustration building. She would usually start whining about shoes on the dashboard, but her worries ran deeper right now.

Laika glanced up, inspecting the bags under her friend's eyes for a moment. "Probably."

Evie's eyes grew bright as the car stopped at a red light, she could feel a swell of amusement coming from her friend. "Really?"

"Yeah, they're good at their job," Laika agreed as the ringtone sounded once more. She burst out in laughter before tapping out a response.

She wanted to give Laika a scathing look. The conversation wasn't having the effect of making Evie feel better. Not while her packmate's words lacked conviction. "This is important," she sighed as the light switched.

"Yeah, I know." Laika didn't even look up, drawing more ire from Evie.

Evie's voice came out as a hiss accompanied by a glare. "You aren't even listening!"

"That sounds good to me."

Laika giggled at the latest text message and Evie took a breath to steady her growing frustrations. She shut down her empathy rather than ride with Laika's emotional rollercoaster. She could be talking about an axe murderer in the backseat and her friend wouldn't notice. "I think I'm going to smash your phone."

"If you say so," Laika automatically replied.

Silence fell from Evie's side for a moment while the metallic click continued to send shivers down her spine. "Owen told me that we can move up to better cases if we join Blood Fang. All you need to do is get their pack symbol as a face tattoo," Evie continued, growing more annoyed.

Laika's fingers still danced on her phone screen and she never even glanced up. "I trust you, Evie... wait, what did you just say?" The distracted werewolf's brain caught up to the words 'face tattoo' like a car crash in progress.

"I knew it!" exclaimed Evie. "You haven't been listening to a word I said all day!" She slammed the brakes fiercely as the Saab screeched into a GPD parking space. Both women were pulled forward by the momentum, but their seatbelts kept them safe. A full force glare whipped in Laika's direction as Evie put the car in park.

Laika looked longingly at her phone before dragging her attention up to her angry packmate. She twisted so that her feet were no longer up on the dashboard, trying to look presentable. "I was listening," she protested, "You said something about your shoes being epic!"

"They are epic, but no, I didn't!" shot back Evie, the edges of her mouth threatening to curl down into a scowl.

Her friend bit her lower lip, knowing she'd already been caught. "Was it about your... hair?" her friend ventured, trying to make her question more like a statement.

Evie pushed her bangs up out of her eyes before folding her arms to huff, "What is so interesting on your phone that you've ignored me all week?" This obsession had started small with a single text message; a week later, Laika was on her phone for hours talking to her new friend. Evie had been so focused on her own mental health she hadn't noticed the unusual aura radiating off her friend until today.

"I'm not ignoring you," defended Laika as her phone chimed again. She glanced down at the device in her lap, trying to disguise the look by brushing a strand of hair behind her ear. The ploy almost worked, but Evie's keen eyes caught it.

"You are too! Even now!" Evie exclaimed, turning her glare onto the tiny device that kept chiming. A pale hand slammed into the steering wheel to accentuate her point. "I have heard that stupid sound a hundred times today alone!"

Laika grinned sheepishly, covering her phone like it might protect it from Evie's wrath. The woman tipped her head and spoke in a consoling voice, "I'm sorry, Evie. I didn't realize the sound was bothering you. You should've-"

"It's not just the sound! You've been glued to your phone since last week!" Evie whined as she threw her door open, silently cursing the bane that was 'Alfred the Moonlighting Vampire.' She tried a different track to explain her frustration. "What can possibly be so funny? Like, read the last three text messages!"

"Oh... well, I said 'Look at this cute cat!' and then sent him this gif," Laika showed her phone screen, where a kitten was rolling around on a blanket. "And then he said, 'That is quite cute.'"

Evie gave her friend an incredulous stare. "Yeah, that cat is adorable. But his response isn't even witty? You've got to be kitten me?"

There was an almost wounded look in Laika's eyes, and she pulled the phone back to her chest. "No! He answers vampire questions too! Here! Watch."

Evie wasn't sure why her friend looked so upset. That pun had been amazing, but went completely ignored. She watched as a question was sent to Alfred.

LAIKA

How do you breathe in your Moonlighting gear?

The response was almost immediate, heralded by that same clicking chime. Evie's brow knitted together in annoyance as she tried to not react. The answer had been so quick, like he'd been waiting for the question.

ALFRED

I do not.

Laika giggled, no longer distracted by the fight she was having with her friend. Evie watched as several messages flew back and forth before her eyes, each more mystifying than the last.

LAIKA

That's hilarious! LOL

ALFRED

How so?

LAIKA

Well you wear a gas mask and those are designed to help people breathe

ALFRED

I see, I suppose that is quite amusing.

I do not actually have to breathe, though, so there are no air holes. Holes would defeat the purpose of a light-tight mask.

Evie cleared her throat, commanding her friend's attention once again. "What am I missing here?"

"It's hilarious! Look... I explained. So gas masks-" Laika began, but was quickly cut off by a sharp look.

Evie's eyes pierced through each word, stopping Laika's explanation before she could repeat her messages. She hated the question before it even tumbled out of her mouth. But she had to ask it anyway, she had to know the truth. "Laika... Do you like this guy?" She couldn't bear to let her empathy check the answer.

"No," Laika rolled her eyes and settled back against the passenger seat with a huff. "I'm just trying to be friends with a fellow moonlighter. You know we don't have a lot of non-wolves!"

"Good, because you're acting like you do. This is the same type of ditzy you did with Zach and we know how that ended," snapped Evie.

Laika flinched visibly at her words. "No, I'm not. I'm just enjoying a conversation with a new friend. There is nothing here."

Evie took a deep calming breath before adding soothingly, "I'm glad because I was worried I'd need to explain the vampire birds and werewolf bees to you."

"Um... what?" inquired Laika as that caught her attention firmly. She managed to ignore the next message, waiting for an answer from Evie.

Evie paused then commented. "You know what I mean. Witches, Elves, and Dwarves are all totally different species. But they are still living 'breathing' people and your new friend, Alfred, isn't one of the living. So he can't do things the living can do."

She didn't actually know if that was true or not, but she said it all the same. A white lie to save Laika from doing something stupid like pursuing this vampire was in her friend's best interests. If she really wanted a new relationship, there were plenty of werewolf boys and girls in Glenwood. Or at least boys, as her packmate's preferences ran that direction.

"Oh. That makes sense. I don't like him like that, though... he's just funny." Laika flushed for a moment, the blush hard to see on her tawny skin.

Evie's silver eyes studied her friend for a moment longer looking for any signs of deceit. She almost considered verifying the answer using her powers... but Laika knew she couldn't lie to her so she wouldn't try... right? "Good," she confirmed again, happy to have quashed any misplaced feelings. Evie finally got out of the car.

The Glenwood Police Department was a small grey box in the oldest part of town. Neat black letters decorated the side informing them they were at the correct municipal building. Nothing inside but the telephones had been updated since the 1950s. Visitors were greeted by a large wooden desk, marred with decades of pen marks and divots. The linoleum underfoot looked aged as well, but every part of this building was well cared for. Everything had a slight sheen from being polished daily, even the sea of desks that formed the bullpen.

Glenwood was not a large suburb and didn't require a large police force. A little over a dozen officers sat in the bullpen, with a handful of offices and interrogation rooms off to the sides. In the far corner, Evie could make out a pair of desks squeezed together and overflowing with paperwork. A little sign hung overhead, declaring it belonged to the "MOONS Liaison" department.

The department didn't even warrant an office. Not surprising, given how most police officers felt about moonlighters. They were kind enough to Evie's face, but Laika swore they grumbled about werewolves taking their jobs. Which the redhead found hilarious because she'd never be caught dead wearing a police uniform.

"Evie! Laika! You're just in time," Owen called once he spotted them from his vantage point in the liaison section. He stood up, waving them back past the officer at the front desk.

Laika, sounding excited they might be in time for something interesting, asked, "For what?"

"Paperwork!" the blonde man declared with a broad grin.

"Ew," both women answered in unison.

Evie had more to say, but her attention was stolen by a crash of exhaustion cascading over her. Someone here hadn't been sleeping well. Aaron walked out from an office on the other side of the room and he looked more tired than her. For a moment, all Evie's annoyance at Laika's phone, new friend, and the woman herself evaporated, as she worried about the officer heading towards her.

He turned a kind greeting in her direction as he approached. Aaron's emotions didn't match that cheery expression, which was uncommon for him. "Evie, Laika, I'm glad you had time to sort out this mess. The captain wants every inch of this case documented right."

"Of course," Evie replied, perching herself on the edge of one of the desks. She tried to return the gesture, "I'm sorry I bailed..."

"I've got the forms right here," Aaron explained without missing a beat. He skipped over the apology, having something more important to handle. The officer held out a familiar packet of papers that needed filling out.

Her smile faltered, Evie took them in hand then asked, "Can I use a desk?"

"Yes, I need to put all of this clutter away anyway," Aaron answered, sweeping other papers into his arms. A quick reassuring look graced his face before he went to work.

"Thanks..." Evie sat down.

Laika had settled into sitting cross-legged on the floor, leaning up against Owen's desk. Her earlier obsession with sending messages seemed to have cooled. The phone lay in her lap rather than glued to her fingers while she spoke with her favorite police officers.

Evie barely concealed how pleased she was, realizing her words had the impact she'd wanted. She focused on the late paperwork that demanded details about her trip up into the penthouse. At least this was just a blank form, and not the case file she knew was sitting on the wooden desk. There were probably pictures and all the other reports in there. Her pen hastily scribbled out words about what she'd felt in that place, as she idly listened to the conversation around her.

"Be glad you never had to go upstairs," Owen teased Laika as he reclined in his chair.

Laika turned curious eyes onto Owen. "Was it really that bad up there?"

Aaron answered, "Yes. That was a massacre like we've never seen in Glenwood before. Our captain wants to pull in moonlighters from LA that specialize in magic."

"Oh? Like more witches?" Laika was pulsing with excitement at the prospect.

"We don't need more witches," snapped Owen, "Glenwood already has *the* top-ranked magic expert in the state. We don't need anyone from LA MOONS coming in to cramp our style."

Laika shifted uncomfortably for a second and Evie wondered if she'd insulted their friend. A small metal clink caught the wolf's attention, breaking the moment. Once a reply was sent off, Laika tried again. "Okay... we don't need more witches, but was it really magic at the scene?"

"Yes," Evie added quietly, "It has to be magic."

"My money is on dwarves," explained Owen with a mischievous grin in place.

"Really?" Laika perked up, "I didn't think they had that kind of magic?"

"They don't," interrupted Aaron, pausing at his desk to pick another paper.

Owen raised an eyebrow, "But they do all the crazy mad science with their 'crafts'?"

Evie's pen stopped mid-word to look at Aaron. He nodded and went back to a grey cabinet, pulling out a form with clean cursive letters. Clearing his throat, the officer recited the words written there.

"Dwarven magic requires physical contraptions when using electricity. Additionally, they cannot create anything from nothing; unlike other races, they may only manipulate pre-existing elements. There was no evidence that anyone had tampered with any of the machines in the home using dwarven magic. I would suggest sending in a proper electrician to double-check."

— KLÍMEK

Three sets of eyes stared at Aaron, trying to comprehend what he'd just said.

Evie broke the silence, "What?"

"Dwarves couldn't have done it because there wasn't a powerful enough machine on the scene," summarized Aaron.

"Oh," Evie looked back at her paperwork, "That's... fair."

Laika stifled a laugh as she responded to another text message. "Do you think it was Pink Magic?"

"Pink?" Owen repeated, "What the hell is pink?"

Evie sighed, "Not this again... that's a myth."

"It's not a myth! It's just really hard and usually takes two witches in perfect sync," hissed Laika. She pushed herself away from the desk so she could spin and look up at both of them. "There are five branches of magic: Green, White, Red, Grey, and Black. Right?"

"Yeah, each has an associated element. So you're a witch expert now?" Owen raised an eyebrow.

"I learned it in my college classes. You can take all the theory classes, but UCLA doesn't allow you to take the application classes if you don't have magic." Laika growled. Evie knew how hard she had tried to get into those classes.

Evie sighed again, "Werewolves don't have magic. I guess I can check them off the list."

"Correct," Aaron answered while brushing past with more paperwork to file, "And it wasn't pink magic."

"It could have been," Laika disagreed, jumping to her feet. "Hear me out! Red magic is fire, and White magic is air. If you combine them, you can make lightning! When you mix red and white, you get pink, so pink magic is lightning!"

"Melinda ruled that out," added Aaron without turning around from the filing cabinets.

"Wait?" Evie asked, "Pink magic is real?"

Aaron shrugged. "Apparently."

"Told you so!" Laika cheered, but her mood was dimmed as it had already been counted out.

"A witch hurling lightning from their hands could have done that," Evie said, leaning back. Her form sat forgotten on the desk.

"You saw the scene," Aaron reminded, picking up more papers and walking away.

"So?" Laika and Evie answered in unison.

Owen gave them a scathing look. "Seriously? Evie, you were there. If a witch had come through throwing around that much big magic, what would it have looked like?"

"Oh," Evie cooled herself back down, "That makes sense. Everyone was so calm and enjoying the party. Someone would have been running, things would have been knocked over, or something would be wrecked... and Harry..."

"Who's Harry?" Laika pressed, but the looks from the others shut her down quickly. Taking the hint, she veered back on topic. "Witches can't do remote magic... by themselves at least. What does that even leave then?"

"Elves and vampires," supplied Aaron helpfully, shuffling more reports into the file cabinets.

Evie burst out laughing, "Elves can't do that, they are barely more magical than us."

Owen stopped her laughter with two words, "Weather Magic."

"What? Elves don't have weather magic. They have those little illusions. You see it all over Hollywood." Evie waved a hand dismissively.

"That's just one of the bloodlines, there are a bunch of different types, and one of them is weather control," Owen countered.

"Nine bloodlines," added Aaron, "But it can't be elf magic either. Skysong magic doesn't work that way." Before anyone could ask, he pulled a different file from the cabinet, rattling off the explanation it contained.

"Elven weather magic, which belongs to the bloodline
   commonly referred to as 'Skysong', requires pre-existing
   weather conditions to affect a large enough area. Or a
   practitioner of higher levels can summon such a storm;
   however, this would have been caught by weather
   systems."

— KLÍMEK

He placed the notes down on his desk and went back to filing away other papers.

"And nothing on the radars when we checked last week," explained Owen, "So no one was playing with the clouds."

"Then clearly this was done by a vampire," Evie decided while her eyes glanced at the papers with the same cursive writing. This must have been the notes from the Glenwood magic expert Owen had been bragging about.

Evie's lips curled up into a satisfied smirk. She felt like she'd solved the case easily while trying to raise morale. "Aren't you glad we were here to help you close this?"

"One problem," Laika shot down her friend's explanation, "I've never heard of vampires having magic like that."

Aaron tilted his head to the side, leaning against his cabinets, "I don't think it was a vampire. Based on the reports from next of kin, this party had been planned for the daytime hours."

"So? Parties don't exactly end just because the sun went down," Evie disagreed. She could tell her friend wasn't sold on the theory either. Vampires being excluded from the list only because of daylight was flimsy.

Laika glanced at her friend, and then back at Aaron. "And it's not like vampires don't come out during the day? You guys called Al- one out to the scene last Friday afternoon. This all took place inside."

"Yes, but in rooms with floor-to-ceiling windows? That doesn't seem likely." Aaron fished another piece of paper out of the filing cabinet. This one was far less detailed in explanation than the rest but was written in the same cursive script. He read out the words.

"There are no vampires in the LA Coven or surrounding areas capable of this magic. Further investigations will be conducted to verify the accuracy of my records."

— KLÍMEK

"That's it?" Laika asked with a look of defeat at the lacking information.

Aaron set the paper down on top of the newly emerging stack on his desk. All the clutter from before was swept away and was already being replaced by new documents. "That's it."

Owen glanced at the mess but didn't seem surprised. "And if our resident expert says it's true about vampire magic, then it's true."

Evie surmised, "So in conclusion, no one did it?" She looked down at her partially filled out paperwork with a dirty look. Why was this taking her so long?

"Or, stay with me," Laika's voice pitched up, giving away her excitement, "It's magic no one has seen before!"

"That's not a good thing!" Owen scolded, placing a hand on the werewolf's shoulder to try and settle her down.

A stern but quiet voice cut across the playful banter, like a bucket of ice water on the group. "Should you two be discussing an active case with potential suspects?"

Everyone's gaze snapped up to the figure that had materialized out of nowhere. The man was tall, with light blonde hair styled with not a single hair out of line. His steely eyes were narrowed, distaste evident as they swept over the scene before him. Evie had seen this man around the office before but never spoken to him.

"Suspects? Lay off Gibson, there's no way it was werewolves," Owen scoffed, "They're about as magical as a rock... a rock that can change shape."

Gibson glared at his fellow officer. "You would say that."

"Hey," Laika bristled, her shoulders squaring off at the rudeness towards Owen.

Aaron broke the building tension. "Thank you, Ms. Belle, for coming in at my convenience to finish up this paperwork," he said smoothly with a raised voice catching the others' attention. His hand swept the paper up from beneath her pen with a quick motion, and after eyes scanned the details, he put it back down. "Please just put your signature there, and then Officer Kirkland will escort you to the door." Evie felt a rush of annoyance sweeping over all the officers.

"Of course," Evie stammered, scrawling down a loopy signature. She wanted away from the agitation clawing at her empathy. "Come on, we should let these officers get back to work."

Laika huffed but moved to follow Evie, allowing herself to be distracted by the metallic clink of her ringtone. Owen also stood up to do as bidden. He exaggeratedly held his arm out, "If you good ladies would follow me." Then he spun around to face the others with a click of his heels and a salute, "If you'll be so kind as to excuse us, Detective Gibson!"

Evie and Laika couldn't help but giggle at the theatrics as they followed their friend. He wove them through the desks without looking back to see if they kept up. "Who the hell is that?" hissed Laika when they passed the massive front desk.

"A pain in my ass," replied Owen with a shrug, "Gibson is your run of the mill racist, and he's got it out for werewolves especially. You can imagine we get along as well as fire and gasoline."

"The captain allows a racist on staff?" Evie questioned, glancing back at the two officers still talking by the MOONS desks.

Owen gave another shrug of his shoulders, already looking bored at the subject. "He's a good detective, and it rarely affects his decisions. He just really hates our department."

Laika changed the topic, perking herself up with a hopeful expression, "So, we're on the case, yes?"

"Nope."

"What? Why not?" Evie huffed.

Owen gave the two of them a look that screamed 'really?', but he answered anyway, "Because you two can do shit all about magic, and this is big magic. Whenever we figure out who did it, I'm going to send the biggest, baddest powerhouses I have to take them down. Neither of you are even rated to handle a magic related mission."

"That's fair," Laika conceded with a heavy sigh, "Someday I'll get my ranking."

"But I have some good news for you," Owen added, flashing a wolfy grin. He flung his arms wide and gestured back towards the MOONS desks happily.

Evie looked back at the messy desks, there was nothing particularly special about them. They were still covered in papers to the point you could barely see the tops. "What?"

"Proof that our beloved Officer Leavenworth has a flaw. He's the messiest partner I've ever had." Owen declared.

"Oh," Evie grinned, "I thought that was your desk."

INTERLUDE - FORGING

The Ritualist
September 24th, 2018
...somewhere in Glenwood, CA

After the Ritualist's last success, she'd tried to communicate more openly with her Love. But they'd been ignoring her again. Why did they always play so hard to get? She'd been trying for years. Even after her Love had run away into hiding and she'd had to track them down again.

They shared so much in common. They were so perfect for each other, but clearly she hadn't proven that yet. Her Love hadn't recognized her first ritual for the present it was, a present to make both of their lives better.

So now, the Ritualist had to finish the second one.

She checked over her scroll one more time to be sure. This ritual was even more important than the last one, because if it worked then the first success wasn't a fluke. For one of the first times in her life it would be real proof that she was special enough, even after so many failures. Her father was WRONG!

He'd been wrong to rip her away from her real mother. He'd been wrong to try and force her to play family. He'd been wrong to deny the feeling that had grown between her and her True Love. He'd just been wrong about everything.

The Ritualist waited for the sun to fall towards the horizon, before her hands swept over a sigil and released chalk to the wind. A surge of power rippled through the circle she had painstakingly built all day. Elation filled her mind, sensing another victory at hand, but the power was just surging, exploding violently outwards before she could brace for impact...

CHAPTER 7
RUST

Laika
September 24th, 2018
Cohen Park, Glenwood, CA

Dark furred paws raced down a familiar path with practiced strides. Claws dug into the hard packed dirt, propelling Laika along faster. She loved the feeling of four legs mid-run after a long day of work. Wind whipped through her amber and brown fur. Exhilaration flooded her, rising up to meet each step. Laika threw her head back preparing to let out a howl to match her joy.

A sound around the bend caught her attention. A pair of grey wolves lazily ambled into view, enjoying each other's company. One of them gave Laika a baleful look as she blazed down the center of the trail. The howl died in Laika's throat, and she let out a huff instead. Her paws slowed their pace to a jog and she skirted around the grey wolves. This was the downside to all run parks, but especially ones with a sundown closing time. They were always busy in the afternoons as people squeezed in a shift early.

Once she was past the couple, Laika picked up speed. Her paws beat a rhythmic tempo as she loped along the well worn path that wound through Cohen Park. The park wasn't large; it was a converted football field for a school long-since gone. Laika's favorite trail followed where the school's track used to be.

Trees had been planted around the formerly plain field, but they barely gave separation to the runners from each other. A tall brick and wrought iron fence ringed the perimeter that blocked the view from the outside. Everything was picturesque, conveniently located in the middle of Glenwood, but not quite the same as running full tilt through a forest.

Still, Laika tried to make time to come to the park at least two or three times a week. Running in her wolf form always lifted her spirits, and she passed the entrance on the way home from work. She couldn't understand wolves who didn't enjoy this, even though she lived with one.

The only real issue with Cohen Park was how boring it could be running in circles. Laika kept her time to around half an hour before heading back to the shifting rooms. She had research to do tonight, which claws and paws weren't much help with.

About twenty minutes later, Laika had dressed and was jogging down the empty street. She had two feet instead of four paws. The late afternoon sun warmed her skin as a gentle breeze lazily wound through her hair. An idyllic day in Glenwood, colored with vibrant greens and golds of early autumn. But her pace was distracted as her phone pulled her attention for the tenth time since leaving the park.

LAIKA

> Coffee is hands down one of the most important substances on earth

Symbols flashed across her screen, marking the message read, and that her recipient was composing a reply. Sneakered feet began moving and picked up speed across the crumbling sidewalk, making her way home. Evie worked late, leaving Laika without a ride once her shift was over. The bus would be quicker than walking across half of Glenwood every evening, but she couldn't stop at her favorite run park that way.

A ping from her cell phone slowed the wolf once more, as her attention switched back to the intense debate she and Alfred were now having.

> ALFRED
>
> Tea does have a better footing with the rest of the world.

> LAIKA
>
> But coffee has way more caffeine!

> ALFRED
>
> Is that a factor in this debate?

The werewolf found herself smiling at the message sent back. Laika's fingers dashed across the screen swiftly, though her feet were meandering lazily down the sidewalk.

> LAIKA
>
> Absolutely!
>
> I mean... it's kind of the point
>
> Don't tell me you don't like coffee!?

> ALFRED
>
> I do not typically partake in coffee unless there is a reason.

A gif quickly answered the last message; a woman shrieking in mock horror. Alfred had limited knowledge of memes and internet culture. Laika took it upon herself to educate him. His responses were refreshing and unique, which amused her greatly.

> LAIKA
>
> How do you not drink coffee????!

ALFRED

I usually do not drink anything besides blood.

Does that truly warrant four question marks?

A small giggle escaped from Laika as she stared at the question. Her speed heading home had diminished with each message sent back and forth. Despite Evie's attempts to dissuade her from starting a friendship, Laika fell back into the rhythm of constant conversations. She wondered what he did all day that meant he had this much free time.

LAIKA

Yes!

You clearly have just never had good coffee

ALFRED

What constitutes good coffee?

LAIKA

The fact you even ask that speaks for itself

If you ever want to try real coffee, let me know

ALFRED

I suppose I shall.

Laika followed the turning sidewalk onto her street. Just five more minutes and she'd be home, but it would take twenty with how focused she was on her phone. Satisfied with declaring herself the victor of the great coffee versus tea debate, the wolf decided to indulge in another question.

LAIKA

I've been curious... It's like you're always awake

What exactly do you do?

Her focus stayed on the screen, waiting for the usual lightning-fast reply. But this time, nothing came. The message didn't get marked as read. There was a slight frown as Laika pondered if she'd overstepped with the question. Alfred had been so forthcoming with answers and they'd just been enjoying a debate.

Laika's frown deepened as she picked up speed. She reminded herself that Alfred would get back to her once he had a minute. He didn't owe her every moment of his time.

"Hello," called a masculine voice as Laika turned up her driveway. Her head snapped up, startled out of her reverie. Exasperation painted Laika's face. Internally she groaned as she realized who was once again standing on their doorstep.

"Hi. Move." Laika tried to step around the invader, "Please."

Jonas stood firmly in front of the entrance with a scarf pulled up over his nose and blackout goggles in place. "Hi," he echoed his earlier statement, "I need to talk to Tor, please."

"She doesn't want to talk to you, just go home," Laika wearily commented as she tried to angle for a way around the man. Just pushing him off the doorstep would be rude, but she considered it all the same.

Jonas answered with confusion evident in his tone. "Why not?" There was a pause and the man didn't move an inch.

"I could think of a few reasons, but mostly because she doesn't want to," Laika quipped as her eyes rolled. She looked to the front window for help. The airy curtains blocked little of the street from the inside. If anyone were in the living room, they'd be able to see her predicament. Based on the lack of rescue, she had to assume no one was awake or home.

Quickly recovering from the insult, Jonas' gaze followed Laika's towards the house. "Look. I need to talk to Tor. It's important. Can you please get her?"

"If she's not answering the door and her bike isn't here, then maybe she's not home?" Laika pointed out exasperatedly. Her sneakers tapped impatiently on the porch waiting for him to move.

The vampire sighed, "Do you know when she'll be back?"

"No. Have you, I don't know, tried calling her?"

"She's not answering my calls," hissed Jonas, his frustrations growing by the moment.

"Sounds like she's just not into you, bro," shrugged Laika.

The longer this dragged out, the more he tested Laika's resolve to be civil. Jonas didn't look particularly tough; she wouldn't need more than one push to get him out of the way.

Jonas stepped back into the shadows of the patio. His hand pulled his scarf out of the way revealing a frustrated expression. When he growled his fangs were visible, "Seriously?"

"Don't do that!" snarled Laika. His aggression had sent a flash of adrenaline through her. She felt the urge to shift crawling up her spine. They were standing in front of *her* home, and every instinct screamed that she should drive away any threats. Werewolf and vampire squared off on the narrow steps. Neither made the first move. Laika didn't know if it was careful restraint or caution that kept her from acting.

"What the bloody hell is this?" yelled a gruff voice from the street. A dwarf stormed up the path flexing his muscles as he did. Laika immediately recognized Fred, her landlord, as he approached, still shouting. "Why is World War 3 brewing on my doorstep?"

Jonas quickly pulled his mask up to hide his fangs.

"Oh..." Laika faltered, "Hi Fred... this is nothing. Just... a um, friendly spat?"

If you had asked the average person about a dwarf before everyone came out of the shadows, they'd describe the little men from Snow White with round cheeks. The reality was much more terrifying. They were usually a foot shorter than humans, but were built of pure muscle and power. Dwarves could withstand a solid punch from a werewolf and were magically resistant.

"Looks a lot like you planned to start a fight on my finely crafted porch," Fred snapped. He squared himself up, ready for a brawl. His biceps flexed causing his anchor tattoo to ripple with the movement.

"No," agreed Jonas, his voice slightly muffled again. He didn't seem keen on going up against the dwarf either. "No fight here. I was just leaving." He carefully walked around Laika, not touching her or Fred as he headed to his car. "Please tell Tor to call me; it's really important."

"Annoying bloodsuckers. Don't do anything stupid like invite one inside," Fred scoffed. He brushed past Laika, unlocking the door with his key. "Are you coming? I got a bone to pick with you and Evie."

Laika glared at Jonas' car as it pulled away from the curb. But Fred's question reminded her of the more imminent threat. She hurried inside following her landlord. "Sorry! ... What's wrong? Evie said she'd sent the rent over last week."

She kicked off her shoes and dropped her bag on the coffee table. Her phone was in hand to send a message to Evie demanding answers about their rent. An error message popped up. Laika realized all her network bars were missing. That was strange...

Fred huffed and puffed, appraising the newly furnished living room. Laika didn't seem too worried about her landlord's inspection. Night Claw had a way of ruffling his feathers, but Fred never threatened to throw them out.

"It ain't the rent. I got an issue with the subletting," Fred grumbled. The dwarf's frown only deepened at the clueless expression on Laika's face. "The roommates!" he shouted as he moved through the house.

"You mean Shelly and Tor? Why are they an issue?" Laika flopped onto the couch, kicking her feet up on the new table.

"Cause I have people staying in my house that I don't know shit about," Fred shot back like a bullet.

"Oh," Laika waved off the anger with a hand, "Evie and I interviewed them. They're legit."

Fred paused at the large television which hadn't been there last month. His eyes glanced where the duct-taped table was missing, then to the new couch. He nodded to himself.

"Did you really?" the dwarf simmered, "You did full background checks and all the credit work?"

"We asked them the important questions," Laika hesitated, thinking back on the interviews. The look on her face was a dead giveaway; they had gossiped about their favorite shows or ones they wanted to see.

Fred stopped and crossed his arms, glowering down at the wolf. "Oh? Like what?"

Laika opened her mouth to offer up some half-hearted explanation; then, her eyes flashed with a stroke of brilliance. "Well, we know they can pay rent, and that they're not criminals." She declared with a smug smile, remembering the random questions that had come after the interviews.

For a moment, the dwarf loosened up, seeming pleased with the given answer. Then his dark eyes narrowed again as he pressed, "You have the paperwork to back any of that up? Like the credit reports?"

"Um," Laika tried to scramble to appease her landlord, "Does a duffle bag of money count as proof of rent?"

"You still got the bag?"

"Yep," Laika pulled herself up, then dashed off to the closet where they'd hidden the next years' rent.

Fred followed, scooping the black bag out of the woman's hands as soon as it was in sight. He pulled out a handful of bills, silently counting how much was actually in the bag.

"It all adds up," Laika offered, perched on the arm of the couch. "I dunno what Tor does, but she's paid her rent. And Shelly works every night, and she did, well, this." She waved an arm at the assembly of new furniture in the living room.

Fred looked skeptical and continued his counting.

"And both swore that they aren't up to anything illegal," Laika continued doing her best to hide her doubts. She loved her new roommates, but she wondered what Shelly was up to on her computer every night.

"Quit while you're ahead, kid," Fred warned while pulling out another few stacks to count.

The front door opened as Tor wandered in dressed in her cycling leathers. "Hey," she greeted as she walked towards the couch. She was unconcerned by the presence of a stranger standing in their living room, despite Fred being a dwarf counting her money from the duffle.

Laika quickly explained to her new human friend, "Um... Tor, this is Fred. He's our landlord, and I think he's, uh, got some questions for you."

Tor looked up at him from where she'd planted herself to sit. A controller was already in hand flipping on the news. "Sup?"

"Is this your rent money?" asked Fred, his gruff voice sounding accusing.

"Yep."

"How dirty is it?"

Tor shrugged, "I don't know. You'd need to ask my ex."

Fred looked unconvinced and pressed for more information. "The blo- vampire who's been at the door a few times?" He glanced at Laika for confirmation.

Laika nodded vigorously, before remembering to pass on Jonas' message to Tor. "Oh, and he's demanding you call him again."

"He knows where to find me at work if it's so damn important," Tor rolled her eyes. She shifted uncomfortably at the message.

"Where do ya work?" Fred interrogated.

"Regis Stunt Show. The one with the bikes and the chainsaws." Tor replied without missing a beat, but her eyes were on the screen. A report of panic downtown dominated the news.

Fred asked, "And when the boyfriend's money runs out, can you afford your rent?"

Tor nodded. Fred opened his mouth for the next question, but he never spoke. The words "Viewer Discretion Advised" flashed across the screen. A blonde elf appeared with a grim expression. She was explaining the disaster unfolding. Laika was transfixed. She lowered herself next to Tor, with Fred settling into the armchair. "As of right now," yelled the anchor over the roar of the crowd behind her, "There is no explanation for the outage of the towers, but the effect seems to still be spreading."

A large metal cellphone tower on the edge of the frame began to lean to the side. Brownish orange spots covered it. Laika's eyes glanced at her phone while listening. She saw a little red symbol at the top and a message: 'CorroNect Network Unavailable'. She wondered if anyone was trying to reach her right now and couldn't get through.

Fred hissed out a breath, causing her to look up as the leaning cellphone tower began to break in half. The top started to fall onto the emptying streets below as the center rusted out. The reddish orange snaked up and down the silvery metal.

"Oh shit," swore the dwarf.

The anchor looked up in shock. "The towers are corroding?! We currently have no explanation for how this is happening." Her scared eyes turned back to the camera, she tried to paint a smile in place. But whatever she saw panicked her. "Emma?" she screamed, "What's wrong?" The camera dropped its view like someone had let go of the machine. The lens cracked on impact with the cement.

Through the lines in the glass, Laika could make out pink high heels rushing forward. Then the feet and legs in view started to turn a familiar reddish-orange. She felt a surge of disbelief as the legs turned to dust. The orange dust dispersed, leaving behind a pair of heels and a dress in the wind. Then a disconnected signal flashed across the TV... "What the hell is happening?" Laika yelled, leaping up from her seat. Her phone was still reading that she had no signal.

"I don't know," Tor answered as her eyes remained on the empty screen. An uneasy silence hung over the room.

Laika was wondering if she could talk Fred into giving her a ride to GPD when the TV flared to life. This time a studio newsroom with two anchors appeared. Both were smiling wide, but it didn't hide how shaken they were. The man on the left started, "We will continue our coverage shortly. Sorry for the interruption... our team... our team on the ground has run into some technical difficulties."

The woman next to him swallowed before picking up, "We have received reports that GPD is already on the scene and has dispatched MOONS. The situation has been contained and is no longer spreading. Officials are encouraging viewers to remain in their homes-"

Fred got up and switched off the TV by hand, "Enough of that for now."

His urgency told Laika that he really just wanted to get out of there. The longer the news was on, the less likely he'd dare drive back to his place. He looked back at the two women. "Imma send over a lease packet for you and the other girl. Sign it, and I'll pick it up next Monday," Fred said, his happiness dimmed despite the pile of money in hand.

"Yeah, sure," replied Tor as she got up, going towards her room. Laika heard the news turn on Tor's room as soon as the door closed.

Left alone with their landlord, Laika pulled herself back together. That had been intense between the interrogation and the report. For now, she needed to make sure Fred was satisfied. "All good then? They sign the paperwork, and we're square?" she asked hopefully, wanting him out so she could turn the news back on as well.

Fred waved a stack of bills in the woman's face, "No. More. Late. Rent! But yeah, we're good." He stuffed the money back into the duffle, leaving it on the table. A hand twitched to grab the handle, but the man didn't follow through.

Laika placed a hand on her chest and sighed in relief. "Okay, good. No late rent and some papers. Can do."

"Next Monday. No later," warned Fred, getting up to leave, then he paused. His eyes glanced around almost as if he expected someone to listen in, "And tell both the girls, the vampire-lover and the nerdy little werewolf, to keep their noses out of the extra room in the basement. No one but me opens that door. You got me?"

Laika's eyes widened for a moment in surprise, remembering the only real house rule from their landlord. Sturdy cement steps led the way down to laundry machines tucked away in the basement. Just at the bottom of those stairs, the door neither she nor Evie had ever opened waited, like a portal to hell. Laika had a thousand theories about what was hidden in that room. But neither roommate had ever worked up the courage to dare touch the door.

"Yes," she agreed quickly, "I'll tell them about the basement door!"

Fred rattled off a few more words before departing. Despite her keen hearing, Laika couldn't remember a single one as her cell phone began an avalanche of notifications. Her service had returned! Hastily Laika pulled the phone free to check her messages. The last one she'd sent to Alfred was marked read as of a minute ago and he was typing a response. Plus there were three from Evie.

> **EVIE**
>
> Are you okay? Is your service down?
>
> Are you at the towers or did you make it home safely?
>
> Call me as soon as you get this!!!!
>
> **ALFRED**
>
> My apologies for the delay. Work required my attention, and my reception died at the scene.

Relief flooded Laika as she idly kicked the front door closed. The report had sideswiped her and only now did she realize she hadn't checked on her friend. A quick message shot off.

> **LAIKA**
>
> I'm totally fine, I was home before anything happened.
>
> **EVIE**
>
> Thank The Moon! I was worried.
>
> Heading home now, might be late.

Those messages were likely typed while sitting in LA rush hour traffic on a freeway. Instead of berating her friend, Laika switched to the other text chain.

She thought she'd fumbled with her earlier question, getting too personal too quick. Flopping down onto the couch unceremoniously, Laika quickly tapped out a response.

LAIKA

It's okay, had some surprise visitors at the house

Scene? What are you doing?

ALFRED

Moonlighting, that is my full-time job.

Laika nearly fell off the couch as she re-read the last message. A jolt ran through her at the thought. Moonlighting as an actual job, not just a side gig for extra income, sounded beyond cool. Tor's stunt show had seemed like the most exciting job in the world just minutes ago, but now it paled in comparison.

LAIKA

Seriously????

ALFRED

You have quite the love for question marks.

Yes, I seriously Moonlight in a full-time capacity.

LAIKA

What was the job? Was it dangerous?

ARE YOU DOWNTOWN RIGHT NOW?

ALFRED

Yes, I am downtown. I will be busy for a while here.

A frown creased Laika's face; this didn't sound like a job you'd send out a vampire to deal with. Had the sun set yet? And what was he going to do about the rusting? Thousands of questions burned in her mind, but she settled for just one.

LAIKA

What happened?

ALFRED

Unclear, the towers were fully intact and functional just an hour before collapsing.

LAIKA

So it really happened as fast as it did on the news?

ALFRED

Not precisely.

A few witches in the nearby area called in a report that there was too much ambient magic in the air.

I arrived just as the sun was setting, and then the towers began to fall apart before my eyes.

I have never seen anything quite like it before.

LAIKA

Woah... so it was magic?

Laika curled around her phone, waiting on each message with more excitement and horror than the last. She'd made friends with a proper moonlighter. Plus, he was a line to whatever had happened downtown.

ALFRED

Most certainly, magic.

But I am unsure what kind of magic rusts metal that quickly.

LAIKA

Black maybe

That deals with lots of metal

ALFRED

Technically, Black Magic just uses metal to focus; it does not easily affect the material.

Black Magic is used primarily for warding and power nullification.

There is a magic that does something similar to this, but to my knowledge, the only practitioner of sufficient power would not remove access to the phone network.

Every text message was a savored treat as Laika read them. She hadn't realized her new friend knew anything about magic. Vampires were not much better than werewolves in the magic department as far as she knew. Alfred seemed to have a working understanding, which meant they could talk theory all day long. She interrupted his explanation of various ways one could use magic to age metal.

LAIKA

Who could then?

ALFRED

I do not know; however, I will find out.

I need to go now. May I text you later?

LAIKA

Only if you have a good story to tell me about what happened?

ALFRED

Agreed.

Laika turned on the news again, wondering if she'd catch a look at Alfred in the coverage.

CHAPTER 8
SCREENPLAY

Evie
October 2nd, 2018
Fashion Prime, Los Angeles, CA

Evie ignored the racks of designer shirts, each just a tiny bit different from the last to maintain the reputation of 'one of a kind.' Every 'stray' stitch was artfully done and the buttons were ever so slightly varied. This store was the sort of place she adored, the kind she used to frequent all through her teenage years.

But right now she couldn't care less as she sat cross-legged on a velvet couch.

Her iPad dominated Evie's view. It was open to a drawing app where she'd written 'Glass People', 'No Damage', 'Limited Radius', and every other detail she could remember from the penthouse. Harry's name was circled twice to remind her how unlucky he'd been on the edge of the spell. Evie tapped her pencil against the edge of her tablet as she tried to connect the dots between what could be responsible.

"Ugh!" came a shout from across the room. Arik stood in front of a trifold mirror, twisting his hips one way and then the other as he scrutinized the pants he was trying on. He'd chosen emerald fabric to accentuate his fair features and match his eyes. However, the elf was less than pleased with the pants. "This is utter trash!" he declared, dramatically tossing his long mane of flaxen hair. His sharp gaze rounded on Tony with the silent demand to fix the problem.

The vampire lazily lounged on another plush velvet couch, a lacy parasol propped behind him. Tony insisted it was to shield himself from the 'deadly' sunlight streaming through the floor-to-ceiling windows behind them; Evie suspected it was more theatrics than actual protection. Even from where she sat, she could see sunlight dappling Tony's face. He'd never admit it, but her co-worker was a daywalker.

Their exchange pulled Evie's attention up from her freelance moonlighting. She wasn't making any progress anyways.

"How is it trash?" Tony asked with a bored expression, typing away on his phone.

That earned him a derisive snort from Arik. "This isn't fit for a runway! They are barely gussied up gym rags!"

Speaking up was futile when Evie's boss was like this, but she tried anyway. "Joggers are very trendy right now. You'll look very chic with the right shirt." She offered a bright smile, but it didn't reach her eyes. Evie had been ignoring the emotions in the room, as she normally did on a day like this. She focused her empathy and was warned of a storm brewing within her boss.

"You're showing your age. No one says 'gussied' anymore," Tony chimed in helpfully, tipping his phone just a moment to look over it. His words egged on their boss to be even more annoyed. "You should be more grateful; you barely qualified to be paid to shop these days."

"Hold your tongue," snapped Arik, throwing the green pants at him.

Evie envied how Tony could get away with sassing their employer so smoothly. The vampire was unflappable in the face of a Taran temper tantrum. He had been working for the elf for decades, and his job was secure through Natasha, Arik's manager. Evie's position as his assistant was much more volatile. She had heard the horror stories of the actor going through a new assistant every week. So in moments like these she held her tongue, despite years of tenure in the position. She'd never say she loved her job, but finding another one would be annoying.

Arik stalked off to the racks behind Evie looking for something else to wear. "It isn't my fault there is nothing worth my time or money in this place." He had enough grace to mumble that. Only elevated werewolf hearing was able to pick it up.

Evie rolled her eyes at the exchange, tuning out her coworkers to go back to work. Everything she'd written in blue was a 'clue' from the penthouse, and she'd scribbled a few notes in orange. Right now she was trying to find any parallels between the radio towers and the first incident. Other than being a large magical disaster, she had nothing.

"What are glass people?" Arik's face appeared over her shoulder.

She nearly jumped out of her skin. "It's nothing," Evie lied, turning off the screen.

This had Tony's attention as he narrowed in on the flare of embarrassment and panic that shot through her. "Is that a new punk band? Should you be buying concert tickets at work? Especially if you aren't about to offer me any?"

"No. It's just an..." fumbled Evie, trying to stop the questions. She groped for an excuse but came up with nothing.

Arik supplied her with one, "Are you writing a screenplay?"

"If there are no followup questions," Evie paused, glancing between them. "Then... yes. I am trying to write a screenplay."

Arik was too excited by the idea. He snatched away the iPad to see what she'd written. "How far along are you? Do you have a protagonist? Action? Comedy? Romance? Action?" He rattled off a million questions as he read over her flow chart.

Tony's eyes narrowed and his smirk intensified. He'd seen

through that lie like he'd been reading it on her face. While Evie was good at reading people's emotions, he was a master of it. Likely a combination of his powers and a few hundred years on everyone in the building. "Oh really? Is our little Evie finally trying to break into Hollywood?" his tone was dripping with sarcasm.

"The idea is actually pretty good," Arik countered while taking a spot on the couch next to Evie.

"Uh... thanks," she replied while dying to pull her iPad back. There were details on that tablet the police hadn't released yet.

"This concept of people getting turned to glass is creepy in all the right ways," Arik continued, "Not so sure about them rusting away though. I'd go with one or the other to not muddy up the theories too much."

"Oh really?" echoed Tony himself, "Inspired by the tragedies in Glenwood?"

"Something like that," answered Evie.

Arik finally returned her device. His stare was focused intensely on Evie. "So who did it? And who's going to stop them?"

"I don't know yet..." admitted Evie, brushing her bangs out of her eyes. She could feel the excitement pouring off her boss. Shutting him down would only set off a bad afternoon.

"Who is the hero of the story?" encouraged Arik.

"I was thinking of making them some badass moonlighters."

"Moonlighters?" Arik said the word like he was tasting it for the first time. "Do they handle things like that? Seems a bit over the average person's head."

Evie snapped before she could catch herself, "Moonlighters are more than the average supernatural. They are the modern day superheroes who step up so that the rest of the population doesn't have to worry about what's going to happen if their werewolf neighbor throws a car or their elven..."

"Their elven what?" Arik prompted. He pressed his lips together in a hard line.

"Oh, oh, oh," Tony's hand mockingly shot up, "Their elven lover might bind them up with some sexy vines for fun?"

Arik glared at him.

"Or maybe he'll throw lightning bolts at you if you cheat on him. I could go on," Tony brazenly continued.

"Please don't," snipped Arik as he rolled his eyes dramatically.

"Is that all real?" asked Evie, unsure she even wanted an answer.

Arik stood up, throwing his hands in the air defensively, "Of course not. That's all just old wives tales about elves."

But behind Arik's back she could see Tony nodding vigorously.

A big clock on the wall chimed 1pm announcing the time for everyone. All eyes fell on the purchase pile. Given how much the store was paying for Arik's presence, it was pathetically small. A few more shirts, a couple of ties, and a pair of bright red pants joined the folded bundles as Evie dashed about grabbing things.

Tony moaned, "We are going to be so late for your next appointment. Natasha is going to kill me."

The only person that Evie had ever felt cause a fear response from the vampire was Arik's manager. Likely because Natasha was the only one with the power to fire him... There was no fussing from Arik despite the lecture. Tony had invoked the name of the only woman able to make him behave. He folded everything Evie handed him over his arms, ready for the promo shots the store would snap of him loaded down with their products.

"I've got our pictures for Instagram already," Evie explained. She had put on a calm front, but she was still in turmoil. Internally Evie was reeling from what she just learned about elves. That knowledge made an elf a very possible suspect. Scooping up the extra bags, she continued, "I'll start posting them as soon as we get back to the house."

Tony steered them to the register for the last photos and then out of the store. They were then onto the next leg of this publicity stunt. The vampire had one hand hovering by Arik's elbow as they stepped out onto the street. A small crowd of paparazzi and super-fans had assembled in the shaded storefront. Evie came clicking after them, the extra bags from the store over one arm, a parasol tucked under the other, and her work phone open. Her eyes were scanning the calendar, realizing they were 10 minutes past due for leaving. She followed the men to their getaway car.

Arik pretended not to notice the crowd for a few seconds. Then a perfect mask of surprise blossomed on his face when he 'realized' they were there to see him. Most of them were women in their 50's and 60's, but it was a decent turnout.

The distraction of the crowd made Evie the first to reach the car. Internally, the wolf was still running in circles about all the ways elves could apparently kill you. She'd need to badger Tony more. The vampire was rarely a font of information, and she needed to know if what he said was true. Evie didn't remember stowing bags in the sleek car's trunk or sliding into the passenger seat. Her eyes were a million miles away as she wished she could google supernatural power comparison charts without her nosy co-worker and boss being so near.

"Remember, this is the first round of discussions with this new publicity agent," Tony chided Arik as he slid into the driver's seat. The vampire had sunglasses and little leather driving gloves, but the parasol was conspicuously missing now. Evie remembered packing it away in the trunk. "Don't be a diva. If you set this bridge ablaze, there might not be a second one."

An answering scoff came from where their boss sat, dramatically sprawled across the backseat. Arik had his phone up in his face, checking how well that little fan meet and greet was trending. "I know how to talk to publicity monkeys," he hissed back. "I've been making a name for myself long before their profession existed."

"Your crash landing from relevance is just bad luck?"

No answer came this time. Arik sat silently stewing as he glared daggers at the back of the vampire's head.

"That's right," gloated Tony, "Respect your elders; I always know better."

"Quit while you're ahead."

"The next big-time superhero has to be nice and clean," Tony plowed onwards as he steered them through LA traffic. "Captain America doesn't go to rehab twice a year. Or cock it up with every middle-aged mom dying to meet her teenage crush... maybe just delete Tinder before we get there?"

Evie had only been half-listening to the conversation. But her focus returned as superheroes joined the fray, snapping her out of her spiraling thoughts. "Wait... What is this meeting for again?" she asked, even as her fingers tapped her work phone to pull up the calendar.

"Keep up," Tony groaned, "It's publicists. Your only job is to sit there and not sleep with any agents."

"Why would I do that?" Evie asked, reading the details on the little calendar box. She didn't know when her boss had gotten this idea to join the skyrocketing number of actors becoming comic book characters. However, the whole concept delighted her, pulling her from dark, drowning thoughts.

"What girl isn't trying to break into Hollywood?" Tony answered with a question, "Why else would you be waiting on him hand and foot for as little as you get paid? Or are you going to stick to your story of a screenplay?"

"Excuse me," Arik interjected, "Evie's script had merit even if she's a terrible writer. But this is supposed to be about me. Can we get back on the topic of making me the next Black Panther or whatever?"

Evie's mouth ran away with her before stopping the words. "You couldn't be Black Panther,"

Both men turned to look at her stunned, before traffic dragged Tony's gaze back to the road. "Why not?" Arik finally asked after a mixture of emotions ran the gambit on his face.

"He's the wrong... aesthetic for you." Evie scrambled to cover her slip up while pushing her bangs over her eyes. If he couldn't make eye contact, he couldn't see the truth.

"Yeah, he's black, and your lily-white ass isn't fitting that bill," Tony added.

Evie swallowed, letting her boss and co-worker continue on their conversation of behavior for the next meeting. She almost revealed her love of spandex-wearing heroes. Even before the werewolf hit double digits, the redhead had an obsession with comic books. During high school she'd also dabbled into the world of art, trying to make her own. That had been a complete disaster when her mother found out and it ended in a backyard bonfire. Evie's mother never had supported her endeavors, so it really shouldn't have come as a surprise.

Tires screeched as the car took a sharp turn down one street, and then up another. The screech was soon echoed by one from her boss, "Tony! If you crash this car-"

"What? You'll take it out of my pay?" The vampire scoffed as he slid the vehicle smoothly through a security gate and into a parking spot. "Natasha will thank me. I got you here perfectly on time. Off you go." There was a wordless grumble from the elf as Arik sat up and smoothed his shirt.

Evie could tell in the mirror that her boss wouldn't be quipping back at Tony now. The actor was putting his game face on. That charming smile had won the hearts of Hollywood decades ago; surely it wouldn't fail him now? A moment later, the door slammed behind him as he made his way to the agency's front door.

Evie sighed, relaxing in her seat. A moment too soon apparently, as she found herself the subject of Tony's attention once more. "So, where were we before I had to play Grand Theft Auto Realism Mode?" His eyes were alight with mischief again.

Questions danced on the tip of Evie's tongue. She was unsure if she could or should ask Tony about more while Arik was out of earshot, but the audible ping of Laika's ringtone derailed her for a moment.

LAIKA

Tor is taking us to a club tonight!

I mean....would you like to go to a club tonight?

Evie felt a bit of warmth flood her mind at the invitation. "There is nothing to talk about. You know I was researching a case," she said, a real smile wrapping her face and eyes still on the phone as she typed out a reply asking for some details.

"Ugh. So boring," the vampire responded, "I don't know why you waste your time playing the hero. You're built the right way to just go be the next Black Widow rather than risk your life."

Evie felt him recoil at the pleasant a calm aura radiating off her, which was normal for him. Anything lovey-dovey made her friend gag. "But then I wouldn't get to go out with Tor and Laika to the club," the woman replied as she answered the invitation with a yes.

"Pity you don't have anything to wear since you couldn't afford all the nice clothing today." Tony changed tactics to try riling her back up.

Evie's eyes glanced at him, then back to the phone. "Yes, I do."
"Oh?"

"I have an epic new top courtesy of Arik," the werewolf bit her lip while grinning.

Sunglasses slid down to the vampire's nose as he gave her a hard look. "What makes you think I wouldn't tell our fearless leader that you got yourself a gift while shopping?"

Evie's expression grew brighter as she assured, "I know you won't tell."

"Oh?" prompted the vampire again, an eyebrow arching.

"Because the red leather pants I put in the purchase pile were not Arik's size. Don't you think you deserve a bonus for getting us here on time?"

Tony's grin matched Evie's as he agreed, "Yes, I do. That'll do, wolf."

CHAPTER 9
TWISTED CROSS

Laika
October 2nd, 2018
Twisted Cross, Glenwood, CA

Laika had been excited when Tor had invited the girls out to a night at her favorite club; Twisted Cross was a mystery to the werewolf. She'd never even heard the name before, nevermind seen the flashy sign with a massive bent iron cross nailed above the door.

The building's front was a boxy plain construction, with black windows so dark you couldn't see through them. Once they were inside, no natural light was permitted past the double-door entry hall.

Instead, the club was lit by track lighting that twisted and turned overhead, casting the room in a dozen different warm hues. They had a coat check room before entering the main hall, where she and the others were greeted by an attendant wearing heavy black makeup. Laika could hear the thump of music from the next room.

Tor wore a leather dress so tight that it looked painted on. A large metal hoop on a zipper from her breasts to her thighs held the material to her. She commanded the room in her eye-catching outfit, which had allowed her to snag them a corner table.

Laika hurried over to join her friends as her eyes roamed the area. The club was modern, with most surfaces a matte black or shiny stainless steel. Red carpet and faux leather seats completed the theme, making the place ooze with quintessential 'vampire.'

Idly she wondered if this was what Alfred lived like, in a world of monochrome and red. Laika's phone was in her hand to ask, but then another hand plucked it out of her grasp. A shot glass replaced it quickly, along with a grinning Tor quipping at her, "Don't be glued to your phone all night! It's girl's night out!" Then she tipped her head back, emptying amber liquid from her cup in seconds.

Behind their human roommate, Evie rolled her eyes and set another shot down in front of Shelly. Laika's friend was usually the one tearing up the club and keeping up on the drinks. But tonight she had a run for the title of Club Queen, not that Laika thought her packmate wanted it at this particular party.

Evie had picked out a lovely white dress for their trip initially, but Tor had made her change into the orange and yellow wrapped outfit she wore now. Matched with the green clingy number that Laika had picked out, the girls were all dressed to the nines and ready for a night out on the town... except for their remaining roommate.

Shelly sat in her usual flannel shirt and jeans regarding the little glass of amber-colored liquid in front of her with apprehension. So far, Tor had gone through three shots while the brunette was still staring at her first drink.

"Not much of a drinker?" asked Laika with curious eyes.

"Uh... no," Shelly answered, "Well... I don't think so."

Tor slammed into the leather seat next to her new friend and threw black boots on the table. "I can totally get you something else to drink? Are you a fruity girl?" She offered with the content air of someone in her element.

Shelly looked confused, "Fruity girl?"

"Shit," swore Evie as she took up the seat on the other side of Shelly, boxing the brunette werewolf into the booth. "You've never had alcohol before!"

The declaration echoed encompassing the mostly empty club around them.

Red burned on Shelly's face as her new friends pegged her for the truth. "Just get me a coke, I don't feel like getting drunk for the first time in a... vampire bar."

Laika reached out to swipe the shot that had been in front of Shelly, "No worries, being a DD is a time honored tradition." Her other hand dropped Evie's keys in front of their flannel clad roommate. There was a flash of a grin as she tossed the shot back to show there truly was nothing to worry about.

"So you've never done the drunken walk of shame in Vegas before then?" Tor asked.

"No... it's on a list of things I want to do at some point." Shelly admitted, her fingers fidgeting on the table.

Evie was halfway through her shot when her hand paused, looking at her new roommate. "Do you have work tonight?" Her eyes were worriedly staring at Shelly. They'd planned this outing tonight clearly forgetting that their roommate worked the graveyard shift, even if it was from the comfort of the living room.

Instantly Shelly's hands raised defensively, as if to wave away the attention. "Yes, but it's fine."

Tor's attention returned to the table, having just rattled off an order for a round of thematically appropriate cocktails, and a complementary coke for Shelly. "Yeah, I checked before we made the plan. Didn't think we'd be closing the club down on your guys' first visit."

"I'll be fine as long as I log on by midnight," Shelly assured.

Curiosity flickered across Evie's face, and Laika's was not far behind it. They both had wondered what their roommate was up to at all hours of the night. They had even made an informal betting pool of guesses ranging from camgirl to white hat hacker. There hadn't been an opening for them to really ask until now...

Laika's mouth opened to start to ask the question, but it was interrupted by footsteps approaching their table. The waiter had drifted back, empty shot glasses cleared away in favor of cocktails that were the same deep red of the rest of the club. Laika gave the drink an experimental sniff, trying to determine what was in the mix, but all she could smell was the astringent whiff of alcohol and fruit.

"So... Shelly. Are you like a hacker or something?" Tor was the one to finally ask something they all wanted to know.

"What?!" shot the brunette, giving the human a look like she was insane. "Why would you think I'm a hacker? I'm way too smart to be a hacker!"

Tor burst into laughter, nearly spitting her drink out.

"Really?" pressed Laika. That had been her actual guess. Which meant no matter what Shelly's actual job was, she wasn't winning this bet...

"Yeah, really," echoed Shelly, shrugging. "Hackers are idiots. They just do the same thing over and over again hoping to get lucky. I don't rely on luck."

"So... you do something less luck based?" Evie tried to push again, "Something more recession proof then?"

"Um..."

Before Shelly could answer, the waiter appeared once more with a round of shots they hadn't ordered. He inclined his head to a pair of men sitting at the bar, "With their compliments."

Evie glanced at the men then back at the shots. "If we drink these, do we owe them attention or are the rules the same in a vampire bar?"

"You know they can hear you," Tor teased, downing her own shot with a single head tilt.

"They can?" Laika felt a jolt of competition at the news. She focused her hearing on the men, trying to cut through the low chatter of people filtering into the club. But the pair was just chatting that one of them knew of Tor. He called her 'a good time,' which pulled a frown from the werewolf.

"Yeah, because one of them is a lotus vampire. They have some epic hearing," explained Tor, giving the boys a wink from where she sat.

Evie finally took her shot. She seemed content with the rules here being the same, nothing owed if you were dumb enough to buy her drinks.

"What's a lotus vampire?" Laika prompted as she picked up her own shot.

She had assumed that all vampires were the same just like werewolves. But as she thought about it her eyes blinked slowly, realizing that all wolves weren't actually the same. Her hearing and speed were different from Evie's empathy, and she had no idea what Shelly was good at yet.

"Lotus is one of my fave types of vampire," Tor continued. Her posture was confident given her expertise on the subject and lack of fear discussing their powers in public. "So basically there are a whole bunch of vampires, and they named their courts after flowers. I don't know why and no one seems to know. I guess it's a secret lost to time or something like that."

"Courts are the different types?" Evie interrupted as she pursed her lips thoughtfully. "Do they all have magic?"

That set Laika's thoughts on fire. She'd never heard of a magic vampire prior to the barebones report at GPD. In college there hadn't been a single class on the history or biology of the undead. Even the generic classes about the Accord signing didn't go into detail about the supernatural races more than naming the five involved. But now, an opportunity to learn presented itself. Her head whipped back and forth between the women waiting for the answer.

"Yeah," Tor replied, going back to her drink.

"Yeah what?" urged Laika.

Tor smirked, "Yeah, their courts are the different types and there's magic based vampires. They're called rose vampires." The woman had the air of a cat who had caught a canary. She had her roommates' attention now, so she left them to spin while she surveyed the room.

Evie sat up straighter. Her curious eyes swiveled around Twisted Cross's growing crowd of both humans and vampires. The distraction allowed Laika to swipe her phone back and she glanced down at her newly recovered device wondering what type Alfred was. But her attention snapped back to Tor with more questions. "Do you know all the ty- courts? You said rose and lotus so far?"

Tor emphasized each by counting them off on her fingers. "Okay so... first we have lotus. They are like the total stereotypical legend. They can't go out in the daylight, have enhanced senses, can walk up walls, and most of them can shapeshift like you guys."

"They turn into wolves?" piped up Shelly, surprise written all over her face.

"No," Evie answered, giving a gentle smile, "They turn into bats. I know that much. I mean it's magic, but not really what I meant."

"Yeah," Tor agreed with a nod. She gestured at one of the men at the bar. "You ask him nicely and he'll show you his wings... well, out back. Twisted Cross has a no shapeshifting inside rule."

"That's... so cool," Laika couldn't stop herself even though she knew now they could hear her. The next question was swallowed as her human roommate continued.

Tor nodded towards a woman with bright red lipstick bouncing coins on her table. Each of them hit an invisible barrier at the edge before rolling back. "Next, you have roses who make up the other half of the standard myth. They do that whole turn to smoke thing and have a ton of magic." She explained.

Evie cut in again, "Could one of them summon lightning?"

"Maybe," shrugged Tor.

"Do you mean like the pent-" Laika trailed off realizing she'd almost spilled the details of a case in the middle of a club, "...like that thing." An apologetic grimace for her packmate followed.

"Yes," frowned Evie. Then she flashed a significant look at Laika. Clearly her packmate was thinking the culprit could have been a vampire.

Given this new information, Laika had to agree it was possible. But they'd need to talk about it in the morning and add it to the 'Mystery Board'. That was what Laika was affectionately calling the big tack board pinned to the back wall of their closet. Every clue the women had was written on a colored sticky note and pinned. A little bit of colored string and they'd be proper detectives soon.

Laika rejoined the conversation as her thoughts stopped wandering. Tor was explaining her favorite type of vampire, "Chrysanthemums are the best hands down. Their fangs aren't that long so they don't leave any scars and they are daywalkers. Also their superpower is basically sex."

"What?" hissed Shelly, looking as shocked as Evie and Laika in that moment. Of everything they'd expected, that hadn't been on the list. Laika felt her cheeks redden a little, and she could hear the men at the bar discussing what her roommate had just told them. That caused her face to go a few shades deeper.

"Okay... I guess sex isn't actually a power. But they control emotions and can read them off people, so that means they know when they got it wrong or right," laughed Tor. "It's a really useful power."

Finally, Evie broke the no cell phone rule as she quickly typed out a message. But the device was just as quickly stuffed back into her little red leather bag with a forceful jab.

Shelly picked up her coke and downed it in a long draw. She looked stressed out by the whole conversation. Words burst out as the empty glass hit the tabletop, her voice was rushed and low. "But I thought all vampires were seven feet tall, with huge claws out of their hands and feet, and maws with rows and rows of fangs. All of them were... are crazed killers?"

"Who told you that?" Laika quickly asked. That sounded like something out of a cheesy horror movie.

"My... father," admitted the brunette. Her eyes were cast down at the table and none of the werewolves needed super empathy to see how embarrassed she felt.

"Those are called peonies," Tor supplied a moment later.

"Those are real?!" exclaimed Evie.

Plenty of the crowd turned their way, looking for the source of yelling. The redhead ducked herself down for a second then looked up trying to pretend she was also searching for the commotion. Once everyone settled and went back to their own night out she repeated her question, but much quieter, "Those are real?"

"Yeah, never met one though," Tor answered as she waved for another round of drinks. "I've heard the names 'iris', 'lilac', and 'orchid' thrown around as well. But I don't know anything about them. It's super rude to ask though, so even if I met one I wouldn't know."

Again Laika's eyes went back to her phone, reconsidering the text message she had planned to send as soon as they stepped outside. Before she could lament how rude it would actually be to ask Alfred, the men from the bar caught her attention again.

"Those chicks don't know shit," the one Tor had pointed out as a lotus said to his friend, "The hot one in black has been around, but she's crazy to bring those three in here."

His friend laughed, "I don't know, they are all pretty hot. Plus, you know werewolves and packs."

A knowing look passed between the two men, half a sneer and half something else Laika couldn't quite place. The lotus knocked back a glass of something that looked a lot darker than any of the drinks sitting on the roommates' table. "Thinking of picking yourself up a moonflower or three?"

"Maybe. They hardly seem like big bad wolves, more like lost lambs."

"Send them another round, see if they invite us to join them?"

Sure enough, a few minutes later a new tray of shots appeared at their table.

Laika was making a face, trying to sort out how she felt about what she'd overheard. It hadn't been... rude per se, not more than usual guy talk at a club... but something about it just felt off. Instead of reaching for the shot, she leaned in toward Tor, dropping her voice to a whisper and hoping it wouldn't carry. "What's a moonflower? They said that before sending these over," her eyes swept the tiniest bit towards the bar to indicate who she meant.

Tor's stare went cold and she gave no answer. Instead, she smoothed out her dress with slow exaggerated motions before getting up from the table. All four shots were taken when she sashayed her way up to the men at the bar, that icy look still in place.

All three werewolves watched her go with apprehensive eyes. Evie put a hand on Laika to stop her from getting up and escalating whatever was about to happen. While the impulsive woman knew she could break free from her packmate's hold, there wasn't time.

"Which one of you assholes called my friends moonflowers," Tor demanded, slamming the shot glasses down on the bar between them.

One of the men had the decency to look embarrassed at being caught, but the other just smirked up at her. "So what if I did?" His voice was cool and a little condescending. The vampire wasn't afraid of Tor, despite his friend giving him a look that screamed to knock it off.

Tor stole back one of the shots and flipped him off as she downed it. Her phone appeared like magic in her hand, then she snapped a picture of him. Another shot was drained while she typed out a message on the phone.

Laika was beginning to suspect that the friend was one of those emotion vampires she'd just learned about. Because he got uneasier by the second, even when it was really just a normal human imposing herself on them.

Suddenly tens of dozens of phones pinged at the same time almost in unison. Laika was startled for a second by the wave of noise, but her confusion faded quickly. "Congrats," Tor informed the lotus with a thread of steel in her tone. "You got yourself blacklisted through Halloween," she spat before picking up the third shot to throw it back.

Her words got a reaction as the vampire's jaw unceremoniously dropped and his eyes widened. "Are you serious, bitch?"

Blacklisted meant nothing to the women sitting at the table, but the angry stares from the humans all around Twisted Cross clued them in that it wasn't good.

Tor picked up the fourth shot, but this one was thrown in the lotus's face before she stalked off. "Good luck getting a date."

The lotus stood up looking livid while swearing loudly. He hissed at the bartender for help, but the large man just shrugged, "Play stupid games and win stupid prizes."

Thankfully, his friend dragged him off so he couldn't chase down the woman who had killed their social calendar with a tweet.

"Who wants another drink?" asked Tor as she sat back down at the table. All traces of annoyance gone, like she hadn't just caused a scene. Laika noted that Evie was discreetly fanning herself and managed to not roll her eyes.

"So what's a moonflower?" Laika asked again. She was pretty sure it wasn't going to be a compliment now. But before she got her answer, the distinct ringtone of MOONS Dispatch called from the red bag.

"I thought you put us on a no-call night?" asked Evie as she fished it out, "Since we were going to the bar?"

"Um... I thought you did it?" answered Laika honestly. Usually her packmate handled all of that part of the paperwork for Night Claw.

"Oh... shit," whined Evie, "How drunk are you?"

Evie didn't wait for a response as she answered the call.

CHAPTER 10
GLASS

Evie
October 2nd, 2018
Pixie Dust, Glenwood, CA

"It's a magic shop?" pressed Laika. Waves of confusion soaked in tipsy energy, crashed through Evie's empathy.

Evie gave her packmate a nod as she read the Google entry again to confirm. "Yep, according to the internet, Pixie Dust is a 4.5 star rated magic shop for practitioners in Glenwood. I guess they've got a lot of varied stock or something."

The call from dispatch had explained this was an open ticket, for the closest pack to intervene in an active robbery. There was one pack a few minutes closer, but Evie wasn't going to let the job go with no contest. They'd paid for their drinks and bundled into the Saab in a flash. The wolves were barely tipsy, and Evie was certain they'd be completely sober by the time they arrived on scene.

"Really? With a name like that, I was sure it was one of those bath bomb stores. Like Lush and Sephora." Laika's eyes lit up. Evie felt confusion twist to excitement. All it took was the 'M' word to have Laika invested in a job.

"Are you sure it's okay to show up to a scene like this?" Tor waved her hand at their sparkly dresses, made for hunting in a club more than hunting down a suspect.

There was a sound of agreement from the driver's seat, where Shelly had settled into her proclaimed role of designated driver. "You guys have been drinking too."

"A few shots, we'll be fine by the time we get there," Evie waved off the concern, "Besides, if we don't go, then Blood Fang gets the job..."

"Oh... Well, we should get moving then," Shelly answered as the car rolled into motion.

There was a sense of determination coming from the flannel clad werewolf. The best that Evie could figure from the nebulous emotion was that Thad and Randall had made an impression on her roommate. Enough so that she seemed eager to get them to the scene first.

Tor sat in the front seat next to Shelly, letting the two moonlighters have the backseat to check details. Google maps was giving directions to guide them through the mostly empty streets.

"This is the downtown shopping area," realization dawned on Laika, "Since when have we had a magic shop here?"

Evie gave a wordless shrug as she zoomed in on the street. As the map narrowed down the range, the names of shops popped up, including a very familiar one. 'Ink & Steel' was where she and Laika had gotten their pack tattoos years ago. The shop had been nestled between a half dozen other boutiques including Pixie Dust.

Now looking at the names, Evie was starting to wonder if they all were magically inclined.

Downtown Glenwood was usually dead this time of night. Most of the businesses closed by eight, leaving the streets empty of people. The lack of traffic and some daredevil driving from Shelly had shaved several vital minutes off the travel time from Twisted Cross.

Shelly pulled along the curb, about twenty feet back from a GPD cruiser. She let out a little laugh, and Evie felt a startling aura of relief. "That wasn't so hard... I knew I didn't need a learner's permit to actually drive."

Tor asked in her usual calm tone, "When did you pass your test?" They'd all known that their brunette friend had been sheltered and was catching up on skills the others had for a decade.

"Uh... it's next week? Well, the written portion of it," answered Shelly, checking her phone for the calendar app.

Evie wanted to scream as a communal spike of fear swept through the car, including the usually calm Tor. But her eyes moved to look out the window realizing they were first on scene.

"You," she snapped at Shelly, "Are not driving home, and don't you dare say a word to Aaron or Owen about your lack of a license." This was tomorrow's problem. Then Evie tried to throw open the side door dramatically, only to remember that the child locks were stuck. Her shoulder smashed into the door with a loud curse.

Tor remembered the issue from when they'd arrived at the club earlier and was already hopping out of the car. A quick click of heels, creak of metal, and both werewolves were freed from the iron prison of the backseat. Tor's green eyes glanced at the waiting officer and she pressed her lips into a tight line. "We'll wait in the car."

"Thanks," Laika groaned as she started to stretch despite her short skirt.

"Laika," hissed Evie through clenched teeth, "Don't flash everyone!" But she kept her posture calm, while popping the trunk to retrieve vests.

Laika just laughed before waving at the waiting men. She didn't seem bothered and her eyes twinkled in amusement. "They'll see more than that if this turns into a fight. Do you really think these dresses are surviving this job? You'll be in Aaron's pants before the night is through."

The little orange and yellow number Evie wore was pretty, but she desperately wished they had backup clothing in the trunk too. Next time they did laundry, she was stealing a few outfits for exactly this. "We need to seriously consider buying shifter tanks and shorts," lamented Evie as she held out a vest to Laika.

Again her packmate laughed at her, "Yeah, when one of us wins the lottery or-"

The amusement died off as a familiar mini-van pulled up on the other side of the street. Their groan was in unison, as two sets of eyes glared at the vehicle. Its suburban soccer mom exterior contained the most terrible thing imaginable... Blood Fang.

Laika snatched the vest out of Evie's hands, realizing what was about to go down. Heels kicked off and arms barely looped through the tactical vest, she took off at a dead sprint for the cruiser.

Before the mini-van's door was even fully open a blur of a person leaped out. Evie recognized him as Joey in his ill fitting vest, with his long dark hair streaming behind him. The race was on, but Night Claw had the head start.

"Go, Laika Go!" Evie yelled, no longer caring about anyone her packmate might be flashing.

"Come on Joey!" A voice called as the most annoying member of Blood Fang slid out from the driver's seat.

Ace Deerling was tall, fit, and gorgeous in every way possible. He had short spiky copper red hair, perfect chocolate brown eyes, and even his scent was enticing with vanilla, roses, and sunlight mixed together.

Trying to pretend he wasn't attractive was a point of pride for Evie, because the moment they made eye contact she felt the usual flare of rage emanate off him. This man had hated her from the first day they met, so she'd met him in kind.

Evie scooped up Laika's heels and left them on top of her car, before taking off in her packmate's wake. Whoever got the clipboard first got the job. That was the rule Owen had set after their 5th or 6th fight about who was here first. Night Claw relied on Laika's far superior speed in these situations, but like hell Evie would be the last one there. She could already feel Blood Fang picking up pace to follow.

Ahead of them, Laika's joy rang out as her fingers closed around the clipboard pulling it out of Joey's reach. "This is our case," she called while waving it above her head.

"Settle down," warned Owen.

He stood in front of his cruiser, waiting for the werewolves to assemble. Meanwhile, his partner was in the car typing away on their console laptop. Aaron was likely pulling up all the known details they had.

"Hold up," Ace called as he came to a stop, standing many inches taller than the policeman. He gestured at the women, "Sorry Owen, but I have to object this time. I know fair is fair, but seriously! They're wearing club clothing, no shoes, are still strapping on their vests, and everyone can smell the alcohol on them."

"Hey," snapped Evie, "We had one drink before the call came in and it was human booze. Plus we didn't drive just to be sure." Her hand snapped up to point back at her Saab, where Shelly and Tor sat in the front seat playing on their phones.

A shadow fell over them as the third member of Blood Fang caught up.

Daniel was a walking mountain. Where his cousin, Ace, had a few inches on the other werewolves, Daniel easily had a foot. He was built twice as wide as Evie in muscle, but she knew he was a gentle giant. The rest of Blood Fang joined in on the jeering and fighting, but Daniel was always just a beacon of soft emotions and embarrassment, rarely saying a word.

Owen seemed content once the five werewolves were standing before him as he cut off the brewing fight. "Alright, alright, shut up," he warned, pulling his clipboard back. A pen was already at work filling out details for who would be working.

"Manners," reprimanded Aaron, climbing out of the cruiser finally with a small stack of papers in hand. But he didn't pursue it any further, instead addressing the moonlighters. "There has been a change of plans. Pixie Dust's owner, Miss Vergas, tapped into her wards to find out how someone had broken into her store. She has advised us that the suspect is a dwarf."

"Oh shit..." Laika swore as some color drained from her face.

Evie swallowed hard and her annoyance flared as she predicted the words before her favorite officer said them. Given the emotions surrounding them, she likely wasn't the only one either.

"Due to this news, both teams will be on the case as neither of you have enough team members present or rankings for solo dwarf combat," explained Aaron.

He held up his clipboard with the image of a man with a squashed nose, shaved head, and a pair of snake eyed dice tattooed above his left eye. "This is Ulric Glasse, aka Unlucky Ulric of the 10th Street Boys in LA. I'm aware how on the nose it is, but his craft is glass which he used to bypass the wards. He has two known associates. While neither of them have been seen at this time, we can't rule their presence out."

Evie nodded along as she noted down everything of importance from the brief. There was a big difference between one and three dwarves if a fight broke out.

Aaron continued, "Right now three GPD Officers are covering the building just around the corner, and that seems to have scared Ulric into staying hidden. Likely he's just looking for another way out of the building. Given the seriousness of the threat, I am greenlighting hybrid forms in advance. But you are not authorized for any lethal force. If you are in too much danger then retreat. Do you understand?"

He made sure to make eye contact with all five wolves.

All of them replied affirmatively.

A pen was still scratching away at paperwork in Owen's hands during the explanation. Then he handed the clipboard around. Anytime they had to use something rated as a 'lethal' power, such as their hybrid shift, there were twice as many forms.

The Night Claw werewolves quickly signed their names before passing it along. Evie's fingers brushed Ace's, and she felt a wave of anxiety mingle with her own. He pulled the form back quickly and while he was maintaining a calm front, Evie knew he was just as nervous as the rest of them.

Once the papers were in Owen's hands, Evie spoke once more. "Alright. So the plan is-"

"Woah, you're not making the plan," Ace raised a hand to stop her in her tracks.

Evie's fierce eyes narrowed, and she saw Laika's mouth open to shoot back a retort. They were on the job now though; it wasn't time to dissolve into bickering. She'd learned this lesson the hard way.

If insults got truly nasty between the packs, Owen was not shy about kicking one of them out. After the first few walks of shame, Night Claw held their tongues. Even if Thad was being a 'Sexist Asshole', neither woman said it aloud. This was one of the unspoken rules of the Clipboard, their fighting stayed verbal and PG-13. Outside of the GPD's watchful eyes, their hurled barbs got much worse. Evie wouldn't repeat the names that were used for her to anyone.

Her hand fell on Laika's arm to hold her friend back. "We don't know where the dwarf is. We have the better powers for sensing him, so of course, we're going to make the plan."

Ace was shaking his head before she'd even finished speaking. "No way. My combat ranking is higher than both of yours. This is a takedown mission, and it needs proper tactics to ensure no one gets hurt."

"I'd also appreciate minimal property damage," Owen chimed in from behind his clipboard, pen scratching out secondary approval on all the forms. "It's a magic shop, you never know what's going to explode."

The packs' bickering waned with that warning. Then Ace set forth a plan with most of them scouting to the front and entering from there. The fastest wolves first to find them a quiet entry while their strongest, Daniel, would cover the back exit. All of them would sweep the aisles as stealthily as possible and when the dwarf was found, everyone would circle up together. Begrudgingly Night Claw relented to Ace's plan, and only a few minutes later the five were-wolves were advancing on the magic shop.

Their hybrid forms were already in place; it had taken them a couple minutes to shift, except for Ace. He had the power of rapid shifting. Less than 30 seconds after he'd stripped off his clothing and resecured his vest, he was a seven and a half foot tall hybrid with sleek copper fur.

Despite their massive sizes, all of them were light on their padded feet turning the corner. Evie heard Aaron calling ahead to tell his fellow officers about their approach, but that didn't stop the crush of fear that echoed into her skull. Three human officers scrambled back into their cars rather than face five hybrids on a dark street corner.

Pixie Dust's lights were out, with only the street lamps for vision. The building was made of grey concrete with some fading due to the sun. A metal door stood to the left of a big shop window. What caught Evie's attention was the spirals of glass erupting forward, creating a translucent staircase.

Unlucky Ulric had 'crafted' the display window into his entrance without causing a single crack in the material. Surprise and awe from the other werewolves informed her that she wasn't the only one impressed.

Joey was up first, testing how sturdy the steps were for them. There wasn't even a crinkling sound as he put his foot down. He retreated so Laika could take his place, using her ears to check for anyone waiting on the other side. After a moment Laika's dark brown fur slipped through the window, and the light grey form of Joey followed.

Next was Evie. She marveled at how smooth the glass steps were as she carefully climbed over the threshold. Ace followed through a moment later, but Daniel's larger form wouldn't fit. He'd be going around back to check for a warehouse entrance he could use.

Evie's eyes scanned around, a bit excited to see what an actual magic shop was like, only to be disappointed at how mundane it was. There were rows of shelves stacked with boxes, packets, and bins of various ingredients. The closest of them contained dozens upon dozens of dried plants. Just looking at them, Evie could feel her nose itch from the dust they surely accumulated.

Further down there was a barrel of large ostrich feathers advertised at $3 a piece. It sat next to a wall of bins with different bits and bobs of metal; everything from spools of wire to smooth rods of silver. Pixie Dust was like a weird mix between an arts and crafts store and a Home Depot.

The store was dark, and the tall shelves cast long shadows. The street light filtering through the front window bounced off mirrors hanging from the ceiling. Like an old movie trick, it gave them light enough to make their way through the shop without knocking over anything.

Ahead, Evie could feel Laika and Joey weaving their way to the back, checking each row. But given all the mirrors above them, it was clear their target wasn't in the front of the store.

Ace brushed past Evie, chocolate eyes commanding her to keep going and stop gawking. This only brought another wave of annoyance but she followed him into the back rows. She lowered herself so that her ears wouldn't stick up over the top of any shelves. They made it to the registers, which surprisingly looked untouched.

Evie slipped over the countertop to check the cash drawer below it, but again it wasn't damaged. Still closed and locked. Either Unlucky Ulric hadn't seen it or he'd been gracious enough to go look for a key first. But neither seemed likely.

She pointed it out to Ace as he checked the door into the back, where the others had gone already. Hybrid faces didn't have the muscles to do a full range of emotions, but she felt the confusion that accompanied Ace's attempt. It was one less problem for the shop owner, but it did mean this break in wasn't motivated by a quick cash grab.

He pointed to Evie, then the back warehouse. Understanding his directions, Evie slid past him. This allowed the more experienced combat wolf to take up the rear position, on the very slim chance that they'd missed their target in the first sweep. Her eyes blinked a few times after she crossed the little hallway to the back.

The doorway was hung with tinted plastic flaps, which blocked the lights in the warehouse. Apparently Ulric had turned them all on, assuming no one would see them from the street front as if the window hadn't been a giveaway.

A light grey hybrid loped Evie's direction, keeping himself low to the ground, his ears perked up in excitement. Joey slid to a stop in front of her then started gesturing back the direction he'd come. He held up one finger while giving a big toothy grin.

She just shrugged at him, having no idea what he was trying to tell her. Blood Fang signals were lost on her.

Ace had seen Joey's approach and both took off at a run the direction he'd indicated before. They had teamwork already worked out from previous missions that Evie had never been part of. Neither stopped to inform her of the plan, leaving the woman to huff then follow behind.

Three hybrids strided into the warehouse's depth, the hum of an industrial fan disguising the sounds of paw pads and claws on the cement. Evie's eyes were greeted with row upon row of industrial shelving. Boxes of every size and color filled these to the brim. What they'd seen up front had been only a fraction of what was being kept back here; Pixie Dust was the Costco of Glenwood magic.

In the shadow of one towering shelf, Evie spotted Laika. The dark wolf was crouched low, ears and eyes trained forward on what must have been their target. Evie followed her friend's laser focus to a more open part of the warehouse.

The gleam of a shaved head was just visible between items.

Ulric stood with his back to them, surrounded by boxes that had clearly been rifled through. He paused and Evie's heart stopped, wondering how he had sensed their arrival. But then the man merely lifted his phone to squint at something on the screen before turning back to the box.

"Is there seriously a fucking difference between twice aged and 2 year old?" Ulric grumbled, throwing a packet on the floor and digging for another.

With a sigh of relief, Evie's attention returned to her fellow moonlighters. Ace's hands were moving in a series of signals, directing Joey and Laika to move out and flank the dwarf. This time they were generic enough that both women could follow along instead of pack specific. His gaze moved to Evie. While the undercurrent of animosity remained, it was stifled by a no-nonsense need to get the job done.

His clawed hand extended towards her, a glittering piece of metal resting in his palm. Evie recognized the item and gave a curt nod to show she understood. Her hands picked up the bespelled handcuffs, running a thumb over the etchings.

These cuffs were only ever employed against targets whose powers needed to be contained, such as Ulric. The runes engraved along the metal formed a circle when the cuffs were snapped closed, which shut down any supernatural powers, from super strength to magic. They gave off a faint golden glow when active, so Evie knew to always look for that before stepping back. Her job was to get them onto Ulric once he'd been restrained. Then they could safely turn him over to the human officers.

Slow shadows began to move into position. The trap started to take shape around the dwarf who was still none the wiser. They couldn't all see each other between the shelves, but everyone had a specific countdown based on how far they had to move.

As the plan started, both Laika and Joey launched forward from their flanking positions. The hybrids' clawed hands closed around Ulric's arms. Werewolf strength was brought to bear as Joey and Laika pulled the dwarf away from the wall of boxes. They attempted to pull his arms back, creating an opening for the next werewolf.

Ace moved forward, long strides closing the distance quickly. He lunged to take advantage of Ulric being thrown off balance. Evie knew what he intended. A heavy hand on the dwarf's shoulder, a sweep of his legs, and the dwarf would be pulled backward to the ground.

Evie had to admit the tactic was well planned, especially since they'd managed to stay out of sight until this moment. At least she would have, but Ulric bellowed with surprise at the initial attack. His reactions were much faster than anyone anticipated. He had a few bracelets with glass beads which began to stir under his magic.

A howl tore from Evie in warning but it was too late.

The beads flattened, creating a thin sheet of glass on Ulric's skin which reduced his friction. He jerked his arm, breaking free of Joey's grasp. His clenched fist gained momentum cracking Laika's snout with a spray of glass shards.

Laika let out a yelp, grip faltering as she instinctively reached for the shards embedded in her face. Her nose dripped blood onto the concrete.

Roaring, Ulric ripped both arms back to his sides, readying for a fight. He sized up all three hybrids descending on him. Then, turning his attention to the most current threat, his hands seized Joey's shoulder. A swift thrust sent the grey wolf flying up roughly, and smashed his head into the wall.

Ace had arrived just a moment too late to save his packmate from the heavy hit. Then he took a hard headbutt to his jaw, staggering him back. Ulric spat onto the ground before squaring up, "Goddamn pack of wolves." The plan was already off the rails but no one was really to blame.

Evie could salvage this if she moved fast enough. Without hesitation she leapt from her hiding place and slid through the narrow gap between the wall and Ulric. There was still glass embedded in Laika's face, but her packmate reacted to her presence. She tried to push back into position. Despite a bloodied nose, Ace was also back in the fight, advancing once more.

This time given three opponents, all posed to strike, Ulric fumbled. His fist didn't reach Ace, who stopped short of the swing. Left open with an arm outstretched, Ulric couldn't do much about Laika's dive forward. Both of her dark furred arms encircled the limb, dragging it down. Any advantage Ulric had evaporated with that movement.

However, Evie struggled to get ahold of the other arm that was flailing around in front of her. She growled in frustration, having to retreat a step back and let Ace take her place.

Spitting with rage, Ulric kept the momentum, clenching his fist like a hammer as it smashed back into the wall of boxes. Cardboard ripped open and potion bottles shattered all over, covering the floor in more glass shards.

Ace sounded a retreat given how much glass was covering the ground. The whole area was now a hazard for the wolves. The danger level was increasing. He'd done exactly as Aaron had commanded if he felt their lives were at risk.

Even Laika let go of Ulric's arm to avoid spikes of glass jetting in her direction. No matter how much strength she had, a well placed attack like that could do her in. The glass bracers had already been a pain, but the floor was now making it impossible for them to pin him. Their options were rapidly crumbling.

Evie took up a position a good thirty feet away from Ulric. She could feel the anger coming off Laika and Ace as they also found a place they could watch the target safely. Joey was starting to rouse, which relieved her. As much as she didn't love Blood Fang, she didn't want any of them to actually get hurt.

The dwarf was radiating agitation, which reminded Evie of a panicked animal looking for a way to bolt. Ulric glanced over his shoulder, evaluating the distance to escape. There was only a single opaque window or the back door. It wasn't far, but making a break for it would mean turning his back on the wolves.

Evie was certain at his first opening, Ulric was going for that window. And no one was in place to stop him fleeing.

A ripple of surprise ran over Ace, which Evie picked up, watching his eyes glance at the back door then to the floor. There was no broken glass on the ground and Ace gave off a muted feeling of anxious energy.

Laika's ears twitched, one swiveling towards the door. There was a sharp jerk of her head, trying to direct Evie's attention, before her packmate rushed forward. An impromptu plan was afoot. Understanding filtered through Evie's mind, and her snarl joined the rest of the pack in pretending to advance on Ulric.

"Fuck off!", hissed the dwarf, throwing his hands up creating a flurry of glass. At first it looked like a glittering hurricane, but soon crystalized into a wall. Ulric took off, trusting his barrier to hold them up long enough for him to make it to the window.

But the three wolves had just been a distraction, as Joey slid into view between Ulric and his escape. Grey jaws snapped viciously, cutting off that path. While the dwarf did have some glass left after crafting the wall, it was not enough to fight his way through. Instead he threw his shoulder into the heavy metal back door.

Evie dropped down and wove her hands together in perfect time for Laika's paw to step on them. She pushed up, helping the dark wolf jump to the top of the wall. Her packmate soared over it, putting more pressure on Ulric to escape. The woman calculated how much time she'd need to run around the shelves for when that door opened.

This would be tight.

To her surprise, Ace had done the same calculation and decided on a faster plan. He put his fist through the glass wall, creating an opening with his super strength. Any injuries from the attack were ignored as he pushed Evie through the opening just in time.

Ulric's shoulder only needed two decent hits before he cracked the frame, pushing himself out into the back alley... Right into the waiting arms of an eight foot tall hybrid. Muscled arms snapped around the dwarf in a bear hug, pulling him clean off the ground with ease as Daniel reacted.

Laika tore out the door behind Ulric, going for the bracelets before any more magic could be thrown about. Claws clipped skin, leaving marks, but nothing too deep. Then she pulled his arms back sharply, making room for Evie to pounce and snap cuffs around thick wrists.

At the first sight of golden light, every one let out a sigh of relief.

Less than fifteen minutes later, Evie leaned on the back of a police cruiser in a pair of sweatpants and oversized shirt, compliments of Blood Fang. Given the sizes, she likely had some of Joey's extra clothing since both she and Laika together could have fit in Daniel's shirt. Right now she was filling out paperwork about what happened inside Pixie Dust.

A few feet away, Laika was giving Owen a detailed blow by blow of the fight and he was recording it for later. Whenever violence broke out there was always more paperwork than usual and everything needed documented. Once they'd tried a body camera but it hadn't survived the first hit, so back to analog the moonlighters had gone.

Unlucky Ulric was living up to his name. He was locked in the back of the cruiser, still restrained. The glowing handcuffs had sapped away the dwarf's magic and strength. After the fight, Ace had shifted back as the fastest among them and gone to retrieve the police officers.

Once they'd arrived and searched the dwarf for more weapons, it was discovered he had glass plates sewn into his jacket and shirt... Which was why he also now had on borrowed clothing. Ulric boiled with nervous energy at having been caught, but as far as Evie could tell he wasn't scared.

"I need your pen," Laika appeared at Evie's side, pulling the implement and clipboard out of her hands.

"Why?"

"Aaron got into the dwarf's phone," replied Laika, excitement bursting from her.

Evie gave her a look, "And?"

She got a dramatic groan in response. "The dwarf was after

ingredients and I need to write them down." Laika's attention was already focused on scribbling fast notes on the back of the form.

"I thought dwarves didn't need spell components," mumbled Evie as she made room for her friend on the back of the cruiser. "Even that guy just threw around glass." Her thumb pointed to Ulric as she tried to remember if she'd ever heard of anything like this before.

Laika smirked, "They don't."

"Then why leave the register and go for twice aged whatever?"

"He must have been stealing them for someone else." Laika shrugged.

Evie pursed her lips, but she agreed with Laika's assessment of the theft. She mused aloud, "If he didn't need them, and stole them for someone else, then it wasn't likely needed by one of his dwarven gang friends... plus, there are like what? 200 magic shops in LA? Why would he need to come out to Glenwood?"

Laika's eyes danced with mischief as they looked back up. She snapped a picture of the list with her phone while answering, "Because there has to be something on this list that's super rare or really specific to the spell the person wanted to cast. If we can figure out what it was, then we can figure out who hired them."

"Great... another case we aren't on, but we'll spend our days solving," sighed Evie.

Laika elbowed her in the ribs before handing back the clipboard, "You know you love it."

CHAPTER II

RITUAL MAGIC

Laika
October 6th, 2018
UCLA, Los Angeles, CA

L aika was enjoying her trip through UCLA's campus, her first since graduating years ago. Everything was as warm and scholarly as she remembered. Sitting in the library doing homework had been fun, and she had all but devoured her classes. She never would have left college. But in one of his many attempts to bring Laika home, her father cut off tuition money. Dreams of a Master's Degree went down the drain faster than the dregs of morning coffee.

At the end of her trek was the familiar library where the werewolf had basically spent her life for a few years. It had the same scent of old textbooks, with the vaguest hint of coffee wafting through the air.

An old student ID was tucked in her back pocket; it was only a few years out of date. Laika breezed through the doors like she belonged here. Her feet led her up a well-worn staircase, weaving through the stacks until she spotted her favorite wing.

This part of the library had once upon a time held language books of some sort. They'd been moved decades ago, as UCLA's magical reference section grew exponentially. These days, the rows of books were piled high with every magical history or theory book a budding magical studies student would need.

And hopefully, one of these would have the answer Laika was after.

Slinging her battered backpack off her shoulder, Laika claimed an empty study table. Her hands fished out the list of magical reagents she'd jotted down after the fight with Ulric.

Despite their best efforts, neither Google nor the Glenwood library had given any definitive answer for what spell this list was for. At best she'd learned it was for a high level spell... probably. In a last ditch attempt to find answers, Evie was at the Central Library in downtown LA and Laika was here to raid the UCLA library.

LAIKA

I'm here and just sat down.

Any luck?

EVIE

No.

Do you know the difference between Argentina Dust and Argent Dust?

LAIKA

One's a country and the other is silver?

EVIE

...oh right...I have the wrong book.

LAIKA

Which one did you actually mean to get?

EVIE

Shut up. Also stay on task, turn your phone
off and get some work done.

Laika scowled at the phone, glancing at the other message
waiting for her. She knew why Evie was telling her to ignore her
phone, and it had nothing to do with the library.

ALFRED

My apologies, I ended up taking longer to fill
in that report than I planned.

LAIKA

Don't worry about it.

Was it a fun job?

ALFRED

Not particularly.

Is your afternoon enjoyable so far?

LAIKA

I'm working on a case right now.

Doing research at the library.

She set her phone to vibrate to not disturb anyone else around
her before disappearing into the rows of books, pulling a few of the
basic books to verify their original findings. She and her packmate
had found the common names and uses for each thing on the list. All
of this was saved on a shared file both of them could update, which
she did for about 15 minutes. So far their internet work had been
mostly accurate, but she'd need more advanced books to get any
further.

When it came to magic, a spell that required this many ingredients could only be a ritual of some sort. Most spells only needed a
handful of items, but this list was dozens of items long. Pushing up

to her feet, Laika wove her way through shelves, snagging every book on rituals that she could find.

The hour wore on, and Laika buried herself in books and her phone. Quick messages were sent back and forth with Alfred as she dug through the books for more information.

She had slouched down in her chair, balancing her notepad on one leg while squinting close at a list of magical plants native to Canada. One of the names looked close, but it was off, as if both names had been translated from something else by different people.

Her phone vibrated and Laika picked up the cell phone to check the latest message. It would be a welcome breather before she started trying to track down the name's etymology. Laika had been chatting with Alfred about the latest books they'd been reading, and she was curious to see what sort of recommendations her friend had.

> ALFRED
>
> I need to ask again, which case are you working on right now?

Laika blinked at her phone, glancing at the past few messages they had sent. That question was so off topic that it deserved further attention. Before she could answer, a grating voice cut through her focus.

"Miss, can you please turn your phone to actual silence. It is disturbing oth-" the words cut off into a hiss of annoyance, "Laika? What the hell are you doing here?"

Laika's eyes flicked up to the source of the interruption. Irritation flashed over her face as her eyes landed on Randall. He looked equally annoyed to see her. Randall narrowed his eyes, the topaz color flashing in the sunlight streaming through the windows.

"Um, same thing as you I assume. Don't be bitter I had the idea first," Laika answered blithely, before pointedly turning her attention back to the book on her lap. Blood Fang was annoying, but causing a scene in the library wasn't high on her to do list today.

Randall let out a scoff of disbelief. "Bitter? I work here! And you still haven't answered my question... Are you even a student here?"

"Work here?" Laika frowned, looked up, and almost immediately had to bite back a snort of laughter.

Sure enough, Randall was dressed exactly like a stuffy librarian, with his dreads pulled back in a tidy ponytail. He even had a little name tag that said "Bellamy" on his chest.

"Yes," snapped Randall, giving her an acidic glare, as if he sensed the stifled laughter. "Why are *you* here?" He started going through the books on the table, putting some of them back on a push cart. His story was adding up about being an actual employee.

Laika frowned, realizing the trouble he could bring down on her. She quickly started to backpedal, "I... have a student ID..." But guilt was written on her face plain as day.

Eyes narrowed as Randall shot back just as quick, "When did it expire?"

"They don't expire. Do they?"

A small trickle of panic ran through Laika as she looked around at the books disappearing off the table. Was she fast enough to steal one? Could she really steal one? What if she stole the wrong one and lost the one that had the answers she needed?

"The library is for students only," declared Randall as he continued to gather books. A small smirk had spread across his face; he was enjoying being able to kick out one of his rivals.

"Students like me?" asked a playful voice from behind them.

When Laika turned, she saw a young girl with a familiar face. A moment later she placed her as the girl who had been vomiting at the Penthouse. A Kelsey or Kayla...

"Keisha, what are you doing here?" asked Randall, pausing in his work.

"Jaci and I are here to stop you from being a jerk," breezed the younger werewolf. She half skipped over to the table, then pulled out the chair next to Laika. Keisha was followed by a second girl who must be Jaci. She looked maybe a year or two older than Keisha, still too young to be moonlighting. Everything about her seemed quiet, plain, and bookish. Her most striking feature was her glasses. Laika couldn't remember ever meeting a werewolf who needed glasses.

As if sensing the scrutiny from Laika, Jaci's grey eyes flickered up to meet her gaze. She looked embarrassed as she stammered out a weak, "H-hello."

"Hi," Laika tried to be warm and welcoming. Any further introductions were stalled as Randall snapped a book shut. The mirth had evaporated from the man, as he stopped taking books from the table.

"As you know," Keisha explained, pulling her own student ID out of her bag, "All students can use the library seven days a week and this section is open until 10pm. Additionally, we are able to bring guests." The girl's bright grin never faltered, as she repeated the information as easily as if she had read it off the school website.

Randall quickly shot back, "Only guests that are relevant to your school work- damn it."

It was Keisha's turn to gloat, though she kept her sweet expression perfectly in place. "Such as an experienced female moonlighter, to help with my Criminal Justice degree?"

Laika's gaze moved back and forth like watching verbal tennis, but in the end she broke into a grin. She could roll with this story. "Exactly. I was just here a bit early to meet Keisha and Jaci." She was starting to wonder if Keisha and Randall were related. They had a similar umber skin tone, but that was where the similarities ended. However, the banter between them reminded her of her own siblings which left the werewolf uncertain.

Crossing his arms, Randall stared them down as fiercely as he could. "I thought you were coming to the library to get a ride home?"

"Whaaaat?" Keisha exaggerated the word, "Me? Bumming a ride home. We would never do that." At her side Jaci stifled laughter behind a small silent smile.

He threw his hands in the air, seeing defeat on the horizon. "Damn it, Keisha. She is the enemy."

"No," snapped Laika, "You guys are the enemy."

All thoughts of figuring out if they were siblings vanished in an instant as Randall and Laika fell back into a familiar antagonistic pattern.

Keisha just burst out laughing at them. "You guys are hilarious with this rivalry," she leaned over to stage whisper to Jaci, "It's so cute to watch the little packs fight."

"Hush you," growled Randall.

"Wait? What?" Laika inquired, her confusion on the rise again. The last few minutes had been a rollercoaster of emotions. But there was something about the younger wolf teasing them that had derailed the brewing fight.

"Moonscent is higher rated than both Blood Fang and Night Claw," explained Keisha with an easy-going wave as she gestured to herself and Jaci.

"Not because of you two though," reminded Randall. He flicked his attention back to Laika before adding, "Their alpha is a badass moonlighter named Nilani. Her ranking is so high it pulls the whole pack up a level above us."

Laika's surprised expression snapped back to the girls, "That's so cool." Admiration and sincerity poured off Laika, though she held back all the questions bubbling up. Now wasn't really the time, after all.

Her excitement was met with smiles from the younger werewolves. Then Keisha pressed on, "So what are we working on then?"

Frustration broke across Randall's face. He plucked off his nametag, shoving it out of sight into his pocket. Then he reached for the radio on the push cart to call in that he was going on his lunch break. Finally, he sat down across from Laika with a sigh.

"Are you helping too?" Laika sounded skeptical. The air bristled as the two rivals sized each other up over the study desk.

"This is *my* library. I know where everything is and I'll save you a lot of time," snipped Randall in a deadpan tone. His stare met Laika's in a silent challenge, "And get you out of here faster. Besides, my pack and I know more about magic than you do. I did a minor in magical studies."

"I did a minor in magical studies," mocked Laika, taking on his tone as well, "So did I. And I've probably spent more time here than you."

"I'm doing a minor in magical studies?" Added Jaci quietly.

Keisha clapped her hands together, trying to get everyone on task again. "Awesome! So please tell me what are you working on? Is this moonlighting work?"

"Kinda..." Laika admitted as she let the sniping back and forth drop. Randall wasn't wrong that he'd save her time... if he actually knew anything.

Randall rolled his eyes and explained, "Laika and Evie have a bad reputation of doing off-the-books detective work."

"We were on this case," disagreed Laika.

"Sure you were," replied Randall, sarcasm dripping from every word.

As they resumed sniping at each other, Keisha got her hands on the ingredients list. Manicured nails ran down each word reading it quietly. Finally she spoke up, "With this much it's gotta be a ritual right? Or someone was opening their own store." She handed the list to Jaci who nodded after reading it over.

That derailed the fight brewing once more and Laika focused her attention back on the list. Eyes lit right back up as well, pleased to find another soul interested in magic. "Right? Imagine if everything here is for just one ritual!"

"What?" Randall's cold exterior cracked. He leaned over the table grabbing the list to scan it, then swore. "Half of this is just reagents for stabilizing magic."

"I know," Laika pressed, skepticism at war with curiosity, "How do *you* know?"

"There are like... three types of dried foxglove, and even more witch-hazel variants," explained Randall, shifting to lean over the study desk. He stole Laika's pencil and started to write the family types next to plants along the list. "I took all the ritual classes that UCLA offers. And I took Latin *and* Elven up to a 300 level."

Keisha looked absolutely lost in that small snippet. Glancing at Jaci and then back up to Randall, she hazarded a question, "Does more types of each plant mean a more stable spell?"

"Uh..." Randall trailed off, the wind taken out of his sails.

"I don't know," admitted Laika, "I mean it should, shouldn't it?" It was easy enough to read the books and know the common use of reagents... But if you couldn't do any of the spells, it was harder to understand the exact interactions.

"Do we ask a witch?" pondered Keisha. She pulled her phone out to check her own contacts, "Jaci, do you know anyone in the magical application degrees?" The quiet girl nodded, picking up her own phone without a word.

"Most of my witch friends were from college. It would be awkward to text them now," grumbled Laika. She should have kept better touch with them. After the move to Glenwood and some other fallings out, she hadn't talked to any of her college friends.

"I'll text Thad," Randall offered. His smirk was back in place, knowing it would annoy his rival.

"Why would you do that? He wouldn't know any more about magic than us," scoffed Laika.

She was met with an exasperated look, complete with Randall rolling his eyes again. "He's our magical expert."

"Are you kidding me?"

Keisha cut in quickly, "Actually, Thad is kinda an expert on this stuff. Even we call him when we have questions. But witches aren't really his speciality."

"Thad knows a lot about all supernaturals," agreed Jaci, but she gave Laika an apologetic shrug for giving her 'bad' news.

"Okay, fine," agreed Laika, "Text your friends, Thad, and I'll ask... someone." Learning that two members of Blood Fang could keep up with her limited magical knowledge irked her. She pulled out her cell phone to shoot a message to Evie, knowing there wasn't anyone to help.

> LAIKA
>
> Apparently Thad and Randall know magic.
>
> Thad's even a 'magical expert'

While waiting on a reply, she turned her attention to her messages with Alfred.

> LAIKA
>
> There was a break in at Pixie Dust.
>
> Trying to figure out what they were doing with all the stuff

ALFRED

Are you working that case?

> LAIKA
>
> I was there at the break in

ALFRED

I see

Have you had any luck then?

> LAIKA
>
> ... not really
>
> I have the ingredients he was after but I can't find anything that needs 20 types of witch-hazel

ALFRED

You would not need that much in any spell.

At most you would use five types of protection, one for each element.

Even then you would only use witch-hazel for metal or water.

Laika stared at her phone like it was tap dancing in her hand.

She started, erased, and restarted a reply multiple times. Fingers moved furiously enough to catch her companions' attention. Was everyone around her today just some secret master of the mystical arts?

LAIKA

HOW DO YOU KNOW THAT?

ALFRED

Because I know how ritual magic works.

LAIKA

I know how ritual magic works, but I haven't found anything like that in the entire UCLA library or google?

ALFRED

I assure you my library is far superior to both.

To elaborate on your original question. Regardless of the brand of witch, elven, dwarf, or vampire, rituals follow similar rules for elements.

Only witches use the specific names, but all types use combinations of elements.

This means that all ritual magic pulls from the same roots and allows for cross magic work.

LAIKA

... so you have a magical library? For real?

ALFRED

You could call it a passion of mine.

LAIKA

I wanna see it!

Laika looked up from her phone with pure joy written on her face. Not only did she have the answer to their question, but she had learned something important about Alfred. He had way more magical knowledge than she'd thought.

Jaci wordlessly shook her head as she glanced up from her phone. Meanwhile, Keisha sighed in defeat, "No luck so far. But a few of them are going to go ask their teachers."

Randall was scowling deeper by the second. Eyes going from his phone to Laika's expression, he seemed to realize exactly what was about to happen. He mumbled begrudgingly, "Thad doesn't know. He said he'll check some books."

Laika's expression quickly shifted to victorious, "Well, as it so happens, you wouldn't have this much witch-hazel in a ritual. It would be overkill and pointless."

She paused as a thought flitted across her mind before returning her attention to her phone.

LAIKA

Why would someone add that much extra?

Would they want different types for different rituals... or would it be more like me? Just not knowing any better?

ALFRED

Interesting thought

If they truly have that many types on their list, then I would assume they were a new practitioner.

LAIKA

Looking for the type that works best for them?

ALFRED

Exactly.

LAIKA

You are brilliant!

Laika explained what she had learned to the other three quickly. "So it seems like most of this list is useless."

That caused Randall to hold out a hand to Keisha, "Give me your notebook."

Keisha dug one out of her bag quickly handing it over to him. "What are you doing?"

"Removing the extra shit," he answered.

Then Randall started making two copies of the list, but left off anything redundant. He detailed out the ingredient families and primary uses for quick reference as well. Once he was done, the man held out one sheet to his rival.

Laika was again skeptical of him, but she took it gratefully, "Thanks." The word felt strange rolling off her tongue, but she meant it.

"Don't mention it," replied Randall, getting back up. "Seriously. Don't tell anyone I was helping you." She noticed the second copy was folded up and put away in his vest pocket. "I need to get back to work now. Jaci, Keisha, I'll drive you home in about three hours when I get off shift, okay?"

"Thanks Randall," Jaci responded sweetly, "We can wait however long you need."

"Don't steal anything. Either of you," demanded Randall sternly. He gave Laika and Keisha one more serious look and Jaci got a nod before leaving them with a head shake. The push cart creaked all the way out of sight.

"He's such a softie," teased Keisha.

"He's such an asshat," corrected Laika, "Is he your cousin or something?"

"Nah," Keisha laughed for a few minutes. "Blood Fang lets the younger girls in my pack go to their training once a month. Nilani trusts Ace to keep us safe at practice, so we know all of them pretty well now."

"Oh..." That had taken Laika aback. Night Claw didn't have much to do with the other packs in Glenwood, and she'd thought Blood Fang would have been the same.

"And Randall gives me and the girls a ride home in his minivan when he works, to save us from the bus. The ride back to Glenwood takes forever," continued Keisha. "They really aren't bad guys. But the feud between Ace and Evie is fairly legendary. I don't think he'll ever forgive her..."

Laika scowled, eyes moving to where Randall had disappeared into the stacks. "What does Ace have to forgive her for? He's the one that came at us with all the rage and fire."

Keisha held up her hands in defense, "I think I've said too much already. I'm sorry."

"No, no, I'm sorry," Laika quickly backed down.

The younger girls had helped her out so much today. They didn't deserve any of the nastiness that sprung up between the two packs. Between letting Laika stay in the library and teasing Randall into helping, Laika felt like she owed Keisha and Jaci big time. "Sorry, Blood Fang just gets me riled up. Thank you, really."

"You're welcome." Keisha relaxed right away. "Let me know if you need back in. I can come hang out for a few hours."

"Me too," Jaci chimed shyly.

"Absolutely. And let me know if you ever actually need an experienced moonlighter... or even just someone to proofread your papers."

Laika thanked the Moonscent girls once again as the three women exchanged numbers. She felt a surge of fondness for the younger moonlighters and while she'd made progress today... It was time to meet up with Evie and explain everything she'd found out.

Laika bid her new younger friends goodbye. "I'm going to head out. I owe you both a drink though."

"I'll take you up on that when I turn 21," teased Keisha as she waved farewell. She picked up some of the books, heading to the shelves to put them away.

Jaci proposed a compromise, "Maybe we can go for a run?"

Laika agreed easily and headed for the exit, making sure to take a large circle around her Blood Fang rival on her way out. She finally got a response from her packmate as well.

EVIE

Seriously?

LAIKA

Yep!

But don't worry… victory went to us.

EVIE

Because we are the best, obviously!

LAIKA

Come get me please

I have a breakthrough.

INTERLUDE - CRACKING

The Ritualist
October 8th, 2018
...somewhere in Glenwood, CA

H er Love was looking for the Ritualist now, even if they didn't know it yet. Maybe she'd send her Love a clue or show off a little bit. If her Love would end up on scene for the cleanup again, then they'd be awed by her power on full display.

Wouldn't that be something to witness? To see the look in her Love's eyes when they beheld the sight of her rituals. Given half a chance, she'd figure out how to get herself to the scene.

Her Love would be so impressed when she finally got to explain how she'd saved them. How the Ritualist rid them of all their enemies and carved paradise out of a crazy world. No matter how much blood it cost in the end.

However, the Ritualist needed to start paying attention to her work. This spell almost hadn't gotten ready in time. She had a tight lunar deadline to follow. Then her usually-solid supplier had an issue with her delivery of components when he ended up in jail. While the others had come through in the end, she'd been short of a few key things.

She'd had to get creative by sneaking into her stepmother's supplies. The old witch probably wouldn't even notice and if she did, then who cared? The Ritualist's 'parents' owed her a lot more than that since they'd stolen her childhood. Ruined her life and never once apologized for anything. Used her as a prop to seal their reputation after they'd failed multiple times to do it themselves.

As the Ritualist invoked her spell, she felt the magic start coursing through her again. It was a glorious feeling of success as it coiled through her muscles and mind. It made her body want to sing and every inch of her skin tingled from so much power rushing from the ritual circle up into her command.

This was the third successful spell she'd manage to activate and this time was easier than the last two. Her previous ritual had gotten out of control and a few changes had been required. Before, she was using the wrong bonding agents to stabilize her five pillars of magic, with some serious side effects. She'd resolved that this time.

The Ritualist's fingers moved, trying to direct her power into a specific spot on the representational map sitting in the middle of the circle. To her immense satisfaction, the place she'd picked started to crumble away on the map and she could feel the ground shifting. *Her* magic was pulsing through the circle and causing a real effect in the world, far greater than any mere witch.

A little bit longer and this magic could be hers to keep, not just borrow for a night.

Three down and two to go...

CHAPTER 12
BREAKING

Evie
October 8th, 2018
Glenwood Police Department Station #1, Glenwood, CA

Evie rapped her nails against the plastic chair arm while she sat in the tiny waiting area of GPD. This was not the first time she'd spent a Monday night waiting to see the MOONS liaisons. The reason why was usually a coin flip. Either Night Claw had paperwork that needed to be signed off on, or Night Claw had a lead they'd hoped would get them onto better cases. Tonight it was the latter.

She glanced down at the piece of notebook paper in her hand, reading over the list one more time. "And you're sure you didn't see anything that would narrow down what kind of magic this is?"

Her question was directed to Laika who sat next to her, half sprawled across two seats and Evie's, typing away on her phone. "No, like I said, it's too redundant to tell. Ritual magic of some sort is the only thing I'm sure of," Laika answered.

"How do we figure out more?"

"By asking someone better at magic than either of us, that isn't a member of Blood Fang." Laika kept tapping away at her phone, but her expression soured.

Evie could feel the growing annoyance rolling off her packmate at her competition for the title of 'most magical werewolf.'

"So we need a witch then," mumbled Evie.

"OR!" Laika added emphasis, "We could just ask Alfred."

A heavy sigh escaped from the exasperated werewolf's lips. "But we don't know how much he actually knows. And what if this is his case already? We could get in big trouble."

"He knew about the redundant ingredients," reminded Laika... again.

They had hashed out this exchange half a dozen times over the past two days. Laika kept insisting on roping in her newfound magical friend, and Evie pushed back against it. She had nothing personal against Alfred; Evie just wasn't sure how much stock she put in this vampire's magical knowledge. The compromise to put this to rest had been to come to GPD and plead their case with Aaron and Owen. They had a solid lead to follow, and if they got assigned to the case officially they could leverage MOONS resources to solve the mystery.

The officer who worked the front desk hadn't been remotely surprised when Night Claw showed up. It was the same grey face who'd been sitting there every other time they'd come in with a lead. He'd simply nodded in greeting and pointed at the aged, orange plastic chairs with his pen.

He informed them that the MOONS officers were in a meeting and would be with them as soon as they could. Evie sighed again, praying for anyone to put an end to this merry-go-round with her packmate.

Suddenly, eight phones began to ring within seconds of each other.

Laika sat up and took notice of the sudden cascading sound. Her expression grew a little distant as she tried to listen in on all the conversations when the phones were answered.

"What's up?" Evie whispered. She didn't want to break her friend's concentration, but was dying to know.

"A disaster? Or an attack? No one is sure yet," explained Laika. Her aura had dimmed with worry. Evie felt the spike of tension as more phones began ringing all around them. As if summoned by the sound, Owen dashed out of a conference room towards his desk. He was a madman packing up a bag with papers, pens, and a radio.

"Call dispatch!" Owen bellowed behind him. Aaron was following at a brisk walk. He had a phone pressed to his ear, already doing exactly as demanded.

Straining her ears, Evie couldn't make out the conversation over the bustling chaos. Normal officers were packing up, orders were being barked in every direction, and even more phones were ringing. A tidal wave of people would soon be crashing through the entryway.

"They're calling in moonlighters," Laika explained under her breath. She was up on her feet now, waving arms for Owen and Aaron's attention.

"What's going on?" snapped Evie. She hated being left out, but empathy was no good in a rowdy crowd. All Evie was getting was waves of worry, anxiety, and urgency. But her packmate's hearing could pinpoint exactly the information they needed.

"The calls are saying that the ground under that mini golf amusement park just gave way," Laika explained as she continued to wave her arms.

"The one by the mall?"

"Yeah, the one with all the blacklights and techno music," confirmed Laika.

Evie bit her lip as she knew the place well. They sometimes went for cheap beer and rides on the weekend. It had built up over the years as the owner kept adding more and more, likely hoping it would be the next Six Flags.

"What are you doing here?" Owen asked as he finally made his way towards the exit. His surprise was evident on his face, never-mind his aura. The man hadn't noticed them waiting as he prepped for the field.

Aaron joined at his side a moment later. "I'm sorry ladies, we don't have time right now. There is a situation evolving at Sync Holes."

"I heard," Laika admitted without even a tiny bit of shame at her eavesdropping. Her eyes were laser focused on the pair, "Can we help?"

"No," Owen replied bluntly, "This is over your head."

"Please," Evie joined in. She kept her attention on the wolfkin, knowing he'd be easier to crack right now. "It sounds like you have your hands full and you're already calling in moonlighters."

It was Aaron that spoke first, however. "We are, and normally you wouldn't get this call." He turned his attention to his partner, "But they're here. Dark Wind is going to be 30 minutes behind us at best."

Silver and amber eyes brightened at those words; both women saw their chance. That had been a pleasant surprise, but apparently their performance at the last few jobs had warmed Aaron up to them more than they knew.

Evie pushed ahead. "At worst we stay in the car and out of the way."

"Or we direct people where to go," Laika nodded along, "We have vests in the car."

Frustration simmered under the surface but Owen relented. "Fine," he barked, "But we need to go now. Get your vests and follow."

"Yes, sir," Evie agreed while grabbing Laika's arm to drag her out before anyone changed their mind.

October 8th, 2018
Sync Holes Amusement Park, Glenwood, CA

Evie stayed hot on the heels of the GPD cruiser as they twisted through the streets of Glenwood at a speed well over the posted limit. This high speed dash was pushing the limits of their aging car, but the moonlighter was focused on keeping up.

She already had her moonlighting vest strapped over her bright orange snaps. Evie gave herself a silent pat on the back for stowing the extra clothes in the trunk after the job at Pixie Dust. If they hadn't kept vests and proper clothing on hand, Owen would have had a leg to stand on in telling them no. It was still very possible they'd not even be allowed to step out into the parking lot, but at least they were prepared.

"What do you think happened?" Laika sat in the passenger seat vibrating with energy. Her phone was sitting abandoned in the cup holder right now. That alone was a testament to how excited the other wolf was.

"I don't know, but it was bad enough to call in Dark Wind."

At a glowing sign, the GPD cruiser swung sharply to the right. The Saab protested at the sudden deceleration, but made the turn as they rolled into the parking lot of Sync Holes. They'd been less than ten minutes away at GPD, but her eyes quickly found they were far from the first on the scene.

Three large red fire engines were already pulled up along the edge of the park railing. Firefighters were running to open the fire exits along the fence. Others were ushering waves of people out in as orderly a manner as they could.

Their car came to a stop a few feet behind the cruiser and Laika was out of the car in a flash. Promises to stay back had been forgotten as her curiosity demanded a better view of what was happening. Evie could hardly fault her either, as her eyes took in the scene in front of them.

The park had never had the grandeur of the larger parks in

Anaheim or Hollywood, but Sync Holes' owners had pride in what they built. The whole park had the air of what someone from the 80s had thought the 2000s would bring. Black railing and structures were splashed with neon signs and fluorescent paint. Blacklights installed throughout the park made the paint glow like radiation in the night, but that wasn't what had caught Evie's attention.

The park's center was the original mini golf course with a ferris wheel, roller coaster, merry go rounds, and other amusement park fare surrounding it. Now those tall structures were all leaning dangerously inward, as if the center of the park was a black hole drawing them in.

Evie scrambled out of the car and a crash of emotions slammed into her. That froze the wolf in her tracks. The crowd being ushered from the park was like a tsunami of panic, with a persistent undercurrent of worry from the first responders. Fear was there, but faint... either weak or far away. With the situation she was looking at, she had a dreadful feeling it was the latter. The redhead quickly shut down her empathy before her own power overwhelmed her.

"Come on," Laika urged, putting her hand on Evie's shoulder. She pushed her forward to catch up with Aaron and Owen.

Once the emotions surrounding them dimmed, her eyes blinked a few times and Evie gave her packmate a reassuring look. "Okay, sorry. It was all too much for a moment."

"It's fine, you've got this," Laika agreed with a smile of her own. The steady feeling of confidence emanating from her packmate bolstered Evie. Both women sprinted after their liaisons, weaving through cars and people.

Ahead of them, Aaron had been stopped by a woman a foot shorter than him dressed in a yellow fireproof coat. She had a no-nonsense bob with matching ebony eyes, but right now they were full of fire.

Aaron's voice was calm, trying to soothe her. "I promise you, Captain Reynolds, that we are going to do everything we can to be team players here. I have only just arrived on the scene and I need to take stock of what's happening."

A finger jabbed into his face as Reynolds hissed back, "Then I need you to be a 'team player' and let my people get to the real work."

"I can't do that yet." Aaron didn't back down, but he did glance over his shoulder at Owen for help.

His partner shook his head with a radio pressed up to his ear. "Still on the other side of LA."

"Melinda?" pleaded Aaron, keeping his voice down.

"Uh... no answer yet. But if she worked a shift this weekend then she's probably passed out."

Reynolds tapped her foot impatiently waiting for a response. "Well?"

The radio crackled to life once more causing Owen to frown. "LA is sending someone over, since they're closer than our magic right now. But they'll still be 25 minutes out, and no promises Melinda will be any faster once we get her to answer."

Aaron bit back frustration, but he stood his ground as he returned his attention to Reynolds. "I don't have anyone who can call this non-magically occurring right now. And after what happened with CorroNect-"

"I don't give a snowball's chance in hell if this is magic or mundane," hissed Reynolds as she cut him off, her frustration growing with every word.

Evie stood back with Laika, watching the exchange with a dawning realization about what was going on. "Oh shit. They don't know if this is a magical or natural disaster, and need a MOONS signoff to let the firefighters on the scene."

"But if it's active magic, then legally she can't enter," finished Laika with a frown.

The feelings of panic and fear were still fresh in Evie's mind. People needed help right now. Without hesitation, she spoke up, "We can."

Officer Leavenworth and Captain Reynolds both snapped around to stare at the werewolves. Her lack of patience was clear and she pressed, "You can, what?"

Evie took a deep breath before stepping forward, "We can enter the park. Night Claw are licensed moonlighters, which means we don't need a magical expert to declare the scene."

"Exactly," Laika quickly added, joining them, "That's why we exist."

Reynolds gave them an appraising look and her lackluster response was evident.

"Hold it right there," Aaron cut in, literally stepping between the women. His back was to the captain as he addressed the werewolves. "I know I said you could come, but I really did mean for you to direct people out here. You aren't ranked to go in there. Stupid isn't a strong enough word for me if I let you go in."

"We know the risks," interjected Laika, "...well, we accept them."

Evie nodded in agreement. Then she gave Aaron an apologetic grimace before swerving around him for the other woman.

"Do you even have any fire training?" demanded Reynolds. She ignored any protests from the police officers. "You're useless to me otherwise."

"Look. I understand we aren't perfect," defended Evie.

"Not perfect is an understatement."

"Laika and I aren't Dark Wind with all of the training in the world. But we are competent moonlighters. We can go onto the scene now. Not in 30 minutes when the better werewolves get here or LA's expert shows up to grant you permission."

The fire captain tightened her lips into the scowl, still unsure about Night Claw.

Laika finally added, "We aren't trying to say we're better than your people. We know we aren't."

There was a subtle shift in the aura around Reynolds. Evie's empathy had reached out just a tiny bit to figure this woman out. As usual her packmate had stumbled on gold. "Exactly, we want to help.

But we can't do this without you and the Glenwood Fire Department."

"I would be completely in charge," commanded the Captain. She was looking between the two werewolves, but her resolve to hate them was cracking.

"Completely," agreed Evie, "Please just let us help. We can take a radio and you can direct us on what to do. Until your people get clearance."

Reynolds looked beyond them at the police officers. "I'm taking your moonlighters. If you've got a problem then file a complaint. Since I'm following all your inane rules there shouldn't be an issue."

"Hold on," tried Aaron.

"Shut up," interrupted Reynolds. "We don't have time to fight about this anymore. I can already see how far that rollercoaster is leaning. It's going down long before your people get here. You two follow me now."

Evie mouthed an apology to Aaron, but she did as she was told. She kept pace with Reynolds while asking what she thought were important questions. "What's the main focus in this?"

"Are we supposed to try and secure the rollercoaster from falling?" Laika added, falling in on the other side of the fire captain.

"You're on Search and Rescue for anyone on the coaster. Those damn things are only safe on solid ground. It looks like the other rides are being evacuated, but we have confirmation from the park operations team that there are cars stuck on the tracks." Reynolds was explaining in the same no-nonsense tone as she waved them towards one of the trucks.

Evie nodded quickly, showing she was following along. "So we need to get the cars back down to the loading zone- No, if it's leaning that much, there's no guarantee the tracks aren't broken." Clarity hit her like a wave.

"Exactly," Reynolds agreed as she hooked a radio onto Laika's vest and then Evie's, before turning to pick up an orderly pack of harnesses. "Werewolves are strong and fast, so I'm hoping you two will be able to climb at least as well as my people. If you can't, tell me now before we waste the time."

"No, we can be quick," Laika assured, studying the gear that was being clipped onto their vests.

"Good. Now these are tandem harnesses. You wear it over your vest with the extra straps and hooks in the front," continued the captain as she gave one over to a tall man dressed in the same yellow coat. He asked Laika to hold out her arms and started to slip the harness around the werewolf with practiced ease.

Evie stood still to allow Reynolds to do the same for her. "So we get up the rollercoaster and then get people out of the cars and into the harnesses to bring them back down."

"Yes. You need to secure them into the harness before you get them out of the cars."

"And you'll be on the radio to explain exactly how to do that right?" Evie felt worry creeping up her spine. If they messed this up then someone could die from a long fall. Her usual missions only endangered herself or ended in some property damage.

"I will be there the entire time. I'm going to hook a camera to your vest so I can see what you're doing as well. If you do what I say, then everyone goes home to their families tonight. Do you understand?"

"You're the boss," confirmed Evie. That stern confidence did more to keep her calm than if the woman had tried to reassure her softly.

"Yes I am." Reynolds clipped the last carabiner into place then picked up a small body camera. She looped a velcro strap through a hook on the werewolf's vest.

"I have a signal," called another firefighter standing at the back of a fire truck, "Image coming through on camera one and two."

Reynolds pressed the button on the radio, "Check."

"Confirmed," the radio crackled back.

"Alright, you're good to move. Get in there and head for the rollercoaster first. I have people working the rides at the edges as close to the epicenter as I'm allowed."

Evie took a deep breath and clamped down on her empathy as hard as she could. The feelings of fear and panic were stronger this close to the disaster, inside of the gates would likely be even worse. A hand gripped her shoulder as Laika tried to reassure her silently. Evie offered up a smile to her friend before putting on a confident expression.

Captain Reynolds moved past the fire trucks to the entrance where people were streaming out. Many of them were crying or panicking as the fire fighters pulled them further away. The woman just pushed through, trusting her people to handle the crowds. Evie and Laika kept up with her in a single file line, making it easier to go against the flow.

"Okay, we're going in," Laika said. She glanced at the captain, "Can you tell Owe... Officer Kirkland that we might need the hybrid shift form?"

"Also, that if a pair of giant half-wolf, half-people come barreling out at full speed not to shoot," added Evie. But neither woman waited for a response as they cut through the mass of people, making their way inside the park.

The initial crush of people at the gates was the worst of it. Much of the grounds had already been evacuated, so while the crowd had bottlenecked at the entrance, beyond the gates the park was nearly empty. Small groups of people came running from the direction of the ferris wheel or one of the other rides, but they were sporadic. Clearly Reynolds' crews were still evacuating rides.

Regardless of the laws in place, saving people was the top priority.

It was eerie as they ran through the park. Everything was lit up in violent hot pinks and hi-vis orange, neon signs proclaiming all the usual amusement park attractions. But the thoroughfares were emptier the further in they went. The roller coaster was straight back at the furthest point from the entrance. If Evie remembered correctly, this main street would take them to the center of the park where the original mini golf course still sat as the central hub. From there, they'd just need to skirt around to the appropriate sign and they would reach the rollercoaster.

An arm flew up, catching Evie across the chest as Laika skidded to a stop. A wave of fear rolled off her packmate, as she spoke in a very faint voice. "Evie, look."

Evie's eyes widened as she realized why the path hadn't looked familiar... The path had been cut off just as they would have reached the center of the park. The golf course was gone, and in its place was a yawning abyss of darkness. No lights escaped the pit before them, leaving Evie unsure just how far down it went.

The radios on their shoulders crackled and it snapped Evie out of her daze.

"Report?" cracked Reynolds' voice.

"Can you see the center?" Laika answered back.

"No."

"That's because it's gone. Hold on, I'll get you a better view."

"I'll keep moving and you catch up," Evie managed, shaking her head clear. Her packmate was faster, so any distance she made wouldn't mean much.

Laika nodded before sprinting forward to the railing of the course. She didn't pause as she leapt over it. Her hands caught on a sign overhang before pulling herself up on top of a crumbling building, half over the edge.

Evie moved on, trusting the other woman to be careful. Especially since Laika was a more competent athlete in the long run.

Since the most direct route had quite literally disappeared, the werewolf wove herself along one of the longer paths, stopping to check the park map. All of the shortest paths were just gone. But there was a far one she could loop out to through the arcade before heading for the coaster.

Empty stalls and rides were even creepier with only the neon lights to light the way. Evie wanted to sprint through the area for her destination. However, after one attempt she nearly broke her neck tripping over a downed vending machine. The werewolf had apologized on her radio before anyone could scold her, then started a safer jog.

She could hear Reynolds and Laika shooting messages back and forth about what they could see as she continued to press forward. Towards the back of the amusement park she found another delay.

'Voyage of the Space Pirates' was one of those swinging ship rides that Evie loved. Usually waiting in the line was the most annoying part, but right now the large black painted ship was blocking the entire route. It was wedged between the arcade and the base of its tower, likely having broken off in the initial destruction.

"I don't see anyone on the ship," Evie said holding down the radio button, "Do you want me to check this out or just go over it?"

"I'll send in someone to follow your path. They can double check the ship," answered Reynolds.

"Understood. I'll keep moving, it appears stable enough to climb."

"No, go around it."

"Are you sure? That'll be slower."

"Yes. I got a good look at what's over the edges from the other girl. If you rock the boat then it might go over."

Evie could not stop herself from laughing, but she responded, "Okay. Got it, I'm going through the arcade. Laika, be sure to follow me that way too."

"Heard," came Laika's voice.

Evie detoured into the arcade doorway. A faded sign proclaimed this as "Ray Gun Games," keeping to the mismatched techno theme around the park. Inside was dim with only the glow of screens lighting up the way. Since the power wasn't out, all the machines were still playing music and beeping. There was a large crack in the ceiling and wall where the ship had hit the building, but it seemed to be holding up for now.

"There's damage to the arcade. I'm going to keep going for now but you might want an alternate path when your people get in here," Evie warned.

A flash of hope sparked through the area, stopping Evie in her tracks. Tentatively, she called out, "Hello? Is anyone here?"

Silence met her question. She lifted her control on her empathy once more, preparing for the fear that would assault her. It crashed into her mind like a sledgehammer, but mixed in with it all was a glimmer of hope that was nearby.

"Hello?" Evie tried again. The emotion flickered up to life to her right and the werewolf scanned her eyes that way. She finally spotted a door hidden in the depths of the dark room with an 'Employees Only' sign. There were three arcade machines fallen in front of the door blocking it from opening; she would have missed it completely if she hadn't been paying attention to the faint call.

"What's the delay?" crackled her radio.

"There is someone stuck in the back office. They sound far from the door, so I'm guessing they got pinned when the ship hit."

"Are you sure?"

"Yes. There is someone alive back there. I can move those machines out of the way."

"I can help," Laika's voice added as she caught up.

"Move quick," commanded Reynolds, "I'm letting my people know. They'll handle first aid. You two unblock the way and get moving."

The werewolves moved quickly, their superior strength coming into play. Normally a woman Evie's size would struggle with pushing one of these heavy booths even a few inches; the game was a few hundred pounds of electronics. Instead, she got both hands under one of them and easily lifted it up. Evie may not have been able to throw one the length of a football field, but she could move it 20 feet without losing her breath.

Laika dragged the other two back with one hand on each. The floor would be wrecked; however, it wasn't like the arcade wouldn't be remodeled if it ever reopened. "I can hear someone yelling for help back there."

Clearing the door took no more than a couple of minutes. Evie pressed an ear to the wood, trying to hear more clearly to the other side before she opened it. But all she heard was a muffled sound. "You're sure it isn't a radio left playing?"

"You told Reynolds it's a person and I don't know any songs that consist of screaming for help that specifically."

"Okay." Evie tried the handle and found it unlocked. "I've got this and you keep moving to the coaster."

"Yep." Laika gave a quick salute before she dashed off to the other exit.

Evie pulled open the door, her gaze trained forward. The room was dim, the track lighting having been ripped from the ceiling when a shelf fell. A desk lamp that had fallen illuminated the area, splashing shadows across the walls. Most outlines were the angular shapes of toppled furniture, but one moved, and this time Evie heard the voice.

"Help me! Please don't leave!"

Panic, pain, and fear was surging out from the far side of the office. Picking her way carefully forward, Evie's gaze finally landed on the source. A man lay half sprawled across the floor with a massive filing cabinet bearing down on him. A sturdy wooden desk was the only reason the man hadn't been crushed. The corner of the desk had caught the cabinet, and kept it from crashing down onto the prone form.

"Sir, it's alright, help is here. Can you move?" Evie's voice was measured as she assessed the jumble of furniture.

"No, my leg..." The man shifted, trying to drag himself forward. An ominous creak echoed from the looming cabinet as he did so.

The radio crackled to life, as Reynolds' voice cut through. "Keep him still."

"Please don't move," soothed Evie as she moved quickly to his side, "I'm here to help you."

Again the radio crackled, "You need to check for blood, if there is none then you can unpin the leg."

"Help," cried the man.

Evie took his hand and dipped her head so they could make eye contact. "Hey, I'm here to help. My name is Evie and I need to check your leg before I move the cabinet. What's your name?"

"Uh... I'm Bradley."

"Are you in pain, Bradley? Where does it hurt?"

"My leg. I can barely feel my toes."

Evie gave him a warm smile before ducking to see the trapped leg. "You might not believe me, but I think it's a good thing you can feel your toes right now."

She felt surprise cut through Bradley's panic. "What? Why?"

"It means you still have toes." The woman couldn't see any pools of blood and pulled out her phone to double check with the light. To the radio she said, "Looks clear, but even without medical training I can see that his leg is broken."

"Shit," swore the man.

"Our expert is supposed to be five minutes out," Reynolds responded.

"I made it to the rollercoaster," Laika cut in, "I'm going to start looking for people." They started a quick conversation about what the werewolf was supposed to be looking for, but Evie tuned them out in favor of keeping her attention on Bradley.

"Don't worry." Evie gave a squeeze to Bradley's hand. "A broken leg is just stumbling around in a cast for a few months. Or one of those cool scooter things."

"I guess that's true... better than needing a new leg." Bradley managed to return a tight smile despite the pain.

"Okay, I need to let go now. I have to move this out of the way so I can get you clear." Evie waited for him to nod before taking her hand back. Then she went to work on the large cabinet, lifting it off his leg as gently as she could.

Bradley gasped in relief as the weight lifted.

"Are you okay there?" Evie asked.

"I don't know. My leg hurts so much..." groaned Bradley.

Evie moved back to the man's side and she could see dark bruises through the tears in his pants. She pushed on her radio for Reynolds, "He's not walking out of here on that leg."

The response came back, "Do you know how to do a safety carry?"

"No," admitted Evie, "Talk me through it. I'll figure it out." She followed the instruction that came, carefully picking up Bradley over her shoulders. Not holding onto his broken leg was the hard part. Reynolds directed the werewolf to take him outside to where she entered the arcade.

However, when Bradley was set carefully down he grabbed her arm. "Please," he begged, "Don't leave me here alone."

Evie put on a soothing tone, "I know you're scared and you don't want to be alone. But there are more people still in danger like everyone on the rollercoaster." She pointed up the leaning structure they could see. "And they need my help right now. Captain Reynolds' people will be here soon and they'll be able to help you. I promise."

Bradley slowly let go. "Okay... just... thanks. I thought no one was going to come for me, no one heard me over all the music."

"Just wait right here. They already know where you are thanks to this camera." Evie pointed at the lens on her vest. "I promise someone will be here for you soon, Bradley." She gave his hand a quick squeeze before heading back inside the arcade.

Her radio cracked to life, "I have him marked. The expert is here and she's checking the scene right now for active magic. My people will be in as soon as I have the go ahead."

"Thank you," Evie responded, swerving through the machines to follow Laika's path.

"How did you find him? I thought werewolves were all punch and vinegar."

Evie laughed, "Oh, I'm totally punch and vinegar in the right situation. But we do have other powers like my empathy."

"How does that work?"

"I could feel his hope when he heard us on the radio before. Probably no one had been through here in a while and the voices caught his attention."

"So you can find people who are hidden. That's good to know," mused Reynolds.

Evie made her way out of the Ray Gun Games at a jog. She could finally see the sign for 'Rocket Coaster' hanging crooked just ahead of her. Now it was time to get to work.

CHAPTER 13
SINKING

Laika
October 8th, 2018
Sync Holes Amusement Park, Glenwood, CA

Laika arrived at the base of the coaster well ahead of her packmate. The Rocket's sign swung on a single nail. Her eyes swept along the twisted frame and even from here she could see the structure was coming down, and soon. Steel girders were twisted; parts of the rail were shattered and tangled in support beams.

She tracked the curves of the track while she looked for the stranded cars. To her surprise, she saw that most of the neon-trimmed cars were sitting in the station. They were thankfully empty. Perhaps the passengers had been close enough to the ground to get themselves out.

Laika let out a sigh of relief, feeling like they might be able to report back that all was clear. Unfortunately, the feeling didn't last long... her ears picked up screams for help coming from far above.

Following her ears over her eyes, Laika could just make out a red spot stuck on top of the steepest drop on the coaster. She swore under her breath, wondering if they could get the car back to somewhere safe. But halfway down the drop a beam had given way, tearing a gap in the tracks.

"Shit," Evie whispered as she came jogging up the path.

"I know," admitted Laika, looking back at her packmate. She raised her hand to point at the steep drop. "I only see one car still stuck. Do you feel anyone else?" Evie came to a stop next to Laika, focusing on the spot of red before closing her eyes. Sight was just a distraction when finding people with her powers.

Impatiently Laika went back to walking the length of the rollercoaster, looking for anyone else. She knew Evie's powers took more time, but she itched to jump into action.

"Report?" Reynolds demanded over their radio.

"I can hear at least one car's worth of people on the drop... the rest of the cars seem to be empty." Laika answered. She wished she knew how many cars there were supposed to be and if any had ended up falling.

Evie finally responded, "I think there are four people up there, but I don't sense anyone else on the coaster. Maybe a few in the surrounding rides though."

"That matches how many voices I can hear," confirmed Laika and let the captain know through the radio.

"We're still waiting for the greenlight back here. Get moving," commanded Reynolds. "I'll walk you through how to hook them in when you get up there."

"Gotcha," Laika said. Again she looked up at the black metal frame. Thankfully, it had glowing blue and pink paints all over so she could make it out even in the fading light. But how was she going to get up there?

"Hey!" Evie caught her attention then pointed at one of the main poles. "That one has a hand railing, maybe for maintenance?"

"Nice!" Laika jumped over the safety railing and placed a hand on the metal peg, testing if it was still stable. With a frown, the werewolf looked up at the long climb. "You know a hybrid form would make this faster..." Her voice was rueful, because she knew the answer before Evie even said it.

"Yes, but even if these harnesses survive the shift... There's no way we can work the carabiners with our claws."

Laika grumbled. "And that defeats the whole point of getting up there." Another shake of the maintenance holds ensured their stability, then the woman pulled herself up the first few feet. The structure creaked, but didn't move.

"Are we good?" Evie asked with a wary gaze.

"Yep, just follow me up." After only a few minutes of climbing, Laika got into a rhythm of testing each hold and moving upward. She picked up speed with every beam they moved between. The metal creaked under her, but it was holding steady.

"Laika! Slow down!"

The distance between her and Evie was growing wider with every passing moment. "Reynolds said to be quick!" Laika shot back, eyes already planning their next move.

Up above them, the maintenance ladder terminated on a small platform. From there it was only a short distance to the car, but the climbing was getting less vertical. The women had moved to part of the frame that was over the open abyss.

"She also said be careful!" snapped Evie.

"I am being careful!" Laika got a hand on the edge of the platform. There was a beat as she tested her weight on the metal. Finally, she pulled herself up, getting a foot on the flat surface.

Only for it to fall out from beneath her.

"Laika!" screamed Evie. She was still about 30 feet behind on the maintenance ladder.

Open air greeted Laika as she began to fall from the Rocket's frame. The platform swung away from its brackets, smashing into the nearest pole. That caused everything to violently lurch to the side. The wind was knocked out of Laika's lungs as she crashed into a beam. Almost immediately, she began to slide back off the beam. Her arms swung wildly for any handhold to catch herself.

Exhilaration rushed through Laika's veins as she managed to catch on with her fingertips. Her legs kicked wildly for a moment, but at least she wasn't still falling.

Evie had made it to the top of the ladder and called down, "Are you okay?"

"Yeah!" Laika panted breathlessly.

The rollercoaster swayed with a creaking that caused Evie to flinch. "How do we get you back up?"

"What the hell is going on?" crackled the radio.

"Laika fell!"

As her packmate and the captain talked about how to get Laika back to safety, the werewolf looked around for an escape. From this angle, Laika could see the people stuck in their car and all four of them were watching her. She gave them a big grin even if they couldn't see her in the dark.

"I have an idea," she called back up to Evie.

"Really?" Evie replied, "What are you going to do?"

"Just hold onto the ladder tight."

"Why?" Evie questioned, but looped her arms around the support beam anyways.

Muscles tensed as Laika did the most important pull up of her life. Her weight rose slowly through the air and she managed to get herself up onto the beam. "Woo!" she cheered.

"Great," Evie snapped, clearly agitated, "But how does this help?"

Instead of answering, Laika gave a wave to the people in the car who had been watching her. Then she jumped as high as her legs would allow, catching onto the next beam and causing the frame to lurch again.

"I'll meet you at the car," she yelled to her packmate.

Evie looked like she wanted to yell all manner of foul things back, but from this distance it was useless. So instead she carefully climbed between the two ladders, continuing on to their target.

From where she was clinging now, Laika was back into the main part of the rollercoaster. If she was careful enough then she could leap from beam to beam to make her way. This far out the structure was leaning heavily on its side, making for an easier climb.

"Help," cried out a voice from just a few feet ahead.

"I'm on my way," Laika assured them. Panicked faces were finally coming into view. She paused in her trek to inform the radio. "I'm arriving."

"Good. Don't pull anymore stupid stunts," snapped Reynolds.

The werewolf didn't respond to that as she pulled herself up onto the top of the track. "Hi," she waved at the people sitting at a 90 degree angle. "I'm Laika, and I'm here to get you out of here."

There was a mixture of crying and relief at her words. The front seat of the car held a couple wearing matching college sweatshirts that looked to be in their early twenties. The woman had herself wrapped around the man's arm as much as she could, while the lap bar kept them in the seats. He was squished up against the side, clinging to their restraints. In the back row were two men who both looked terrified and were straining to hold onto their lap bar. All four of them had been hanging over the open maw of death for a while now and had likely seen people fall in already.

Reynolds' voice commanded, "You need to calm them down. Ask their names and start telling them the plan."

Laika shook herself to action again, realizing she'd been staring. "Okay, my packmate and I are going to hook you into our harnesses and then climb back down with you. See? They are designed exactly for this."

The man in the front row asked, "Are you with the rescue?"

"Mostly." Laika carefully lowered herself off the edge of the track so she could brace her feet on the center railing.

"We're moonlighters with Glenwood's MOONS, working with the fire department," Evie picked up the question. She'd caught up finally, reaching the top of the tracks.

"Thank god," one of the men in the back exhaled with relief.

"These chicks are werewolves!"

"Yep," Laika confirmed. She knew that her packmate could read the people better than her, but she thought the woman in the front might be their biggest hassle. Confidently, the werewolf pushed herself along the rails so she could get up the side. A leg hooked over a bar gave her enough support to lean and reach the car. "Hello, what's your name?"

The woman's eyes were pleading with Laika for help. "I'm Molly. I want to get down now. Please!"

Metal groaned in answer, causing her to scream.

"Okay, okay," Laika tried to soothe, "I'm going to get you down. Captain Reynolds is going to tell us exactly how to strap you into the harness with me and then I'll do the work. You'll just hold on, alright Molly?" She waited for confirmation and let the firefighter know she was ready for instructions.

Reynolds walked them through getting Molly into the harness. It was a struggle to get her to let go of her boyfriend's arm long enough to loop her own through the straps. A few precious minutes ticked by, but the last buckle eventually clicked into place.

Glancing to Evie, she found Molly's boyfriend was also ready to go. Normally Laika would take the taller guy to save her packmate the hassle. But she had a feeling Molly wasn't going to keep still on the way down. There was an internal sigh as she assessed their final obstacle: the lap bar. Moments like this she wished her packmate could affect emotions and not just sense them.

"Laika." The redhead gave the tiniest frown in the direction of her packmate. The unspoken reminder to focus hung in the air. Evie was stern; perhaps the emotions from the car were getting the better of her.

Laika nodded and spoke in a calm and level voice, her words directed to Molly. "Alright, we have to lift this bar so we can hook the harnesses together. Are you ready? I promise, we won't let you fall." She offered an arm to the woman to brace herself.

Their eyes met and Evie started the countdown, "On 1, 2, 3..."

The bar's safety locks were no match for werewolf strength. It jerked up enough for the two humans to start sliding out of their seats. Molly's nails dug in deep on Laika's arm; the woman had her in an absolute death grip.

Reynolds barked directions over the radio for the two humans to wrap their arms around the werewolves' necks. Then magnets helped guide pieces into place so that they could be locked into the tandem harnesses.

Molly clung tight, throwing her legs around her savior as well. She was 140 pounds of shaking deadweight for the climb back down. "Just a couple minutes and you'll be safe on the ground." Laika tried to give the woman a reassuring look, despite Molly's face being buried in her shoulder.

Her eyes swept up to the two men who had been patiently waiting their turn for rescue. It felt cruel to leave them behind. There just wasn't a way to clip two harnesses to the werewolves, even if they could climb while so encumbered.

"We'll be right back. Just sit tight; we're going to move as quick as can be," Laika promised.

"Where else are we going to go?" one of the men joked with a scared smile.

Laika turned her attention to navigating back to the ground. There would be no daring leaps this time. Instead she followed the path Evie had found to get up here. The frame was now leaning further, making this more like a horizontal crawl to the maintenance ladder.

Evie was having an easier climb as the man she'd saved was following directions. He was holding onto the beams and moving as commanded, instead of just dragging her down. Meanwhile Laika had to muscle her way every step, wishing she could swing her passenger to her back. Thankfully, once she got to the ladder she felt that grip on her neck loosen a fraction.

"Are we almost there?" Molly asked, opening an eye when she felt the metal rung under her foot.

"One more ladder and then you'll be safe on the ground. Promise." The climb down was blissfully uneventful. Laika's boots hit the cracked pavement with a gentle thud. The woman wrapped around her was still shaking like a leaf, but that choke hold had shifted into a hug.

In the time it had taken Laika to get back to the ground, the first wave of firefighters had booked it through the park. They'd followed the path the werewolves had scouted earlier and arrived on scene in force.

Evie tapped her on the shoulder before pointing towards the edge of the abyss. "Is it just me, or is that bigger than before?" She was already freed from her passenger, and two of the first responders swarmed around Laika to remove Molly from her harness.

Lakia's head swept around, looking for the building she'd originally climbed back at the center of the park. However, it was gone... and the only place for it to go was down. "Yeah, it's bigger."

The radio crackled and Reynolds' voice cut through the noise. "Our expert should be arriving on scene. Once she gives the all clear, you're going to hand off the scene to my people."

She looked up sharply at Evie. Laika covered her radio for a moment and hissed, "We promised we'd be right back up!"

"I know! Just give me a moment." The moonlighter reached for her own radio to respond. "Do you want us to wait or go back up for the other two? We know the safest way up now."

"As soon as the expert says it's safe, then *Evie*, show my team the path up."

Laika's frown deepened and her mouth opened to argue. However, her train of thought was derailed as a strange figure marched onto the scene.

A blonde woman with a long braid made her way towards the rollercoaster with a quick click of heels. She wore well-fitted jeans and a low cut top, showing off her neck and shoulders. The only thing that marred her sunny appearance was the heavy, black, long coat that hung open. Its style looked oddly familiar, which made sense a moment later as the woman opened her mouth to speak and revealed long fangs. "Quick like bunnies, out of the way."

Evie hesitated a few times then looked at her packmate to see if she heard the same. Laika met the look with a bewildered one of her own.

"Well, I would say that is more like a turtle than a bunny," scolded the vampire as she breezed past them to the edge of the rollercoaster.

"What are you doing?" Laika followed along, realizing this had to be the magic expert. Was this the one from LA that Owen and Aaron talked about? She'd certainly never seen this woman around the GPD before.

The blonde woman gave her a wild-eyed expression as she stopped on the very edge of the dark abyss. "Testing how strong this ritual is."

"Wait... this is a ritual?"

"Yes," the vampire answered shortly, her head snapping down to the abyss. Then she spun around and put a vice-like grip on Laika's arm, dragging her back a few steps as the ground started to crumble again. "It's picking up speed again. Whatever was holding it back is failing."

Laika swore and scrambled back to the safety of the solid ground.

Above them, the Rocket's frame gave a loud creak as the crumbling stability took out one of the major support beams. All the black painted poles began to violently lurch to the side.

"We need to get up there," one of the firefighters shouted as he finished buckling in his harness for the climb. "Hazel, give us the green light!"

"No," the blonde vampire answered, "That's going down now due to magic. I can't let you go." She and Laika had made it back to the rest, and only then did the vampire let go of the werewolf.

"But there are people up there," he insisted. There was no way he'd make it past a vampire, though, if she didn't let him. Laika knew that as strong as he was, this woman outmatched them both.

"What's going on?" Reynolds' voice cracked through the radio.

All of that faded into the background as Laika remembered the two men she'd left back on the drop. Ignoring everyone else she dashed forward, no longer taking any care about rocking the coaster. She knew she'd never make it up as she was now, so the werewolf started her shift.

Making the shift to hybrid form was not impossible while moving, but it would be painful to do. She swallowed that pain, allowing the fire to burst through her muscles as she leaped up into the collapsing beams. Fur ripped out of her skin as bones cracked and stretched, but the werewolf just kept moving.

By the time Laika reached the top of the maintenance ladder, she had fully turned. Using her longer reach she didn't have to pause and balance her way along little paths. Instead, her powerful legs pushed her into another jump. The werewolf launched herself up the side of the coaster, barely stopping to catch hold before leaping again. All the while she could feel the rollercoaster becoming more unstable as more of the ground gave way around the supports.

The top of the frame had fallen so far the two men waiting were almost upside down. They screamed when Laika's massive form appeared. Or perhaps it was cheering...she could barely make out what they were saying in the rush of adrenaline. One clawed hand dug into the track as she swung into the open air, trying to reach them. The other reached out as a lifeline.

Both men had a look of panic, but between the hybrid werewolf and the certain death below them, they made their choice. Quickly, one threw his arms out, grabbing her hand and twisting himself out of the lap bar. The car gave an ominous groan as he kicked free. Laika pulled him to her and onto her back. The man held on for dear life.

The other was more reluctant to leave the safety of the car. So Laika's claws took hold of the restraints, ripped them away, then grabbed the human as he began to slide free. He'd probably have a scratch, but as he joined his friend clinging to her back, she assumed she'd get forgiveness.

Laika tried to warn them to hold on tight, but it came out as a growl. With both hands on the edge of the track, she pulled herself up above the tangle of support beams. She looked down at the drop below, then back at where Evie and the firefighters waited.

A small quake shook everything and the fragile but solid spot she stood on began to fall away. The Rocket had reached its limit between rapidly decreasing supports and the hybrid werewolf jumping around. Everything started to sink.

The world felt like slow motion as Laika wrapped an arm around each man holding onto her, eyes scanning for the next safe place. She took off, pushing her legs past the normal speeds she ran at.

Most werewolves were blessed with just one major power such as her keen hearing, but she had two. Laika was not just faster than Evie or the members of Blood Fang; she was faster than almost every werewolf she knew. Kicking into super speeds she reacted on instinct, racing forward, leaping from beam to beam.

Behind her, poles and track fell away. The drop to the yawning abyss chased close on her heels. As she reached the spot where the maintenance ladder began, the destruction caught up. Laika watched as her landing spot twisted then cracked, disappearing into the darkness below.

"JUMP!"

Laika did as bid and jumped anyways. A beam to her left bent at a strange angle, but it was perfect for her to leapfrog back into the air. Again another beam twisted unnaturally to her aid. That was enough to give the werewolf the distance for one final leap.

Excitement mixed with fear, while Laika flew forward without knowing if it had been far enough.

People scattered in every direction as the hybrid form hurtled like a cannonball towards them. Laika put her hands over her passenger's heads to protect them from the impact. A moment later, she hit the ground hard. There was a crunch as her nose snapped, but she forced herself not to roll.

Voices yelled above Laika and she felt people trying to push her onto her side. As the fog cleared, she realized that the firefighters were pulling both the men from her grasp. They looked bruised and a bit scared, but both were alive.

Then Evie was above her and Laika felt a swift kick into her shoulder.

"You moron," fumed her packmate, "That was beyond reckless!"

Laika held up her hands defensively as she started the shift back into human form. Her shoes and outfit were long gone, but her modesty was preserved since someone had thrown a safety blanket over her massive form.

Evie wasn't done shouting though. "Never, ever do something that stupid again! And I won't hear any crap about how it was the right thing to do, because *I* know that *you* loved every minute of that!"

Her words fell on deaf ears though, as Hazel the vampire captured Laika's attention.

The woman was glowing with silver and green light; it danced up and down her arms. Her coat lay forgotten on the ground, showing off tattoos up her back and arms almost like Melinda's. Words poured from her lips in some foreign language before the crumbling ground abruptly stopped. Whatever had been causing the sinkhole cut off with the end of the spell.

Now that Laika had her human vocal cords back, she asked, "What is she doing?"

"I don't know," Evie sighed, seeing her lecture was pointless. "She was singing earlier too."

"Singing?"

"Yes, and I swear that beams were bending to her song."

A laugh escaped Laika. "That's so cool!"

"I guess," Evie agreed, but she looked uncomfortable. Her eyes flickered to where the vampire stood, still at the edge of the crumbled ground.

Wrapped in a blanket, Laika pulled herself up to her feet. First, she counted off the people from the rollercoaster, pleased to see all

four were being taken care of. Then she approached Hazel with gratitude. "Thanks for the assist up there."

The vampire waved her off with a distracted tone. "You're
welcome. You are a very fast bunny."

"I'm a werewolf."

A large smile crept onto the woman's face and Hazel laughed,
"Yes, like I said... a very fast bunny." The vampire's eyes hadn't
moved from the hole in the earth. She looked vaguely bemused more
than anything.

Laika pressed on, "Did you stop the collapse too?"

"I didn't not stop the collapse. More like I ripped the hooks out of
the rocks," Hazel answered easily, with another wave towards the
edge of the hole.

"Uh... thanks for that too." Laika's amber eyes scanned back over
the people who were closest to the edge. If it had continued picking
up speed, they would have been lost within minutes. Curiosity
perked up now that everything seemed safe. "What kind of magic
was that?"

"Them or me?"

"Both?"

"I don't think we're both today... maybe them, then me... do I
know you?" Hazel's gaze had turned to Laika and then sharpened
like she'd seen the werewolf for the first time.

Laika couldn't suppress the confusion blossoming on her face.
Was this woman insane? Or just LA manic pixie?

Before more could be said, Reynolds' voice cut over the radio.
"Laika, Evie, get your asses back here, right now."

"Uh... excuse me." Laika backed away, realizing that the camera
was still hung on her chest. So the captain had seen every moment of
her disobeying orders...

Hazel did not move to follow, her eyes just studying Laika with
vague confusion of her own.

Evie came to her packmate's side with a panicked look. "Shit.
How bad do you think we screwed up?"

Laika shrugged, the motion a little lost in the blanket. There was nothing to do about it now. It had been the right thing to do anyway... Neither of them could have lived with themselves if they'd let those guys plummet to their deaths.

Both women wasted no time running back to the Sync Holes gate where Reynolds was already waiting for them. Her arms were crossed and she tapped her foot like a mother who'd caught her children coming in past curfew. Behind her, police cars, ambulances, and news vans filled the parking lot.

"First I just want to apologize," Evie started, only to be cut off.

"That was dangerous," interrupted Reynolds, giving both of the werewolves an even stare. "It was a stupid thing to do, especially with an expert on the field saying it was too dangerous."

"I know, but..." Laika tried to defend herself only to be shushed.

"And thankfully everyone lived. Good job ladies, maybe all moonlighters aren't complete wastes."

Evie responded with a bit of a dazed expression, "Thank you?"

The ghost of a smile pulled at Reynolds' lips. "I'm pulling you out of the field. My people can handle it from here. Go get checked out by the medics before you go."

Laika held back a step, meeting the captain's eyes. "Thanks for giving us a chance to help. I know it was unconventional..." She trailed off into a shrug.

Reynolds gave her a nod before walking into the amusement park. When she passed, she patted Laika's shoulders and dropped her voice. "Keep yourself safe, but never lose that momentum you have. I can't condone your actions but... Best you believe I was cheering you on when you made that first jump."

CHAPTER 14
DEAL

Evie
October 9th, 2018
Taran Estate, Los Angeles, CA

Evie sat in her car grimacing at her phone. She was tired, sore, and late for work. While the first two could have been handled by another few hours of sleep, that might mean the end of her paycheck. When she hit the parking lot there was still hope she could sneak in without being noticed. But a voicemail derailed Evie's entire morning.

Everard Belle had called Evie while she slept. In the mad rush to get out of the house, she hadn't noticed this bombshell. His message had been short, but she listened to it three times. "Hello Evette, this is your father. I saw you on the news. I hope you are well and please call me back."

The news? When had she been on the news? Evie had reported back to Reynolds last night then to Owen. She was sure she'd avoided all the news crews as she and Laika slipped out of the scene after midnight.

Evie popped open her car door while swiping to the internet, looking for any clips of last night. The Sync Holes Collapse was big news in Los Angeles, so most of the sites had it featured. The news had dubbed whoever had done this as the 'Glenwood Anarchist'. Evie felt it was a silly name, but it wasn't wrong.

The reporter on screen was interviewing Reynolds set against a backdrop of the crumbled park. By the time they'd gotten the fire captain's attention, the roller coaster was completely gone. Only the ferris wheel was left standing in the dark.

Evie could see the GPD cruisers, fire trucks, and ambulances parked everywhere. Reynolds mentioned moonlighters where there and thanked them. However she didn't use any names or pack names, just said Glenwood and LA MOONS sent people. So where had her father seen her?

Then Evie spotted it.

At the back of an ambulance a man was getting his leg in a splint while sitting on the edge of the vehicle. Evie remembered him as Bradley, the poor guy trapped in the arcade. She'd gone to check on him while working on paperwork.

There she was, full faced to the camera with a clipboard, giving Bradley a high five as they laughed together. Her vest had the big reflective letters of 'MOONS' perfectly displayed, and the screen caption read: "Firefighters and moonlighters pulled survivors from the wreckage."

"Fuck my life," Evie groaned as she dragged herself up the steps. She needed to tell Laika about this and fast. Her key opened the front door as she started to type out a message.

"YOU!"

Evie nearly dropped her phone as Arik screeched at her from the top of the stairs. His home had one of those movie perfect entrances like you'd see in a castle. A grand, sweeping staircase dominated the front room. The elf had one hand on his hip and the other pointing dramatically down at her. He didn't look like he'd just rolled out of bed either. Dressed in a bright silk shirt and long blonde hair swept back into a perfect braid, Arik looked like he was ready for an interview... or interrogation.

"Uh... me? I know I'm late. I'm sorry. It won't happen again." Evie rambled looking guilty. Her mind raced to try and remember if he'd had an early appointment today. That would make her tardiness even more egregious.

As Arik continued, he radiated a lot of loud emotions. "How could you?!" Graceful steps carried him down to Evie. "How long has this been going on?"

"Almost never." But Evie's words were pointless; he was gearing up into a rant.

"I don't believe that for a second!" Arik jabbed a finger at her again. "Complete betrayal and deceit, all happening under my own roof!" The elf raised a hand to his forehead, feigning as if he was going to faint as he reached the bottom of the stairs.

Evie stood frozen, unsure if she was about to lose her job or even what he was talking about right now. She'd already been on uneven footing coming in the door; now Arik was assaulting her with both words and waves of excited emotions. Was he actually happy to have caught her and now had a legitimate reason to let her go?

"I'm sorry?"

Arik came to a stop in front of Evie, emerald eyes staring at her intensely. "You're sorry? Is that all you have to say for yourself?"

"I'm *very* sorry for being late," Evie tried to emphasize her apology better. However, she was starting to think he wasn't talking about her tardiness at all. In front of her was a minefield and usually empathy allowed her to navigate it. But Arik had the upper hand today. Evie scrambled to excuse her actions. "I had a late emergency last night and it kept me out much later than I planned."

"So you admit it?!"

"Admit what?" Evie could feel glee coming off Arik. Then she noticed he was holding something in his hand. He had a wild grin as he held out his phone. On the screen was the same video Evie had just been watching, paused perfectly on the frame that showed her face.

Her heart dropped.

"Oh... I can explain. I have always had a second job and I had cleared it with-"

"This is wonderful!" Arik cut her off.

Evie struggled to keep up. "What?"

"Absolutely amazing!" He continued on, ignoring her question. Evie tried again for an explanation but a hand raised to stop her in her tracks. More excitement built up from Arik, sending his hands moving through the air wildly. "To think, you've been here under my nose this whole time. We need to talk... I haven't had coffee yet..."

Evie was feeling overwhelmed, still not sure her job wasn't on the line right now. Her boss was a neon sign in a dark room with how much energy he emitted. She took the opening to claim some distance and recover. "I'll run out and get your usual then? Let me just-"

Arik clapped his hands together again, stopping her from speaking. He called loudly up the stairs. "Tony! Tony, whatever I have going on this morning, cancel it! We're going out for coffee!"

The vampire was leaning against the railing at the top of the stairs. His arrival had been masked in the madness below. Smugly Tony replied, "Certainly boss, I'll pull the car around."

"Don't bother," Arik waved him off as he strode past a stunned Evie. He picked up keys from the wall. "I can drive."

Tony bid them goodbye with a finger wave, before disappearing back to wherever he'd come from. "Have fun!"

"Come on then, Evie," proclaimed Arik, putting on his jacket.

"What?" She was stuck on repeat. Her boss never drove anywhere, preferring to be shuttled by one of them. Did he even have a license? Did he even know how to drive?

Before Evie could protest more, his arm looped through hers. "Oh, this is going to be amazing."

Evie was caught in a whirlwind of confusion. As she was pulled outside to one of the many cars she thought were for decoration only, she tried again. "What's going on?"

"Perhaps one of the most important events of either of our lives!" Arik gave a vague answer, still smiling.

Digging her heels in, her eyes shot daggers up at the man. Werewolf strength beat elven every day of the week, so Evie forced them to a stop. "NO! What is going on?"

"What do you mean, what's going on?" inquired Arik.

"I meant exactly that," Evie felt her agitation rising even as she fought it down. "You haven't said anything that makes sense since I got here. What's so amazing!?"

"Your 'screenplay,' of course."

"My what?" Her eyes went wide as Evie finally caught up. Arik had seen her iPad when they were at that shop. And now, he'd put all the pieces together from the news reports to her case files.

Arik's smile returned. He started walking again dragging an unresisting werewolf with him. "Exactly. We must talk about these cases of yours and how we make them into the first big moonlighter blockbuster."

"But I'm not actually writing a screenplay..."

"You are now."

Evie paused at the side of the car, staring at Arik like he had a second head. "What?"

"You are now." Arik gave her another flare of excitement before he climbed in the driver's seat. "Hurry up."

Evie looked at her Saab parked only a few spaces away. She could make that sprint, and as a bonus she had all her belongings still in her arms. He'd never be able to stop her from running. Then she sighed and got into the passenger's seat.

Evie had sullenly stayed quiet during the entire drive out to the coffee shop. She'd listened to Arik talk a mile a minute about all his plans for 'her' screenplay. Barely five minutes into the trip she learned it wasn't really about her.

He'd explained how he believed her original script would make a big splash. Especially if they added super realistic characters, compelling storylines, and used her own experiences in the field. The catch was, he wanted the main protagonist to be a tall blonde elf, not a werewolf.

"A few changes and you'll have an absolutely perfect script," Arik finished with a flourish. He pulled them into one of the parking spots outside his preferred coffee shop. Expectant eyes turned on the woman.

Evie saw her only opening and took it. "Let me think about it. I'll just pop in and go get your usual!"

A quick click and the werewolf was free of her seatbelt. Evie was out the door in a flash, heels clicking across the pavement as she beat a hasty retreat. She welcomed the distance just to get her head around everything. Then a hand reached past to open the door to the coffee shop. Arik held it open with a bright, optimistic expression in place.

"After you," the elf chimed in an uncharacteristic picture of chivalry.

A startled expression flashed across Evie's face. She had been lost in thought about how Arik hadn't been angry about her being late, or her second job. She should be relieved... But she knew how unreasonable her boss was about his pet projects.

"It's alright if you wait in the car," Evie offered.

"Yes, but we still have so much to discuss. This is a very important time in the creative process, when the ideas are still fresh and flowing!"

Evie glanced around checking if anyone had noticed her boss yet. So far all the emotions inside were the usual hum of content, friendly, or bored. Nothing that said 'Arik Was Here', but that would change if she held them up at the door any longer.

"Fine," Evie relented. Arik followed her inside, still talking a mile a minute about his ideas. She surveyed the room, but no one had taken notice of them. She whispered, "Do you have your sunglasses?"

"They're in the car."

"Go and get them." Evie was cursing internally at her terrible day.

Arik followed on her heels, giving a theatrical sigh. "You do know that the hat and glasses draw *more* attention than not, especially in the middle of downtown LA?"

She wanted to literally growl at the man. Instead, she parked herself at the end of the line with a huff. Clearly Arik just wanted an impromptu public meet and greet. Or he'd just lost his mind this morning while watching the news...

"So. As I was saying, I think if we frame this screenplay right, we can kick off a new Moonlighter Cinematic Universe," the elf prompted, trying to get Evie back to the topic dominating his own thoughts.

Finally, Evie snapped, "I don't know the first thing about writing, never mind something as complicated as this. People go to school for years to become professionals and never have a script published."

"Those are unlucky fools who don't have one of Hollywood's most beloved faces backing their project." Arik was frustratingly single minded when he picked something to dig his heels in.

"Even you couldn't save the train wreck of a script I'd write. You were looking at my case notes." Evie hissed.

"I can save anything," disagreed the elf. But he kept his voice low.

"Really?" There was a sharpness to the werewolf's tone.

"Yes."

"Name the last action movie you starred in!" Evie was done dancing around the fact her boss had never managed to break out of his role as a romantic lead. He'd been firmly typecast long before she was born.

Arik's eyes narrowed dangerously. Evie was saved as they reached the front of the line. She automatically placed their orders as she'd done hundreds of times before. The girl behind the counter kept glancing at her companion as she repeated the order back. Arik pulled out his card to pay for the drinks making sure his name could be seen. With a toss of his braid, he huffed before heading to find a table for them.

Scowling, Evie moved to the counter to wait, trying to come up with a way out of this mess. Her boss was being petty now by refusing to go back to the car. She glanced at him, feeling the storm clouds gathering in his mood.

"Evie! Long time no see!"

A voice cut through the werewolf's thoughts like a knife. Today wasn't her day. Slowly the redhead turned around to greet the newcomer.

Becky had just left the counter to wait by the window for her drinks. There was something different about the woman that took a moment to place. She had the same overly excited energy, but this time it was mingled with a calm aura of the man whose arm she hung off.

"Hi Becky..." What had Evie done to deserve both of her least favorite elves on the same day? She focused on the person she hadn't met yet and her frown deepened.

Another elf greeted her. He had long golden blonde hair and multiple piercings along his ears. Unlike the excited woman and her impatient boss, this man didn't look like he'd care if the roof came crashing in on them. His eyes were glued down on his phone, allowing himself to be led.

"Petronius Dufort," Becky supplied, "Babe, say hi."

"Hey." Petronius didn't look up.

"Hi," Evie replied, feeling awkward in this conversation already. She couldn't help but judge the odd pair of Bel Aire Becky and her tatted up boyfriend. That's when she realized what was so different about the woman.

Becky had bright pink streaks through her blonde hair. They looked perfect in color and artful spacing; no doubt she'd gone to a salon to do it. There was also a small flash of silver when the elf tilted her head, showing off new small nose ring. Becky caught Evie staring. "Oh, do you like it? It's still healing, but I thought it was so cute."

Evie felt like her brain was imploding for a moment. "Um... yes. It's totally cute."

A wave of pure happiness washed over the shop from Becky. "Thanks. I'm really glad you like it."

"It's hot, babe," Petronius added again, not looking up from his phone.

Evie felt the flash of annoyance pulse from Becky, but as she looked back the emotion faded into a content lovey-dovey feeling. This was clearly a new relationship still feeling itself out as far as Evie could tell. Thankfully, before she was forced into more small talk two cups were placed at the window. "Well, this was fun. We should do it again. I need to get this to my boss. Bye!"

"Oh totally!" agreed Becky. Her blue eyes watched Evie as she headed for Arik. "Bye!"

Picking up her pace, Evie retreated to the safety away from the counter. She sat and handed over the extra coffee keeping her eyes down. Why was she drowning in a sea of annoying blonde elves today? Then a flicker of disdain dragged her attention back up to Arik. "Friend of yours?"

"Not exactly." Evie mumbled before taking a drink.

"Ex-girlfriend or one night stand?"

Evie choked on her sip of coffee, before leveling a sharp look at her boss. "Neither. We just keep running into each other. It's honestly starting to get kind of weird."

"You should be more polite. Elven ears are very keen."

"What?"

"I can hear them talking, so why wouldn't they be able to hear us?" Arik smirked, taking a sip of his coffee. "You really don't know anything about elves, do you? How long have you worked for me?"

"I'm your assistant. You being an elf doesn't really matter."

"But if you knew I could hear you, you might be more careful about what you mutter under your breath around me."

Shock and embarrassment spread across Evie's face, as a few of the more nasty comments she'd made came to mind. "Your hearing isn't that good. You're just trying to piss me off."

"You're lucky I'm such a magnanimous boss. A more petty one would fire you for it." Arik kept his composure and emotions calm, making it impossible for Evie to read how truthful he was right now. "Should we get back to the real subject at hand?"

Evie's shoulders tensed. "I told you I don't know anything about writing. Those were my case notes, not a script."

"Are you sure? Because what I read was an extremely compelling story about a horrific tragedy."

"That was Laika." Evie stirred her coffee while trying to explain. "We share our notes and she gets a little crazy on her theories sometimes. I just do the outlines and she adds the details."

Arik wasn't giving up. "That's easily resolved with a good editor, and I know plenty of those."

"That's not the only problem. You're looking for some grand screenplay that lets you be an action hero." She waited for a response, looking up at him. There was a long moment before the elf begrudgingly admitted to his plan. "See right there! I'm the wrong person for the job!"

"Why?" Frustration was beginning to build up with Arik again. His coffee was forgotten on the table.

"I don't know shit about elven powers. So even if I could cobble something together, it would have to be werewolf centric."

"Really?" huffed Arik.

"Yes, which is why I can't help you with your plan." Evie stated flatly, releasing all the tension built up in her shoulders since she'd unlocked the door this morning.

Arik leaned forward and kept his voice to barely a whisper. The words were almost lost in the sounds of the coffee shop. "And that's why you are at a dead end on your case?"

Evie frowned, unable to refute the point. She and Laika had made no headway in the past few days. And Owen had firmly refused to put them on the case despite the lead, citing the Sync Holes as being 'enough excitement from Night Claw for one month.'

"So I'll make you a deal," Arik continued with the same unconcerned air. "You help me make my project a success, and I will help you with your problem."

"I can't discuss an active investigation with-"

"What are you talking about? I'm helping with your screenplay." A sly smile was in place on Arik's face.

Evie stared openly at the grin mocking her from the other side of the table. In the years she'd worked for him, Arik had never done anything magical even once. Now he was openly claiming he could help with the penthouse murders.

She shook her head, "I don't believe you."

"Who else are you going to ask about the elven elements of those rituals?"

Silence fell for a moment as Evie considered the offer. Where else was she going to get an insider look at elven magic? What was she going to do? Ask Becky? Then again, the young woman might tell her.

"Well?" Arik pressed.

He was met with an annoyed stare before Evie looked over her shoulder. The couple was nowhere to be seen. That removed all temptation from her view. "Fine."

"What?"

"I said fine, we have a deal. I'll write you a screenplay using my 'expertise' in moonlighting and you'll help me with anything elven that comes up."

"Wonderful." Arik finally picked up his coffee. "Where do we begin?"

Evie gave him another hard look as she reconsidered this deal. Could she trust her boss on this? She tested the waters with the only information on elves she had. "With you telling me honestly if elves can throw lightning around."

Arik scoffed, "Are you really asking *me* that?"

"Yes? ... Can *you* throw lightning around?" Evie pressed.

"That wasn't your question," he mocked her tone, "Of course *some* Skysong elves can. A simple google search could have told you that. 'Skysong' is the common name anyway, but it sounds so much better in its native tongue."

Evie felt the exasperation, superiority, and smug aura coming from the elf across the table. Not a single bit of guilt or deceit, though. Either he was a master of lying with his whole body and soul, or Arik was telling the truth.

"Okay. What are the other eight bloodlines? Do they all have big crazy magic like that?"

"Get me the first 5 pages of my screenplay and I'll answer." Arik countered her request smoothly. Only the first answer had been free.

Evie found herself face to face with a stone wall. "Seriously?" She'd need to bring her laptop with her tomorrow and research how to write a script today. "Fine. I need to loop my packmate in."

Phone in hand, the werewolf started typing out a message explaining this revelation to Laika. Evie glanced back at Arik and her frown returned stronger. If she was going to make this deal, then they needed to use every resource at their disposal.

EVIE

> Okay, long story and I'll explain tonight but I have a source for elven magic

LAIKA

What!? No way!

EVIE

> Yep. Can you contact your magic source?

LAIKA

You mean Alfred? I thought you didn't want to ask him stuff... Why the change of heart?

EVIE

> A weak lead is better than no lead. I'm not thrilled about it, but we can compare notes between them.

LAIKA

Oh trust me, he's not a weak lead

But yeah, I'll see if I can set something up for this weekend!

EVIE

Don't do anything extreme.

Maybe a phone call will be enough.

After I finish five pages of my screenplay

LAIKA

YOUR WHAT?

Evie looked up at Arik, and then back down at her conversation. The things she did for moonlighting...

CHAPTER 15
INVITATION

Laika
October 9th, 2018
Moonbeans Warehouse, Glenwood, CA

Laika had spent her morning laughing at Evie since she learned about the 'screenplay'. Night Claw had been moonlighting for around five years now, and Laika's work had known since day one. Hell, Laika gave Boss blow-by-blow accounts of their missions. It was harder to keep things like a second job quiet when you worked for the family business.

Evie keeping moonlighting a secret from her day job was bound to end up like this eventually. Laika was glad she'd never made a bet on how Evie's work would react to the news; she never would have guessed Arik would be excited about it. While Arik was an endless source of amusing work horror stories, this one was extreme. But even though the 'screenplay' meant she'd be hearing Evie complain for months until the plan inevitably failed, Laika's mood was sunny.

For the last week Laika had been half begging to ask Alfred about the Pixie Dust case. Normally, Evie didn't have any control over

Laika's actions or friends, but this was 'their' case. There was a small chance it was also Alfred's case as well.

Which could be a disaster... Especially if he mentioned to the GPD officers that Night Claw was still working on this case off books.

Sitting on the top of a delivery truck, Laika basked in the midday rays of sun. She was at peace as she watched leaves fall from trees. But internally, Laika's mind was hard at work scheming. Evie had given her permission and she intended to pounce on the opportunity. If Laika could just figure out a good plan of attack. Before she could decide, a voice cut through the autumn air.

"Laika! What the hell are you doing?" Her boss's voice floated up from the ground, sending a grin across Laika's face. Leaning forward, she peered down at the dwarf, calling back, "Just hanging out. You need something?"

"Did you just tell me, your boss, you're slacking off on the clock?" The man crossed his arms as he squinted up at her.

"I'm taking my lunch!" She gave a little wave, with her hand holding a silver foil packet. As the light of the sun flashed on the wrapper, it was like a lightbulb had gone off in Laika's head.

A scoff echoed up as the man shook his head. "Just don't hurt yourself... or the truck!"

She could hear him muttering about stupid jumpy werewolves as he left. "No promises," Laika replied breezily, before flopping back onto the warm metal. One hand raised the half eaten poptart to her mouth, staying true to her story about being on lunch. Her real focus, however, was the phone in her other hand. Clicking through, she found where she'd left off in her messages.

LAIKA

What are you doing on Saturday?

ALFRED

I am picking up a book in LA. Why?

LAIKA

So! Remember when you asked me about that case I was working on?

ALFRED

This would be the Pixie Dust break in?

LAIKA

Yep that's the one.

ALFRED

I do recall.

LAIKA

Are you assigned to that case?

ALFRED

I am not, no one is on the Pixie Dust break in.

The last I heard regarding that case, it is no longer open.

LAIKA

That's what Owen was saying, but that's totally beside the point This is perfect!

ALFRED

What does all of this have to do with Saturday?

LAIKA

Since you aren't on the case you can come over for lunch Saturday and we can talk about all my notes.

ALFRED

You are inviting me for a meal? Me?

Laika stared at her phone and the odd question. Why would it be strange to invite him for lunch? She eyed the poptart in her other hand before taking a bite. Then it hit her like a brick to the head.

LAIKA

Oh... Shit, was that rude? I'm sorry. I didn't think to ask but, can you eat?

ALFRED

Everyone eats, even the dead.

LAIKA

...do you eat food?

ALFRED

I can eat food.

Laika sighed in relief. That had been two steps from a disaster if it turned out that he couldn't eat.

LAIKA

Okay! So we could do a backyard BBQ!

ALFRED

For lunch?

LAIKA

Yeah. Is that a problem?

ALFRED

How shaded is your backyard?

LAIKA

We have an amazing view at sunset and... oh.

We have pretty good curtains in the kitchen?

Laika groaned loudly. How had she forgotten something as simple as most vampires don't go out in the sun. She'd seen all that leather gear and he'd even explained once in a previous message it was light tight.

ALFRED

Should I bring something?

LAIKA

Nope. I'll text you the address.

That had gone much worse than Laika had planned. She'd nearly insulted him three times over, but Alfred had agreed to come to lunch. A giggle crept to her lips as she sent the information and started a chain with Tor and Shelly for planning.

Evie was always wary of allowing supernaturals in the house, even though two... no, three werewolves didn't have much to fear. So she'd let her friend know before Saturday.

Probably.

October 11th, 2018
Night Claw Residence, Glenwood, CA

Laika stretched out on the couch, enjoying how relaxed her muscles felt after a run. Shelly had met her at Cohen Park after work. It wasn't the same as a big pack run, but it was so enjoyable to have someone to run with. Especially someone like Shelly, who embraced her 'inner wolf' far more than Evie would ever allow.

The pair had indulged in a nice long race through the park's paths. Shelly couldn't keep up with Laika in speed, so Laika had slowed down to not leave her too far in the dust. Once they were both tired, the women had shifted back and come home to prepare for Trashy TV Thursday. Shelly was helping with dinner and Laika had crashed on the couch after cleaning up the living room.

This was a new tradition in the house which Laika was enjoying. Before, she and Evie had gotten cheap pizza and some beers to sit and watch their shows. They'd enjoyed the terrible TV, getting more invested in it than they should have.

But now that Shelly and Tor were in the house, the weekly block of new episodes had turned into quite the event. Either their human roommate cooked or they got some exciting take out. Desserts and drinks followed.

Tonight's festivities were about to get started; the scent of nearly finished dinner wafted out of the kitchen. Laika glanced at the door straining her ears but there was no sign of her packmate yet. So she picked up her phone.

LAIKA

Have you left yet?

EVIE

I'm leaving in 5

LAIKA

You're going to be late!

EVIE

Arik is demanding a page before I leave.
What do you want me to do?

Laika groaned, sinking back into the couch. She'd been excited about this deal at first. It let her rope Alfred into investigating and gave them insight into elven magic. Or at least, it was supposed to. Instead, it had just kept Evie late at work almost every night this week as Arik badgered her over the screenplay.

LAIKA

I don't know! Do you want me to call with an 'emergency'?

EVIE

Do you really think he cares?

LAIKA

No, but I could call Natasha and say I can't get ahold of you?

EVIE

… Yes. I am so far into overtime. She'll kick me out at top speed

Sitting back up, Laika wracked her brain for some excuse that Natasha would buy. The excuse wouldn't need to be life-or-death, just enough to warrant the manager to go free Evie. After a few moments of thought, Laika's fingers scrolled through her contact list and hit the one labeled 'Natasha Perez'.

A voice answered after two rings. "What?"

"Hi Natasha, this is Laika."

"Who? Are you from the Parker Agency?"

Laika paused, realizing that despite having met Arik's manager multiple times over the years, Natasha had no idea who she was. She contained her amused snort. "I'm Evie's packmate. Arik's assistant?"

"Oh, you're the moonlighters causing me a fucking headache this week." There was the sound of nails rapping on a desk. "So, what?"

"I'm sorry to bother you. Evie has been getting home later and later all week. Now I can't even get her to answer the phone. Is she still at the office?" Laika rushed out the words trying to sound concerned.

"Define later?" Natasha's voice was sharp.

"Oh," the werewolf could feel a swell of victory, then tried to drag it back in, "... um... she's been at work for like 60 hours already this week. I'm just concerned about her."

The line cut off as Natasha hung up.

Not even five minutes later Evie sent a message.

> **EVIE**
>
> I'm free! Natasha was pissed I was still here. I got tomorrow off!

> **LAIKA**
>
> HURRY!

> I can't promise I can keep Shelly from starting.

> **EVIE**
>
> On my way

LAIKA

Now that I have you in a good mood and you have a whole day off.

Alfred is coming over for lunch on Saturday.

I'm hanging your blackout curtains in the living room

EVIE

WHAT THE HELL?

Laika knew that her friend would come home screaming at this news. But at least she had the drive to take it in.

Until the redhead got home, they couldn't kick off the festivities. So Laika decided now was the time to handle the chores for Alfred coming over. The curtains wouldn't steal themselves. Laika dragged herself up from the couch, heading for their shared room. As her hand pushed the door open, a thought struck her. Her other hand fished her phone out of her pocket and dashed off a text message to Alfred.

LAIKA

Do you actually need an invitation into the house?

ALFRED

Only criminals do not wait for an invitation before entering a home.

However, to your point, I do need a verbal invitation.

LAIKA

How does that even work?

ALFRED

Any form of 'Enter' or 'Please come in' is good enough.

LAIKA

No, I mean why would you need one.

ALFRED

The dead are weak to thresholds. I assume
that is the universe balancing the scales.

LAIKA

Okay... but what does that mean?

While Laika worked on taking down the deep green curtains, she
continued the conversation with Alfred. He explained briefly that
homes had a natural living energy around them that protected the
people who lived there. Vampires couldn't enter without permission;
it was like an invisible wall. This helped pass the time as Laika
climbed ladders, pulling down the sunlight protection.

Her phone rang as the werewolf went back into the living room
with heavy curtains draped over her arms. She juggled the fabric and
pulled her phone screen up to read, 'Dad'.

"Hey Dad!" Laika threw her burden over the couch to answer.

"Hey Kid." Luca Lowell called every other week to check in on his
daughter. Rarely on a Thursday since she had her TV night. "How's
work?"

"The warehouse is the warehouse. Easy work and easy money."
She went to get the ladder as they caught up.

"I was talking about your other job."

"Oh... it's fine too."

"Nothing you want to tell me? About your second job?" Luca
pressed.

"Not really." Laika tried to play off that there were no exciting
stories. She busied herself hanging up the curtains. No point telling
Luca about the strange happenings in Glenwood just yet.

Luca sighed loudly, but he let the topic go. "Alright. I'm here if
you 'think' of anything important. But that's only part of why I am
calling-"

Evie rammed her shoulder into the door, throwing it open loudly.
She looked like a shark hunting prey as she turned on her packmate.
"Those. Are. Mine!"

Laika's father was talking in one ear and her friend was screaming in the other. Laika could see the bomb primed in the living room. She needed to give this her full attention.

"Did you hear me? Is that alright?" Luca probed from the phone.

"Yeah Dad, that's fine. I gotta go." She hung up as soon as Luca said 'bye'. Laika would sort out whatever he needed later. Right now she had an angry werewolf on her hands.

"I said those are mine!" Evie snapped as she slammed the door loud enough to rattle the frame.

Laika defended but she kept her tone light, "I heard you. But I need them and I don't have time to go buy some."

"Why are you hanging them in here!?"

"Because vampires burst into flames in the sunlight and that would be super rude of us." Laika rolled her eyes as she stuffed her phone into her back pocket.

Evie looked like she had another scathing comment but swallowed it back down. Instead her friend replied, "Are you going to put them back?"

"Of course I will," assured Laika. She could hear Shelly and Tor pressed up against the kitchen door listening to the argument.

"This is such a bad idea." Evie was whining now, likely about to gear herself back up into a fight.

"No! It's not a bad idea. There are three werewolves in the house and he's one vampire. Who can't even come in without an invitation."

Evie opened her mouth, but she got cut off.

"We are an hour late to start." Shelly pushed her way into the conversation.

Tor was close on her heels. "Dinner's done. I'm putting it out now and if you keep fighting then you'll eat it cold."

Laika was standing on the top of the ladder, considering just leaping at Evie. They'd been behaving with their new roommates, but it wouldn't be the first spat to devolve into fists between them.

However, all her aggression faded at the interruption. She could see that Evie was deflating as well.

"Okay," Laika agreed. "Let me just finish hanging this since I'm up here. Then food."

Evie took a calming breath. "I'm going to go change and then we can watch all our trash TV."

The others settled into the couch and chairs waiting for Evie's return. Tor broke the silence. "So you want me to cook for Saturday?"

"Um... sure? But you know I can just order pizza or pick up something from the deli." Laika answered with a shrug.

"None of the delis do vampire friendly food. The VF is for vegans."

"I know that," Laika countered.

Shelly added, "Why would that matter?" She already had her phone in hand looking up the words she didn't understand.

Tor leaned back regally keeping a neutral expression. She looked between the two women before asking. "What do vampires eat?"

"Oh... but he said he could eat food..." Laika stared at her roommate before mumbling, "...Tor ...can you cook on Saturday?"

"Yeah."

October 13th, 2018
Night Claw Residence, Glenwood, CA

Laika sat perched on the arm of the couch, playing with her phone. This was the excuse she used to check the time constantly. She'd been there for the last 10 minutes, so if anyone approached her keen ears would pick up the footsteps. Right now the clock on the screen said 1:00 PM.

No one was ever perfectly on time. Laika knew that even as she felt a bit more excited. She'd had witch friends before to talk with about magic, but nothing like this. They'd all been college students figuring out the theories together. Alfred seemed to know investigation skills for criminal matters, so he'd have new insight.

With another glance at the clock Laika knew she had to get herself back in control, but it only read 1:02 PM.

She ran through the list of preparations they'd made. The dining room table was set for lunch. The curtains were drawn to block out the afternoon sun. Tor bustled around the kitchen pulling things out of the oven. There was a wonderful scent of tomatoes and cheese coming from her direction.

Even Evie was already sitting with her iPad full of case notes. Her friend had relented after an evening of promising the progress they'd make on the case was worth it.

A knock sounded on the front door, sending Laika to her feet. She hadn't heard a car or footsteps coming up the walkway. How could she have missed his approach? Her phone read 1:04 PM, which meant Alfred preferred punctuality over the social norms.

She could hear Evie muttering at the table but ignored it, instead springing up for the door. "Hey!" Laika greeted, as the door swung open. "You're right on time! Come on in!"

Alfred stood on the doorstep dressed in the long black leather coat she'd seen at their first meeting. There was no extra car parked out front either. Laika wondered if he'd walked to their place.

In the shade of the porch he'd taken off his helmet before knocking. There was a small surprised expression for just a moment. Then it transformed into a polite smile, with just a hint of fangs. "You should be more careful about inviting strange vampires into your home. Or at the very least, be sure it was the vampire you were expecting to see at the door."

"You said you needed an invitation," countered Laika, feeling herself beaming. "It would have been so rude to make you wait on one when you got here."

"I suppose so."

They'd spoken almost daily for the last month, but in the first few words at the door Laika now could place his voice to his text messages. He spoke the same way he wrote to her. Her eyes sparkled with amusement at that fact, as she stepped back out of the doorway. "But seriously, welcome."

Alfred gave her a polite nod as he stepped over the threshold without pause. Her invitation had done the trick apparently. He began to loosen a buckle near his throat on the long coat with practiced fingers. Laika closed the door, cutting off any extra sunlight into the living room.

This close to him, the werewolf could see multiple heavy duty buckles and buttons securing his coat in place. With matching gloves and what looked like leg guards, Alfred's outfit looked more like armor than anything.

Gesturing to the coat, Laika asked, "Do you need to hang that up?"

"No, if you do not have a coat rack then the back of the couch is fine."

Laika realized Alfred would need a few minutes to get his coat off. So she took advantage of that to finally get a good look at him. The vampire was older than she remembered, maybe in his mid forties when he stopped aging. He was handsome with high cheekbones, and- the werewolf shut down that line of thinking quickly. Instead she turned back to her roommates to let Alfred unbuckle in peace.

Evie was giving Laika suspicious looks from the table, but Laika ignored her. "So I think I mentioned everyone before. But these are my roommates. Tor, Shelly, and Evie."

Shelly had headphones on while she sat on the couch with a laptop on a tray. Colors were flashing rapidly across her screen as she played some new game. A quick hand went up in greeting, but she focused back on the match.

"Yo," called Tor from the kitchen. She popped her head through the open doorway to greet their guest. "Lunch will still be 15 minutes."

"Thanks," Laika called back. She made her way to sit down with

Evie and the case notes. They could get started on some of this before food.

Both women received a polite nod from Alfred, but he left them alone to their activities. Under his coat the man was dressed in a clean white shirt, grey vest, and matching slacks. He spent a moment rolling his sleeves up before turning to the werewolves at the table.

Laika thought he looked good, but realized she and her packmate looked underdressed for the occasion. Which was silly since it was a work lunch at her own house... but her jeans and poncho shirt just didn't stand up to a suit.

"Thank you for the invitation," Alfred said, catching her attention again. His eyes were looking down at the screens with notes. She thought for a moment he was reading them upside down. "What are you working on here?"

"A few things," Laika admitted, "The break in at Pixie Dust seemed really strange. You remember the whole list of items that we had?"

She pushed forward the list with the groupings she'd gotten at UCLA.

Evie was scowling before she forced her expression back to neutral. Something was bothering her beyond worrying about their visitor. She flipped her iPad around showing a list of possible rituals. "Laika said you were part of figuring out everything was redundant?"

"That is correct." Alfred stayed standing, but he took the paper.

"Well, so far we have grouped the list into categories of the types of components," Laika continued.

"Is there a particular reason you two think the break in case should not be closed? Officers Kirkland and Leavenworth believe it to be a simple robbery." Alfred's question was polite.

"There is something really off about that robbery," Laika shrugged.

Evie frowned again. "We've worked a few and who leaves a

register full of money completely untouched? Why bother stealing dried flowers and feathers?"

"Certain magical items can be worth far more, depending on the preparation for them," Alfred answered without missing a beat.

"Not this stuff," Evie disagreed. She was openly glaring at Alfred now.

Picking up where Evie's short argument had left off, Laika tried to explain. "I checked the prices online and nothing here was even that expensive as far as we can tell."

"Mr. Glasse is a dwarf and likely untrained in ritual magic of this nature. He may not have known that." The vampire seemed calm as he countered points.

"He wasn't stealing for himself. There was a list on his phone so someone probably hired him for the break-in." Frustration was building in Evie's voice as she pulled her iPad back.

Laika didn't need to be an empath to see the disaster coming. The whole interaction was disconcerting. Evie normally had far more patience than Laika did when explaining their theories. This wasn't even the first time someone was poking holes either. They'd run this one by Owen and Aaron already.

Before the tension could escalate any further, Laika cut in. "We found two other break-ins. And everything missing was on this list."

That detail gave Alfred pause as he inclined his head with a curious expression. "That is strange. Where did these break-ins occur? I assume not in Glenwood?"

"They were both in LA, so they fell under their MOONS department," Laika explained quickly.

"More likely the LAPD handled them, unless they were active crime scenes," Alfred clarified.

"I had a day off yesterday," Evie added, "So I did some sleuthing. I called around the public records and got the files that reporters use."

There was a flicker of disbelief in Alfred's eyes. "How did you get this level of detail, such as the list of the stolen items?"

"Oh, that was easy, I..." Evie trailed off mid-sentence, glancing at her packmate.

Laika knew the truth; Evie had called the stores saying she was Glenwood MOONS. But Alfred knew they weren't on this case. Laika stepped in quickly to cover, "We got them from the police reports."

"Do you have copies of these reports?" Alfred inquired.

To Laika's eyes, he looked slightly more interested in the case now. Because he suspected they broke the law, or because they were on to something was unclear. "We have them pinned on the murder board-"

"It's a *mystery* board, Laika!" Evie interjected sharply.

"That's what I said," Laika waved her hand, grinning cheerfully. The tension was diffused with her bad joke. "I can show you if you want?"

Alfred's smile went from polite to warm. "Yes, I would like that."

Popping up from the table, Laika motioned for him to follow her into the hall. She could hear Evie sighing loudly, but again ignored her. The mystery board was in their shared bedroom. Once they were out of the earshot of the main room Alfred added, "I also keep a murder board at home. I rarely bother calling it a mystery board, even if technically correct."

Laughter rang out as Laika led them down the hall. "Oh my god, that does sound so bad out loud... but I'd really like to see it sometime."

"Perhaps if we are working the same case then we can share one."

"I'll hold you to that." Laika pushed open her bedroom door and headed straight for the closet. They had a small walk-in with one side for each woman, and the back wall had the cork board they used to track cases.

She then realized that he hadn't followed her. "Something wrong?"

Alfred was standing in the hall. "Not particularly, but we may be better served if you bring it out here."

"Why?" Laika looked around knowing the room wasn't too much of a mess.

"You have no curtains in here," he answered.

Laika's head snapped around, realizing she'd taken them down. "Whoops. Yeah, we put them up in the living room for you."

"Very kind of you, but it does prohibit me as much as social standards do from entering your bedroom." He flashed her a quick grin.

The chime of the doorbell reached Laika's ears, but she didn't react. Her mind was still processing Alfred's words. Her roommates were closer to the door anyway. Was he flirting with her? This was the second time since they left the table he'd said something that, if you squinted, was flirty. She was sure of it, and if she thought back on their first meeting he might have been doing the same then.

She felt certain she was right while staring back at that easy smile. Laika took a moment to duck into the closet and gather her thoughts. Did she want to respond? If Alfred was just naturally flirtatious that was fine. But if he was serious, Laika wasn't sure she wanted that.

"Laika, were you expecting more guests for lunch?" Alfred asked, keeping his voice low enough that she'd hear but it wouldn't carry.

Those words were enough to shake her back to the present. Laika unhooked the board off the wall. She had all of their lunch to decide if she was actually interested in Alfred beyond magic. Then her brain caught up with the question. "No?"

"Are you certain? There are more people in the living room."

Laika strained her ears for a moment then swore. She rushed out of the room, handing the murder board to Alfred as she ran past. Why were they here?

"Hi, Baby!" Lavender Lowell was standing in the living room as Laika burst in. Luca was eyeing the leather coat on the couch with suspicion.

"Mom! Dad! What are you doing here?"

CHAPTER 16
LUNCH

Laika
October 13th, 2018
Night Claw Residence, Glenwood, CA

This was the most awkward lunch of her life. Laika wanted to curl up in a ball and just hide under the table. Introductions had been crazy enough with her new roommates, never mind Alfred following her out from the hallway.

There wasn't room for seven people around the table, so Shelly had taken her plate with thanks back to her room. She claimed she had a game raid to plan for. Even Tor had run off after ten minutes, swearing that work needed her there early.

Lavender Lowell was the queen of the table, dressed in a skin-tight leopard print dress. While Laika loved her mother, the woman was loud and whenever she came out to California she dressed like something out of a bad movie. At least she'd dished out food for everyone before chatting with Evie about her flight earlier.

Her father, Luca, picked at his food. He kept glancing at her, then Alfred, and back down at the meal. She could tell he was annoyed she hadn't listened to him warning her they'd be here today. "So... how's work?"

"Same as last time you asked," shrugged Laika.

"Really? Nothing you want to tell me about... at all?" Luca pressed once more. That tone and those furrowed eyebrows warned his daughter he knew more than he'd said.

Laika swore under her breath.

"I heard that!" Luca shot back. Embarrassment colored Laika's face. She had just been thinking it would be fun to work on her case. Now her father was interrogating her lifestyle instead. Without missing a beat, Luca clarified, "Climbing collapsing roller coasters?"

"I had to! And it was only one job," Laika quickly defended.

Her mother cut in praising Laika. "See, I told you she'd have a reason. She had to." There wasn't an ounce of sarcasm in that statement, only pride.

Shaking his head in disagreement, Luca countered, "That's not a good enough reason for you doing anything that dangerous."

"You wouldn't care if I did these 'dangerous' things in Denver," Laika snapped back. She knew Luca was worried about her, but she also knew he had ulterior motives. Her father wanted her to move back home. He'd tried everything from guilt to cutting off financial help to make it happen. The Lowell family had, once again, dissolved into a run-of-the-mill argument. They hadn't sat down to a meal in years without some variation of this.

"You'd have your aunt if you were in Denver. Cheyenne is one of the best moonlighters out there and you know she'd take you into her group," Luca reminded.

"But it wouldn't be California," Laika pointed out.

Evie spoke up, "This might not be the right time to talk about this."

Laika watched her packmate look pointedly at Alfred. That dragged everyone's gaze to the vampire. Laika thought her face would catch fire when she realized she'd been fighting with her parents in front of him.

"I do realize this is none of my business," Alfred was unfazed by the looks, "but I may be able to offer an explanation for why the Night Claw pack was active at that particular situation."

"You can?" Laika's eyes went wide. She hadn't expected that at all. He hadn't been there as far as she could remember.

"Yes. Laika and Evie were already on the scene because they were with Officers Kirkland and Leavenworth at the time of the call. All Senior Moonlighters in Glenwood were at least 30 minutes behind them in arriving."

Laika was surprised Alfred had remembered so many details from the little she'd texted him. Maybe he'd read the police report as well. His blue eyes glanced down to meet hers, and she could have sworn Alfred's smile brightened for just a moment.

"We only went to help with organizing people," Evie added.

Laika continued, "But when we got there no one could clear the scene to let the firefighters in."

Alfred picked up the explanation, "The policies do state that until a magically rated moonlighter or officer clears the scene, no one is allowed to enter. To prevent more loss when lethal magic may still be active, as I'm sure you know. Only moonlighters could enter and, given the times on the report, if they had waited for others then no one would have made it off that roller coaster."

Silence hung in the air.

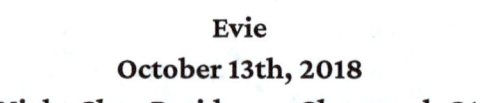

Evie
October 13th, 2018
Night Claw Residence, Glenwood, CA

Evie's head was pounding. She knew better than to let her empathy run free during a Lowell family fight. As much as she loved Luca and Lavender, more than her own parents, this was a common problem.

Her surrogate mother gave off emotions that were like flat notes with no detail. Pride, anger, joy, and other basic feelings. Solid walls with no cracks or deceit. Some people were like this and Evie assumed it was just they honestly felt things without worrying about them.

Luca and Laika were both more chaotic in their feelings, like hurricanes crashing into each other. Her friend wore her emotions on her face. But her father was calm on the surface and spiraling on the inside. Evie assumed he'd learned to hide them after years as the alpha of the Red Earth pack. Together... they were enough to make her head ache.

The real cause of the throbbing, though, was the last person left at the table. Alfred was a black hole. Evie could see him react to the conversation. A crinkle around the eyes when listening, but no emotion behind it. Even when he gave her friend a smile, there was nothing. From the moment he walked through the door he'd thrown her off. The longer they sat here, the creepier it got.

No matter how much Evie turned up her empathy, the vampire was devoid of emotion. Finally, she turned it back down to a manageable level to help negotiate the brewing fight.

Luca was the first to speak, "And you would know this how?"

"I am one of the Senior Moonlighters in Glenwood MOONS," answered Alfred.

Laika stared at the vampire and Evie could read shock mixed with admiration coming from her friend. He'd offered up an explanation that Luca could hardly argue with, easily putting an end to this argument. A renewed wave of annoyance at Laika's fascination with the emotionless void she was sitting next to bubbled up. There was nothing exciting about Alfred other than the fact he moonlighted. Shaking her head slightly, Evie forced herself to focus back on the conversation.

"Well I'm proud of you, baby," Lavender praised her daughter, then patted her arm.

Sensing he was outnumbered, Luca threw up his hands in frustration. "Alright, alright. But you two don't need to be doing dangerous missions like that. You know you can always come home. The cost of living is better in Colorado."

Evie was reminded why she felt closer to these two than her parents. He'd meant those words, despite no blood bond existing between them. If Evie moved to Colorado, then Luca would make sure she had a roof over her head and could get on her feet.

"We know. But what would we do in Denver? There's not even a beach," Evie teased with a smirk.

"We have better coffee though," Luca shot back. But amusement was already pulling on his lips. Moods in the room were lifting. "You could still visit LA when you wanted the beach."

Laika interrupted. "Speaking of visiting. Why are you here?"

With a snort, Luca's attention turned back to his daughter. "Why do you think we're here? There's been two dangerous magical events."

"Three," Evie corrected, then internally groaned. That wouldn't make anything better.

Laika mumbled under her breath. Even though the redhead couldn't hear it, she saw Luca frown and Alfred pull a smile under control.

"Were you here on council business?" Evie asked. She was starting to put together the events of the week. There were only two events that brought Luca out to California: Laika asking, and the supernatural council.

"Uh... I probably shouldn't talk about it." Luca looked uncomfortable at the line of questioning.

That brought a frown to both women. Evie knew for sure based on Luca's emotions and expression that she'd guessed correctly. Her eyes dropped to the barely touched meal in front of her. Talk of the council soured her mood for more than just the change in Luca's demeanor.

The council was made up of representatives of all the supernatural races on the west coast; every member was powerful, well-respected, and influential. So it was only natural that Evie's father, Everard Belle, was also a member. She hated that her favorite dad knew her biological father, because then he got to see the worst of what Evie could be.

"Are you seriously not going to tell us?" Laika pleaded.

Luca waved a hand, "If I could, I would, Kid. Things are serious and events have the council worried."

"Oh you're being dramatic," Lavender laughed, as nothing ever brought her mood down.

"I'm not being dramatic." There was a big spike in Luca's aura as he disagreed.

Evie looked up with concern. "What's wrong?"

Luca put down his fork before folding his hands. He looked every bit the concerned parent as he turned to Evie. "The council is pretty sure that all three of the major events that happened recently are connected. There is a good chance that whoever is doing this isn't done."

"Okay?" Evie was surprised that he was telling them so much after saying no.

"A lot of people have died and specialists are being pulled in from all over the country." Luca crossed his arms with a frown.

Laika cut in. "You mean like Hazel?"

"I would not call her a reliable specialist," Alfred sharply disagreed. When everyone looked at him to continue he waved it off. "Apologies, you were saying."

Picking up his story, Luca continued, "Yes, Miss Amadori is one of the specialists that the LA vampires called for help. I think she's from the east coast."

"But there are plenty more on their way," Lavender added with a reassuring nod.

"Too many people," her husband sighed. "With all this firepower on the way, it seems pretty clear to me that Glenwood could end up a warzone soon. That's why Everard asked me to talk to you."

Evie stared back at the worried eyes of Luca. Her world began crumbling as she silently clenched the table. Her next words were chosen carefully. "Why did he want that?"

"He asked me to let you know that he's concerned about your safety. Your father really wants you to call him to let him know if you need anything."

Everything around Evie went hazy as the words struck her like bullets to the gut. She had desperately needed her father when she lived in his house, but he was never there. There was always a business trip or council meeting he needed to attend.

The woman Everard married was an abusive shrew who denied her daughter even the most basic affection. Years were spent having small pieces of herself ripped off by Sylvia Belle. She was the reason that Evie had hated everything about the way she looked and the hobbies she liked. Even when Evie was showing signs that she'd be able to shift, her mother had berated her, making her feel unloveable. Only years of unconditional love and acceptance from the Lowells had begun to heal that damage.

Now, her father was crossing the line by going to her surrogate dad to force contact she never wanted. "If I need anything? Is he serious?"

Lavender reached out a soothing hand to rub along Evie's arm. "Honey. Calm down, you're close to a frenzy. When was the last time you ran?"

Rage was sweeping through Evie's mind even as she heard the truth behind Lavender's warning. She hadn't run all month, being far too busy with work. But despite knowing that a frenzy was really possible, she felt her hands go through the table with a loud crack.

"Evie," Laika's voice was in her ear on the other side, "It's okay. You don't have to call him back. Right, Dad?"

"No, you don't. I delivered the message but I never said I'd do more than that," Luca clarified quickly.

Evie's emotions were too riled up, making it impossible for her to calm down. She couldn't find good words, but she managed, "I'm not hungry anymore."

Before anyone could poke her wounds again she practically sprinted out of the room.

Laika
October 13th, 2018
Night Claw Residence, Glenwood, CA

"I'm so sorry," Laika said for the fourth time.

Alfred was putting his coat on, taking his time to do the buttons. "It is quite alright. You need to take care of your friend and family. I need to make it into LA today anyways."

"Still... I'm so sorry. This entire day has been a mess."

Pausing to give her a warm smile, Alfred suggested, "Perhaps we can try again with dinner on Friday?"

"This Friday?" Laika pulled out her phone. She was glad he was giving her a second chance to sit down and talk about the case. They'd barely gotten started when her family hijacked, and then crashed, lunch.

"Yes, the 19th." Alfred finished with the last of his buckles but waited on her answer for the rest.

"Yeah, I can do Friday. I have work so it would need to be in the evening."

The vampire flashed her a teasing look. "That is usually when dinner is served."

"Oh..." Laika flushed for a moment. "I'll text you later and we can set up the details?"

"Of course." Alfred clicked his helmet into place. Laika opened the door as she bid him goodbye. She wanted to know if he'd really walked here in that gear, but her remaining guests needed her attention.

Once Alfred was gone, Luca descended like a vulture with more questions. "Who was that exactly?"

"Shush. He can probably hear you still." Laika scolded her father, realizing he'd heard the entire conversation just now.

"So? It's not a rude question to ask my daughter why she's got older men over."

"Dad! He's a moonlighter like me and he came over to help us with a case involving magic. I thought it would be polite to at least feed him while he was here."

That brought a concerned look to Luca's face.

"Dad!" Laika rebuked again, realizing where his mind had gone. "I was talking about the lasagna. It had blood in it for him!"

"What?" Her father's face turned a few shades of green.

This was Laika's turn to give him exasperated looks. As if she'd feed everyone at the table human blood... "Relax. Tor added it to the tomatoes in the red dish. We only ate out of the white dish. That's why she brought his plate from the kitchen."

Recounting the events in his head, Luca seemed happy enough with that answer. "Still, you shouldn't be inviting any vampires into your house. At the very least you should put up a hexed mirror on the door."

Laika rolled her eyes at the suggestion. Hexed mirrors revealed people for what they were supernaturally. Plenty of shops hung them over the registers, but for werewolves at most they had glowing eyes. Done with this conversation, she headed back to where her mother was clearing up the pieces of the table. "Need help, Mom?"

Lavender had kicked off her leopard-print high heels near the door, put the dishes in the sink, and was stacking pieces of IKEA plywood in the corner. "No baby, I have it under control. Who hasn't broken something in a rage before? I need to check the floor for glass to be safe then I'll put it out in the trash can."

"Thanks. I'm sorry about all this." All Laika felt like she was doing was apologizing to everyone.

Lavender shrugged, "We all knew it was a sore spot for Evie. That 'wolf' is lucky I didn't take a swing at him myself when he asked."

"I held her back," Luca explained.

"I wish you hadn't," Laika growled.

Luca groaned, "Both of you realize that attacking Crescent Bell's alpha could be seen as an act of war, right?"

Laika bit out, "If he deserves it, then no one would blame you."

"That's not how it works. You can't always punch your problems away," reminded Luca, as he always did.

"It works for me," Lavender and Laika spoke in unison.

Luca sighed.

INTERLUDE - BUILDING

The Anarchist
October 16th, 2018
...somewhere in Glenwood, CA

"You fucked up last time," whispered a voice in the Ritualist's head, "You barely completed my spell."

"I did complete it," snapped back the Ritualist. She hadn't expected after the last ritual that she'd make contact. Since then, this... passenger had been living inside of her head, making her feel crazy.

"You almost didn't. You need to be more focused, my little Anarchist," the voice teased her with that stupid name the news had given her.

"Stop that," she hissed back.

"Annnnarchisst," droned on the voice again. She could hear laughter behind the word and for a moment rethought if she wanted to continue.

Names and faces rushed to the front of her thoughts. Her Love was depending on her to become powerful so she could save them.

Her REAL mother, who lost her way so long ago she didn't even know how lost she was. Her father, who had dragged her kicking and screaming into his family so she could carry on *his* name. All of the people trying to stand in the way of her happiness.

The Anarchist wanted to cast the next ritual in her summoning.

Her last ritual had been a mess of almost epic proportions. She'd poured so much time into studying and preparation, only for a barely passing grade. The magic had come to her so easily but forcing the earth to move hadn't been as simple as she first thought.

If there hadn't been a delay in traffic slowing down the response teams, then everything would have been a total failure. Even when the Anarchist had finally gotten the right rhythms during the last ritual, she'd had to give up or be found out.

"You're distracted again," pointed out the voice.

"Only because you're distracting me. This one is going to be a lot harder than the last," reminded the Anarchist, trying to center herself again. The voice in her head was starting to vex her.

"The last one shouldn't have been that hard. You just aren't very good with earth magic. Not in the blood, I guess," the voice teased.

She worked on the fourth circle, trying to ignore the voice. The next element was very malleable, but hard to get a physical reaction from. The book laying open next to her showed old symbols that were all but unreadable. Thankfully, the Anarchist had tracked down a better dwarven to elven dictionary that actually included magical text. She didn't have to guess on the stroke order of the runes anymore.

With every stroke of the Anarchist's paint brush she got closer to starting. This time she'd be more careful not to drag her Love into the action again. If she'd been a little slower last time killing the ritual, she may have hurt her Love. But this time she'd make her Love so proud.

Just a few more minutes and the Anarchist would turn up the pressure on the people trying to ruin her plans.

CHAPTER 17
PRESSURE

Evie
October 16th, 2018
Hot of the Presses, Glenwood, CA

Evie had been in a spiral for days now. After she'd ruined lunch it had taken hours for her to calm down. She'd tried a shower, worked out, and finally just caved to curling up with a book in bed for the rest of the day. Laika had coaxed her out to say goodbye to Luca and Lavender, but it had been an awkward parting.

The Lowells were the picture of patience with her. Not another word was spoken about Evie's outburst, or her father's request for contact. They'd just made her promise to take a run soon. In turn, they promised that they'd have all her favorites for Thanksgiving when the girls went out to Colorado next month. The warmth radiating from them had only made her feel more guilty.

'Blindsided' wasn't a strong enough word for what Evie had felt sitting there. She'd made a scene, not only in front of a practical stranger, but her two roommates knew too. Laika had stopped any questions about the missing table, but the redhead wouldn't blame either of them for taking off after that.

"Penny for your thoughts?"

Tony's voice brought Evie's focus crashing back down to the present. The pair were sitting in the back of a cafe at their boss' latest publicity stunt.

"Not today," she protested.

"But you're in such a delectable spiral today." There was an edge of mockery to the man's tone.

Evie tried to ignore Tony as her eyes trailed to their boss.

Arik was up front, charming the guests flooding in for Hot off the Presses' grand opening. He had been annoyed he only ranked enough for a cafe slash bookstore opening. However, Natasha had reminded him that beggars couldn't be choosers when they were trying to maintain relevance. He'd shut up and put on a smile.

Evie focused on how much the elf was secretly enjoying their trip to block out her pity party.

Pressing again, Tony needled for more information. "I might go as high as a nickel if you have some juicy drama going on."

"My thoughts are worth more than your pocket change."

"I doubt they're that unique."

"Then they aren't that important for you to know."

"Oh boo, you're just no fun right now," Tony held up his hand to stop any retort. "Let me guess anyways."

"Please don't," Evie begged.

The vampire held up his hand, ticking off possible reasons. "Perhaps it's trouble in paradise, sharing a bed with Laika isn't half as fun as you thought. Either you need more space or less."

"No," Evie rolled her eyes. Laika had crashed on the couch the night of the outburst but they'd been back to normal by the next morning.

"What about that new 'hottie' I saw on your insta? The one that took you to the club but is only into the fashionably undead." That was Tony, always focused on her current lack of a love life.

"Dating Tor would be a bad idea, it doesn't matter how much of a 'hottie' she is." Evie had admitted a couple weeks into living together that as pretty as her new roommate was, a fling would cost them stable rent.

"Is it just your time of the month?"

"Tony!" Evie whipped her head back around, ready to tear into him for that one.

"What? You're a werewolf and your mood changes like the moon, and since it's half full, you're only half sane." He dazzled her with a toothy grin.

Her silver eyes glowered at the vampire. "Are you done?"

"On a scale of Warm to Scalding, how close was I?" Tony shined with joyful energy.

Admittedly his teasing had raised Evie's spirit a little bit. Her co-worker was a kid in a candy store when it came to drama. Nothing the woman said would stop him from gorging himself. But that didn't mean she'd be telling him about her family drama.

"Well?" The vampire insisted.

"Ice cold." Evie scanned his aura and face, looking for a way to distract him. Her eyes settled on his tiny fangs and an idea flashed into her mind.

Tony scoffed, "You lie; I am amazing at this game. It's like I can read you like a book."

Evie paused, knowing it would annoy him. This could be shifted into a win for her since Tony was the most experienced empath she knew. Even if their powers didn't work exactly the same.

"What's bothering you?" Tony dropped the mockery as he reacted to something in her mood.

"Have you ever run into anyone with absolutely no emotions?"

"Is that all?" The vampire rebounded his teasing by laughing loud enough people turned to look at them.

"What do you mean is that all?!" Evie felt her cheeks redden.

"Sweet summer wolf, there are plenty of people out there that are just quiet," explained Tony.

Evie bit her lip trying to gather her thoughts. "No, he wasn't just quiet. I've met quiet and low before, but this was empty."

He raised an eyebrow, "I sincerely doubt that. Only the upper echelon of the LA Coven can block out people like us. Well, them and some powerful witches."

"This guy was a vampire," Evie quickly pointed out, "That new friend of Laika's."

"The boring one?"

"Yes, but I swear to you. Tony, I had my empathy on full blast and I got nothing!"

Again Tony gave her a skeptical look. "He's probably just one of those quiet people. Who else was around?"

Evie started listing, "Well, Laika and her parents-"

Raising a hand to cut her off, Tony shook his head. "So... you were sitting at a table with loud ass werewolves and couldn't hear a vampire? Honey. I've met your friend. Her emotions are like having a loudspeaker plugged into my head. Is her family really any better?"

Evie couldn't argue with him anymore. Not that she didn't have more to say, proving she wasn't crazy. But a wave of fear suddenly pressed down on her from all sides. Given how Tony's eyes widened, she wasn't the only one feeling it either. She went into work mode, scanning around them for the cause. She was expecting screaming to follow a moment later.

But there was a sudden lack of voices as silence fell over the cafe.

Evie felt pain in her chest like her lungs were struggling to get air. Heavy pressure was starting to push down on her. She forced herself to slow down and take a deep breath, feeling momentary relief. The invisible force bearing down on her was intensifying with each passing moment.

"Evie?" Tony placed a hand on her arm. He seemed unaffected by whatever was stealing the breath from everyone else. "Honey, what's wrong? Why are you panicking?"

The redhead gave him wide eyes as she realized whatever was causing the air pressure to rise on her wouldn't affect a vampire. He didn't rely on his lungs to breathe. Evie took another deep breath and managed to gasp. "Call 911."

"And tell them what?"

People around them were grabbing at their necks and trying to fill their lungs. Fear and confusion were building just as quickly as the air pressure. A few were already on the floor or with their heads between their knees.

Evie managed to send a text.

EVIE

help

bad air

LAIKA

What's going on?

Before the werewolf could send more details, Arik appeared at her side ripping her purse out of her hands. He was holding his breath which seemed to have insulated him from the pressure just enough to get across the room. His hands tore through the contents of Evie's bag.

Tony voiced what Evie was thinking. "What are you looking for?" Even he sounded a little strained as the pressure continued to climb.

Arik didn't answer, or even glance up. His hand closed on something and a jolt of relief rolled off the elf. He lifted the object free, popping the lid off of it in a smooth motion. Confusion colored Evie's face as she recognized her lipstick. A lovely pink she'd only used twice. What the hell did he want with her makeup? Glee radiated off Arik as he pulled up his sleeves quickly. He brought the new lipstick down onto his arm. Drawing rushed lines, he stained his skin with the pink pigment. The symbols looked too purposeful to be random.

Evie opened her mouth to scold him, but felt the pressure collapsing her lungs again. What were you supposed to do in a high air pressure situation? Was it to take deep breaths, or hold your breath? The lack of air was already affecting her thinking.

Just as suddenly as it started, all the crushing weight lifted up.

"There," Arik sighed. He was gulping down air with quick breaths. "I managed to push back some of that. But I don't know how long I can hold this."

"You did what?" Evie pressed after she could speak again.

"He used his magic." Tony answered for the elf. He'd jumped up from his seat, grabbing all their bags in the process. "Get up."

"Your magic?" Evie did as she was told, reaching for her purse back.

Arik didn't give up the lipstick, instead repeating the same symbols again on his other arm. "Yes, I already told you that Skysong elves have weather control. I am pushing back against the caster so that we can breathe. Someone took control of the air to turn up the pressure on us, and once they break through my magic we have minutes at most."

"Can you dispel all of this?" Evie asked, feeling tentative hope forming.

"Hell no. I'm not combat trained. It's a miracle this worked given the actual caster hit such a large area this hard." Arik continued writing the symbols.

Evie pulled her phone out to relay the information.

EVIE

> There is a magical attack happening right now.

> Arik says that someone just jacked up the air pressure.

LAIKA

Can you call Owen and give him the details?

He knows something is up.

Get out of there now!

EVIE

I'll try.

"How many people can you fit under your bubble of protection?" Evie's eyes were sweeping through the cafe. People looked almost normal again after a few lungfuls of air, and far too calm for what was happening.

"I have no idea," admitted Arik. He copied over the symbol again on his arm. "I don't push my limits. Why would I?"

"For moments like this?" Evie glared at him, but pulled herself back in check. Why would he assume some normal day someone would try to explode his lungs? That wasn't reasonable.

Arik shrugged, "I still don't know how big I can get this or how stable."

"He's got a range of about a store and a half on either side. I can feel those people starting to wake up," Tony answered again. His gaze was distant and his words slow.

"Are you sure?" Evie needed to know so she could plan how to save the most people with them.

"Yes, because I'm keeping them all calm," Tony snipped.

Arik gave his assistant a level stare and warned. "Tony. You know the consequences of this many people."

"Do you want them to trample us like a frenzied pack of idiots? Or do you want them to walk calmly to the exit?" the vampire snapped back.

Evie looked between them, catching up on what Tony was doing. Compulsion or emotional control against someone's will was illegal. People could press charges against Tony if they realized what happened later. She should have told him to stop. But he wasn't wrong, people would get hurt in a panic right now.

"I'm not paying for your lawsuits," Arik stated. He looked a bit tired already from the few minutes of holding the pressure at bay.

Evie took control. "Alright. Here's the plan. Arik, you'll need to stay at the center of our group so we can get the most people in your radius. Tony, you'll need to lead the way while you blanket everyone with your powers. Exclude me if you can and I'll get people into the safe zone as we go."

Both men looked skeptical at the werewolf's bid to be in control.

"I'm a trained moonlighter," Evie reminded them with a hint of steel in her tone. "Any other day of the week either of you can boss me around. But today I outrank you. Any questions?"

Arik sparked up in a moment of excitement, likely as he realized he'd be doing actual moonlighting work. He nodded, "Of course. I'll need more lipstick to keep this up."

"I can handle that. Go put yourself at the front door." She pointed at the doorway.

Evie took a deep breath, watching them do as she said before climbing up on the chair so she had height over the room. The werewolf had a plastic MOONS ID that she kept tucked in her vest... which was sitting in the trunk of her car back at Arik's house. She pulled out her wallet knowing this would be a bold faced lie, but time was essential right now. This was a desperate situation so hopefully no one looked too close. Clearing her throat, Evie pulled her driver's license out and held it up. "Everyone! I'm Evie Belle with MOONS Glenwood. Me and my colleagues are going to get you all out of here safely."

Eyes turned in her direction. They all had placid looks but she could feel hope, worry, and relief filter through the forced calm.

"I need everyone on their feet. If you can't live without it, then leave it behind. The only exception is your lipstick. Ladies and queens: if you got some, then get it out. My colleague can keep us in a safe zone, but he needs it for his magic. Understood?"

Everyone nodded slowly as her words sunk in. Then they started to do as she instructed, picking up purses or children who couldn't move quickly. Evie had half expected the crowd to move like they were drugged given how calm they acted, but they followed directions like someone running a few minutes late for their next appointment. Just not running for their lives.

Her hand swept towards Arik, "Please head to the front door and stay close together around my colleague."

"Aren't you just Little Miss Bossy?" Tony commented, offering a hand to help her down.

"It's that or we wait too long," Evie reminded.

The vampire had no response to that. His attention was focused on keeping everyone calm, which was easier while they could breathe. Scrolling through her phone, Evie found her contact for Owen. The officer had gone drinking with them a few times when he wasn't working. She thanked whatever power was listening for that, as she pressed to dial.

The phone rang once before Owen answered. "Evie! Laika said you were on scene? Are you alright? What's the situation?"

"Yes, I am on scene at Hot off the Presses' Cafe. For the moment I'm fine, but I don't know how long that'll be true," answered Evie.

"I don't know that place. Hold on, I'm pulling up the location." Evie listened to him muttering to himself as he worked. "Found it. Shit, you're at the epicenter of this based on the reports we're getting from the edges."

That got a heavy sigh from Evie. "Of course I am."

"The pressure zone is about a mile wide and grows every couple of minutes. I'm not even on the scene yet so this is all based on 911 calls. I think your best bet is to go north and meet up with us," commanded Owen.

"I'm not alone. I managed to get a lot of people into my safe area." Evie was unsure how to explain everything. She stuck to the truth. "I am, or was, at a thing for my day job. My boss is here and he used his own magic to get things under control."

"That's lucky. How many are injured where you are? With the radius, we are contacting LA for medical backup."

Evie cut him off. "We don't need them..." The words matched the empty cold she felt in every direction surrounding her.

"Why not?" Owen's tone was careful as he waited for the answer.

She looked around at the people who were crowding towards the door and lowered her voice again. "No one outside of where I am made it past 5 minutes. I could barely breathe when Arik managed to push the air pressure back."

"... Shit."

"I'll keep all my senses open just in case someone else is still alive."

The line stayed silent while the officer found words. "I need you to stay on the line with me. You're my eyes and ears inside of this."

"I understand," Evie confirmed.

"Evie, we have to go," Arik's voice called out from the door expectantly. He'd just traced another layer of symbols on his arms.

She held up a hand in acknowledgement before jogging across the room. The unusually calm crowd parted easily, letting her pass to the front. Likely Tony had his attention half on the werewolf so that the people bent around her.

Evie realized she needed to tell Owen what was going on with that magic. She picked her wording carefully not to give anyone ideas. "Officer Kirkland, there is a secondary magic being used by my current team. Approved by me to keep everyone focused and I'll give you the full run down when we arrive safely."

"Okay?" Owen sounded uneasy. He took the hint not to press.

"I need to switch you to my bluetooth as well." Evie fumbled around with the work issued earpiece. She'd been given one so that she could use both hands while on the phone for Arik. Once it was secured to her ear, she tested, "Can you hear me?"

Owen responded affirmative. His voice was muffled after that, likely turning away to relay the information to Aaron on the other end.

For her part, Evie turned her attention to getting the crowd moving. "We've got to go about half a mile north and we'll meet up with Glenwood's first responders. Everyone needs to stay calm, close, and keep moving. If you need help then call my name."

"You heard the lady," Tony urged. He was a few steps ahead of them trying to stay in the lead. At his command the crowd started forward, filing out the doors into the streets.

Evie counted how many people were with them as they exited. Then she weaved forward to whisper to the vampire. "Do you sense anyone else we need to help?"

"There is no one else, Evie." Tony's voice was flat. She knew his range of sensing was much wider than hers.

Evie frowned but let it pass without comment. "Go north along this street. When I get our next directions I'll let you know."

"I know how to make my way out of downtown." The bite was back in Tony. "You go make sure Arik keeps his shit together."

The elf had just exited and was already starting to walk in the wrong direction. All of his arms were stained in pinks, reds, and purples.

"This way," Evie urged him, taking his shoulder, "Just follow Tony's horrible shirt." Arik gave her a small smile in response, but Evie could see the strain weighing on him.

The street looked like a typical day in Glenwood at a glance. Midday sun shone down on sidewalks devoid of people. When she looked closer, the signs of disaster were more obvious. Across the streets, spiderweb-like cracks were growing in the glass window panes. Even the thicker windshields had small lines forming. There was an unnatural silence.

Evie kept Owen updated in a low voice as they walked. She even asked a few of the people to take photos on their phones.

"So far so good," grumbled Arik.

"Let's hope it stays this way," Evie replied. But her wishes died in her throat as she kicked a tire sticking out from an alley between buildings. Her gaze followed the tire back to a downed bike. A spike of fear shot up her spine as the werewolf took in the collapsed rider.

Before she could do anything a wave of panic surged from her all around her.

Then Arik stopped dead in his tracks. "Oh..."

Forcing her eyes back to the path in front of them, Evie felt her stomach churning. This was the end of any denial about what happened. The next street wasn't lucky enough to have a skysong elf capable of buying them time to escape.

The first of many casualties was upon them. A figure lay crumpled against the side of a bakery. The woman had raised her hands to her throat, as if expecting a physical cause for her lack of breath. But there had been nothing there. She'd died minutes ago where she'd fallen. Further up the street, the scene repeated over and over.

Fear grew as Evie took in every terrifying detail of the silent streets. A primal energy clawed at her mind, trying to push its way up. This was wrong on every level. She needed to run and if she let the wolf in her go free, then they'd run far and fast. The werewolf fought through the feeling.

Fingers gripped Evie's arm. Arik had paled to almost sheet white as he saw the scene as well.

"It'll be okay." There was no conviction behind Evie's words. They were the only two not under Tony's control. The crowd behind them was able to block everything out, but they could not.

"I-" The elf was still staring, in a state of shellshock at the sight.

"Arik! Snap out of it!" Evie's voice was stern. She had no idea how often he needed to keep repeating the spell, but now wasn't the time to find out.

"But..."

"But nothing. We can't do anything for them now. We can only save ourselves and everyone else who came out to see you today. Do you understand?" Evie put her hand on top of his.

That seemed to crack through the haze. Arik's gaze went to her as he realized what she'd implied. All of the people in his bubble were only alive because they'd stopped in to see him.

"You are their only hope right now. You wanted to be an action star? This is it!"

His emerald eyes blinked slowly, and after a long beat, Arik nodded. "Y-yes."

Evie took his hand off her arm, curled her fingers around his, and gave him the best smile she could manage. While her boss needed a firm hand most days, the little bit of warmth had a greater impact on his emotions. He squeezed her hand in return.

"I will keep myself together," Arik assured. He used his free hand to keep redrawing the symbols that prevented their deaths.

"Good," Evie agreed.

The group continued for two streets before they hit their first blockage. Three cars had smashed into each other, taking up the entire road and both sidewalks.

"Owen. I have a problem. Alder is completely impassable," Evie explained to her bluetooth.

Owen asked, "Can you backtrack and take Willow?"

"We can, but there is another problem."

"What?" Owen waited for the other shoe to drop.

Evie looked up at her boss clinging to her. "Arik is exhausted and I don't know how much longer he can keep this up."

"What are your choices?" Owen pressed.

There weren't any good options. Evie looked ahead at the blocked roads. She could try to get people over the cars, but they had elderly and children. However, turning back might be too much for Arik.

"How close are we from the edge?" Evie asked.

"It's still growing... right now it's about a mile and a half wide." Owen explained.

"Seriously?" Evie forced herself to lower her voice after that outburst. "Okay. I'm sorry, but I can't keep the collateral damage down. I'm not strong enough to do this otherwise."

"I don't care. Smash down the damn walls if you need to," Owen commanded, "Just get yourself and the others out."

Evie took a deep breath trying to calm herself. Her eyes looked up at Arik and she said, "I'll be back in a minute. Just stay here."

"Stay alive," demanded Arik, letting go of her hand.

She wove through to where Tony led the group. He looked pissed off at the obstacles before them. "What's the plan? I can't keep this powder keg from exploding all day."

"I'm going to clear the road. Just don't let anyone follow me." Evie laid out the plans for him.

Tony groaned, "Yeah, I got it. Go be a big bad wolf, just be quick about it."

Evie had a decent idea where the edge of their safe zone was; she paused there. In front of them three cars were piled up, needing to be cleared. There were people in those vehicles so she couldn't just throw them around carelessly. She needed to shift to make this happen.

Quickly she pulled off her shirt, shoes, skirt, and undergarments then packed them in her bag. The bluetooth followed a moment later since it wouldn't fit in her ears in a few minutes. Normally Evie wouldn't undress in public, but this was desperate times.

She prepared herself for the shift she'd need to reach hybrid form, hoping that it would be fast enough. The invisible timers were ticking down, fueling her urgency. Either Arik or Tony's powers could run out at any moment...

The wolf rose up to meet Evie's call in an adrenaline induced rage. Changes raced out from her shoulders and down her arms as they started to shift much faster than normal. Was the pressure in the air causing this, or her stress?

Knees buckled then Evie hit the asphalt of the road. She heard yelling, but she couldn't respond. Her voice was lost to a wordless snarl. A spike of worry shot through the werewolf's mind. She'd been so focused on getting the strength to clear the street, she'd forgotten she would lose her ability to communicate with the others. Evie just had to pray they could keep it together without her voice of calm reason. As the last ripples of change ran along her skin, she pushed herself to stand again.

Massive hybrid hands stretched out in Evie's view. They'd be capable of pushing cars out of the way. Again she felt a spike of fear rushing around as all of Tony's emotional zombies caught sight of her form. Even his power couldn't fully squash their gut reactions. She hoped the vampire would keep everyone safe.

A run and a leap over the wrecked cars later, Evie landed neatly on the other side, putting the vehicles between her and the crowd of people. Maybe that would help them stay calm?

"Evie! Don't go that far!" Arik's voice called out as she dug her claws into the bumper of the first car. She glanced back but kept to her work. With a mighty heave, Evie began dragging the car further up the street. One of three cars was out of the way...

Arik called again, "I'm not kidding, if you go any further then I can't protect you."

Another car was already in process of being moved. The pathway would soon be opened enough for everyone to pass. Evie let the cars settle against the sidewalk. She could feel the pressure increasing as she reached the edge of Arik's magic. Her eyes swept up the street and to her dismay, she saw more cars strewn across the road.

Tony approached, shepherding his flock forward. "Can you move all of those?"

There was a half strangled sound before Evie just nodded.

"Can you move them quickly?" clarified the vampire.

Evie didn't have any conviction this time, but she was standing in front of everyone trusting her to save them. She nodded again.

"Off to work with you then." Tony shooed her away.

Arik tried to pull her back, "Evie. If you keep going out of the circle I can't keep the pressure off you."

A clawed hand raised up to stave the elf off. She knew the dangers already and directly looked at the crowd of people, then back at her boss. His eyes followed her gaze and he sighed.

Evie took her escape with a breath. She ran down the street trying to keep ahead of the group. Her shoulder smashed into car after car, forcing them out of the way before returning to the safe zone for a few seconds. This caused her lungs to scream at her with every step as her body rapidly shifted between pressures. Only her enhanced healing was keeping Evie moving.

Moving further and further down the street brought more sounds of freedom. The wail of police cars and people called them forward like a siren's song. Finally, as Evie heaved one more vehicle out of the roadway, she spotted her salvation. A GPD cruiser sat on what she assumed was the edge of this mess. Two familiar figures stood next to the car.

"Evie," Aaron yelled. He didn't rush forward, but his eyes were sweeping the street.

Glancing back at her charges, Evie felt her lungs burning again. She needed to make a choice quickly. Back to Arik's magic she went.

"Do you know them?" Tony asked. He could see the path to freedom as well. "They're tasty." Evie swirled her head to glare at him from a few feet above. Tony had his priorities in the wrong place, even at a time like this. "What? Did you call dibs on both of them?"

"Tony, shut up," Arik hissed. His arms were smeared with a rainbow of colors. Blues and blacks added to the mural now. He was dripping with sweat from continuously pushing his powers.

Safety was so close, but Evie could tell that Arik was at his limit. She made a judgment call and hoped that the vampire would catch up, in a literal sense. Two large hands grabbed Arik around the waist, before hefting him up over her shoulder. Then she ran for the edge.

Swearing followed her before Tony commanded his horde to run. There was a stampede of footsteps chasing her every step. Evie led them forward weaving through the path she'd created. She knew that the run would be rough on Arik. Similar feelings to sitting in the cafe were already creeping over her. The pressure was starting to build again.

A faint pop rang through Evie's ears as she passed an invisible barrier, signaling that she'd made it out. But she kept moving another ten feet before putting Arik down.

"Evie," Owen said as he appeared at her side, "Is this everyone?"

By the time she'd turned around Tony was out as well, but still controlling people to move forward. The werewolf scanned the crowd, counting them again. Then finally she nodded at Owen.

Aaron was noting down the counts and ushering people forward.

"Please keep moving. The incident zone is still growing and we can't stay here for long." The pressure zone wasn't even two miles wide yet and had already claimed more victims than any other case Evie had been on. How much worse would this get?

"Magic incoming," Owen yelled. As he did, a blue car with pitch black windows pulled around the corner.

Evie's head whipped up at the screeching of tires. She recognized it as a model with cameras installed to allow for daylight driving. Most vampires who had a car had this upgrade. Sure enough, when the door opened a feminine figure emerged wrapped in a long black coat, high boots, and face coverings. Her words were a little muffled but understandable. "Hi bunny; I see you're still running for your life."

The werewolf attempted to say "Hazel?" but it was more like a strangled yelp.

"Save your breath. I don't speak your language on Tuesdays." The vampire strode past, ignoring both officers as well.

Tony had released all of his minions, which meant they'd all started falling apart. He was sitting on the ground with his head between his knees.

All of the crowd was crying, collapsing, or screaming in some variety. None had gone after the vampire who took over their will yet. But the mess had created enough of a distraction that Aaron let Hazel pass undeterred.

Meanwhile, Owen had his hands full with Arik. The elf was being loaded into the back of the police cruiser just so he could sit. Again, no one was there to block the vampire's advance.

The bizarre words from Hazel had left Evie frozen with a stunned expression on her face. But seeing the scene falling apart, she pushed herself back into action. Her shift back to human form was slower than her shift before. She hid behind the cruiser to change. It must have been the adrenaline earlier causing the speed.

Fumbling with her bag, Evie retrieved her shirt and skirt. She didn't have time for a full outfit. When she rounded the car once more, Owen had finished loading Arik in.

Hazel had reached the invisible line of pressure. If it was closer than before, it was impossible to tell. The vampire's face coverings hid her expression, but it didn't matter much. The woman was chatting quite happily with the air.

"Oh my, oh my, someone over did it. Who makes a balloon like this?" Hazel was running her hand through the air, as if she was touching a wall.

"She's as screwy as the last time," Owen mumbled to Evie as he fell in pace with her.

"She's a little quirky," corrected Evie. Their last meeting had been strange with all the magic being thrown around. But it had saved Laika from death by a long drop. The pair caught up to Hazel, stopping a foot behind.

"You don't fill a balloon like this," Hazel scolded, but she never looked back at them, "Because someone will just come around and....POP!"

At the last word, one of her gloved fingers darted forward. There was a flash of greyish-blue light.

Evie grabbed her ears as it felt like a mountain of pressure crashed onto her. But it evaporated in seconds, leaving her with a headache. By the sounds of the surrounding people, they'd felt something similar.

"Sweet jesus," swore Owen. Both hands covered his ears and he still managed to put a glare in place for Hazel. "What was that?"

"I popped their balloon," Hazel answered, completely unapologetic.

"What balloon?" Owen hissed.

"That one!" Hazel wildly gestured back at the empty air.

Evie cut in. "Thank you, I know that wasn't pleasant for us. But now it can't hurt anyone else."

She tried to focus on the vampire's emotions to make sure they hadn't upset her. But all she got was white noise; her emotions weren't missing, but there was so much there it all jumbled together into a blank feeling.

Aaron joined them a moment later. "Are we good here?"

"Yeah," Owen answered, "Miss... eh... Hazel handled the zone." The wolfkin fumbled with a last name realizing even from their last encounter he'd never gotten it. "At some point our Glenwood magic needs to show up to one of these."

"They did," Hazel shrugged. She pointed to the east and then west. "Both of them went to separate areas to try to disarm the ritual. I saw Her and stopped."

"I understand," Aaron beamed with gratitude, "Thank you for stopping. You really helped us keep these survivors safe."

"Her who?" Owen prodded.

Hazel carefully extended a finger to point at Evie. "The zone was following our bunny here."

"What? Why?" This was Evie's turn to look annoyed and partly shocked. She'd been so focused on the strange white noise style emotions that she'd almost missed the explanation.

"How should I know?" shrugged the vampire.

"That does make some kind of sense," admitted Owen, "You were at the center as far as we could tell. Plus, the pressure kept extending wherever you went."

"But why?" Evie tried a different question.

Aaron spoke up this time. "That's a good question, and when we find this ritual master, we can ask."

CHAPTER 18
LINKED

Laika
October 16th, 2018
Glenwood Police Department Station #1, Glenwood, CA

The space outside of the Glenwood Police Department was chaotic, mobbed by police cruisers, news vans, and more middle-aged moms with cellphones than Laika had seen outside of a PTA meeting ever. She'd had to muscle her way through the crowd just to make it to the front door, and even then she'd had to dig out her moonlighter ID. The normally friendly officer who manned the front desk looked harried as he let her in, a cold glare stopping a swarm of photographers from overwhelming the door.

"I hate when we get celebrities involved. It's always a madhouse," the officer grumbled, mostly to himself. He pointed towards the familiar orange chairs that Laika knew well. "Everyone is swamped; you're probably going to have a long wait."

"That's fine, I just came to pick up Evie," Laika replied easily. She made no fuss as she took up her usual spot, being the picture of compliance. "What exactly is going on?"

Sometimes the officer would indulge in a bit of gossip, but today he shook his head as he resumed his post at the desk. "The vultures can read lips." There was an uneasiness to the way he sat, watching the horde of people outside the station doors.

LAIKA

I'm here!

It's crazy outside!

Laika waited for the indicator to flicker to 'read', hoping that Evie would give her the details she craved. She'd gotten the barest explanation of a magical attack hitting downtown Glenwood where Evie had the misfortune of being at a work event. The death toll hadn't been announced yet, but the numbers being thrown around on the news were high. Arik's presence escalated the situation and explained the mob outside. Fading celebrity or not, he was putting a sympathetic face to these attacks.

Her phone was silent and focusing her hearing wasn't getting Laika much. Eavesdropping on a conversation on the other side of the bullpen was easy for her keen hearing. However, every office door was closed with multiple conversations creating a wall of sound, none of it intelligible. Evie was still in one of these rooms waiting for her rescue, but Laika would have to wait or start knocking on random doors.

A door opened and Laika caught Owen's voice as he backed out of the room. "No, no. Just stay here for one minute!" He sounded frustrated and Laika wondered if he'd been saddled with Tony. That vampire could make even the straightest man blush. Owen had his back to her, but he should be in earshot.

"Owen! Do you need help?" Laika called. The last time she'd tried this had been before going rogue at Sync Holes; she half expected him to ignore her. Especially in the madness of the attack today.

Owen's head turned and he stared at her like she'd just rode in on a white horse. "Laika! Yes, get over here! I need your help." He turned back to whoever was in the conference room with a polite nod before closing the door.

Laika was on her feet in a flash, the front desk officer just waving her past. She made a beeline for Owen, dropping her voice to a normal volume as she neared. "What's up? How can I help?"

"I need you to sit with Miss Amadori," Owen jerked his head towards the closed door, "She's giving me a headache. Everyone's busy with their own questioning at this point and I need to rescue Gibson before we have another murder on our hands."

"Rescue Gibson from what?" Laika asked. Her eyes and ears were already scanning the remaining doors. If Owen had Hazel for her report, then who was Evie talking to?

"A catty Chrysanthemum who declared he's only going to talk to me," Owen sighed, "Because I didn't have enough problems. I have every senior moonlighter in the building working on witness statements and every senior pack out with rescue crews clearing the streets to find people. Now I've got the vampire who won't write her report and the vampire who's more interested in flirting than helping. So can you sit with Miss Amadori until I get back?"

"Does this mean I get to be a Senior Moonlighter?" Laika pressed. She had a wide grin on her face because in the last minute she'd learned more about the attack than in the last two hours of texting Evie.

Owen grimaced as he saw the trap Laika was trying to lay for him. "You can be the Senior Moonlighter of keeping LA's expert on track. Our own expert won't even be in the same room as her."

Laika nodded her agreement and patted him on the shoulder. "I accept this promotion with grace."

"Only until I get back," reminded Owen, but he didn't have any more time to bicker with Laika. He headed to a nearby room and forced a happy grimace onto his face before opening the door. Laika heard Tony cooing a greeting just before the conference room closed up again.

She needed to focus on her own task. Making someone write a

report wasn't that exciting, but seeing as Hazel was LA's magical expert, then she likely had a ton of information about what happened. Plus, Hazel had been receptive to Laika before so she might listen to the theory Night Claw had about the magic store break ins. Laika put her own smile in place before opening the door to the tiny room.

There was one table, only big enough for two chairs and a large mirror on the wall; this had to be one of the interrogation rooms. Laika's ears strained to pick up sounds of anyone on the other side of the glass. Despite the constant buzz of indistinct voices, she couldn't pick out anyone in particular that might be standing that close. Owen seemed way too exasperated to be playing a prank.

"Hi bunny!" Hazel raised one hand to give a tiny finger wave, spinning a pen as she did so. The woman was dressed in her heavy leather coat buckled up to be light tight, but her shoes and bag were bright green today. Despite being on the scene of an attack, Hazel didn't have a hair out of place.

"Hello, Hazel. Owen said you needed some help with your report?" Laika pulled out the chair across from her. As the werewolf sat down, she spied the stack of papers that formed their usual moonlighting debrief report, covered in idle scribbles but no actual words.

"I do not need your help, bunny. I've already solved the case and once my detainment is done then I'll be chasing down the suspect," Hazel explained.

Laika's eyes went wide... What did she just say? "You know who did this?"

"I know who did this, but I need to go sniff out their name," lamented Hazel. She sounded bored and was tapping her pen on the metal table.

"Oh, so you mean that you know what type of magic this is?" Laika tried to follow the conversation. Their first meeting had been confusing. But Laika had been so pumped up on adrenaline from running down a rollercoaster, she'd thought that her memory might be wrong. Hazel was just as difficult to follow a second time around.

"Silly bunny, can't you see the pattern already. All the circles..." Hazel's pen came down on the paper, drawing a series of rings that went from perfect circles to lopsided, malformed squiggles. "See? It's starting to decay. So many worlds all orbiting around each other. Pulled by the gravity of four moons in perfect balance, always getting closer. Only to miss each other by a breath every single time... But there is a dark star consuming a dying sun as it eats away at her light... The balance is getting worse and worse..."

Laika hesitated, having no idea what Hazel had just said. She didn't sound sane, more like the mad rambling of a drunk at 3 AM. "Are you okay?"

"I'm fine, bunny, why do you ask?" Hazel answered.

"You just seem a little more erratic than usual," Laika admitted. She'd only spoken to the vampire once before, but this entire situation was getting uncomfortable.

Hazel shrugged. "The moons aren't close enough today. I suppose I better finish this report so I can get out of here. No ritual is going to wait on me, and I only have 364 hours."

Again Laika's head was spinning from this 'conversation', but she was saved by her phone. A message appeared allowing her to bury her nose in her screen.

ALFRED

I intend to offer Evie a ride home since we are both at the GPD right now.

Will you be home this evening, we could finalize the plan for Friday in person?

LAIKA

You're here too?

So which of Evie's coworkers are you stuck with?

ALFRED

Why are you here?

I took a statement from her employer, his retelling of the incident has taken longer than I would have liked.

LAIKA

I have been promoted to a Senior Moonlighter!

ALFRED

Oh? Who promoted you?

LAIKA

Owen. He's entrusted me with highly important top level moonlighting stuff

ALFRED

Are you doing reports or witness statements?

LAIKA

…reports

ALFRED

That is a highly important task.

Will you be here much longer?

Hazel mumbled, "That's concerning…"

Laika looked up from her phone. She'd almost forgotten the headache-inducing vampire sitting in the room with her, she'd been so consumed in the text messages. Laika asked, "Something wrong?" When she got no answer from Hazel, who was focused intently on writing now, she went back to her messages.

LAIKA

Not sure. I brought Evie her car, but she's still off in one of the rooms

Why? Need help?

ALFRED

No, I can handle my own reports.

I have chosen Longtooth Steakhouse for our plans on Friday. Is this acceptable?

LAIKA

Of course!

They have the best chocolate lava cake!

ALFRED

Shall we meet at 7pm?

LAIKA

We could meet up tonight if you're free?

ALFRED

Sadly, I will be here for most of the night.

LAIKA

Then yeah, 7 on Friday is good

ALFRED

I am heading back to the scene, but I do not see you in the bullpen to say goodbye. So I shall see you on Friday then.

Laika bit her lip. If she asked, maybe Alfred would let her tag along to the scene with him. She could leave Evie's keys with Owen easily enough, and then she could get plenty of time with Alfred. Instead of waiting until Friday, Laika could try to explain the theory she and Evie had been crafting for a while now. Still, she was supposed to be doing a job right now... even if it amounted to babysitting.

As if on cue, Hazel's voice stole her attention back. "My, my, my, bunny, what big teeth you have."

"What? Are you talking to me?" Laika forgot all about her plan to beg for a trip to the scene.

"Yes, bunny... but that's not right is it?" Hazel put down her pen and all of the cheer drained out of her tone, "You aren't a bunny are you? I'm not sure what you are just yet... A snake waiting to strike or a fox already mid-trick."

Laika felt like she should be insulted, but she barely understood what she was being accused of. She'd been as polite as she could by sitting with Hazel and listening to her ramble on pointlessly. Yes, she'd been on her phone for a few minutes, but at that point Hazel had been working on her report. It wasn't like they had been talking. Laika frowned, "Did I do something to offend you?"

"Not yet," answered Hazel. She seemed more focused than before, almost like a different person. "Your pretty amber eyes are wandering from our work."

"Like what?" Laika felt herself getting heated. What had happened to change the atmosphere between them so much? "I'm completely focused on this case. I've been begging for anyone to give me a chance to help and I've been doing my research. Don't tell me I'm not being focused."

Her words seemed to settle Hazel down. "Like I said, not yet. But there's blood in the water and you need to stay your course."

"Blood in the water?" Laika asked.

"Not yet, but soon. Give that to the nice officer for me, will you?" Hazel handed over her report to Laika before pulling her face coverings into place quickly.

"Where are you going?" Laika asked she got to her feet, report in hand. She wasn't sure if she should, or even wanted to, stop the vampire from leaving. With the paperwork complete, Owen probably wouldn't be too upset and Hazel was making her extremely uncomfortable now. The vampire had gone from lovably quirky, to drunken poet, and finally disappointed mother all in the span of two conversations.

"I told you. I have 364 hours to find my summoner," answered Hazel. She snapped her goggles over her eyes before breezing past Laika to the door. "I need to put all the orbits back on track, before the corruption worms its way into everything. It would be nice if you were a bunny again next time I see you."

And with that, Hazel was gone out the door. She moved like liquid bending around people to escape the police station. Laika let her go. What the hell just happened? She looked down at the report in hand, only to find it had actually been filled out. Owen still wasn't back and he'd never said that Laika wasn't allowed to read what Hazel wrote down.

Laika scanned the page and the first detail that came to her attention was also the first non-nonsense scribble.

"The attack using air pressure to crush individuals is linked
to the previous three attacks in terms of ritual magic."

—AMADORI

That confirmed it. The media had been correct when they dubbed 'the Anarchist' as a singular entity behind all the attacks. Whether it was literally one person or a group was still in the air... Hazel had mentioned a summoner, and Laika turned her attention back to the paper, searching for more details.

"The ritual magic fused multiple elements to cause effects of
this scale. Requires considerable materials in addition to
magic to power the spell."

—AMADORI

Laika blinked in surprise. If she was understanding this correctly, then someone doing these rituals would need a ton of components. Just like the dwarf who broke into Pixie Dust was trying to steal. Could she and Evie really be onto something chasing the break-ins? They'd already confirmed there was more than one looking for the same list. If Laika could get real clearance, then she could dig into past break-ins the weeks before the other attacks, or maybe the police officers had already tried to dig those up...

Not being allowed any information was so frustrating!

She skimmed the rest of the report, but it was far less coherent. She didn't spy any other statements about a summoner or the oddly specific '364 hours' Hazel had been on about... But Laika couldn't be sure it wasn't there in the rambling sentences. This was more like a riddle than official documents.

This was still perfect! LA's expert was saying that the rituals were linked and that they needed a lot of supplies. Laika and Evie had an entire murder board of break-in reports for magic stores-

"Laika? Where the hell is Amadori?" Owen asked as he stepped through the door.

"She left," Laika answered honestly. She quickly held out the report to the officer, "And she said to give you this. It's finished... kinda."

Owen had looked annoyed when he'd spoken to her earlier, now he looked on edge. "Are you kidding me? I needed her to stay here until I checked over the report!"

"Oh," Laika gave him an apologetic look. She wasn't sure if she wanted to explain why she'd just let the vampire walk away.

"Now I have to track her down again," grumbled Owen. He stalked out of the room heading for the front desk and Laika followed at his heels. She knew he was disappointed in her for not keeping Hazel contained, but maybe he'd listen anyways.

Before she could get a word in, Gibson joined them at the front desk. "Kirkland, you need to go deal with the vampire again."

"No, it's your turn. I've got to go find Amadori; she took off while I was saving you from the least dangerous type of vampire," snapped Owen. He grabbed a pad off the front desk and started to write down a description of Hazel.

"Hey Owen," Laika tried to get his attention. Now wasn't the perfect time, but if she could just explain then he could follow her lead. And she could go find Hazel, since she had superior speed and it hadn't been that long.

However, her favorite officer stopped her mid sentence. "No. I don't have time for you today, Laika. I need to get some real work done and clean up this mess. I've got a rogue vampire out there who could talk to the press at any moment. Plus, I need to save Gibson from the big bad Tony and his terrible shirts."

Laika might as well have been slapped for how quickly she shut her mouth. She really hadn't thought that letting the other woman go once she'd written the report would be that big of a deal. "I'm sorry?"

"Just go home. Evie will be out in a minute, so take her and *go home*," Owen demanded and gathered himself again to address Gibson. "Do you want to deal with entertaining Tony or go find Amadori?"

Gibson scowled, "I'll baby sit, you go find your missing expert." He paused long enough to shake his head at Laika and left back to the conference rooms. Laika glared daggers at the back of Gibson's head the whole way. Why was *he* shaking his head? Like he was doing any better given that *Tony* apparently was too much to handle...

As Gibson disappeared behind one door, another opened and a disheveled Evie appeared. She blinked in confusion as her eyes met Laika's. There was a tired edge to her movements, but her feet carried her towards Laika. "What are you doing here?"

"I was talking to-" Laika turned her head to find that in the moment of distraction, Owen had disappeared, leaving Laika standing on her own. Dammit... She turned her attention back to Evie and sighed before offering up a wry smile. "I was waiting for you. Ready to go home?"

"Yes, take me home. I want to be anywhere but this stupid police station right now. I've been answering questions for the last two hours. Like I had any idea what happened," complained Evie. She looked at the front door and all the news crews outside. Laika followed her gaze with a frown; they were going to have a fight back to the car.

"Should we try for the side door?" asked Laika.

CHAPTER 19
WHITEBOARD

Laika
October 18th, 2018
Night Claw Residence, Glenwood, CA

L aika stood in the middle of the living room, staring daggers at her whiteboard. So far it had not been providing the answers she'd expected.

"Where are you planning to put that?" Shelly pressed. She sat in her usual spot on the sofa with two TV trays; One with her laptop, and the other prepped with snacks for Trashy TV Thursday.

"I thought we'd just leave it in the living room against the wall." Laika shrugged as she marked off another 'x' on her new whiteboard.

After trying to show off her last murder board, Laika had decided that a more mobile version was needed. A wheeled teaching board was promptly purchased and was delivered today. For the last two hours, the household had sat in front of it marking down which races were capable of the recent string of attacks.

	FULMINO APT.	CORRONECT TOWERS	SYNC HOLES	HOT OFF THE PRESSES
DWARF	?	✓	✓	✗
ELF (AMBERGLADE)	✓	✓	✗	?
ELF (HAVENLARK)	✗	✗	✗	✗
ELF (SILVERTIDE)	?	✓	✓	✗
ELF (SKYSONG)	✓	✗	✗	✓
WEREWOLF (NORTHERN)	✗	✗	✗	✗
WEREWOLF (SOUTHERN)	✗	✗	✗	✗
WEREWOLF (WESTERN)	✗	✗	✗	✗
BLACK WITCH	✗	✗	✓	✗
GREEN WITCH	✗	✓	✓	✗
GREY WITCH	✗	✗	✗	✗
RED WITCH	✓	✓	✗	✗
WHITE WITCH	✓	✗	✗	✓
VAMPIRE (ROSE???)	✓	?	✓	✓

The Murder/Mystery Board

"Nope," Shelly quickly rejected the plan. "That's going back to your room. We are not living with the newest murder of the week on display."

Tor commented, "I think it could be fun. A real conversation starter, like a book on the coffee table."

"I agree," Evie added to the vote, "So that's three against one for keeping the Mystery Board out here."

There was a defeated sigh from Shelly before she sipped at her drink.

Laika turned her attention back to her whiteboard. She'd added every race and powerset they knew anything about already. But so far, no one lined up perfectly. "Are we sure that this isn't a group of people working together?"

"No," admitted Evie as she tapped away on her keyboard. She had her own tray set up so she could keep googling questions as they arose.

"So a group of witches could pull this off then?" Laika added notes to the side of the chart. She calculated how many it would take to cover all these events. Three or maybe four?

"Maybe... but we don't know if they can combine magic like that in a remote spell," Evie remarked while she tried to search for the answer online.

"Who can we ask?" Laika pondered.

Evie bit her lip before answering, "I asked Owen for Melinda's number. But he said he had to check with her first."

"Let me text Alfred. He knows a lot about witch magic," offered Laika, picking up her phone.

She heard Evie mutter, "Of course he does. You talk to him more than you did your ex-boyfriend." She'd tried to keep it under her breath, but Laika's keen ears picked up every word.

Laika frowned, wishing whatever this unknown issue Evie had with her new friend and amazing resource could just go away. That was the second time she'd compared Alfred to Zach. But the men weren't even the same species and she wasn't in a relationship with the vampire. Their friendship was nothing like her disaster romance with her ex. She decided to ignore the comment.

LAIKA

Good Evening!

Got a minute for some questions?

Before she even closed the screen, Laika saw the read icon appear and the dots of a response.

ALFRED

I have more than a minute. How can I help?

LAIKA

Can witches pool their magic?

ALFRED

Yes, witches of the same circle can easily pool their magic together.

That is a benefit of when they bind themselves to an element.

LAIKA

Right, and if they don't bind then their powers fade around their late 20's?

ALFRED

So I have heard.

> LAIKA
>
> What about witches in different circles?
>
> Can they pool their power the same way?

ALFRED

Yes, but it is much harder.

The witches need to be in perfect sync with each other. Or complex rituals are involved to sync them.

> LAIKA
>
> So it's possible for 5 witches to work together with rituals. Awesome!

ALFRED

May I ask why you want to know?

Laika took a step back, stopping when she bumped the back of her calves on the coffee table. Her phone snapped a quick picture of her new board before sending it off to him.

ALFRED

I see.

What have you concluded?

> LAIKA
>
> That this might be a bunch of witches?

ALFRED

I reached the same conclusion during the events at the amusement park.

> LAIKA
>
> Okay...so are you going to admit you are working on these cases yet?

ALFRED

I was not aware that was a secret?

You had been following the case?

LAIKA

But you never said it was your case?

ALFRED

You never asked?

LAIKA

I asked about Pixie Dust?!

ALFRED

Which has nothing to do with this case?

LAIKA

Hold Please!

Laika tossed her phone at the safety of the couch cushions before taking a running leap over their sofa. Her aim was down the hall to the original murder board that was still on the closet floor.

"What the hell?!" Evie screeched. Her cries went ignored in pursuit of proving Laika's theory.

The murder board appeared first as Laika returned. She propped it up on the tray meant for markers, then snapped another picture of all their ritual research for the vampire.

ALFRED

You believe you have singled out the ritual?

LAIKA

Nope, I'm not even close

But there is enough here that I think whoever hired those dwarves to rob Pixie Dust is part of your case.

ALFRED

I am skeptical of that. Nothing on that list is illegal or even particularly hard to find.

Shelly sat up to attention as she realized what was going on. While she'd barely spoken to their new vampire friend last time he'd been over, so far all interactions had been positive. "What does he think?"

"Skeptical," admitted Laika. There was a slight frown to his lackluster reaction. She'd wanted him to be more excited.

"I told you that he wasn't going to believe us," gloated Evie. Her baleful expression flickered up from the screen. "He's too 'senior' of a moonlighter to take us seriously."

Laika protested, "He doesn't know the whole theory yet. Just let me finish explaining it to him."

LAIKA

But what if you didn't want someone to know you'd bought everything?

ALFRED

That is not an uncommon tactic if someone wanted to hide a ritual.

May I have the full list of stolen items? Not the cut-down version.

LAIKA

Sure, let me go type it up.

"There!" Laika exclaimed.

"So?" Evie had closed her laptop to watch the frantic typing. "He magically changed his mind?"

"He wants the full list to check out if there is anything dangerous that can be made with all these ingredients. That's at least him considering it!" Triumph was written on Laika's face.

"So we might be right?" Shelly added. Her fingers flew on her keyboard as the woman pulled up more information. "I am almost done with some code that will check those ingredients against the spellbook sites, but I need a few more days."

Laika nodded her understanding. "It's okay, even another week is still faster than us trying to search by hand." Their roommates had been helpful in the search for knowledge; even Tor had managed to get them some answers from her friends. Again Laika's phone vibrated.

> **ALFRED**
>
> Can you give me a copy tomorrow?
>
> Assuming we are still meeting?

> **LAIKA**
>
> Oh...right!

"Well?" Evie pressed. Her lips had turned into a thin line and no magical empathy was needed to determine she was annoyed.

"I'm meeting up with Alfred tomorrow," explained Laika. She was irrationally happy about that, even if they were only meeting up for the case.

"A date?" Tor piped up. She sat flipping through a Spells Weekly, looking for anything relevant to the case. Her vampire knowledge had been called on earlier, but now they were firmly out of her realm of expertise. This was all Tor could do at the moment.

Waving them off, Laika responded before turning back to her phone. "No, it's a work thing."

> **LAIKA**
>
> Do you still want to go to Longtooth? We could just meet up here?

> **ALFRED**
>
> Longtooth would be my preference.
>
> I will send you the address? My treat this time.

> **LAIKA**
>
> I'll bring a copy of the list with me tomorrow!

> **ALFRED**
>
> Wonderful.

"I think my parents' crashing scared him off from coming here. So he's sending me a place to meet up."

"So you're meeting a stranger at a secondary location?" Evie teased, but her smile was flat.

Shelly came to her aid. "But he's been in the house before? And shared lunch with your parents... is he really still a stranger? It's not like you don't even know his last name."

Silence hung in the living room.

"Right?" Shelly pushed again, glancing between her roommates.

"We have no idea of his full name, Alfred is a stranger who wore a three thousand dollar suit to lunch here. We don't know anything about him other than he moonlights." Evie's tone was sour and she gestured at their meager living room.

"Ummm... I just never got around to asking him." Laika defended. Her phone saved her from further inquisition with multiple rapid pings.

ALFRED

Also assuming you do not mind:

A dwarf could have caused the Fulmino incident, but there are none of a poworful enough craft in LA. They tend to live in the New York area.

Amberglade elves do not possess the power to manipulate air pressure. Only Skysong and Windswept may do that.

Silvertide elves do not possess the power to generate lightning.

"Oh shit!" Laika moved into a flurry of motion to update her whiteboard. She almost couldn't believe Alfred was handing her the remaining question marks.

Evie was standing next to her a moment later to read over her friend's shoulder. "See? He doesn't have a clue what he's talking about!"

"What?" There was a skeptical look from Laika in return. "This is more than we've gotten from the internet."

"No, it's useless if it's wrong. Windswept and Skysong are the same things. According to Wikipedia, Windswept are just a subset that is better at wind magic in general," Evie disagreed.

Laika huffed. "Why would he give us wrong information?"

"Because he's an emotionless void and possibly a sociopath." Evie had herself worked up, on the edge of ranting. She got like this sometimes when she pushed out her runs too far.

"You are being crazy right now," Laika snapped back, putting her hands on her hips aggressively. "Is it possible that you just need to run?"

"When *was* the last time you ran?" Shelly inquired as well. "I don't think I've ever seen you run."

"I don't need to run!" snapped Evie, taking on her own aggressive stance.

"Are you moonburnt right now? Is that why you are being so cruel for no reason? You should come running with me, Keisha, and Jaci next time we go," Laika glowered at her friend, ready for the monthly fight. But she still asked for clarification on her phone.

LAIKA

Really? I thought Skysong and Windswept were the same powers?

ALFRED

No, they do have some overlap. But are separate bloodlines with different invocations as well.

Skysongs are inscribers, they must draw their symbols in some manner on their skin.

Windswepts are somatic casters who invoke through dance-like movements.

> Unlike dwarves who only have a single craft,
> an elf could use multiple bloodlines if their
> invocations were different and they had
> lineage in the magic.

"Are we really supposed to trust him over Wikipedia?" growled Evie, still spying on the message chain.

"Yeah! Because he's got no reason to lie to us and doesn't seem upset we want to help on his case." Laika knew that her packmate was just trying to distract from the run conversation brewing.

"There is an easier solution," Tor cut into the conversation. "Ask an elf?"

Both Laika and Evie turned to their human roommate.

"You could ask an elf and settle it once and for all," agreed Laika, taking the offered de-escalation.

Evie looked annoyed, but she shot off a text message to her boss. Laika read over her shoulder this time.

EVIE

> Are Skysong and Windswept elves the
> same?

ARIK

> EXCUSE ME?!

> Wash your mouth out and never confuse me
> with airheads like that bloodline again.

EVIE

> Okay sorry.

"So, Alfred is correct over Wikipedia then?" Laika gloated, not restraining her smirk.

Ignoring the jab, Evie insisted on a new line of questions. "Ask him about rose vampires then? If he knows the ins and outs of dwarves and elves, then he should know that."

"Oh yeah!"

> **LAIKA**
>
> What about rose vampires and CorroNect?

> **ALFRED**
>
> I suppose, that is possible. But I highly
> doubt a vampire did any of this.

> **LAIKA**
>
> But one could be capable of it?
>
> Miss Hazel broke two of the rituals already,
> so she's got the right magic.

> **ALFRED**
>
> I suppose, but a rose vampire would need to
> be on-site for each of these incidents. Other
> races would not.

She updated the whiteboard with his answers.

"Ask him about other magical vampires," pressed Evie as she was still reading the entire conversation second-hand. "Tor mentioned there were other types, but not what."

"As far as I know they don't come around a lot. Probably scarier than peonies," Tor added.

> **ALFRED**
>
> I will see you tomorrow.

Laika sighed. Her window for questions today had closed up. When Alfred cut off a conversation, then something was usually on fire. He wouldn't be back for hours. They'd be distracted by trashy TV before he returned.

"It's fine," Evie assured, finally looking away from Laika's phone. She headed back to the couch with her mood seeming to be lifted up, then opened the lid of her laptop to go back to her searching. "I can just ask him tomorrow."

Laika felt like a deer in the headlights. "You're coming? As moon-burnt as you are?"

"You said it wasn't a date and I want to know more about what magic needed those ingredients. I can feel that we're right about the break ins being connected." Evie kept pressing the subject.

Laika felt her patience fraying and knew she had to decide if they were fighting about a run or dinner tomorrow. A choice was made for her.

"Excuse me," Tor cut in while raising her hand, "Ignorant human here. What's moonburn?"

All three werewolves turned their attention to the woman. Expressions ranged from embarrassed to open confusion that Tor didn't already know. Having a human in the house meant informing her fully of the dangers of living here.

Shelly's cheeks tinged pink as attempted to explain. "Sorry. Sorry. You know the story that werewolves need to run on a full moon?" Tor nodded, her magazine placed on the coffee table. Shelly glanced at the other wolves for help before continuing, "It's not really like that, but werewolves do need to run about once a month."

"We get bitchy when we don't," Laika was glaring openly at Evie now. She was certain she was right and Evie had been putting off her run for work or research. "My dad says back when we were all in the shadows, full moon runs were common because we got the most natural light and that's where the stories comes from."

Evie defended, "I'm not moonburnt."

"The longer you push your run, the more likely you get an involuntary shift," explained Shelly for Tor's benefit. Her attention moved to Evie, "Do you want to go with me? I can take you out to the park?"

"I hate those run parks," Evie whined.

"And we come full circle," Laika said, "That's why we end up like this every 30 something days. I'll check if we can rent that woods plot this week."

"You can rent space in the woods to run?" Shelly was fully interested in this. While Laika had shown her where the run parks were, both of them had talked about how confining they felt.

Rubbing her temples, Laika glared at Evie. "Yes, but it isn't cheap.

I'll get us some time this week or next at the worst. And you are going, end of the conversation."

Evie rolled her eyes, "You are being dramatic. I'm not that bad right now."

Laika sat down in an empty spot on the couch. She was calling her friend's bluff about dinner as well. "If you can't behave you aren't going tomorrow either. I want a good working relationship, here."

CHAPTER 20
DINNER

Laika
October 19th, 2018
Longtooth Steakhouse, Glenwood, CA

Laika was certain she was staring a trap straight in her silver eyes. Either her face or 'aura' was probably telling Evie just how skeptical she was right now.

Despite Laika skipping lunch so she could leave an hour early, Evie had somehow beaten her home today. Her best friend was fully showered, dressed, and made up already like she was ready for a night out. Pieces started falling into place when Evie began to badger about tagging along to dinner tonight.

Laika did her best to tune out Evie's demand to go. She busied herself with digging through their shared closet to find something to wear. She picked a nice sundress and flats. In the mirror she liked what she saw when she put them together. Laika might even dare to say she looked 'cute', but this was for a professional dinner.

No matter how hard her best friend pushed, Laika held strong.

Evie was moonburnt and the slightly manic way she was

pleading made that obvious. But then she made a compromise so tempting that Laika considered it. Her best friend would drive her there and back. She'd be able to avoid an expensive Uber ride on her cheap budget and these shoes would be terrible to walk that far in. They could go over their evidence one more time in the car too.

Laika agreed and they drove to one of the social hubs near their home with a big movie plex and lots of restaurants. Evie pointed out the Longtooth Steakhouse as they parked. She got out, following Laika, refusing to let go of the tote bag that carried their research.

"I'm already here and I can help," she urged again.

Laika's gaze was on her phone and she decided another compromise might work. Fingers tapped out a message to Alfred. "Okay, I'm pretty sure I can convince him our theory is right, but if you can keep your cool then you can come."

LAIKA

Hey! Just parked!

ALFRED

I am already inside.

"I'm always cool," Evie interrupted, but Laika didn't believe her.

Laika surged forward towards the restaurant. The front door was just a short distance away and she hoped he hadn't gotten a tiny table. Why hadn't she double checked if Evie wanted to go days ago instead of an hour ago?

She reminded her friend, "Do not be that super intense crazy person you are when you don't run. I know you say you're fine, but just trust me... You're moonburnt even if you won't admit it."

"I am not moonburnt, and I am already here," Evie dismissed with a scoff.

Laika sighed deeply, stopping them before they got to the door. "Yes, you really are. You promised mom and dad you'd go, but both times I've gone this week you claimed work to get out of it. Runs are not that bad."

"You're being dramatic." Evie closed her hand on the brass

handle to Longtooth. Before she could open it, Laika's hand fell on her arm to stop her.

Her amber eyes looked up pleadingly at Evie, trying to force sincerity and worry behind every word, "Look... I'll drop the run for tonight, just promise to tell me if you feel a shift starting? I can handle getting us to a park in an emergency."

"I'm not going to shift, and I'm not going to piss off another moonlighter," Evie promised. Under her breath she added, "Not that he'd even feel it..."

"Evie!" hissed Laika. What was Evie's problem? They stood in front of the door blocking the entrance way, but Laika wasn't going to budge.

Evie turned defiant eyes on her. "What?"

"Please, I mean it," Laika pleaded. She didn't want this night to go wrong. If Alfred got offended by them, then that would be the end of their budding friendship.

"I want us to get on this case and that means us putting our best foot forward on this," Evie relented finally.

Laika gave her a suspicious look; there was another reason her friend wanted to be here beyond getting them on a case, and she wished for just a minute she could read people half as well as Evie. Just to get an idea of what was going through this moonburnt werewolf's head...

She allowed Evie to pull open the door to the waiting area that was warm with comfortable seating. Even at this time of the night, the restaurant was getting busy. She couldn't find Alfred standing in the crowd.

LAIKA

Are you already seated?

ALFRED

Yes, if you check in with the hostess. She will lead you to the day-proof room in the back.

LAIKA

The sun's already down though?

Why do you need the day-proof room?

ALFRED

Company policy and thankfully it is very
uncrowded.

LAIKA

No screaming to be heard over everyone.
Nice!

Longtooth Steakhouse was a regional chain, which claimed to cater to a werewolf appetite. Everything was clean, cozy, and had all the trappings of a safe and fun time. Including a friendly hostess at the podium who was expecting her. She bid Laika to follow her.

"Come on," Laika beckoned Evie. They cut a path through the full dining room back to where the day-proof rooms were protected by heavy glassless doors.

Inside was a well-lit, spacious area with four tables. They weren't very big, giving lots of room for privacy. All but one table was empty.

"Good evening," Alfred greeted as he stood up. He looked nice dressed up in a different suit than she'd seen before. This one was more formal than the one he'd been wearing at her house. Maybe it was for going to nice places instead of work?

He'd sat so he was facing the door with the table between them. Only two place settings were there... shit.

Laika internally scolded herself for not warning him that it was her *and* Evie coming, "Hello. Um... I should have confirmed earlier... that uh... both of us were coming. I'm sorry."

"Do not worry, there is plenty of room," Alfred assured. His attention moved to the hostess that brought them in and he asked for a third setting. Then he greeted Evie politely, "Nice to see you again."

"You too," Evie responded with a bright smile. Laika knew that tone and barely concealed a groan; her friend wasn't being sincere.

Which, given they'd just added a whole person to pay for and he wasn't making a big deal, was kind of ungrateful.

"Again, I'm really sorry. Don't worry; we'll cover ourselves," promised Laika.

"No need," assured Alfred, his eyes trained to the hostess as she left. Then he moved to pull out chairs like a movie character from a forgotten era. Laika knew she should roll her eyes, but the action was a little charming as he waited for them to sit. Had he been this formal last time?

The first couple of minutes of dinner was tense. Laika glanced between her packmate and her new friend; she didn't need powers to feel the ice building up. Alfred seemed stiffer than before, his words a little more reined in. Perhaps that was just how he was? They'd only spoken in person twice before and this was a fancier setting than either time. Why did that bother her a bit?

Evie wasn't even trying to pay attention. Her eyes were glued to her phone as she shot off message after message. After two hours of harping for an official invite to dinner, her friend was ignoring them. The responsibility for conversation would fall to Laika. "So... Come here often?" The question was aimed at Alfred with a bright grin.

His lips curved up. "No, sadly this is my first time here."

"Why here of all places then?" Laika quizzed.

"My quick research garnered that you would get a filling meal here versus other places." Alfred had explained before he *could* eat, but didn't do so often. "Do you have a suggestion on what to order?"

There was a momentary glint in Laika's eyes. She didn't normally go out to dinner with someone as prim and proper as Alfred. The impulse to suggest ordering something messy like hot wings tempted her. The mischief got stifled very quickly though. Alfred had a sense of humor in text, but she was unsure that would translate over. What if he wasn't as funny in person? Why did that matter to Laika?

"Most of their steaks are really good, I don't think you can really go wrong with those..." Laika paused and then a follow-up question flowed before she could think twice. "If you eat a rare steak, does that count as drinking blood?"

"No more than it does for you," Alfred responded without hesitation and for the first time tonight he warmed up.

That pulled a hint of amusement from Laika. "Huh," she looked thoughtful, "So animal blood is no good for you?"

"I suppose that depends on your definition of animal," Alfred clarified with a smirk.

Evie interrupted loudly. "Here is that list you want." She placed a stapled packet in the middle of the table.

"Oh yes, thank you." Alfred picked up the papers so he could flip through them. His expression went back to politely neutral. "Allow me a few minutes to check these ingredients."

Laika glanced at her packmate, feeling irritation rising unbidden. That forced her to stop and assess why she cared so much. That interruption got them back on track. She'd never cared for small talk before? They were supposed to hand the list over as an olive branch as they maneuvered to get onto Alfred's case officially.

"So, can you figure out which ritual from that?" Laika asked hopefully.

"Perhaps," Alfred kept his eyes moving along the page, "But I suppose that will depend on the brand of magic."

"Are some harder than others?" Evie wondered aloud.

Alfred flipped the page then answered, "When it comes to formalized spells, then yes. Many races hide their secrets even when another could not use the rituals. Knowledge is power where magic is concerned."

"...so what's your speciality?" Laika sat on the edge of her seat hoping he'd give a clue. Clearly Alfred had to have some magic, given how much he knew on the topic.

"You need to stop getting distracted," Evie hissed while keeping her voice down. She'd leaned in closer so they could talk quietly, forcing attention away from the vampire with another interruption.

Red colored Laika's face for being told off and knowing Alfred could hear them clearly this close. "Ssshh!"

"Don't you shush me!"

"Evie, be quiet!" Laika tried again to get her friend to shut up as they glared at each other.

"No, just because you want to make bedroom eyes at a guy who's like 10 times your age doesn't mean I have to be quiet," hissed Evie.

"He can hear you, shut up!" Laika had no idea why her friend had gotten so spun up. She had half a mind to march the redhead back to the car for that comment.

All the color drained out of Evie's face, "What?"

Not bothering to whisper anymore Laika explained. "Alfred's got enhanced hearing like me."

"Oh... I'm so sorry." Evie looked mortified.

"No need to apologize," Alfred shrugged, but he didn't look up from his reading. "I know how to pretend I cannot hear conversations not meant for me."

A waitress appeared to rescue them all from this disaster by asking for their orders. The woman busied herself taking down drinks and meals, giving everyone a few minutes to calm down. Laika silently thanked her for her amazing timing and swore she'd sneak an extra twenty into the waitress's tip. Once they were alone, Alfred continued on as though he hadn't just been insulted by the two werewolves trying to get onto his case. "I hope that no one is attempting to use this specific list to cast a ritual."

"Why?" Laika felt a jolt of excitement again. That meant the ingredients might be a lead just like she'd suspected.

"This ritual lacks the protections that modern day magic has learned. Unsupervised practice of this could drive a person insane. No master practitioner in their right mind would teach it to anyone."

Laika pushed, "I don't understand. Why is it dangerous?"

"When you originally sent me part of this list, I explained that it had too many redundant components to be for a single ritual. However, if you look at this as a whole it reminds me of some old magic that was used to wage wars between various races. While it has powerful effects and stops outside forces from creating backlash on the ritual casters, there is nothing dampening the magic that's coursing through them. That much unfettered magic would drive anyone insane," Alfred explained.

"So whoever is casting that is killing themselves in the process?" Evie seemed interested in the conversation at last.

"Not precisely. A human would die if they tried to channel magic like this. But if they had even a drop of supernatural blood in them, then they would survive." Alfred paused as he looked back at the papers.

"Do you know what that one does?" asked Laika. Her hands were gripping the sides of her chair. She wanted to ask a million questions but needed them to stay on topic.

"This would crumble the ground below your enemies," admitted Alfred. His lips were pressed into a thin line.

"So it is related," Laika cheered. She threw both of her hands in the air for victory ignoring Evie's glare. "The break-in happened a couple of days before Sync Holes. I bet if we looked, there would be more cases in the weeks before the other attacks."

Alfred seemed distracted, staring at the papers again as he asked offhandedly, "Why have you not?"

"Owen wouldn't give us any information," Evie answered. They'd taken this theory to GPD shortly after the sinkhole, but the officers had been too busy. "And... I couldn't get away with lying to the LAPD again."

"We did try, but we don't have the connections," explained Laika.

"And if you had those lists? Then what?" Alfred's attention pulled up from the papers, settling on the pair of werewolves with a curious expression.

"I don't know," Laika admitted. She gave him a sheepish expression as she continued, "But you might know if those rituals caused the other attacks right?"

There was a thoughtful look before Alfred agreed, "Perhaps. If there is a pattern with the break-ins, then someone could track future ones and know about any more attacks that are coming."

Laika felt overjoyed that he'd followed her thoughts. "Exactly!"

Then Evie interrupted again, "And we could do all the legwork of getting you information?"

There was that feeling again. Laika felt an intense surge of irritation at her packmate speaking up. Aside from their whispered fight, every word had been polite and to the point of what they wanted out of tonight. A valid reason to join the case even if they were just doing some running around. What the hell had her so hostile at every interruption?

Her gaze trailed back to Alfred looking over his face again and the answer clicked into place.

Laika had a crush.

Evie
October 19th, 2018
Longtooth Steakhouse, Glenwood, CA

Evie was torn about how she felt right now; she'd suspected she was crashing a date when they arrived at Longtooth. The moment they'd walked into the day-proof room, that suspicion had been confirmed. Her only saving grace was that Laika didn't seem to realize it. Even if her best friend was dressed for the occasion.

Why did this have to be a date? Part of Evie rebelled hard against the thought of Laika dating again. Her friend hadn't shown more than a passing interest in anyone for the last three years. The more reasonable part of Evie wanted Laika to be happy. But there was no way that Laika could be happy for real with a vampire. Relationships like this were doomed to fail in dramatic heartbreak and a call to the GPD. You could have fun but you didn't date dead men...

Alfred had reacted calmly to her arrival with a polite greeting for Evie like she was expected at dinner. But she knew better, she'd just derailed his date plans and he should be livid. Instead, he was an empty void of emotion again. They weren't faint, they weren't there. She wasn't crazy. Alfred had no emotions at all.

Laika had been a literal roller coaster of emotions, excited, interested, annoyed... and the strangest thing was that the last part seemed to be directed at Evie. It made no sense. The packmates were normally on the same page, and right now, everything was looking up. So why would Laika be annoyed with her?

Evie didn't need her empathy to read this situation. She saw a man interested in a woman, and that woman was about to get her way... Which meant that Night Claw would possibly get their hands on the information and case that they wanted.

She'd never admit that pushing off her run for a month could cloud her judgment. But right now it was kind of hard to ignore that she was not on her A-game. Between the table, the emotions, and her phone, she couldn't decide what she cared about more. Her mind was a jumble.

After Evie's conversation with Tony, she was even more confused.

She'd texted him a hearty 'I told you so' earlier. He'd fought her on the void theory again, saying she was just a weak empath. But he'd finally laid out options if she was correct and all of them were bad. From an ancient daywalker that could hide his emotions even from empathy, to elite LA vampires with expensive shielding in place, all were dangerous. She was sure that Laika leading this vampire on would end badly.

But at the same time, Evie couldn't just get up and drag her friend away like Tony was demanding. The prospect of real cases was within reach. An honest detective work case, instead of just being muscle for domestic disputes.

Alfred finally answered in his same infuriatingly polite tone. "I would have to give this some consideration. Pulling junior moonlighters into a case of this level is not something I would normally advise."

Evie wasn't able to contain the frown at the non-committal answer as he dashed her hopes of real work. Her gaze dropped back to her phone while letting her excitement cool off. She was pretty sure if Laika had asked, he would have just said yes.

As if she had read Evie's mind, Laika spoke up again. "But you know we're just going to keep researching this even if you don't let us help, right?"

"I had suspected that may be the case," Alfred mused.

Laika leaned forward, "So wouldn't it make more sense to just let us work with you? So a 'senior' moonlighter can keep an eye on us?"

There was a moment of silence, and then Alfred gave Laika a bemused look. "I suppose that would be safer for all parties involved."

The two dissolved back into their oddly comfortable rapport. It had been a long time since Evie had felt like such a third wheel. But she was sticking to her guns on interrupting this date at this point. Fingers drumming against the side of her phone, she resumed her conversation with Tony quietly.

EVIE

I hope you're wrong. I'm sitting across the table from him

Well how would I figure out what situation this is?

TONY

You don't

You get up and get your ass out of there

EVIE

You're being dramatic!

TONY

No honey, dramatic would be calling a bomb threat into the restaurant

Get your fluffy tail up out of that chair and drag your friend out by her ears

EVIE

Wouldn't that just piss off this super dangerous guy?

TONY

Who cares?!

Evie looked back up at the conversation, realizing Alfred and Laika had gone off topic again. Was he trying to distract them from the case for some reason? Why didn't he want them to talk about it?

EVIE

Can rose vampires hide their emotions?

TONY

Wait! Wait! Wait!

Is this guy a super well-dressed rose vampire?

EVIE

I mean I don't know for sure, but all signs point to magic vampire.

He's got on some stupidly expensive suit for Longtooth.

I think he's just trying to impress Laika, but she'd never know the difference.

TONY

I know of one

EVIE

And?

TONY

I'm sure it's not him, but that guy is bad news.

Just in case, be nice, get through dinner, and go home.

Evie's eyes widened as she stared at her phone. Be nice? Tony had never uttered those words once in the years she knew him. She looked up at the conversation debating her next move, but her mouth spoke before her brain could catch up.

"Why do you keep changing the subject?" Evie demanded, leveling a glare at Alfred.

A flicker of surprise crossed the vampire's face as he cut off mid sentence. It was almost like he'd forgotten she'd been sitting there. "Do I? My apologies. That had not been my intention."

"Evie!" snapped Laika, spinning around in her chair. "What the hell? I changed the subject while you were on your phone again."

"No," Evie shot back. She wasn't backing down; there was something really off at this table. "Since we got here, Alfred hasn't wanted to talk about the case all night. He was barely interested in the ingredients *he* asked for and I've had to put us back on topic multiple times."

"That's not true," Laika defended. But Evie could feel the worry building up in her friend as the events of the night ran through her mind.

"If I may," began Alfred. His voice was still that polite, unemotional tone that was starting to grate on Evie's ears.

"No, you may not. We came here to get on the case and our theory was good. But he's denying us anyway even though we can help." Evie stood up with enough force that her chair toppled backwards. She hastily jammed papers back into the tote bag and stormed out the doors of the day-proof room.

Servers scrambled out of the angry werewolf's way as Evie furiously marched for the front door.

"Evie!" yelled Laika, trying to catch up only a second behind her. "Where are you going?"

"I'm going home!"

"Seriously?"

Evie didn't answer as she let the door fall back into her pack-mate's face. Even the cool fall air of the evening didn't sober her up.

There was something so off about this night and it wasn't just that she'd crashed a date.

Falling into step beside her, Laika tried to calm her again. "Please tell me what's going on?"

"He's lying to us and stonewalling us from this case!" Evie had reached her car. She ripped open the back door to hurl the tote inside. "Why? Why would he do that?"

"Where is this coming from?" begged Laika with a bewildered look.

"I think that's more than obvious at this point?" Evie exploded, uncaring if anyone was watching them.

"Not really!"

The women were standing ten feet apart and yelling at each other in the dimly lit parking lot. A few bystanders rushed past to safety where they could gossip in peace about the lunatics screaming outside.

"Think about it," spat Evie. She tried to lay out her case, "We did the possibility board and there were what, three options? A circle of witches, some elves, or a rose vampire."

"So?" Laika crossed her arms. Right now her emotions were hard to read because of how upset Evie was.

"Oh come on? You've noticed by now that Alfred has the answers to all the magic questions right? He gets called to all the big magic cases in Glenwood." Evie presented her evidence at the top of her lungs.

Her packmate shifted uncomfortably, "I mean, yeah I'd noticed. But Tor told us it's rude to ask so I haven't asked him."

"You don't need to ask, he's advertising it for us. So we've got a rose vampire in Glenwood who has avoided telling us multiple times that a rose could do all of this shit. We found a way to link all the cases and predict them, and the same person doesn't want to pursue it?"

Laika reminded, "Evie, you're really moonburnt right now. I

know you don't want to hear it, but you are and you're not thinking clearly. Why would Alfred do any of this? He's got no motive?"

"I don't know! Yet! Maybe he wants to be the big hero around Glenwood when he stops the attacks. Or maybe he wanted to meet a pretty moonlighting werewolf!" Evie could hear the crazy coming out of her mouth, but she couldn't stop it.

"Evie," Laika tried to soothe her again, "Please calm down so we can talk about this rationally."

But Evie needed to get away from this dinner, this fight, and everything else going wrong today. She pulled open the driver's side door with a huff before slamming it and hitting the gas, peeling away from Longtooth and not looking back.

CHAPTER 21
DATE

Laika
October 19th, 2018
Longtooth Steakhouse, Glenwood, CA

L aika stared open-mouthed as the Saab sped away. Evie had just left her stranded at a restaurant like a bad date. And for what? Blowing up in a conspiracy theory fueled rage? Her packmate desperately needed to run and Laika sent her a message emphasizing that. She needed to catch up quickly before Evie did something stupid. Or dangerous, such as crashing the car.

Staring down at her phone, Laika considered just sending a text to Alfred so she didn't have to face him. How embarrassing was it going to be to explain what happened before calling an Uber? But he'd been so polite all night and he was inches from letting them join the case. With a heavy sigh, Laika turned around to face him with the truth.

As Laika went back inside, she could hear all the whispering about her exit. Rumors flew from table to table, and even the hostess was debating with her co-worker. One of them was sure that Evie was the wife who'd met her husband's mistress and they'd confronted him together. The other swore that the scene was a breakup between the two women because Laika wasn't really gay.

Fighting off any reaction, Laika made her way back while pretending to be as deaf as everyone else. She kept her eyes on the floor, refusing to look at people. Even when she bumped into another woman with pink streaks through her hair, Laika barely glanced up to apologize before brushing past.

Laika paused as she reached the door Evie had stormed out of not five minutes prior. Her hand hesitated on the handle, taking a deep breath. Alfred had been so unflappable with everything, he'd understand surely. "Hey, I'm really sorry about that," Laika began as she pushed the door open.

Only to find Alfred wasn't alone anymore. Their waitress was tying up two plastic bags that likely contained their dinner. Meanwhile, Alfred was signing the check and leaving the waitress's tip on the table. "Do not fret about it."

There was a tinge of disappointment as the steak disappeared into boxes. Which was silly, since Laika had come back in to say she had to leave. Either way, it was the end of dinner.

"I assumed you would need to leave. So I had the dinner boxed to go, so you may at least enjoy your steak at home." Alfred gave the waitress a tight lipped smile as he handed her the signed receipt and she left them.

"Oh... That was very thoughtful, and yes... I need to call an Uber. Evie took the car already, but first I feel like I owe you an apology." Before Laika could say any more, she was waved off.

"Please. As I said, do not fret about it," Alfred reassured. He seemed calm despite the second meal ruined within the span of a week. "May I offer you a ride home?"

Laika paused, looking up at him with a flicker of surprise. Every time they met up a disaster had or was happening, putting an end to the day quickly. For all she knew he'd heard them screaming in the parking lot.

After her internal revelation about the crush, she'd found it easier to let go of any awkward feelings. Alfred was tall, he was handsome, and so far had rolled with all the crazy in her life. A chance to talk to him a bit more would be welcomed. Maybe even figure out if he'd be interested in more than just case work after all of this was over.

Laika offered up a quick grin as thanks. "Sure, if it's not too much trouble. It would be nice to not end the night on such a down note."

"No trouble at all." Alfred checked over the table, making sure he had everything and picked up the two bags then added, "I feel I should warn you about my car."

"Why?" Laika's curiosity immediately piqued. She knew that Evie should be the priority, but until she got home there was nothing to do about that. Especially since her messages had still gone unanswered.

"Are you familiar with day-proofed cars?"

"Not really..." Laika admitted.

Alfred's face brightened enough she could see his fangs. "Then I will not be offended if you change your mind."

Laika mirrored the warm expression. "Really? Is it that bad?"

"Most of the living find it dreadfully uncomfortable." He held the door open for Laika as they made their way into the restaurant proper, then to the parking lot.

She peppered him with questions trying to guess why, appreciating the distraction from the gossiping people all around them. Once they reached the cars, Laika looked around for something that screamed 'vampire'. Nothing stood out, though.

When Alfred came to a stop, she almost did a double take. The town car was in good condition, clearly well cared for, but it was easily a decade old. At first glance it appeared to be just a normal black car; then she saw the issue. "All of the windows are blacked out?" Laika tilted her head to the side while he put their dinner in the back. "How do you see? Can you see through all that tinting?"

"No, there are cameras along the outside that feed screens so I may see around the car during the day," explained Alfred. This was the closest to uncomfortable he'd appeared during their conversations. "Some people find it unnerving, but as the sun is set we can roll the windows down."

Laika blinked as she studied his face. There was honest confusion at why this, of all things, would make him uncomfortable. She cracked a grin before responding, "If that's all that's 'dreadfully uncomfortable' I think we'll be fine. Plus if we have the windows down it'll be hard to hear each other, even with our hearing."

"You may change your mind in the car," warned Alfred.

"No I won't. I was half expecting a hearse with your vague comments," Laika answered by sliding into the passenger seat. As he'd said, there were nine screens up front that came to life with the engine. Each one held a different angle, giving a decent 360 view around the town car.

"A hearse? That would draw quite a bit of attention for no reason." Alfred checked his screens before backing them out of the space.

"Well, next time be more specific!"

"I believe you will find I am rarely specific about anything," Alfred replied. His tone almost sounded teasing.

Laika gave him a look that read as a challenge. "So I'll just need to get more specific with my questions then?"

"If you want specific answers, I suppose so."

"I'll keep that in mind then." Laika's eyes were now roaming over the interior. The seats and dashboard were clean and well kept. There wasn't much light inside though as the windows blocked out everything, even the street lamps they drove past.

Alfred's gaze flickered from the screens to his passenger. "Is it too dark?"

"No, not at all," Laika responded without hesitation. She drug her eyes from scanning the car and back to her friend. "It's just you can tell a lot about a person from their car."

There was the slightest hint of challenge on Alfred's lips, at least as much as she could make out from the glow of the screens. "Is that so? And what have you learned?"

"That either this is a rental that you got just to go to dinner... Or you're an extremely tidy person. Not even a scrap of paper on the floor. Which is it?"

"Is your car covered in paper?" His eyebrows furrowed in confusion.

Laika's eyebrow raised in response as he side stepped her question. It wasn't the first time, but it seemed like a harmless one. Still, that was a strange question to avoid, so Laika put a pin in it for later. "Well no... Because I don't have one. Evie's car on the other hand..."

"Ah. What does Evie's car say about you two then?" Alfred encouraged.

Laika pushed back. Two could play this game. "What do you think it says?"

"That Evie may have some abandonment issues." His line was delivered with a straight face, but the teasing tone gave it away.

Laika couldn't resist laughing. In between laughs she scolded, "That's horrible... and maybe a little accurate."

Alfred gave a shrug in response. "So is inviting yourself on a date without asking, storming off in the middle, and stranding your roommate without a ride home."

"Well, moonburn is kind of unpredictable. It's half my fault for not stopping her-" There was a pause as the gears in Laika's brain caught up. What had Alfred just said? "Wait... date?" Laika echoed the word back.

Alfred kept his eyes on the screens. "I suspected when both of you arrived that my invitation had been misunderstood."

"I thought you wanted to work on the case, since we hadn't gotten to actually talk about it," Laika trailed off.

Her mind ran through everything that had been said while planning the meeting. Nothing he had said screamed 'date' at her... But it did explain the awkwardness at the table.

"In all fairness, I did enjoy the case working part of the evening and most of the conversation," soothed the vampire.

"So... That was a date? Like a date date?"

"No, that was not a date, as I do not date multiple women at the same time."

"Oh..." Laika fell silent. She felt a bubble of excitement grow, but worked to keep it from creeping onto her face. "Well, that's good. Because I do not date men who date multiple women at the same time."

Alfred managed to turn his full attention to her as they stopped at a red light. "I am glad we can both agree on that point. Perhaps I can try this again then. Miss-"

"Do you want to go out to dinner?" Laika knew what he was about to say. She rushed her words, beating him to the question.

That gave the vampire pause. His expression moved to surprise as his second attempt to ask her out died on his lips. Then Alfred cleared his throat, "Yes, Miss Lowell. I would enjoy that."

The part of Laika that had realized her crush earlier screamed happily. But another part of her mind had caught on something else. "I don't recall telling you my last name."

"Your full name was on the Pixie Dust report," supplied Alfred quickly.

Laika went pale. She should've been riding high on him accepting the invitation. However, right now she wanted to sink into her seat from embarrassment. "Ah... my full name?"

"Yes, your full name. Obviously, I have realized you prefer your middle name." Alfred's face stayed perfectly straight.

Laika leaned forward glad the light was still red as she tried to keep Alfred's focus. "You don't understand. That is like the most top secret information. Half of my siblings don't know my first name!"

"That your first name is Lulu?" Alfred looked confused. The light turned green on them and the car started moving, pulling his attention back to driving. Only the fact that the vampire was driving stopped Laika from reaching up to cover his mouth before he could say her name. Probably for the best; that would be a little too touchy too soon.

"Shh! If word got out here... I mean Owen and Aaron know obviously, but if Blood Fang found out? I'd never live it down!" she lamented.

"I see. Then I shall be sure never to mention that to them. Still, this could be much worse. At least your initials are only LLL; one letter back in the alphabet and you could be stuck with something less polite in the current day," Alfred teased. The smile that he'd had since they left the restaurant was still resting comfortably on his face.

Once again, he'd disarmed her with a joke. Laika relaxed back against the seat, laughing at how he'd said such a thing with a straight face. "I guess you're right... but 'Lulu' is a pretty terrible name."

Alfred turned the car onto her familiar street. "I find it pretty."

Laika felt her cheeks grow warm. "You don't have to lie to spare my feelings... or are you trying to butter me up?"

"If I intend to ask you to join my case to do the less than glorious work of running down leads, then you being in a good mood would be preferred." He stopped the town car in front of her house.

"Join your case?" Laika echoed the words, a grin spreading across her face in a flash. On the screen she could see Evie's car was parked on the driveway, diagonally, but she was in no rush to get out of Alfred's car just yet.

"As you said, you are going to keep looking into the break-ins. If that is true, then I might as well have you look into them for me and save me the time," reminded Alfred.

"That's true... You're awesome! I promise, you won't regret this!" Laika was practically dancing in her seat with excitement. A date and a case! Even with Evie's freak out, this day was panning out amazingly.

"I will inquire with the GPD in the morning about adding the

Night Claw pack." Alfred gave her another warm look, all of the stiffness from dinner long gone.

"And I will make some plans for our date. No tag-alongs this time, I promise." The amber of Laika's eyes sparkled.

This was much more like how they spoke in text messages. Any worries Laika had earlier were gone. The conversation was comfortable and fun. If they hadn't been parked in front of evidence of a disaster she needed to handle, she could sit here and talk for hours.

"Wonderful. We can attempt to plan for next Friday?" He reached behind the seat to get both bags with all three meals for her.

"Sounds like a plan," Laika agreed readily. She had considered countering with something like 'why not tomorrow?' but there was a good chance she'd be dragging a grumpy werewolf out to a run tomorrow. "If you need any help with your case, you know how to reach me?"

"Of course."

Laika was handed the bags and seriously considered ripping into her dinner now. She'd been hungry when they arrived at Longtooth. Everything was so clean in here though; it would be a shame to stain the seats. "I guess this is good night?"

"Sadly, it does appear that way. As much as I would enjoy another few hours of sitting here, I believe you have a packmate to attend to," Alfred said as he popped the locks open.

"Yeah," Laika sighed as she unbuckled her seatbelt. Each motion was slow, dragging out the departure. "But we are on for next Friday right?"

"I will be looking forward to Friday all week."

Finally, Laika opened the door and gave an awkward wave. A glance at Evie's car reminded her she did need to move, so Laika got out of the town car. "Sleep well!"

"Good night," Alfred returned the wave.

Laika was halfway to the door when she remembered the most important question she'd meant to ask all night. Kicking off her flats, she turned running back to the window with a knock. "Hey! One more thing?"

"Yes?" The black glass lowered to show a curious Alfred.

"What's your last name?"

"I was wondering when you would get around to asking. My last name is Klímek," answered Alfred.

CHAPTER 22
MOONBURNT

Evie
October 20th, 2018
Night Claw Residence, Glenwood, CA

Evie felt awful. Her head ached like she'd been drinking heavily all night. The words would never leave her mouth, but she knew that Laika and Shelly had a point about being moonburnt. She stared at the bathroom mirror, annoyed at how bad her skin looked from terrible sleep. A reflection of smeared makeup and frayed emotions glared back. Her wavy red strands couldn't be tamed into place, either.

Last night, Laika had followed her home pretty quick after being abandoned. Then she'd tried to get Evie up for a run then and there. All Laika's effort only got her head bitten off. Her friend had gone to sleep on the couch. Evie owed her an apology for that behavior.

Evie cleaned her face with warm water while she made a list of things to do today. Making things right with Laika was at the very top. That meant coffee and food before even attempting to talk to her.

Once she deemed herself passable for her roommates, Evie made a beeline for the kitchen. She tiptoed past the others, who were chatting in the living room. A quick read of emotions came back with a mixture of concern, amusement, and the usual calm that cloaked Tor.

A tray hit the countertop first, followed by four mugs for coffee. Evie busied herself with preparing a pot of the expensive moonbeans blend that she usually saved for guests. While the pot bubbled away, she picked up her phone.

This was a little excessive, but since she was trying to smooth things over... An order was placed for donuts from Laika's favorite shop. Expensive and frivolous, but a sure-fire way to win her pack-mate over. Evie paced the kitchen as she waited, watching the app to be sure the driver brought the donuts around to the back. Running through the day before, she had to admit that she had flown off the handle.

Tony had spun her up, not the first or the last time she was sure. She needed to get actual explanations out of him instead of vague texts. If Alfred was this dangerous rose vampire that Tony meant, she needed to know.

A knock at the back door caught Evie's attention. A few minutes later she was armed with a tray of fresh moonbeans coffee and warm donuts. Taking a deep breath, she nudged the kitchen door open and made her way out to the living room.

"Good morning." Evie's voice was sweet. "I have coffee and donuts."

Laika looked up from her phone screen. She was still wearing the sundress from last night, but it was wrinkled now. There was a sharp spike of annoyance, likely from sleeping on the couch and not being able to change all night. "It's morning, at least."

Evie put the tray down on the coffee table. "I know. I know. I'm sorry."

"What are you sorry for?" prompted Laika.

Shelly looked up from her laptop, watching the women with a carefully neutral expression.

Evie sighed again. She knew she had to just own up now to her bad behavior. "I'm sorry for insisting on coming with you last night. After we got there I knew it had been a mistake, but at that point I was there."

From the armchair near the couch Tor spoke up, "So it was a date?"

"No," Laika shot back quickly, "That wasn't a date."

"It doesn't matter," Evie tried to move on, even as she felt a flicker of relief. If that hadn't been a date, that was one less thing to worry about. "At the end of the day, I was out of line. I shouldn't have shouted at you, or left you stranded."

There was a momentary hard look from Laika, but it faded with a sigh. "It's okay Evie, I mean... It's not okay, but I forgive you." The wolf reached to snag a donut from the tray at last.

"Thank you!" Evie felt relief flooding through her for the first time today.

Laika continued, gesturing with the donut, "You are moonburnt and while it's not an excuse, it explains why you're so frazzled."

The instinct to refute that she was moonburnt was on Evie's lips in an instant. But she caught herself. "Okay, okay. We can head out to the park once you're done with breakfast."

"What?" Laika raised an eyebrow as she took a bite out of the donut. "There's no way you're going to a run park."

Shelly cracked up from her spot on the couch. Her coffee barely made it back onto the table as she half toppled over. "A run park? Seriously?"

"Excuse me?" snapped Evie. The calm atmosphere was evaporating fast.

"Evie. I know you are trying right now and I appreciate it," Laika's tone was sincere, matching her emotions, "But... you aren't stable enough to go to a run park right now."

"I'm fine! I just need like thirty minutes of laps!" insisted Evie.

"No," Shelly threw her arms up in an 'x' in front of her. "You need 3 to 4 hours of running, playing, and maybe even a nap in wolf form."

"At least," Laika agreed with a nod.

"Why can't she just sleep in the front yard?" Tor spoke up, her voice laced with interest again.

"Do what now?" Evie looked shocked at the suggestion.

"Like Shelly does? I find her out there most days either sleeping or playing fetch with the neighbor kids," Tor explained.

Everyone turned to look at Shelly, whose face was turning red rapidly. "I... um."

Tor looked taken aback. "Is that not normal?"

"No," Laika and Evie echoed each other. They shared a quick look before the redhead added, "Why would you do that?"

"It's complicated," Shelly tried to wave them off, "I'm careful about it and no one gets hurt."

"Is that something your family does?" Laika asked, curiosity was dripping off every word.

Shelly shook her head vehemently. "Never. My father would disown me again for letting human children touch me while I'm on four paws."

"So why then?" This time it was Evie who tried to understand. She could feel how uncomfortable their new roommate was, but she had to know.

"Because I don't know how to socialize with humans at all. Before leaving home, I'd seen about two people who weren't related to me in my whole life. And now I don't know how to even stand next to them without being awkward... the kids are easy," shrugged Shelly.

Evie understood. "Oh... okay then. Just be careful, because parents could get really scared if they learned you weren't just a big dog in the yard."

Shelly nodded, "I know. I shift in the house and leave the back door open."

"Back to the subject at hand," Laika cut in. She also seemed at peace with Shelly's answer. "Evie, you can't go to a run park right now. If you snap then you'll hurt someone, since everyone around here is a domestic wolf and you're a trained moonlighter."

"So? What does that mean?" Evie felt her frustration culminating faster than she wanted. Another sign she needed this stupid run.

Laika groaned, "It means we need to find land to run on! Far away from everyone, just to be safe."

Tor chuckled this time. "You picked a bad week for that. Every cabin in the state is booked for Halloween parties already."

"I know, but I'll find somewhere," Laika lamented as she pulled her phone back up to her face.

"So I just need to keep my shit together for another couple days? Easy," Evie nodded.

---———( )———---

October 23rd, 2018
Taran Estate, Los Angeles, CA

"I don't know how you did it," Owen said for the third time.

Evie's phone sat on speaker so she could free up both hands for writing. "I told you. Night Claw was always meant for more than cleaning up physical fights."

"This case is so far over your rank. I wouldn't have ever let you near it, but the lead moonlighter asked for you and Laika." Owen's voice was filled with disbelief.

"I know, can you repeat that number again for me?" Evie was taking note of all the release numbers she'd been given. With these she could call up the surrounding areas' police stations and actually request the records she was looking for. They could deny her with a valid reason, but likely no one cared about a few robberies that much.

Owen repeated the number once more before pressing again, "Are you not going to tell me how you pulled this off?"

Evie pursed her lips, trying to decide how to answer the question. She hadn't done anything to make this happen, and had probably hurt their chances more than helped. However, telling Owen that the lead moonlighter was looking for an excuse to spend time with her packmate sounded bad.

"Evie?" Owen prompted.

"We had a really promising lead, alright?" She defended.

"The whole break-in angle?" Owen sounded skeptical, his emotions were miles away and out of range to confirm.

"Yes, the break-ins. Obviously, Alfred agreed there was some merit here and he's letting us pursue it for him. Rather than waste his time if we're wrong." Evie smiled, knowing that had a certain logic to it.

A heavy sigh answered her and Owen added, "Yeah, that makes sense. He's been denying LA's expert's help since Hazel got into town, and has been on this full time when he's not at another scene."

"Really?"

"Yeah. So I guess any lead is a good lead when you're into your second month of dead ends."

"That's weird right?" Evie prompted. She started thinking of ways to get more information out of the officer.

Owen responded, "Which part?"

"That he doesn't want LA's help. This is a huge mess and we should be accepting help anywhere we can!" insisted Evie.

Laughter rang out before Owen answered, "Actually, it's not that weird. Alfred works part time at LA's MOONS, and from what I hear they hate him."

Evie frowned. "Oh."

"Alright. I need to go, I have more cases than just this one. And I can't stand around all day gossiping about boys," teased Owen. "Don't do anything stupid with your new powers of research. Bye!"

Evie's eyes glanced at the phone with a deeper frown on her lips. She'd wanted more information. Her theory about the vampire wasn't dead in the water yet, even if she wasn't bringing it up around her packmate right now. But Evie had another matter to attend to presently.

"You can come out now," she called towards the door of the kitchen. Evie had sat down at the high counter when the phone rang originally.

Arik appeared a moment later. Every inch of him radiated excitement, from his expression to the aura bomb exploding with every step. "Do we have a case?"

"You already know I have a case. Since you've been listening at the door the entire time," snapped Evie. She deftly started folding up her notes before the elf could see them clearly.

He placed his hands on his hips defiantly. "You took a work call on my time," Arik countered.

"I am entitled to a fifteen minute break once in a while."

That seemed to take the wind out of the Arik's sails for a moment. She felt the flicker in his aura before he regrouped. "Do you want to be able to work that case during the day or not?"

Evie's head snapped up and she spun the chair around to face him. "What?"

"I said, do you want to work on that during my time or not?"

Her eyes narrowed as Evie sensed a trap beginning to unfold. "What's the catch?"

Arik's lips spread into a predatory smile. "I get to be involved in every minute for research purposes. Every phone call, every report, and every minute of the action."

"This is all just going to be boring research," Evie reminded him. She hadn't been cleared for any field work. There was no point in lying to her boss either.

"But that's where all the details are right? A good story comes down to the little things and how realistic and relatable they are." Arik looked completely serious.

"I guess..."

"Good, then it's settled. You give me all your research so that I can use it for the script, and you get to work on your research here.

We have a deal!" Before Evie could even think to disagree, Arik walked back to the doorway and yelled to the rest of the house. "Tony, cancel all my appearances this week!"

The vampire screeched back, "ARE YOU KIDDING ME!?"

Evie knew that tone too well. Tony's aura flared up like an inferno from the direction of his ground floor office. A second later, she felt the heat start moving their way.

"Of course I'm not kidding," sighed Arik. He glanced back at Evie with a look that read how obvious that should be.

"All of your appearances?" Tony was visibly annoyed when he joined them in the kitchen. His expression was dour. "Do you know how hot you are right now after your brush with death? We literally couldn't pay for this much attention! And you want to just throw them away? For what?"

"We have a case!" Arik declared brightly.

"A case?" Tony approached the other two at the countertop. "What case?"

"The same one as before," admitted Evie. She put her iPad down for both men to see while pulling open her folder of notes. "But I've been officially assigned to it and all the reports just got sent to me."

"So let me get this straight," Tony said. He was pretending to be calm right now as Evie could feel him boiling under the surface. "You want to blow off your fans and all the attention they'll give you, to play private dick for the week?"

"No," scoffed Arik. Again he gave Evie a look like he couldn't believe how dense the vampire was right now. "This is research for the screenplay."

Tony snapped, "We both know that the screenplay is going nowhere!"

Internally, Evie agreed with Tony. The script was a complete nonsensical mess that would never see the light of day. But she'd only agreed to write something, not something good. A side eye from Tony meant he'd read something off her. He didn't comment on whatever he got, though, as he continued to bicker with Arik.

"Come now," Arik half pleaded. "That's what editors are for. I'll hire a good one to take the raw draft from Evie and clean it up a bit. Have you read what she's got so far?"

"No. I prefer my fantasy with a lot more undressed men in it and less murder," Tony hissed in a mocking tone.

Evie giggled against her better judgment.

"Oh, don't be like that. Hold on; I have the latest copy around here," Arik promised as he got up from the countertop. He was already searching the rest of the kitchen with his eyes.

"No, really it's fine," dismissed Tony.

"Just a moment. I'll get you the script to read while we start our research. If by the time you're done you don't believe we have something real here, then I'll go to my appearances this week." Arik's declaration was accompanied by a wave of sincerity that neither empath could mistake.

Tony gave the elf another skeptical look. "Those terms seem fair."

"Good," Arik said. He was halfway out the room looking for the physical screenplay before they'd even finished talking. The entire way, he mumbled to himself about the last place he'd been reading yesterday.

As soon as her boss was out of sight, Evie moved to defend herself. "This was not my idea."

"I know it wasn't," Tony rolled his eyes, taking up the empty seat. "Arik is a damn addict and moonlighting is just the latest in a long line of drugs."

"He'll get bored quickly. I only got permission to look up some break-ins and compile a couple lists for Alfred," Evie explained, hoping to reassure Tony.

Tony nearly leapt out of his skin at her words. His chair toppled to the floor as the vampire scrambled away from her, while fear enveloped the kitchen. "What did you just say?"

Evie was on high alert now. "I said I was only allowed to do research?"

"No!"

"No, I can't do research?" Evie was inching away slowly, "Or no I can't do research for *Alfred*?"

"I told you on Friday! Turn and run as far and as fast as you can from that guy!" reprimanded Tony, fear rippling from every word.

"No you didn't," Evie shot back.

Their text conversation was a little fuzzy from before, but she remembered Tony saying it couldn't be the guy he thought. Or did she misunderstand? She wasn't on her A-game and still hadn't been for a run. Everywhere was booked solid for the season. Another couple days and they'd risk the run park anyways.

"Yes I did! If he's an emotionless void of a rose vampire, then get up and leave! Don't look back! Don't care about how 'rude' it might be! Your life was on the line." The initial shock had passed Tony now. But his aura was still swirling with intense concern and a lot of genuine fear.

"Why?"

"You don't need the details. You just need to detangle yourself!"

"It's more complicated than that... is Alfred dangerous? I mean, he's a moonlighter so of course he's some level of danger. But I mean to me? Or I guess to us?" Evie felt her own emotions rising, feeding off the panic radiating off of Tony.

Tony picked up the chair before retaking a seat at the countertop. He reached out his hand, placing it millimeters from Evie's without making contact. "There is a chance it's not the guy... but LA used to have a rose vampire named Alfred in the coven. He was bad news, like, the big bad guy in the worst horror movie you can think of." Evie inched herself towards Tony. His story was enrapturing her and she wished she could record it for later. "LA has a lot of scary powerful vampires in it. We have like three iris and a handful of peonies in the LA Coven! But even with all that, he was the worst of them and he's responsible for I don't even know how many deaths."

"And you think this is the same vampire?" Evie whispered.

"I don't know for sure. I never met him personally, but I heard all of the stories. If even half of them are true, then you're fucked if you keep messing around with him." The warning Tony gave was resolute.

"Why isn't he still in LA? Did the coven drive him out?" Evie wanted to reach out and take Tony's hand but she resisted. If he'd wanted contact, then he would have initiated himself. Tony's fear was infectious, creeping along her spine like roots trying to take hold in her skin.

"Here we go!" Arik declared in triumph. He split the tension in the kitchen clean in half as he took a bow. "I left it in the bathroom upstairs. You read this while Evie and I do research."

"Uh... sure," Tony mumbled, stealing his hand back to take the stack of loose papers. His usual demeanor was muted by the heavy conversation.

Meanwhile, Evie was feeling herself getting spun up on the fear and uncertainty of everything. She had to force the calm back into her system before she did something humiliating like shifting. While Arik was talking a mile a minute at her, Evie wasn't listening as she put herself in order.

"So I'll make the calls then?" Arik put a hand on her shoulder jarring Evie back to the present.

"What calls?"

Arik clarified, "To the police stations! Haven't you been listening to a word I said?"

"I'm sorry," Evie apologized. She gave herself a quick shake trying to keep calm. "Tony had just been telling me about the types of vampires and I got distracted by it."

Tony rolled with the lie. "Yeah, I was just trying to be helpful."

Arik's interest was piqued by the news. "Oh really? Trying to rule them out or in?"

"Either," Evie latched onto any thread of conversation. She opened up the copy of the mystery board to explain what they'd done already and the holes still there.

"I see," Arik nodded along before taking the device for himself. "And Tony, you know all about the missing ones?"

"Did you just ask me if I understood how vampires worked?" Tony was getting back in his element.

"Uh... yes?" Arik shrugged unapologetically. "Could an iris do these attacks?"

"I couldn't find much about them online," admitted Evie. Everything she'd found said they had long fangs and dealt in blood. But what vampire didn't?

"They are creepy as all hell," exclaimed Tony.

"How enlightening," deadpanned Arik. "Evie, we should get back to our own research now."

Before the werewolf could respond, Tony cut back in. "Excuse me, I wasn't finished. Irises are creepy as hell because they have blood magic. Like, actual magic that requires blood to do things like turning people into puppets."

"Like you?" Evie wanted clarification on what that meant. She'd been sure Tony was a chrysanthemum vampire.

"Both of you bitches are trying to be ignorant today. No, nothing like me." Tony huffed at them.

He abandoned the script on the kitchen counter so he could gesture with both hands. "I am a beautiful emotional manipulator. People do as I say because I can literally charm the pants off them."

"And?" Arik prompted him to continue.

"Irises are brutes who take over your motor control with blood magic. It's not even close to the same thing." Tony rolled his eyes as if this should have been obvious.

"So no turning people to glass then," Evie mumbled more to herself while she took notes.

"Peonies are the ones with the claws and rows of fangs. I don't think they've got any magic other than being able to clear a crowded dance floor in seconds." Tony went on to give the little he knew about them.

Evie crossed them off the list as well. They sounded all physical, which made it unlikely a peony was behind the attacks in Glenwood. "What about lilacs?"

"Lilacs are daywalkers and as far as I know they're one-trick ponies with no real magic," Tony scoffed. Evie looked expectantly at him for what trick that was. "They are the guy at the party who never stops talking about his bottled ships collection until he's killed the vibe and everyone is nodding off."

"Uh..." Evie wasn't sure how to even ask for a clarification on what that meant, so she prompted, "And orchids?"

Tony paused to bite his lip. Finally he said, "They might not even be real."

"What?" Arik again pushed him to explain. "What do you mean? I have always heard there are seven types of vampire. I just don't know a lot about the last one beyond my grandmother ranting hatefully."

"I've never met or seen one before. They supposedly can steal your face and powers if you have contact with them," Tony shrugged. He clearly didn't believe the last court was real because he continued, "But I think it's just a scary story people tell new vampires to keep them in line."

"But an orchid could be behind these attacks. Since they could copy the magic needed for each one of these rituals?" Evie tried to wrap her head around that. Then she marked them as possible on her notes. She'd update the shared document once she got her iPad back from Arik.

"Yeah, I guess," Tony agreed, "But I seriously doubt a vampire is doing this. You don't piss off the food supply if you don't have to."

Evie nodded, her attention firmly on the papers in front of her. Right now they had two types of vampires, four types of elves, and an angry circle of witches that could be blamed. Evie needed to find a way to cross something off the list, but that meant more time with her nose in a book. "Thanks, this was really helpful!"

Arik surprised her by speaking up a minute later. "I can help with these missing elves you have on here. But I'll need to reach out to my family for more details on them, and we're in different timezones right now. Send me a copy of this."

"Sure," Evie agreed, finally getting her hands back on her iPad. "Thank you both. For now, though, I need to start making calls to request reports."

"I'll take half the list," Arik quickly interjected himself, "It'll be faster this way. Just in case Tony tries to cheat and speed reads our screenplay."

Evie rolled her eyes at the 'screenplay' going from 'hers' to 'theirs' in less than a month. But at least she had help for the fifty phone calls she had left to do today. "If anyone asks, you are a werewolf and you belong to the Night Claw pack."

———•——◡——•———

October 25th, 2018
Taran Estate, Los Angeles, CA

"I've got coffee," Arik's voice called into the big living room. Whenever research got too boring for his attention span, he went to get everyone food and drinks. Yesterday he'd declared the kitchen wasn't comfortable enough for them to keep working. So Arik had moved their efforts here and had some ancient chalkboards and a fax machine pulled from storage. He, Tony, and Evie had a decent system in place for organizing the records they'd received so far.

Evie sat on a plush couch with her legs pulled up and files on every surface in reach. Her main job was to do the initial read and decide if it was worth further research. Anything that fit the timeline was then passed to Tony.

The vampire made follow up calls to precincts to see if any leads had panned out in those cases. Then he updated their copies and checked for a full list of stolen ingredients.

Finally, Arik wrote out a clean copy of relevant information for

Evie to pass along. He had the best handwriting among them by far, and if he did this boring job, then he could steal ideas from the cases for their screenplay unchecked. Coffee runs had become his secondary job when he needed a break.

"Thank you." Evie took the lukewarm drink offered. Her boss hadn't learned to pay the extra quarter for a heat-em-up charm on the bottom of the cup yet.

"Guess who I saw?" Arik sat across from Evie, sipping at his own drink.

"Who?"

"Your ex was there again with her boyfriend. She must love that place or is really trying to make you jealous," he teased.

"Who?" Evie echoed herself before remembering the last time she'd been to Last Drop. "I told you Becky isn't my ex. I barely even know her. Hell, even if she'd gone to my high school I wouldn't be able to tell her apart from anyone else."

"Cold as ice," teased Tony. He'd just hung up with a detective from the latest case. She could see him writing in some updates, but the break-in at that particular store seemed pretty unlikely to be in their pattern.

"I'm not being cold for the sake of it. I had a lot going on with my family when I was in high school. My sisters had moved out and never looked back, leaving me alone with my mother and younger brother all the time. She went out of her way to make me hate myself every single day of the year," complained Evie. Only years of time and space allowed her to talk about this. "Especially after I started shifting. I didn't have a large social circle by the end. While I wasn't a raging jerk to anyone, I basically kept to only my close friends before I ran away."

"You're a runaway?" Arik seemed surprised by that. Then he added, "I also ran away from my family for a while. Sometimes you just need the distance to finish growing up."

"Yeah, something like that," muttered Evie. She'd run for her life more than her sanity. Then continued after a moment, "But either way, I don't remember any blonde elven Beckies at school."

Arik tutted before correcting her, "Becky is not an elf. She's a half elf."

"What's the difference?" Evie asked, "And before you get on me about not knowing there is a difference, I assumed there was but I don't know what it is, so I'm asking."

The scowl forming on Arik's face melted away. "Pureblooded elves like myself have two elven parents and will inherit their magic, while half elves are born of only one elven parent and do not have the ability to use any magic."

Evie was itching to pick up her notepad to write all of this down. But her boss would probably find it rude so she resisted. "And Becky is a half elf... how can you tell?"

"Her ears are too short and that blonde comes out of a bottle. Usually, I can feel the lack of magic in them as well. But anyone who comes from Bel Aire money can afford magical trinkets to pretend to have power. She had a few of those on her," explained Arik.

"I guess that makes sense."

Arik shrugged. "I'm surprised you would have any half elves living in the hallways of Bel Aire. She's likely her elven parent's bastard child."

Evie didn't even know what to ask to follow that up. The statement had been delivered with a cold indifference from Arik. She fumbled with words. "Ummm... why would you think that?"

"Elves don't marry outside their race unless they are of no consequence. Everyone living in Bel Aire has an old and proud bloodline. No one would get away with having a half elf child around unless they'd failed to have any other children."

"Again with all the bloodline politics. Elves are worse than vampires about blood purity," grumbled Tony.

"It matters," defended Arik. "How much elven blood you have and which bloodlines determine how powerful you can be. If two elves can't have their own children, then they'll try outside their marriage looking for help from a brother or cousin. If they still can't conceive, then a half elf daughter is better than nothing."

"Why?" Evie hated everything about this conversation. Every word was completely backwards and insane to her. She forced herself to keep calm by holding onto the arm of the couch. The moonburn was rearing its ugly head again; Laika was still searching for somewhere safe for her to run and they were on dozens of waiting lists. For now all she could do was breathe deeply and focus on staying sane.

"Because a daughter can have more children and keep the bloodline alive. Elven society is a matriarchy because you can always know for certain who the mother is and trace back her bloodline. Even if their only child is a half elf, she can be paired up with a full blooded elf, like her boyfriend."

Evie gave Arik an incredulous look. "So you think Petronius is going to be Becky's baby daddy?"

"Probably, and it does explain why he's so uninterested in her. Must be the least favorite son if he got stuck with the half elf," concluded Arik. He still sat unfazed and drank his coffee.

"All of that is so messed up!" Evie looked to Tony for help, but the vampire only appeared put out, likely having heard all of this before.

Arik's response was to shrug.

"What about you, then? Have you been paired up with a nice elven girl to 'keep the bloodline alive'?" Evie knew the question was possibly over the line, but this whole conversation had her on edge.

"That is none of your business!" Arik shot her a stern look, everything about him read to drop the subject.

"Okay," Evie went back to her coffee. She watched him out of the side of her eye as another thought occurred to her. "If two elves have different bloodlines, what magic do their children inherit?"

"Both or all if the parents have more than one bloodline," answered Arik, "But it would be a far less powerful version of the original magic."

"Theoretically, one elf could have all the bloodlines and use all of them?" Evie's eyes glanced back at the mystery board, considering how that changed things.

"I suppose, but some combinations work better than others and some can't be used at the same time," clarified Arik.

"What about the bloodlines needed for the ritual? Could one elf do all of this?" pressed Evie.

Arik picked up his tablet, opening up his copy of the mystery board and scanning what was there. "Yes, but they'd never be powerful enough on their own with this many bloodlines. It would take something like divine or demonic intervention to pull that off."

Evie grabbed her notebook and furiously wrote everything down.

* * *

October 26th, 2018
Night Claw Residence, Glenwood, CA

Evie pulled into her parking spot on the driveway, killing the engine before grabbing her bag off the passenger's seat. Today she had precious cargo in the form of a fully completed report proving her theory.

Every day this week she'd gone to work and used her bosses as free labor, then came home to Laika with stacks of cases. Together they'd gone over the new ingredient list, finding the most promising ones. Those got sent to Alfred who would give them any idea if something was possible with it.

Now, Evie had multiple robberies the week before each attack with the same list of missing items. The three rituals they'd found matched the CorroNect, Sync Holes, and Hot of the Presses attacks. What she'd found today was going to match the Fulmino Apartments for sure. Again, three spaced out break-ins all with similar lists of taken items. As soon as she ran this by Laika, they'd have four for four.

Evie locked her Saab's door before heading inside. She was home later than everyone else today, so thankfully she wouldn't have to wait long to work over the last cases. The living room was empty except for Shelly, who was sitting where she always did on the couch with her laptop and headphones. The brunette waved, but her attention was the screen containing whatever game she was playing tonight.

Evie didn't remember seeing Tor's bike outside, but that wasn't strange on a Friday night.

"Hey," Evie called to her roommate again.

Shelly obliged by uncovering an ear, "Yeah?"

"Where's Laika? She didn't text me saying she'd be this late tonight?" A thread of worry was already worming through Evie's stomach. Pushing out her run another week made everything feel bigger, even the little things. "I could have gone to pick her up on my way home."

"She's home and gone already," answered Shelly. Her eyes were on the game and her hands flew across the keyboard.

"Gone where? Did she go to Tor's show? Or is she out running with the Moonscent girls again?" Now Evie was feeling a bubble of anger at not having her roommate's attention and Laika wandering off when they had work to do today.

Shelly seemed to notice because she told her friends she'd be back in a minute then paused. "No, she went out on a date. Didn't she tell you?"

Evie felt her bag slip from her fingers as her mind went blank. "A date? No... she didn't say anything to me."

"Probably since you think Alfred is mass murdering people in Glenwood. She probably didn't want you to worry about her."

"A date... with Alfred?" Evie was trying to force the calm back into herself. She'd misheard that. She had to have misheard that.

"Evie?" Shelly's voice sounded far away this time, "Are you okay?"

No, she wasn't okay...

EPILOGUE

Waiting was so tedious, but the Anarchist had little choice left at this point. She still had 120 hours left until she could start her final ritual. Lazily, she flipped to the next page of reviews on Yelp, searching for security information on her prospective target.

"You're distracted," whined her passenger. The voice in the back of her head dogged every step of her day at this point and it had an opinion on everything.

The Anarchist sighed heavily, "No, I'm not. I'm just deciding where to place our last ritual. I think this tacky club, 'Twisted Cross,' should be good enough."

"No," the voice was like a spike into her skull. "You need to do better."

Clutching her temples, the Anarchist sucked in a sharp breath;

her head felt like it was going to split in two. She took a moment to respond, "It'll be full of people that night, both humans and vampires."

"No," her passenger spoke softer now, almost apologetically. "Each ritual needs to be bigger than the last and your last one was impressive. The souls reaped were so high... It was delicious. So we need somewhere with real fangs..."

Reluctantly, The Anarchist closed the window she'd been browsing and moved to the next. Anywhere with a great review wasn't going to be good for her ritual. Places like that had lots of security against anyone losing control or posing a danger. She'd need to go out on foot and find somewhere that wasn't on Google for her real target.

Only one more ritual and she'd be done. But these corruptions were only the first stage of her plan... Next she'd visit her Love and make a proper declaration. She was practically giddy with the idea.

Don't like Cliffhangers?
Corrupted Moons is Available Now!

...we promise the next one doesn't end
in a cliffhanger

Did you know that Moonlight in Glenwood has free bonus chapters and novellas available?

Get your claws on these Freebies!

About the Author

Aynsley & Lita are a collaborative duo that have worked together for nearly a decade. Their creative projects span from art to role-playing games, and now the world of urban fantasy literature. This is their first attempt to write a book and no, they are not a couple.

—–—–——◡——–—–—

Join the Night Claw Pack!
https://moonlightinglenwood.com/

instagram.com/wolfandrosebooks